ARCHITECTURE
FOR BEGINNERS

Robert Cohen

HOBART BOOKS

HOBART BOOKS

ARCHITECTURE
FOR BEGINNERS

First Published in 2023
by
Hobart Books, Oxfordshire, England

hobartbooks.com

Printed in Great Britain

With limitless love and thanks to
Ma Cohen (née Williams), Pop Coco (né Cohen),
and the superb Jenny Rowe.
Without these, there would be nothing.

– Encounter –

4 February 2008, 10:44am

I'm reminded now of an episode of *Thunderbirds* I saw one time.

There'd been, I recall, some kind of disaster. A plane, perhaps, or maybe a rocket; *something*, at least, had dropped, undue, from the sky, and out of this something crawled a man; out he popped, our little puppet voyager, gratefully tumbling through hatch unto dirt – and fell straight from one to another inferno. For, yes, as fate would have it, his refuge was the Devil's anvil; into a scorching desert he'd descended.

Who he was, this man, I cannot say; nor do I know the name of the desert in question – I know only that he crawled from the wreckage and, once having done so, he kept, kept, kept on crawling – crawled and crawled across that arid landscape, his fibreglass face pricked in sweat as the camera toggled ruthlessly back and forth between he and the roaring sun above.

Or am I getting muddled up with *Lawrence of Arabia*? Easily done.

One thing we can say for sure: never was a marionette more needful of International Rescue's tender mercies. What tarries in my mind, though, is not so much the nail-biting rescue as a tiny detail of what went before: the fact that, as he crawled across the screen, the little lost voyager was heard repeatedly to mutter, 'Water... Must... get... water'.

And I remember asking myself, why does he say such a

1

thing?

'Water... Must... get...'

He *knows* what he needs – water, of course; why waste precious energy reminding himself?

Well, now I understand. Down here in the darkness, trapped amongst the intermingled shards of a broken building and a shattered career, here now in the hacking, groany gloom, I see all too well the logic in the actions of that desperate marionette. For in speaking his needs aloud – I see this now – he was arming himself with a *focus:* a means to keep his mind alive, to keep his head from bobbing further groundward with each gruntful elbow thrust, and thus to save himself from dozing to death.

And I must do likewise.

I can't speak my thoughts aloud, the way he did (I've tried; my mouth's too caked with powdered gypsum) – but, if nothing else, I can *think;* I can keep my mind active, stay awake and thus alive till they dig me out.

Alive, though – that's a good one. Alive – to what end?

Oh, don't be daft. There's plenty to live for. Plenty. Make a list.

Okay, I will. Er... Er...

Mog! Yeah, Mog. Imogen – her and the girls. Rachel and Lulu.

Good.

Good. Um... Um... Mum and Dad – yeah, live for them... they're the best parents anyone ever...

Don't cry. Don't cry now.

No, no, but really, why should they have to lose their only

child? They're the kindest, sweetest people who ever – who ever – notwithstanding they play their electrics too loud – how can a person do any *work?* I mean, yes, okay, I know, a roof over my head, they – they – I'm *grateful,* I am, they've given me everything – *everything,* yeah, and that's the point: the least I can grant them is the right not to have to exhume then re-inter their only son.

Okay. Okay. Right, then, so...

1. Mog.

2. Rachel and Lulu.

No, no, one each – the girls... a number for them each – thus they go further.

Oh, and Mum and Dad, of course. They can be 4. No – likewise – diversify:

Let Mum be 4 and Dad be 5.

Right. And then...?

Then *what?*

What *else?* What else to live for?

Well, not much. I mean, *they* are, of course – that lot – they're much much more than much – they're everything, without a doubt, and yet... and yet, beyond that sanctified handful... I mean, really – what *is* there? Man cannot live by love alone, and let's face it, I may yet be brought out breathing from this premature grave, but as to my *career...?*

No. No. No question, I'll do *time* for this mess.

Not that it's my fault – well, not *entirely.* Mog, of course, *she*'d say that...

She'd...

But no. No. One list at a time. 'Whose fault?', that's another

3

one altogether. This one's 'What to live for?'

If only... If only I'd recognised, back then – if only I'd *seen*... If, say, if the Good Witch of... of... of whichever – North? South? whichever it was – had she only come bubbling down and said to me, in that smiley, twinkly voice, 'Alex, all you need – your heart's desire – it's right here at home, you don't need to go searching for it...'

Yeah, thanks, Witchy. *No place like home?* That's easily said. My home, back then, a year and a bit ago... well, *what* home? I wasn't *living* at home. I'd *played away* from home and got caught – sent off, in fact, chucked out – a *fait accompli,* a free transfer, that's what they say – forced to decamp up the road to Mum and Dad's, there to sleep once more beneath the Dogfight Doubles, fit only to dream of a time in a far-off future when the marital minefield once again would be safe for democracy.

A forlorn hope – and though I could (and no doubt *will)* list many prime 'drivers' toward my current poignant status, I think we may say, with high-precision hindsight, that its inevitability was sealed on the day we buried the marriage: Boxing Day 2006.

Fresh from lunch – a lovely quiet cold-turkey lunch with Mum and Dad – I'd denied myself the temptation of a dozy armchair and set off instead on my pilgrimage: off to see Mog and the girls, weighed down with pressies and hopes of a Christmas truce. And truce there *was,* indeed, but not like Tommy and Fritz – no time for a spot of footer. Should've *made* the time, I guess. Instead, we sat down to a game of Sorry.

Sorry. *Sorry* – was ever a game so aptly named? Hard to credit now, yet I'm sure I haven't imagined it: we wound up on the doorstep, Mog and I – barrister and architect – wrangling physically over the Sorry set, each claiming title, each with an absolute faith in this tatty old game as a relic of our lives before each other; I from my childhood, she from her days in uni digs.

Slouching back from that encounter, I was probably more than a little preoccupied.

4

Exclusion zone? Restraining order? That's what she threatened as I left her there, picking up the little round cards. She could do it as well. No grounds, but so what? She's a QC, is our Mog; she'd know the right people to talk to. Chrissake, it wasn't even me who broke up the game – it was *Rachel;* Rachel – spicy-tempered Rachel – swept the whole lot off the table – and why? What had I said? I asked her to get a move on, that's all. Just 'Get a bloody move on!', nothing more. By no stretch was it my fault – any more than it was when, just a few minutes later, those gaily coloured counters, so freshly scooped from the living-room carpet, went soaring once again, this time to end up strafed across the driveway.

Not my fault at all, yet here I was, trudging 'home' beneath a lading of liberal guilt; infected by her rhetoric and, despite myself – despite mere facts – feeling shabby, feeling tainted, feeling (just as I know she'd have wanted) like a domestic abuser – and why? Because I'd gently urged my progeny to play up, play the game and stop boring me to death.

Surprising, in a way, that it took me so long to lose it. That game was merely the tip of a viciously jagged iceberg; throughout the preceding tea-time my betrayed-and-still-steaming better half had kept up a constant barrage of verbal assaults, cleverly designed to fly above the heads of our children whilst taking full advantage of their presence. How could I possibly fight back? Only by calling her bluff – by inviting her to come clean, stop talking in riddles and explain to the girls that yes, their old man was a shit who'd shagged another woman, though, in his meagre defence, it might be noted for the record that their mother had withdrawn all such domestically-sourced privileges many months before.

Yeah, that really would've made all the difference to my standing.

So in truth, the mood I was in – *stompety-stomp*, head no doubt a-zing in wobbly lines of comic book fury – I'm sure it was I, and not the other guy, who failed to look where he was going. There again, it *was* Stevenson Road – a road I've crossed a million times, a road I could cross with my eyes shut – I really didn't *need* to look where *I* was going. All I really needed – all I might've meekly asked – was for drivers to take a modicum of care, not scorch round the corner like the fucker in that Porsche.

'Oi!' I reeled back onto the kerb. 'Oi! You missed me! Come on, come back and have another go! ...Oh, right, that's it, go on, take off. You wanker! You *know* you're a wanker, don't you! That's why you're so keen to get away, cos you're so embarrassed about being such a – such a – a – a...'

Yes, of course, he stops.

And not just stops... starts backing up.

The car draws level.

Downward whirrs a smoked-glass window.

I tell myself to fret not – no need to panic; they're maybe in need of directions.

A yobby voice now, from within. Deeply male, chillingly subdued.

'Got a problem, mate?'

Says I, now self-preserving, sheepish, 'No. No, that's okay.'

Would I *could* have left it there, submissively secure; but no. Something within me – something I hate just as much as I sort of respect it – compelled me to enlarge on my position: 'No, no problem,' I said. 'You nearly killed me, that's all. No 'problem', as such.'

A pause, just a fractional pause before the voice was heard again – 'Fucking hell!' – and a door flew open.

So swiftly did it move – this Mystery Voice – so keen was its owner to reach me that he barely wasted time straightening up before he started round the car toward me; hence the full might and height of what I'd messed with was only apparent when the monolithic being came to within a yard of my face and vital organs.

'Reggie Cullen!' he yelled.

'No,' said I, in my dimness. 'Alex Broughton.'

A loud, barking laugh came forth; the colossus reached out, took me by my cowering shoulders and shook me like a new Christmas toy.

'*I'm* Reggie Cullen,' he said. '*I* am. *I'm* Reggie Cullen, you tosser!'

And, of course, he was.

– Quality Time –

Ah yes, the old chestnut. Perhaps the oldest of *all* the chestnuts. And oh, so eloquently phrased.

'You architects – yeah? – your problem is, you don't live in the places you design; cos I tell you, mate, if you did – if you actually *lived* in them places – things'd be well different.'

We're sitting, by this point, in The Flock of Geese, barely two pints apiece into our resurrected friendship, and Reggie Cullen is presuming already to tell me what's up with my profession.

'If you actually *lived* in them places – if you actually *lived* in them...'

'Yes...?'

'Well, you'd be more careful, wouldn't you – how you planned stuff, all that.'

Now, I could, at this point (if so inclined) have embarked on a description, pitiless in its detail, of the RIBA stages of development; I could've suffered him to know just how carefully we *do* plan 'stuff'. That, however, would've bored us both; instead, I went straight for my ace.

'I *do* live in a place I designed.'

'Oh.'

'Or, I *did*, at least – and will again, I'm sure, once I sort things out with Mog.'

'*Mog?*'

'Sorry, my wife – Imogen. I call her Mog; it annoys her.'

'That why she chucked you out?'

'Who *said* she chucked me out?'

En route back to the bar I pondered, more or less aloud, why it should be that I was unfolding my most personal griefs to a man I'd not seen in half a lifetime; a man, at that – a fabulously wealthy man – who as yet was showing a remarkable reluctance to put his hand in his pocket; thus far the drinks were all on me – and it wasn't even me who'd wanted to come. He'd all but twisted my arm; it was, he insisted, his treat.

Taking the wide-angle view, of course – looking back on the past (and final) year of my life – this is not at all an unfamiliar scenario: me providing pocket money to a multi-millionaire...

Heading resentfully back with the drinks, I was met by the curious sight of Reggie, on his feet, squared up before a picture on the wall adjacent to our table. His head jutted forward; his face contorted in apparent disbelief as he peered deep into the ancient photo. It was a group shot, a Victorian boys' cricket team – possibly a relic from some long-gone local prep school, more likely part of a cache of antique bric-a-brac imported for a heritage refit. Either way, I didn't like to interrupt, such was the clear intensity of whatever Reggie was taking from the experience; I merely hovered, pint-handed, until the moment passed.

As he stepped away from the picture, he seemed to be shaking his head in bewilderment.

'Anything wrong?'

'What? Oh, hullo, mate. Drinks – great!'

Resuming his perch, he gestured back to the picture and, as if in explanation, muttered, 'Snobs!'

He tucked into the new pint.

'Thanks, mate. You're a good lad. Listen, sorry it's been a while. I've been, y'know... busy.'

Such odd phraseology: 'busy' – 'been a while'; terms you'd employ after a gap of, say, six months, maybe even a year or two. Me and Reggie, it was getting on for three decades.

'Been kinda busy myself,' I said. 'University, career, getting married, breeding...'

'Tell you what, mate, you're a cool customer. You playing hard to get?'

'*What?*' I said. 'What d'you mean?'

He said, 'Let's face it: I'm an icon – that's what they tell me, at least. I'm a football legend – *not,* I admit, for all the right reasons, but a legend all the same. Most people, when they meet me, they want to *know* stuff. They say, y'know, 'What was Cloughie like?', 'How's it feel to play at Wembley?'. You, though, you're sat there half an hour – not a single question.'

'Well...' I said. Well *what?* As if I'd had the chance to *ask* him any questions.

'I mean, I don't *mind* – I'm not being funny, y'know; I'm just surprised, that's all. Mind, I don't imagine you're that keen on football – you never was back when. 'Ere, d'you remember, back at school, back in the old days, when they was picking teams? It was always us – you and me, yeah? – always us got chosen last. The fuckers!'

Ah yes, the second great chestnut. If only I'd a tenner for every self-deluding jackanapes I've heard to lie through their revisionist teeth about school football. I mean, really – an England international, claiming he was never picked? Okay, I concede, there *was* a grain of truth in it – a *grain;* we were, on a number of occasions, the last to be picked, he and I. That much is true, I concede, but in Reggie's case it really was a very, *very* few occasions. Being as he was a big-eared new kid who smelt quite forcefully of wee, it naturally took several games for his obvious talent to transcend our colleagues' personal prejudice; once his gifts were established, he never looked back – least of all at *me.* Young Reggie Cullen had not the tiniest qualm about yanking up the ladder behind him. Even when he himself was one of the two captains, I was still the last to be picked – no, not even 'picked'; by that point it was just a matter of me, the runt of the litter, being assigned to whichever side had lost the toss.

'We was best mates, then – eh? – you and me?'

I smiled – well, kind of *simpered*, really – and waited for him to move swiftly on to some new, less contentious observation. He didn't, though; he just sat there, beseeching confirmation.

Well, what could I say? Best mates? Okay, we *were*; we were, indeed, at one time, the best of friends – but surely, even after all these years, he couldn't have forgotten how it ended? Surely, I wouldn't now be forced to *remind* him?

He slumped back in his chair. The moment had passed.

'I love this place,' he said. 'D'you remember when we used to come here and play pool – when we used to bunk off?'

Again. Again with the bullshit.

'No,' I said, now peeved into action. 'No.' I reached for my coat. 'No, I *don't* remember that – but then, why would I? The truth, I'm afraid, is that you and I –'

'What's this? Where you going?'

11

'Got to get back. My folks – they'll be expecting me.'

'*What?* What're you – eight years old? Fucking hell, chill out.'

This, be it noted – this moment here: me, on my feet, ready to flounce out of the pub – this moment's rage at amnesiac insult piled on ancient injury (cos let's be clear: I *never* got to play pool with Reggie, here in this pub or anywhere else) – this moment, I now see, is my inaugural escape hatch – my first chance to duck out of a decades-dead friendship that ought never to have been resuscitated. Later attempts would come to seem as daunting as a dive off the Hoover Dam, but this here, on this Boxing Day evening at The Flock of Geese, this was a mere step down off a low wall – and I flunked it.

'Come on, mate, take a pew. Please. It's not often I get to see the old crowd. I should make more effort, I know I should, being as how I'm down here so often. I told you my kids are living here?'

Indeed, he had – though, oddly, he hadn't said *why*. Perhaps he just assumed I'd know already, courtesy of the all-intrusive media circus that surrounded the death of his wife, almost exactly two years before. Theirs was a famously volatile marriage, but it was during one of the seemingly more stable periods that Denise Cullen one day loaded her three kids into the family Range Rover and set off from their Bedfordshire pile, bound for the south coast; arriving in Godham Malpass, she stopped briefly to offload the offspring on her parents, then got back in the car *(car? jeep? tank?* whatever you call it) and carried on down to the seafront; once there, she just kept on going.

And where was Reggie during all of this? It became a very hot question in the days to follow. Buying toys for the kids, insisted the grieving widower; while several on the Street of Shame insisted just as firmly that, according to *their* sources, he'd in fact been procuring Christmas cheer with another woman.

In the end, of course, it was academic, at least for the press: just a few days in, 'Tragic Denise' was bumped from the front pages by a tale of many drownings more – for this was the year of the Boxing Day tsunami. What a story! What a feast! Reggie, of course, was less equipped to move on and leave the story behind. He couldn't cope at all, in fact – hence the kids, at least 'for the time being', remained with the in-laws.

'Tell you what, it's nice to be able to come in here and not get mobbed any more. Now I come to think of it, that's why I stopped coming here – I couldn't come in and have a nice quiet pint. They always wanted a piece; y'know – do this, do that, take a picture, fuck my sister, all that. I tell you, it was mental back then. Now it's just...'

With a sigh of contentment, he sat back in his chair, as he did so allowing his gaze to unhook from mine and settle on the fire. I thought once more of taking my leave.

'Y'know what, mate...' He sprang back up in his seat. 'Y'know what: you were my friend when no one else wanted to know me.'

'Well, I, er –'

He fixed me anew in his sincerity beam.

'I'll never forget that,' he said.

'Well, I'm glad... y'know, glad I was able to...'

'The great thing is, we both got what we wanted out of life. Two completely fulfilled human beings, me in football, you in building stuff.'

'*Architecture,*' I said. 'It's called architecture.'

'Yeah, yeah, architecture. 'Ere, you should see my place, in Bedfordshire. You'd bloody love it, mate. It's really old. Jacobean. Old manor house – I mean, it's *grown,* of course, down the years – there's been improvements, not least from my good self – but I tell you, it's fuckin' gorgeous. You wanna come see it.'

'I'd love to,' I lied.

'Two hundred acres I've got, near Woburn. Woburn, yeah – you ever been there? It's magic. Well good. They've got lions and tigers and bears and everything – you can drive round and look at 'em – it's just like being in Africa – least, going by what Dave Beckham told me that time.'

'Oh yes?'

'Yeah, that time we went to Jo'burg. We played this friendly – right? – in South Africa; the locals arranged all kinds of stuff for us – trips and shows and tribal dancing and what-have-you – only *I* stayed put at the hotel, cos, well, I wasn't gonna have people tell me what to do. Then, of course, later on, late at night, back comes Becks from this safari thing, and, I tell you, he was so fuckin' over the moon – these lions he'd seen; I was well jealous. Course, after that, he couldn't shut up with that song – y'know, the three lions on his shirt, all that; I'm trying to sleep off a hangover, he's bustling around the place, tidying up, lining our shoes up by the door – I tell you, that guy's got issues – and all the time warbling that fucking song. Still, after that I told myself I'd always go on the cultural things in future, cos you might not get the chance again. Course, I never *did.'*

'Did *what?'*

'Get the chance. I never got picked again. Least, not *yet.'*

I am, in truth, a bit of a sucker for stories about the rich and famous; thus, for a while at least, I was content to let him steam ahead with his anecdotes. As the pints wore on, however, these stories began to take a turn for the repetitively belligerent; he was, I think, on his fourth witty put-down of a freshly ex-boss when I finally felt obliged to call time.

'Right!' said I, slapping the table decisively. 'Time for dinner!'

Where did I go wrong? In cutting off his anecdotal flow I'd been – or so it seemed to me – abrupt to the point of rudeness. And yet, as quickly became apparent, he hadn't even clocked I was saying goodbye.

'Dinner? Great!' He bounced to his feet. 'Where d'you wanna go?'

Oh, what the hell. It's been 25 years since last we met, and with any luck at least as many more would elapse before it happened again. What's a kebab between ex-friends?

Bundling back into the Porsche, we slalomed down to the town centre – and it was there, outside the Viking Fish Bar, that we had our first tiff.

'Fuck off,' says Reggie. 'You're not getting fish juice on my seats.'

'*Fish juice?* What d'you mean?'

'Ketchup as well.'

'I won't. I won't get 'fish juice' on your seats – nor ketchup. I'll be careful, I promise, really careful. C'mon, it's freezing, let's get in the car.'

'Sorry, mate, it's a Porsche, I'm not taking the risk.'

'Right, so, driving it while you're drunk, *that's* not a risk?'

I upped chips and stomped off down the high street.

'Where you going?'

'Office.'

And, without further comment I cut through St Alfred's churchyard and led him forth to the premises of Ingalls Broughton Grant.

A good move, was this. Aside from the warmth factor, it granted me licence to do some showing off. Okay, so I couldn't drop the name of 'Dave' Beckham, but I could at least invite my erstwhile friend to eat dinner off the impressively large desk in my impressively large executive office, affording on one side a smoked-glass vista of the entire work floor, and, on the other, an all-encompassing view of downtown Godham Malpass.

'So,' says Reggie, swivelling back and forth in my big comfy power-chair, 'you're the big boss-man, yeah?'

'Yes. Well, no, not exactly. I mean, I'm *a* boss – *one* of the bosses – one of the *founders*, in fact; I started the company, with my friend Oliver.' *Friend*, right. 'We got into a bit of trouble, though, had to sell out; moved too fast, y'see – *grew* too fast – bit of an Icarus thing, y'know...?' He didn't, pretty clearly. 'Officially,' I said, 'it was a merger; officially we're on equal terms with the others, but, well, we don't call the shots anymore – though, in some ways, that's not such a bad thing. In any case, there's safety in numbers; we're the biggest practice in town, and we're on the up. C'mere – look at this.'

I beckoned him back through to Reception, there to focus attention on the lovingly crafted model of our flagship project.

'Wossis, then?'

'The new civic centre.'

'Oh, right – what you were talking about earlier?'

I was pleasantly surprised; he'd actually absorbed one of the few slivers of information I'd managed to squeeze onto the agenda at the pub.

'Yeah,' I said, 'yeah, that's right. I designed it.'

He leaned over to examine the model, which, like all the best of its kind, had a beauty more intense and perfect than any finished building ever could.

'Nice. Really nice. This what done for your marriage, yeah?'

'Er, yeah.' He really *had* been listening, far more than I thought. 'Yeah. Yeah, we, er, we got the go-ahead just before Christmas – for the second phase. The car park's in place underneath, but they managed to stall the next phase. We had to go to the High Court and get it unstuck.'

'Right. And then she chucked you out?'

'Well, it's a bit more complicated than that...'

'You filthy fucker – don't tell me you was playing away from home?'

'I was, er... Er, well... I was very stupid. It's over now, but –'

'*Stupid?* What you on about? Listen, mate, if the old lady ain't coming up with the oats –'

'When did I say that?'

'Didn't *have* to, mate. Story of the world.'

'Right. Yeah. Shall we go?'

Having earlier disputed Reggie's fitness to be driving, I now found myself keener than keen to get him back behind the wheel. He, however, seemed reluctant to be away. As we progressed back up the high street, he took to quizzing me about the buildings en route.

'What's that?'

I squinted across the road. 'Toilets,' I said. 'Public toilets.'

'Yeah, yeah, toilets. I know they're toilets. What kind of architecture we talking about?'

'Oh, I see. Well, it's... it's sort of 1950s municipal *faux* vernacular. They've tried to make it look like –'

'What about the town hall?'

'Ah, well, now, the town hall, we're talking late Victorian neo-gothic. Course, they ran out of money, that's why it looks a bit funny, with that stump at the end. There was meant to be a big, spired tower; they only got two storeys on it, though, before they ran out of funds – had to shove a flat lead roof on it.'

'Brilliant. What about *that,* then?'

He was pointing now to the far end of the central reservation, the island that divides the carriageways; the island on which... which... which is where...

'This,' I said, wandering across to stand in front of the William Terriss Memorial Theatre, 'is the source of all my pride – well, *most* of it, at least – and all my woes, as well. It's the work of Frank Matcham, England's foremost theatre designer. Opened in 1900 as a tribute to William Terriss, revered Victorian actor-manager, who was murdered outside the Adelphi Theatre in London by a man called Richard Archer Prince.'

'Christ on a bike! Know a lot of stuff, don't you?'

'I should hope I do – especially about this place.'

'Tell you what – d'you ever do a football stadium?'

'*Do?* Design, you mean? No, can't say I have.'

'Fancy having a go?'

'Dunno. I mean, yeah, in principle – I like a challenge – but it's not like it'd never come up; there's any number of practices they'd seek out before us – ones that specialise –'

'*Specialise?* What d'you mean? I don't want no 'specialists'. I want *you;* you're my friend. I trust you.'

'What're you saying? You... you want a...?'

'A stadium. A football stadium. For football.'

'Football, okay, I get it – but *where?* Where d'you mean to put this stadium?'

'Where d'you think? In my house. Well, no, not *in* my house, but *next* to it – *near* it – y'know, on my estate. There's plenty of room – two hundred acres. So, what d'you think?'

'I think it'll be a wonderful opportunity for someone – someone who knows what they're doing. As for me, I'm afraid my hands are rather full at the moment.'

'Full? With what?'

'With *what?* With *this!*' So saying, I bestowed a fondly paternal pat on one of the iron columns supporting Matcham's portico.

'*This?*' He shuffled backwards, seeking, it appeared, to take in the entirety of the theatre and thereby understand what I was on about.

'*This,*' I repeated. 'This is what I'm working on.'

'How d'you mean, *working?* It's already here. How're you *working* on it?'

'You saw the model. This is where we're putting the Civic Centre.'

'*What?* You're kidding? It's nice, this; you can't knock it down.'

'Oh, don't *you* start.'

'You can't knock down the theatre.'

'No one's –'

'It's part of our history. Don't you remember – they used to bring us here with school. That time – right? – what about that time – d'you remember? – that time we got detention for throwing Smarties!'

'*What? We?* No. No, I don't – not *we*. But *you: you* I remember – *you* getting detention – getting us *all* detention. The entire Fifth Form *detained* – and all because of *you.*'

'No, no, no. No you don't – it was more than just me. You was involved as well. You and –'

'I assure you I wasn't, and I'll tell you why I know – cos – No. No, fuck it, never mind about that. The point is –'

'No, you can't just –'

'Forget the Smarties and listen: we're *not* knocking it down. No one is demolishing this theatre. Quite the reverse: we're *protecting* it. It's a Frank Matcham, for Christ's sake. We're gonna *preserve* it: wrap it in a glass envelope, buffer it with offices on either side, lay a conference centre across the top. It's gonna be safer than it's ever been.'

Reggie laughed – a big, barking laugh. 'You really do talk the talk, don't you. Is that what you tell people – you're gonna *protect* it?'

'Well, yeah.'

'And people believe you?'

I shrugged. 'Well, yeah. I mean, *sometimes*. Not my wife, unfortunately. Anyway, look, I need to be getting home.'

I walked off in search of the car.

'Ere, Al! Hang about! Listen, mate, what're the chances of crashing at yours tonight?'

'*What?*'

'I'm too far gone to drive. Yeah, I know, I know, you said – and you were right: I'm wrecked.'

'What about your in-laws?'

'They're up the other end of town. 'Sides, I don't want the kids seeing me like this.'

Odd, that. If only half the tabloid tales were true, Reggie's brood would have seen him drunk and worse on countless occasions – on quite a few of them locked in verbal or even physical conflict with his equally inebriate wife. Popular chatter suggested he'd never spared his kids a thing; why so squeamish now, then? Indeed, I was all ready to put this to him for a fatal intervention which had the effect of causing me to feel sorry for him.

While we were talking in front of the theatre, some boy racers had been patrolling the high street, down one side and up the other, searing the midnight clear with the dual exhausts of their funked-up Fiesta. On perhaps their fifth time round the strip, while we were in the process of discussing Reggie's sleeping arrangements, one of the boys leaned out the window and started yelling, 'Reggie! Reggie! Oi, Reggie, my man! Reggie! Oi, Reggie, over here! Reggie!'

Finally Reggie looked round and waved – 'Hello, mate!' – whereupon the young man concluded his address with a warm and witty 'Reggie, you WANKER!'

***

Mum and Dad were long since departed for bed. Reggie and I talked some more over a cuppa and a slice of Mum's Christmas cake – 'Fuckin' magic' – then we too retired.

Though the evening's exertions had left us both with barely the energy to heave ourselves upstairs, the sight of my old bedroom, so little altered over half a lifetime, gave Reggie a new lease of annoyance.

'Blimey,' he said – bouncy now as Tigger – 'look at this: still got your dogfight doubles!'

'Yes,' said I, rather less bouncy as I worked to remove two months' detritus from the spare bed. 'Why she never hacked them down, I don't know. Maybe she knew I'd balls up my life and end up back here one day.'

'Yeah, or maybe she just likes 'em.'

'Don't know about that. She doesn't really share my nostalgia for the Second World War – but, then, she *lived* through it.'

Now turning round, to offer the new-found bed to my guest, I was more than a little surprised to find him standing tall on mine. He was inspecting the Airfix Spitfire that dangles, to this day, from one corner of the ceiling – dangles, diving, in eternal hot pursuit of an eternally doomed Me109.

'What're you doing? Get down!'

In vain I hissed my exhortations; he was in another world – that other happy long-lost world, a tiny, short-lived world for two, where every school day, more or less, would end at this house, the two of us labouring side by side in the assemblage and loving decoration of Airfix planes, tanks and warships.

'Chrissake, get *down!*'

'Oh – what's that there?' His gaze now had shifted towards the airborne tableau in the opposite corner. 'Is that a Mirage?'

'Yeah, that's the Yom Kippur War.'

'Right. Yeah, right – so what's that: a MiG 15?'

'Correct. Now, if you don't mind –'

He leapt down – I thought he was going to go through the floor – and scurried over to lavish attention on the war in the desert.

'Egyptian, is it?'

'*Syrian.* But the Egyptians were in on it too.'

'Yeah, course.'

'Listen, here's your bed. If you need another blanket –'

'Is that one of mine?'

I followed his gaze to the top of the wardrobe; there, from amongst a pile of books, games and other relics, could be seen protruding the bashed-in, bladeless nose of another, larger Airfix Spitfire.

'*Yours?'* I said. 'Course it's not yours.'

He extracted the model, turned it over in his hands, started gently blowing away the dust of decades.

'*Sure* it's one of mine.'

'No,' I said, hovering nervously. 'No, it's not. You always took yours home.'

'Yeah, you're right; *usually* I did – only, now I come to think of it, I'm pretty sure I was working on a Spitfire last time I was here.'

'*Precisely,'* I said. 'Precisely. *Last time.* You never came back. Someone else had to finish it.'

I grabbed back the plane and made to return it to the top of the wardrobe; just as he was reaching out to yank it from my hands once more, a voice from the corridor whispered, '*Reggie?*'

'Oh,' I said. 'Hi Mum. I hope you don't mind. I thought Reggie, maybe he could...'

No need to complete the sentence; of *course* she didn't mind – that was clear from the hungry embrace in which she was already wrapping the prodigal.

'Look at how you've grown!' she muttered. 'I used to be able to get the whole lot of you into one hug. Look at me now – barely up to your chest!'

Though it was Mum who'd started the hugging, it was Reggie who held it the longest. He seemed unwilling to let go, finally doing so only in order to shake the hand of my father, who had now appeared, dazed, in the doorway.

'Well,' said Dad, 'this *is* a surprise. We haven't seen you in years. What is it? Ten? Twelve?'

'Pushing thirty, Mr B.'

'Well, don't leave it so long next time. See you in the morning.'

Mum, meanwhile, had bustled to the airing cupboard and back. 'Here's a towel,' she said. 'D'you need some pyjamas? I'm sure Alex won't mind if you borrow some of his.'

'*Mum...*'

'What, then?'

'He's about ten sizes bigger than me.'

'That's right,' said Reggie. 'And besides, I always sleep in the buff. Don't worry, though, I'll keep me pants on tonight!'

If it somehow enhanced his sense of manhood to impart such details to my 70-something mother, his sense of manhood was considerably undercut by waking the next morning in a patch of piss. I've got to hand it to him, though: in like position, I'd have done anything to avoid owning up – blame someone else, steal the sheets, whatever; Reggie just confessed.

'Sorry, Mrs B. Think I had a bit too much to drink last night.'

'Don't fret,' said Mum, ever the one to put folk at their ease. 'No doubt it was that cup of tea that did it.'

'Maybe you're right, who knows? It's never happened before, I know that.'

I didn't trouble to challenge that particular fiction. Incontinence is rarely, if ever, an apt topic for breakfast debate – in any case, Mum had already hurried off in search of a pair of pants for him to squeeze into.

Over breakfast, Reggie was grilled about his celebrity lifestyle. Occasionally, from behind Dad's *Daily Mail*, I would urge my parents to leave him alone, though in truth I knew he was quite happy, batting back fulsome answers to their rapid-fire enquiries. Having not been much in company the past two years, this was likely something of a treat for him.

Breakfast done, Reggie took his leave. The tainted pants being already in the wash, Mum promised to send them on to him.

'Don't be daft,' he said, 'there's no need for that; just bring 'em when you come to the party.'

'*Party?*'

'Didn't I say? I'm having a New Year's do. At the country pile. It's a yearly fixture, *chez* Cullen. You've gotta come, all of you.'

'Oh,' said Mum, 'a party? That sounds lovely – doesn't it, Alex?'

'Yes, Mum.'

'We'll have to see what we've got planned.'

I kept Reggie company, wandering back down the hill with him to fetch the car from the town centre. As we pressed forward into the biting wind, he told me, 'I've half a mind not to go back, y'know. They're so lovely, your mum and dad. Maybe I'll chuck in the mansion, move in with you lot.'

I laughed nervously.

'I've got to get them something,' he said.

'Sorry?'

'Something to show my appreciation.'

'Don't be daft. They were happy to have you.'

'They *were*, weren't they? They were really pleased to see me. I love your mum and dad.'

'Yeah, me too.'

'What about a sunbed?'

'A sunbed?'

'Yeah, yeah – a sunbed. I'll get 'em a sunbed – like I did for the in-laws.'

'I don't think they've really got room for it.'

'Funny, that's what Jack and Monica said – Denz's parents, y'know. I got 'em one anyway.'

'Did you? That's lovely, but, really, we don't have the space.'

'What about *your* room? You don't need two beds.'

'Where're *you* gonna sleep next time?'

'Fair point. Still, I want to get 'em *something* – I want to show my appreciation – y'know, for having me there –'

'Believe me, they were delighted –'

'Yeah, but the sheets – being so nice about the sheets; I wanna thank 'em for that.'

'No need.'

'For that, and, y'know, for keeping quiet about it – which I'm sure they *will,* but, y'know...'

I laughed out loud. 'What – you think they're gonna go running to the papers?'

'No, no, I *don't* – that's just it, they're diamonds, your mum and dad.'

'Yes, they are.'

'On the other hand,' he said, '*no one's* incorruptible.'

– Janus –

11:06am

Funny thing is…

I mean, not funny-ha-ha…

What I mean – what's funny is, I'm lying here, half-buried, surrounded by blackness and cadavers and groaning cadavers-to-be; my reputation's in bits both real and metaphorical, while inside me must be fuck knows how many shattered bones and punctured organs… In short, there's a lot for me to chew on in the time I have remaining; and yet, at this moment, all I can think of is the way Reggie used to ridicule me in front of the girls at our school.

And it makes me flush with embarrassment.

No, not *flush*. Not *just* flush. I'm sweating – actually *sweating*.

I picture myself proceeding down a corridor, 13 years old, every bit as spotty as a spiteful God could ever have meant me to be; and somewhere down that corridor I see my erstwhile friend, towering as ever above an admiring phalanx of pretty girls. He's already getting his first taste of fame: the girls adore him, the guys revere him – yeah, even those who once abused him for his wingspan ears and piss-stench cologne. In short, Reggie Cullen has no need to score points off me in order to enhance his feel-good factor, but he invariably does it all the same – and, as I hear his stage-whispered bitchery echo down that 30-year corridor, beads of sweat break out – I can *feel* them; beads of hot humiliation breaking forth amidst the dust grains on my brow.

So it was on that December morning a year and a bit ago, trying to explain to my parents why I'd no desire whatever to attend Reggie's party. The line I sought to spin was of the 'Not my scene' variety, but the sweat now annexing my distinguished executive pate hinted at deeper concerns.

Hinted? More like *screamed*.

Mum thought I was having a turn. *Sit down,* she said.

Don't *need* to sit down.

So what's wrong, then?

Nothing's wrong, I said, nothing, leave me alone.

No good, though. Even now, at a point in my life when I'd got to be as big and cool as I'm ever going to be, I could no more confide in my parents – lay bare those childhood shamings – than I could when first they were minted.

I was forced, instead, to fall back on generalities.

'What d'you mean you don't like him?' said Mum. 'He's so *nice* – even now he's famous. How can you not *like* him?'

'And if you don't like him,' spluttered Dad, 'why'd you invite him back last night?'

'I don't know. Old time's sake.'

'Exactly: *old times*. You two were inseparable.'

In that, at least, he was right. Inseparable. We *were*: me and Reggie, inseparable. All but. For about a year. A year, it was, yeah, give or take, a sweetly happy year; a well-nigh golden age it was – and, perhaps unusually, I pretty much *knew* it for such at the time: a golden age, in which almost every school day would end with Reggie coming back to the old Broughton place, there to have his tea, do his homework, play war and make models. About the only thing he didn't do at ours was sleep; for that he'd return to the bony bosom of his family at the local TA centre (his dad was the RSM). For those brief months, Reggie was, to all intents and purposes, a member of our family. Not even his burgeoning football career could keep him away completely. More and more of his evenings came to be devoted to training and away matches for the County Juniors, but still he would pop round when he could to do a bit of Airfix and savour Mum's cooking.

Yes, Reggie was very much a member of the family – right up until the day he discovered Woman. Once having crossed that particular bourn, he didn't stage another appearance for the best part of three decades. And that's what gets to me, even after all this time: not so much that *I* was unwanted on voyage, but that my parents too were cast overboard. They'd treated him like a son, and *he* treated *them* like week-old dogshit on his shoes – though of course, with his growing attention to fashion, he would've devoted a lot more care to brushing off dogshit than he did to brushing off my folks.

And what was their response to this? Nothing. No, not *nothing*; far worse than nothing. *Absolution*. Saintly forgiveness – though, in truth, that doesn't cut it either: to forgive, there has to be some sense of offence, and my parents gave not the slightest inkling of such. For all I know he'd hurt them deeply; for all I know they may have died inside each and every time he oafed his way onto the TV screen, but if so they weren't letting on. I sincerely hope they were genuinely unaffected by Reggie's behaviour, for if it were otherwise then I must conclude that they consciously used me as a kind of psychic punchbag to exorcise their pain. At any rate, I couldn't begin to count the number of times, in my lonely, spotty late-teenhood, when my parents all but forced me to bear witness to the gallingly meteoric rise of Reggie Cullen.

There I'd be, minding my business, when – 'Alex!' – a yell

from below – one or other parent – 'Alex! Alex! Quick!' – I'd stumble down the stairs, nearly breaking my neck – 'Alex, come on, you'll miss it!' – I never learned, I should've ignored 'em – 'Alex!!!' It might be something good – a clip from *Dr Who,* perhaps – from the Hartnell years – or maybe the bear from Andy Williams – remember? – 'Alex! Alex!' – almost there now, a step or two more – I'd explode into the sitting-room – 'WHAT???'

And there would he be, with his famously powerful, well-nigh-invincible left foot: Reggie Cullen, the teen sensation, a national treasure in the making!

All those years, they never heard a word from him – not one that wasn't transmitted via the TV or smudged across a page of newsprint. As far as I could tell, it bothered them not one whit. So why should I be surprised – why should I be so *annoyed* – when he walks back in after 30 years and they greet him with open, all-forgiving arms?

'Well, what d'you expect?' said Dad. 'You brought him home. He was your guest. What d'you want us to do – beat him with the phone book?'

'Er, no...'

'Well, what, then? Why'd you bring him home if –'

'I don't know. I was... drunk.'

'*Drunk,* were you?' said Mum. Well, however drunk you were, you never would've invited him back unless you were actually pleased to see him.'

My mother can be very perceptive.

'Yeah,' I said. 'Yeah, but – he took me by surprise; I'd just had all that business with Mog, I wasn't thinking straight. But I am *now,* and Reggie Cullen is *not* someone I want back in my life.'

***

Many was the time, over the course of that first drive up to Bedfordshire, when I considered turning back. On one occasion I actually *did* it – I turned off and left the motorway; and yet, after three circuits of the roundabout, I somehow found myself heading back up the northbound ramp and rejoining the pulse.

I'd been compelled – here's the thing – *compelled* – no other word – to weigh my resentment of Reggie against a number of other factors.

For one, there was the prospect of spending a nice quiet New Year with my parents. This, I'd come to realise, was liable to turn out much like any other nice quiet evening with Mum and Dad: he in the lounge with his Sky Sports; she in her kitchen lair listening to Classic FM. That's how they do things. Apart from meals and reception committees for washed-up footballers, there isn't a big communal vibe in my parents' house.

Not that *I* was entitled to complain. They'd granted me shelter in a time of direness, and it was for me to be grateful – for me, more than that, to minimise my sponging, make swift peace with Mog and get out of their hair. Which indeed I sought to do: once having opted to stay in Godham Malpass for New Year, I lost no time in making fresh overtures to the opposing camp. However, my peace offering – lunch out with Mog and the girls on New Year's Day – came to nothing; efficient as ever, she'd made early plans for a trip to her parents in Devon.

Well, I thought (whilst sobbing in the hallway and banging my head against the wall), if that's how it is, then sod it – and sod them all: I'll go to bloody Bedfordshire. *Maybe I'll never come back!!!*

Of course, I knew I *would*, if only for the partners' meeting

32

that loomed just a few days into January. And therein, of course, lay the most powerful motivation for attending Reggie's do; for however nutty, vague and tenuous was the great man's professed desire for a garden stadium, it would, I felt, be folly to dismiss it without at least a nod toward investigation. For here's the thing about architecture: it's not like football, there's no George Best factor; you can't live and be loved for ever more on the basis of increasingly distant past glories. You have to keep on proving yourself. Even at the best of times, you have to be looking ahead; and *this,* of course, for me, was nowhere *near* the best of times. True, the Civic Centre design had brought me kudos, but much of that had been squandered through my dalliance with Charlotte. It wasn't that people disapproved, exactly – nobody, at least, said so *out loud*; but it did seem to me that all of a sudden people were voicing opinions they'd not have chosen to air when my stock was at its height; the general tenor of these opinions was that, since signing off on the final plans for the Civic Centre, I'd been resting more than a little on my laurels.

In a way it was true – though not so much in the sense that I'd been *lazy*. Far from it; I had, in fact, helmed a number of smaller projects while the Civic Centre was slothing its way through inquiries and court hearings – but, crucially, I'd failed to make sure I was *seen* to be doing all that I was doing, and thus protect myself from the snake-like manoeuvrings of Oliver Grant.

Oh, Oliver, are you dead? I do hope so. You poor, sad man. You'll be better off, you really will.

He, of course, was far too smart to accuse me directly of failing to pull my weight, but the fact that *lesser* beings were willing to do so told me that the notion had almost certainly originated with him.

Oliver – here's the point – has never really forgiven me for 'betraying' the partnership we founded together, back in the early '90s. And it *was* a glorious thing we had: so far we went

33

together – so high and so young – *too* young, perhaps, but no matter – we reached for the sun (of course we did), and we grabbed a good handful of fire before crashing back down to earth. Crash we *did*, though, and the clean-up was ugly. I wound up going to court with Mog to apply for power of attorney; I didn't want to, but Oliver was beyond control – what few assets were left to us he was stuffing up his nose. In spite of all that, when negotiating the take-over, I insisted on something for him in the new set-up. He had to get *clean*, of course – that went down in writing – but once he'd kicked the Ajax, there was to be a place for him at the table.

What's that they say, though – no good deed goes unpunished? 'Tis true, oh, so true. He got himself clean, did Oliver, and like all addicts, he found himself a new, less toxic addiction to feed. As with so many, so it was with Oliver: religion – a *new* religion – a sacred mission to undermine and finally destroy Alex Broughton.

Thus my New Year odyssey, more than anything, was a tardy recognition of the malevolent power opposing me, and the need for true resolve in fighting that power. I had, as the pundits might have it, taken my eye off the ball. As a consequence, I found myself on the verge of losing everything. If this trip to Reggieville was a clutchment at straws, so be it – I would clutch at any straw necessary.

And so I headed north, propelled above all by a growing desire to vanquish Oliver Grant – to kick him in the balls, push him to the ground, then rub his smirky face in glass-strewn mud (figurative or literal, no matter).

***

11:22am

I am *so* uncomfortable. My back...

Probably a good thing. Keep me awake.

Yeah, that or the other way – take comfort in sleep – which, obviously, well, I can't, can I? Can't sleep, gotta stay awake, or... or never wake up, so...

Something...

Something to prop my head up.

Something...

Any...?

Ah!

Uh! Uh! Uh! Uh! Wet! Wet! Uh! Uh! Uh! Uh!

Uh!

Uh. Oh God.

Oh.

Uh.

Uh...

Whose *is* it, anyway? Hope it's not Charlotte.

No, can't tell. Too dark. Short hair. Too short. Bloke, most likely. Odds are.

Face. Nose. Must take a while – blind people – get used to this.

Stubble. Yeah, it's a bloke.

Head, right. Well, any port in a storm. Shove it under my... If...

That's it.

Better. Little bit. Bony, but...

He'd done alright, had Reggie. Electric gates and a half-mile of woodland before you even got a *glimpse* of the house – which itself, I had to admit, was something of an eye-opener. I seem to recall, in fact, that, as I emerged from the woods the word 'Wow!' actually passed across my sophisticated lips.

So often the backdrop to its owner's tabloid self-trumpetings, Cullen Place had always been easy for me to dismiss: *yes, yes, Jacobean mansion, yellow stone, very nice – nice but unexceptional...* Sheer jealousy. The place was *magnificent.*

Just a shame about the extension: that flat-roofed, mock Tudor abomination on the west side. In the already gathering gloom, tall, narrow leaded windows were casting ghostly pale shimmerings across the gravel from what I assumed to be a swimming-pool. Could be worse, I surmised – a single storey, only; but it *was*, for all that, unfortunate. Tosser as I am, I like a bit of symmetry, and sadly, at some point in recent history, someone had chosen to piss all over the symmetry of that rather fine house.

So, there I was, idly pondering whether or not Reggie was the 'someone' to blame for this inappropriate development, when the man himself came bounding out of the house, a pack of assorted dogs leaping about in his jetstream.

'You made it – fucking excellent!'

He wrapped me in a crushing embrace.

'Good to see you, mate. Just admiring my spa, yeah?'

'*Spa?* Right, thought as much.'

'Yeah. Got a pool and a sauna – gym, too. Yeah, I'm well chuffed with that. Course, it's made for a bit of hoo-ha with the local commissars; it's out of keeping, they say – it's, er – it's 'unbalancing', it's got an 'unbalancing' effect. *You* don't think that, do you?'

'Well, I, er –'

'Maybe you can help me – with the planners, y'know, seeing as you speak the lingo. They want me to pull it down, the fuckers.'

'Well, I'd be happy to help, of course...'

He plucked up my hold-all.

'You don't mind dogs, do you? Come on, y'cunts!'

I followed the pack back through the front door. We emerged in a flag-stoned hall, where a number of white-cloth'd trestle tables stood ready for a feast. Flanking the space was a pair of elegant wooden staircases, each abundantly wrapped with variegated tinsel. To one side, stretching almost up to the second floor, stood a Christmas tree so intensively baubled that hardly an inch of green peeked through. At the back of the hall, two large wooden doors opened into another cavernous room beyond, from which were now wafting the clipped abstractions of a band in soundcheck mode.

'The alternative,' said Reggie, who hadn't yet drawn breath, 'the alternative – this is just one idea I've had – is to make the whole house like the extension; if they don't like the differentness, we can unify the whole thing – y'know, bung a bit of plaster and some wooden beams across the front of the house, make the *whole thing* look Tudor.'

'Yeah, well, I can tell you now, there's no way I'd help you do *that*.'

Reggie halted.

'That's what I like about you; you're not afraid to tell me what you think.'

I laughed. '*Should* I be?'

'You hungry?'

'I *am* a bit.'

'Come on, then.'

Dumping my bag on the floor, he dragged me toward a corner of the hall, where, beneath the left of the two grand staircases, the wooden panelling opened discreetly onto another, more rudimentary set of stairs. I followed Reggie down to a large, high-ceilinged kitchen, where, in contrast to the bustle above, the only sound was of a clock gently ticking above the hearth. The long, sturdy wooden tables looked as if they'd been in use since the time of the Prince Regent, likewise the cupboards and the dressers – and yet everything else in the room was shiny up-to-date state-of-the-art.

'Lilian! Lilian! Got another snout for the trough!'

'There's no need to shout,' intoned a deep, patiently commanding voice from one cosy corner of the otherwise ill-lit vastness. In an armchair by the hearth, ensconced between an electric fire and a tall brass reading lamp, I beheld a large black woman, sizing me up over half-moon specs. Only slightly lowering the newspaper between her hands, she said – to Reggie, but without taking her eyes off me – 'This be your old friend you was tellin' me about?'

'Yeah, that's right: my friend – my very best friend, from school. He came, just like I said he would.'

'And like I said he *wouldn't.*'

'Right – so you owe me a fiver!'

'Fiver? I never bet you no fiver.'

'No, no, just having a laugh. A *tenner,* it was!'

'Get out of my kitchen, now.'

'No way. Got work for you. 'Ere, hang on, what's all this?' He was looking now at the heater on the floor. 'What's with the electric? You've logs coming in the window – use 'em.'

'I'm happy as I am.'

'*Happy*? Do me a favour! I mean, look at it – two puny little bars. You want a *proper* fire!'

'Do I?'

'Course you do. You're from Jamaica.'

'Is that right?'

'Well, more or less.'

'Where am I from, Mr Cullen? You know precisely well.'

He sought in vain to weather the heat of her tractor-beam glare.

'Yeah. Yeah, of course. You're, er... you're from Barbados.'

This, apparently, was the right answer. With a sigh, she folded her paper, shoved it down the side of the armchair, and got to her feet.

'So, Mister Schoolfriend, how much he paying you to come here?'

I laughed; she did not.

'Oh. Er, nothing. Nothing.'

'Yeah, nothing,' said Reggie, 'so lip up and get him some grub.'

'Fine,' said Lilian, fighting back a yawn; 'fine, I will feed this friend of yours.' She trudged across to a big, steely cooker and removed the lid from a king-size copper saucepan. 'He can have some of this, from earlier. I made it for –'

'Perfect, thanks, you're an angel. Listen, mate, I'll show you the house when you're done. Just a coupla calls to make.'

And he went, leaving us to face one another in the silence.

'I'm Alex,' I said.

'Welcome, Alex.'

'Reggie and I were at school together.'

'I know. He told me that.'

'Oh. Right. Yes, of course.'

She lit the gas beneath the saucepan. After a few moments, a gentle plopping sound began to issue forth. Strange, I thought, that aside from what was on the hob, no food preparation was in evidence. Upstairs, it seemed, they were making ready for a feast; down here, but for the plopping saucepan and the gentle ticking of a clock above the fireplace, all was quiet.

'So, uh, how long have you been working for Reggie?'

'Five years, more or less.' She bade me take a seat at the kitchen table. 'I used to have a cafeteria in the town.'

'*Town* – what: Luton?'

'Luton, precisely. I set it up with my husband; we ran it together for three years.'

'Fantastic.'

'Then he went off with the waitress.'

'Oh. Oh, I'm sorry to hear that.'

'No need to be sorry. He was useless.'

'Right.'

'Like everyone in that Luton. People in this country, they don't appreciate good food.'

'Right. So, you had to shut down?'

'Didn't *have* to. Just *did*. Got a better offer – from Mrs Cullen.'

'Right. So, a happy ending after all!'

'What?'

'A happy ending.'

'She drowned.'

'What? God, yes – I mean, *no*, not Denise. *You*, I mean – *your* story... A – a – a happy, er, er...'

I looked desperately past her to the cooker, where the plopping of the saucepan was now grown urgent – big, red, angry globules of liquid were hopping forth onto the hob and the floor beyond. Lilian sighed and turned away.

'Thanks,' I gasped, as a plate was dumped before me.

From the pan unto the plate were slopped out several large ladlefuls of thick orange substance. *Substance*, I say, for in the mid-winter gloom it was at first unclear what I was about to receive.

'Is this your own recipe?'

'No. Mr Heinz's recipe.'

Beans! Of course that's what it was. Beans. But some kind of innovation was in play, surely? What were all those dark bits?

Well, as it turned out they were *burnt* bits – though whether new burnings or ancient spirits stirred up from the bottom of the pan, it was really no easy thing to say. What was all too clear was my need for an exit strategy. Right now, she was stood beside me, but if perhaps, I could create some kind of diversion, get the beans in the bin while her back was turned...?

'Please, don't worry about me. Carry on – whatever you were doing...?'

'Too late.'

'I'm sorry?'

'You disturbed me now – you and Mr Cullen. He tell me look after you, that's what I do. I'm all yours. Anything else you want, I get you.'

'Well, that's... that's very kind, that's, er...that's, er...'

Unbearable – that's what it was. Burnt beans in abundance, and the forbidding searchlight of an old woman's waste-not-want-not glare.

Salvation, when it came, just a few disgusting forkfuls later, was through the stair-clumping intercession of a man (to use the term loosely) the size and shape of a small hot air balloon. If he wasted no time with introductions, it wasn't a problem, for I knew him instantly. Ever since the dawn of Reggie's celebrity – ever since the very first time he was papped on the threshold of Tramps or Stringfellows or whatever alternative shitespot, Festus was to be seen lurking in the rear of the frame. They'd met when both were apprentices at Tottenham, and though Festus never made it – primarily for lack of the necessary weight discipline – he followed Reggie almost everywhere from then on.

'What's going on? Is he eating my beans?'

Lilian reassured him. 'Plenty more where that came from.'

Festus, however, was not so easily put at ease. He came

right up to the table, allowing his ample belly to rest on the woodwork, and glared down at my plate.

'Look at him, he doesn't even like 'em. He's hardly touched 'em. Don't you like 'em?'

'Well...'

'Here, *I'll* have 'em.'

He sat down opposite, stretched his tits across the table, and grabbed my plate.

Lilian swiped him across the top of the head. 'Bad boy!' she barked, though she couldn't entirely disguise her gratification. She watched him for a moment, and I did too. Then, for the first time, she tipped me a smile.

'I get you some more.'

I tried to protest, but Festus pulled focus: 'Me too!'

'Don't you worry, now; there's plenty for everyone.'

And so another plate of beans appeared before me. Had she, I wondered, picked up on my unenthusiastic vibes, or did she truly believe she was doing me a kindness? I stared bleakly down into the orangey new abyss.

'Ain't you done yet?' Reggie was back in the room. 'Come on, never mind that. We need a hand.'

With a rueful smile back at Lilian, I allowed my host to drag me forth. My parting vision was of Festus reaching across the table to secure a third helping.

Upstairs, a caterers' van was backed up to the front door. Reggie and I helped ferry trays of cakes and sandwiches to a bespectacled young woman in a black beret.

'How was the lunch?' enquired my host, as he handed me another tray.

'It was... It was...'

'Fucking disgusting, I'll bet. Sorry, mate, I forgot, you're an architect.'

'I don't really see what that has to do with...'

'Out of practice, that's the trouble. She used to do fine when the kids were here; Festus, he ain't so fussy.'

'What about you? Aren't you fussy?'

'I eat a lot of take-aways.'

'What – so you've got a cook who...?'

'I know. I know what you're thinking – why'd I keep her? Denz, that's the answer.'

'Denz?'

'My old lady. *She's* the one who took her on; she'd go mad if I gave her the push.'

This, it seemed to me, was unusual reasoning – Denz, after all, was some way beyond 'going mad' on anything. But perhaps I just didn't understand the finer points of grief. In any case, the task in hand was done – the catered goods were through the door – and Reggie was moving on. He beckoned to the woman in the beret.

'C'mere – say hello to Alex. Al, mate, this is Shelley, my all-round Wonder Woman!'

Wonder Woman chuckled. 'I'm just his PA.'

'*Just my PA?* Fuck off!' He tugged her to his side. 'I wouldn't be fuck all without this girl.'

She shifted the agenda.

'You're Reggie's friend from school? I'm so glad you came. He's been on about you ever since he got back from Sussex.'

'Course I have,' said Reggie. 'I've been telling everyone.'

'Reggie says you were his only schoolfriend.'

'Well, it's not quite that simple...'

'It's every bit that simple,' said Reggie. 'When no one else wanted to know me, this guy stood tall. We were soulmates. Blood brothers. You should've seen us on the games field, week-in, week-out, every other bugger getting picked ahead of us.'

Shelley gasped. 'Really? That's ironic.'

'Say the least. Bunch of wankers. Right, then – Alex, me old mucker, let's be sorting you. Where we got him, Shel?'

'Oh, I made up the bed in the Blue Room.'

'*Blue Room*? What d'you mean? They're *all* made up, aren't they?'

'No. Why?'

'You're kidding? Where're the others gonna sleep?'

'Alex is the only one staying.'

'You sure? I told people they could stay the night.' He turned to me. 'I said on the invites: bring a bottle and your PJs, and they don't even need the bottle, not really – we've got Champagne and everything.'

'It's actually *Cava*,' said Shelley. 'I hope that's okay.'

'Yeah, yeah, whatever. Oi, fuck off, you lot!'

From under the nosings of assorted dogs he seized my bag

and, yelling 'Come on, Al!', he selected a staircase and bounded upward, two or three steps at a time.

'Come on, keep up! Tell ya what – by the time people get to crashing out tonight, they won't *care* where they're gonna sleep. Least, that's how it usually works out, *chez* Reggie.'

At the top of the stairs was a gallery bounded by two doors – these, apparently, leading to the master bedroom and the master bathroom. On the wall between hung a row of canvases, mostly antique depictions of elegant males sporting beards and/or wigs. Centrally placed, however, was a rather more recent group study of Reggie, his late wife, and their three children.

'D'you like it?' said Reggie. 'It's a Bryan Organ – he's the one done Prince Charles. Princess Di, an' all, in her trousers. Them there's my little ones: that's Conrad, he's the oldest, real chip off the old block; then there's Daisy, she's ten I think – ten or eleven; and that's Chico, he's my little baby, he's six.'

Such was the warmth now infusing his gruff tones, I wondered, not for the last time, why he was content to have his children living so far from his protection.

'Right, let's get you settled.'

He about-turned and led me down a corridor into the east wing of the house; we passed between a succession of doors on one side, and on the other a series of large, Georgian-era windows offering what, in spite of the failing winter light, were spectacular views over rich Cullen parkland.

'Here it is. The Blue Room – which, as you can see, is painted bluuuuuuue!'

Plonking my hold-all on the floor, he proceeded then to plonk himself down on the bed. After a couple of happy bounces, he stretched himself full-length.

'Make yourself at home,' he said. 'There's loads of storage –

46

cupboard, chest of drawers. There's drawers under the bed, too. I think.'

He leaned over to look.

'Oh. Some of them have drawers under. Not this one. Sorry.' He pulled himself back up. 'You can stay as long as you like, by the way.'

'Oh, thanks. I, er... thank you. Actually, I have to be back the day after tomorrow; we've a partners' meeting, so...'

'Yeah, yeah, course. Still, it's great to see you, mate.'

I busied myself putting stuff away. Only after a few moments did I register the silence. I looked round; he'd turned over on his side and was directing his gaze through the window and onto some far-distant point.

It was a while before he became once more aware of my presence.

He sat up on the bed.

'Means a lot to me, you being here.' He smiled sadly. 'It's important, this party. It's the first since Denz... She was, er... It was just before Christmastime that, er... I mean, obviously the party got cancelled, and, well, I wasn't up to it last year – first anniversary, all that – but I told Shelley, I said to her, y'know, save the party poppers, cos I knew there'd be other times to come. And we did have a thing in the summer this year – a sort of midsummer do, a soirée. This, though – this – this here's the first New Year – well, the first actual New Year party since, uh... So I don't mind telling you, mate, I'm a bit nervous.'

'It's gonna be fine, I'm sure.'

'Yeah, well, hopefully one or two of the luvvies'll come bearing gifts – y'know... gifts from, say, Colombia...'

'Oh, like coffee, you mean?'

He laughed. 'Yes, mate. Coffee.'

After he left, I took a bath and changed for the party.

When I got downstairs, Reggie was in the ballroom with the musicians, regaling them with anecdotes about his own singing 'career'.

'Yeah, Parky said to me would I do a song, he'd heard I could hold a tune, how would I like to do My Way? Dunno, I says; maybe – maybe, if you sing it with me. Tell you what, you never seen a guy crap himself so comprehensively. Still, he couldn't say no, not in front of – Ah, there you are, mate! What d'you think?'

He gave us an Anthea, twirling about in knowingly camp honour of his unquestionably elegant white tuxedo.

'Nice,' I said. 'Very nice. Very *Diamonds Are Forever.*'

'Oh, I was thinking more *Great Gatsby*. Yeah, alright, don't look so surprised. I've read books. That one, at least – had to, didn't we, at school?'

With a while, as yet, before anything was due to happen, I was granted a tour of the house. It revealed, to my great gladness, that the spa block was the only major example of Cullenian tampering. Granted, it was a fairly major bit of tampering, but, at least, the only one to date – and, if nothing else, it was self-contained. In any case, as I told him (in a moment of uncharacteristic obsequiousness), there isn't a great house in England that's not been altered radically down the centuries. It's not true, of course: much of Hever Castle remains as Anne Boleyn would've known it; Longleat, on the other hand...

'Longleat, yeah? With the lions? Tell you what, I've gotta take you to Woburn. They've got lions, tigers, bears, the lot. Hippos!'

At seven o'clock, in the ballroom, the musicians – known

collectively as Panache – kicked off their first set. Approximately two minutes later, roughly halfway through The Doors' *Roadhouse Blues,* they were silenced.

Reggie emerged from behind the stage, brandishing the plug he'd just ripped from the wall.

'If I want deafening,' he quipped, 'I'll stick a fucking pencil in me ear. Just chill out, you lot, wait till we've got a few guests. Have a sandwich, yeah?'

In a way, there were two parties that night. The first saw Reggie, his household, myself and the band 'chilling out', downing sarnies and nattering. Lilian made a brief appearance, enjoying just the one glass of cava before returning to her subterranean lair. That, it would transpire, was very much par for the course. The entire basement area was her domain – the kitchen, the old butler's parlour, and an en suite bedroom; she was at home down there, and, as I would come to see for myself, she rarely left it when not on official business.

Festus, of course, availed himself fully of the layings-on. Sturdy as a golfer on the tee, he established himself beside the food table and proceeded to work his way mechanically through row after neat catered row of triangular sandwiches, desisting only when Reggie, mid-way through a sentence he was speaking at me, asided loudly, 'Festus, get away from them fucking sandwiches!'

When the first guests arrived, Reggie let the band out of the trap. Over the next few hours he was to be (or so it appeared) the life and soul of the party. It thrilled him to see all the faces, famous or otherwise, who'd turned up to help him usher in the new year – though he was also a little perplexed that none but I had gone for the sleep-over option. His occasional showbiz bathroom visits made him increasingly 'up-beat', and several times he stormed the stage to press-gang Christine, the Panache vocalist, into an unplanned duet. *You Got Me, Babe*, that was one of them. *My Way* was another – complete, of course, with the rambly intro about Parky. But it's the last one that echoes most vividly.

Shortly before midnight the band was once again silenced, this time in order to allow some words from our sponsor.

'Listen, I just wanna say thanks – yeah? – for all you coming here tonight and joining with me to celebrate the new year. As you know, it's the first New Year shindig we've had here since I lost my lovely Denz. Now, uh, where did I...? Where did I put her...?'

He smiled in acknowledgement of the tumbleweed silence. 'It's alright, guys, you *can* laugh... I mean, Jesus, you can't mourn for ever, can you? That's the last thing *she'd* have wanted. I'm over it – yeah? – and it's you guys helped me get to that place of safety. So thanks. Thanks very much.'

A sustained and generous ovation ensued. Reggie basked for a while, then begged silence. 'And now, if you'll make sure you've got something in your glasses, we'll count down to the... Oh, hang on...' He looked at his watch. 'Fuck, we're nearly there. I make it... Seven! Six! Come on! Five! Four! Three! Two! One!'

The room exploded in a frenzy of New Year hugging, snogging and party-popping.

I watched from the doorway, detached, suddenly much aware of just how far I was from any kind of home.

'What's wrong with you?'

Reggie was standing in front of me. I met his gaze but couldn't speak.

'Come on, what's up?'

'Nothing,' I gulped. 'Just...'

'Missing your old lady?'

'Well...'

'Tell me about it. The kids too, yeah?'

'Well, y'know...'

'Oh, *mate!*' he said, moving in for a hug. The guy really doesn't know his own strength – and yet, despite the lack of breath, it *did* seem to make things better.

He let go, looked me deep in the eyes. 'Everything's gonna be fine, mate. Don't worry, it's gonna be great – 2007. It's gonna be the best year ever. Believe me. *Do* you believe me?' I shrugged and forced a smile. 'Good lad. Hang about, what's this...?'

The band, it appeared, were having a go at The Smiths' *There Is A Light That Never Goes Out.*

'Fuckin' yeah!' – and away he went, bounding through the crowd, invading the stage, commandeering the mic and letting go with a performance which, in passion and commitment, made up in full for what it lacked in perfect tunefulness.

Drifting forward to watch the show, I found myself standing next to Shelley. Gazing up at her employer, she yelled aside to me, 'It's great to see him enjoying himself. It's been so long.' Then, without taking her eyes off the stage, she said, 'It must be strange for you, seeing him again after all these years.'

'Yeah, it's a bit weird.'

'So you were actually at school with him? I can't imagine him going to school!'

'He *did,* though. He's human, y'know – just like you and me.'

Now, for the first time, she detached her gaze from the stage.

'Reggie's been very good to me,' she said.

'I'm sure. Yes. I'm sorry.' So much for my powers of gentle satire. 'I didn't mean to be rude, I just... I can see you're very devoted to him.'

'In my *work*, you mean?'

'Absolutely.'

'Because there's never been anything else. I know *Denise* thought...'

Her voice, hitherto directed into my ear, began to wander off as we both became aware that Morrissey and Marr were no longer guiding Reggie in his account of their lyrics. In fact, Reggie wasn't even singing the same song. While the musicians were hanging on with *There Is A Light That Never Goes Out*, he seemed to be singing *Baby Come Back* by... by The Equals, I think – though, before long – *whoever* recorded it – before long, even *that* was going by the board. Essentially it was becoming a spoken word number.

'Come back,' he intoned, 'come back, baby, come back, come back, come back come back come back COME BACK! Alright, then, don't, fucking don't, fucking leave me alone, you bitch. Fuck off and leave me alone, you fucking... you fucking – you – you – you fucking wifemotherfuckingbitch FUCK OFF and leave me aloooooooone!'

Now, at last, he appeared to register the silence surrounding him.

'What's wrong?' he said. 'What's wrong?' He swung round to address the band. 'Come on, play some music! What – are we gonna to let that little tart spoil everything? I don't think so. Play some music, we'll dance on her grave!'

If something hadn't occurred, I'd have been compelled to *scream*; anything – just *anything* – to break the silence that continued to pervade the air for three or four eternally excruciating seconds before the guitarist, for want of any better idea, started up again with his part from *There Is A Light That Never Goes Out*.

'That's better,' muttered Reggie as the rest of the musicians joined in. 'Now dance. C'mon, dance. Everybody dance! Come on, don't let me spoil your fun. I just live here, that's all!'

With that he slapped the mic back into the hand of a shell-shocked Christine, jumped down from the stage, and wobbled his way toward the stairs. As he went, the crowd parted before him like the Red Sea; an apt metaphor, come to think of it, for even before he'd reached the top of the stairs, the exodus was getting under way.

– Navigation –

First memory of 2007: wandering into the lounge at Cullen
Place, there to be met with the sight of Festus, jellied out on a
sofa and covered with dogs. Two of them were draped across
his legs, a third curled atop his tor-like stomach, moving
gently up and down to the rhythm of the wheeze. There were
others of the pack, assembled on another sofa nearby, who
took the trouble to tumble down and greet me from their
perch of lesser privilege, but those who'd bagged a place on
Festus declined to move – and sensibly so, I thought;
although, in contrast to their host, even *they* at least cocked
their heads up to check me out.

In time I would come to know that Festus was no fonder
than I am of dogs; dogs, however, rated *him* most highly as a
source of warmth and tummy-comfort, and he'd long since
ceased wasting energy on their removal. Provided they didn't
actually obscure his view of the TV, he'd let them be. What
else had he to do, after all, than lollop downstairs from time to
time and hassle Lilian for food?

'Morning,' I said. 'Happy New Year!'

He looked up, just long enough to see I'd no grub to
covet, then returned his attention to the screen, mumbling me
back the vaguest of New Year greetings as he did.

'Seen Reggie?'

'No.'

'Thanks.'

In the ballroom, Shelley and Lilian were clearing up post-party. Like a good boy I helped out, filling bags in abundance with bottles and cans and the foul afterbirth of other people's tobacco habits.

Regarding the Lord of the Manor, Lilian was marginally more helpful than Festus, if not much more encouraging.

'You won't see Mr Cullen, not today.'

'Oh.'

Shelley was a bit more PR. 'I'm sure he'll put in an appearance, at least.'

'Not a chance,' insisted Lilian. 'Last time, he was in his room for two whole days – I had to leave his meals outside the door; even when he took them in, he ate hardly anything at all.'

'Well,' I said, 'that's New Year for you!'

'New Year? I'm not talkin' about New Year. I'm talkin' about the summertime.'

'Oh, yes, right – the summertime.'

Now I came to think of it, Reggie *had* made some vague allusion to a midsummer event – some reference to 'saving party poppers' – and though Shelley was reluctant now to go into details, I was pretty sure I got the picture: like the New Year bash just gone, the event had launched on a wave of hype and new beginnings, only to end in a similar outburst of wild, uncontrollable anguish. It made sense of the fact that nobody had chosen to stay over this time; they'd obviously reckoned – wrongly, it transpired – on being able to turn up, show their support, have a drink and a line, then bale out before things got awkward.

'How long d'you reckon...?' I said.

'Two days,' said Lilian.

'*Two days*?'

'No, honestly,' said Shelley, 'don't worry, he'll be down.' Upon which optimistic pronouncement, she bounded from the room, leaving me and Lilian to fill the unforgiving minute.

'I've, er... I've got a partners' meeting tomorrow.'

'That right?'

'No, not tomorrow, sorry. *Wednesday*.'

From upstairs there echoed a knocking on wood, followed by an apologetically timid '*Reggie...*?'

'Wednesday, yeah. But, y'know, I've got to *prepare* for it, obviously.'

'Obviously.'

'Reggie, it's Shelley... *Reggie...*?'

'Not having much luck, is she. You don't suppose he's, er...?'

'He's what, now?'

'No. No. Just joking.'

'You didn't *say* nothing.'

'Sorry?'

'You didn't *make* no joke.'

'No. No, not explicitly.'

She picked up her rubbish bag. 'He's not going to build no stadium, y'know.'

'Oh.'

Shelley reappeared.

'Sorry, Alex, he's really gone to ground. I'll keep trying, though. You just make yourself at home.'

'Right. Okay – though I don't have much time.'

'He's got a board meeting,' said Lilian.

Lacking cooperation from the 'client', I decided to seek at least a degree of usefulness in exploring the house. The stadium, more than likely, *was* a mere pipedream, but the spa block was something I could help with, and the more I knew about the main building, the better equipped I'd be to fight a claim of inappropriate development.

Cullen Place, I guessed, had originated as a large but probably not ostentatious farmhouse late in the reign of Elizabeth I. It had clearly been the subject of major aggrandisement during the baroque period, making Reggie's recent mock Tudor contribution all the more incongruous. That said, the external vulgarity of the spa block belied a surprisingly elegant interior. Rising up like a battleship from the floor, the pool was clad in a rich black Chinese slate, with a series of large portholes set into its outer walls. Arranged along one side were treadmills, rowing machines, assorted other gym gear, and, at the southern end, where the poolside steps began their ascent, a bar area looking out (via those unfortunate leaded windows) onto the surrounding parkland.

Stood there, minding my client's business, quietly taking in the facilities, I found myself pounced upon by a lanky young man with blonde hair.

'Hi, I'm Curtis!'

He looked vaguely familiar from the night before – I'd had him down as one of Reggie's metropolitan coke-hounds.

'Would you like an induction?'

'I'm sorry?'

'I manage Mr Cullen's spa for him. Would you like an induction – to the gym? We like to give people an induction, show them how the machines work – try and make sure they don't hurt themselves! If you like, we can book you in for later today.'

'Oh, no, that's okay. I'm only here till lunchtime.'

From the guileless disappointment in his face, I could see he wasn't exactly fighting off the inductees.

I continued my recce. On the far side of the house, a service door led me out into the courtyard. Across the way, in the stables, I encountered another member of Reggie's extensive staff: Harriet this one, a plump, ruddy-faced teen imbued, like Curtis, with a missionary zeal for her duties – surprising, perhaps, given that when I found her, she was wrist-deep in excrement.

'Every morning,' she laughed – 'every morning, bright and early, here's me, picking up plop!'

She introduced me to the means of production.

'This is Dobbin and Jasper' – she pointed to a couple of ponies standing in the stall next door – 'and down the end there, that's Brian.'

Brian was a donkey. I patted him.

'You gonna have a hack, then?'

'I'm sorry?'

'A *ride*? I thought maybe you...?'

'Oh. No, sorry. Not now.'

'Right. Sorry, I just assumed...'

'No.'

'Right.'

She sighed.

'They don't get much use these days – not since Mrs Cullen. They were *her* thing, y'see. I was teaching her to ride – Conrad, too, the older lad. I was going to teach them all, but *now*, of course...'

I shook my head. 'Tragic. It's a tragic story.' Then, for quick want of something less stupid, I said, 'My girls'd love it here.'

'Oh, well, bring 'em along, do.'

'Right. Yes, I will.'

'Any time. Any time in the morning.'

'Right.'

'Well, between ten and eleven. I just do the one hour now.'

'Right.'

'*Weekdays*, that is. Shelley does it on the weekends – and of course I'll get a day off in lieu of this – y'know, what with it being a bank holiday.'

'Right, right.'

'So, y'know, any time: weekdays, ten to eleven.'

'Right.'

At this point I withdrew; much longer and she'd've had us comparing diaries.

And so to the big metal shed. *Nothing to see here*, I figured; just hay bales and tools, and maybe – who knows? – maybe one of those jumbo lawnmowers, with a tractor to drag it along in its wake.

That, in fact – *that*: the big, draggy lawnmower – that was nowhere apparent, but there was ample compensation – for in that shed, by the light of the weak winter sun that followed me through the door, I counted at least a dozen other assorted motor contraptions.

'Oh, of course,' muttered I, full of green-eyed contempt. 'Of course – a playboy football legend; why would he *not* have his own motor museum...?'

Not that they were *all* museum pieces. Reggie's Porsche was there, stashed alongside a white Range Rover – but practical items such as these were far outnumbered by the vintage exhibits, which included a DeLorean, a sand-yellow BMW motorbike and sidecar, something ancient that looked like a Model T... and... and... and I wonder, am I souping this up in my delirium? No – no, I'm not: it *was* – it *was* – it really *was* Chitty Chitty Bang Bang!

Surely, though, not the real thing? I don't mean the *real* real thing – I didn't expect it to fly or anything, but, maybe... No, no, it *must* be a replica – not the actual one from the film? That, for sure, he'd keep in the house? He'd park it in the hall; he'd make it the focus of any and every media call he granted. It *couldn't* be the real thing – he'd not just shove it up the end of a shed, leave it there neglected.

I picked my way through the other exhibits and stood – just stood there, staring. I stared and I stared – and then, once having glanced around to confirm I was alone, I clambered up into the driver's seat.

Now, what could I say? I wanted something to *say*. Something American – something to quote from Dick Van Dyke.

Nothing. Nothing was coming to mind. All I could think of was the Child Catcher. 'Chil-dren! Come and get your custard!' No, not *custard*; what was it he said...? 'Ice creeeeam! Lollipops! All freeeeee!'

'They made six of 'em, y'know.'

I nearly shat my pants.

'For the film, I mean – they made six. Not all of them worked, of course.'

Where was he? I couldn't see a thing – could barely even hear, he was talking so gently.

'Yeah, there was one fully driveable – one they could take on the road, y'know; there was another, smaller one; there was one on that blow-up raft – that was just a shell... Don't remember about the rest. That there, of course, that's a replica.'

'Of course,' I said, only now starting to make out the silhouette of a head and an arm lolling out the driver-side window of the Range Rover.

'Sorry,' I said, suddenly aware that I'd had no formal permission to be where I was. I clambered to my feet.

'No, no, stay where you are.'

I sat down again, though feeling now a bit stupid and not at all like being Dick Van Dyke, let alone Robert Helpmann.

'Scrubbed up well, this old girl.' He patted the sill of the Range Rover. 'I mean, considering it's been under the sea – bit like Chitty! Or, no, not Chitty – more like that Lotus in *The Spy Who Loved Me*.'

'Both Ian Fleming.'

'You what?'

'Ian Fleming books. Both of them; both based on – y'know, *Chitty Chitty Bang Bang* and *The Spy... The Spy Who...* Sorry, are you...?'

I'd only now digested the significance of Reggie's previous comments. 'You're saying, *that* Range Rover...?'

'Oh, yeah, she done it in this. Drove it into the sea. Course, it wasn't under for long – couple of hours, if that; took a lot of flushing, though. Weeks, it took 'em; even though they'd told me – *promised* me, absolutely promised – it'd be done real quick. It's important, I said, I need it back in a week – after all the *doings*, I mean, after the coppers've had it, make sure there's no foul play or anything.'

He paused. Was he *crying*, I wondered? Crying, or simply taking a breath?

'So they says to me, 'A week? No problem. No problem at all, my man!' Fucking grease-monkeys. Six weeks later, they show up, pleased as Punch: *There she is: see what a great job we done!* I think, alright, I'll let it go, no harm done, not really, no one died – well, not *that* week, at least! Only, then, of course, I get the bill: it's twice what they said at the start. I told 'em, you can whistle for it.' He sighed. '*Another* lawsuit.'

'I thought you were still in your room,' I said.

'You what, mate?'

'I didn't expect to... I thought you were still in your room. *Everyone* did.'

'My *room*? Why'd you think that? I've been here all night.'

'In *here*? In the *car*?'

'Posh seats. New upholstery, everything.'

'Right.'

'Listen, mate, I'm sorry; really sorry.'

'For what?'

'What d'you think? Last night, of course.'

'Oh, don't be silly.'

'No, I was out of line, totally – and believe me, I don't care what all them coke-hounds thought; I'm just sorry to have embarrassed you. Stupid musos.'

'I'm sorry?'

'The band. They weren't to know, of course – no malice aforethought – but, see, that song, that was special for me and Denz. Sang it at our wedding – duet. That and *Something Stupid*. Course, when they started up with it, I was delighted – you saw me – but then... I dunno, all them words about dying in cars, it just...'

He started gently weeping.

Awkward. Awkward, for sure, at the best of times – but all the more so when you're perched in a fantastical flying car, way over on the far side of the room from the afflicted...

I climbed down from my mount and began to weave my way across to the Range Rover. What I might do when I got there, I could only guess. Hug him, perhaps? *Through the window?* Awkwardness on awkwardness – what had I embarked upon?

To my immense relief he started talking again.

'Funny,' he sniffed, 'I did think, at one time, of turning this into a motor museum.'

'Oh, did you? Good idea.'

'Yeah, but, y'know – health and safety: it's more trouble than it's worth.'

More trouble than it's worth? And he's after a *football stadium?*

'Listen, Reggie, I've had a great time – thanks so much for your kindness, but I really will need to be getting back, so if we could maybe go in the house and have a chat about your various projects...?'

'Projects? Oh, no, sorry mate. Not in the mood.'

'Well, I appreciate that, but I really *do* need to be...'

'Tomorrow, yeah? First thing tomorrow? Right now, I – y'know – I just want a bit of 'quality time' with the old girl.'

Old girl. Quality time with the old girl. *Now*, of course, hearkening back with wiser ears, I've cause to wonder: was his allusion to the car or to its former owner?

Retracing my steps along the side of the barn, I found myself once more in the courtyard. Shelley, dressed up in riding hat and boots, was talking in urgent murmurs to Harriet. Jasper, the larger of the two horses, stood saddled and quietly waiting.

'I'm sorry,' she was saying, 'I know, it's not fair. I'll make sure you're top of the list next time.'

Harriet, I sensed, was about to insist that 'next time' wasn't good enough. At that moment, however, the pair of them spotted me, and normal service resumed. Harriet smilingly took her leave, and Shelley asked if I fancied 'a bit of a hack'?

These people, with their 'hacking'!

Fact was, I'd not been on a horse in *years* – not since Mog and I took Rachel pony-trekking on Dartmoor, just before Lulu came into our lives. As Shelley so breezily observed, however, you never lose the ability to sit on a horse; so, having saddled up Dobbin and sourced me a helmet and some boots ('These were Denise's!'), she swung herself up onto Jasper, and away we clopped.

Our route took us round the back of the house, across the deerless deer park and down toward the lake. All the way and all the while, Shelley showed little inclination to talk of anything but Reggie.

'What was he like at school? It must've been so exciting!'

'*Exciting*? Don't know about that. It was... *okay*, I suppose. We had some fun. But what about you?'

'*Me*?'

'When'd you come on the scene – with Reggie, I mean? When'd you get the calling?'

She looked at me askance, but chose, on this occasion, not to engage with my irreverent tone.

'Nearly fifteen years I've been with him. Since I was at school, more or less. He came, one time – when he was playing for Fulham – he came to our school to do a talk about bullying – I went to a sixth form college in Fulham, you see – and, well, I don't know, I just fell in love with him there and then. I don't mean – y'know, *love* – I just – I mean, I just thought he was *wonderful*, so *energetic*, such a force of nature. I started going to see him play after that. Of course he was only there for the one season, then he moved on. By that time, though, I was already running his fan club. It was after he married Denise – when they bought this place – that I went full-time. Of course, she never wanted to move here; she wanted him to move back to Godham Malpass. Oh, but I'm sure you know all this – in fact, you must've *known* Denise – she was at your school.'

'Actually, no, I didn't.'

A lie, that. I *did* know Denise, but only as one of the gaggle of supermodels Reggie used to hang with after he graduated from my companionship. If it fits the legend to call her his teenage sweetheart, then so be it, but in fact she was just one of the many.

'He loved her so much, y'know. She was the love of his life. Of course, they fought a lot. All the time, in fact, towards the end. I think, in a weird kind of way, it sort of... sort of...'

'Turned them on?'

'Well, I, er... D'you know how they got together again? Reggie went back to school – your old school – he was invited back to do a talk...'

'About bullying?'

'No. No, about, I don't know, aspirational something-or-other, and afterwards they were going to take him out for a posh lunch, but he said no, that's alright, I'll eat in the dining hall with the kids – because, y'know, Reggie, he's very down-to-earth; and he was queuing up, and there was this lady behind the counter, serving the food, and at first he didn't recognise her, though of course *she* knew *him* at once, and she was just about to say something when he said, oh, that's not very much – she'd just given him some mashed potato, and he thought it was a bit, well, y'know, *mean* – and he said can I have some more? – rather, y'know, like Oliver Twist – and she said no, I'm only allowed to give one scoop per child. And he said, look, I'm a guest, surely I can have a bit more mash, and she said I don't care who you are, you get the same as everyone else. Of course, by this time he'd realised who it was, but he wasn't going to let on, any more than *she* was. So you see, that's what happened: they fell in love arguing about mashed potato!'

'And they never stopped.'

'Well, no.'

'Arguing, I mean.'

'No.'

'Not necessarily about...'

'Not about mashed potato, no, but...'

'No.'

We came to the lake and dismounted. Though I'd made no commitment to anything at all, my mind was already racing ahead, assessing possible locations. 'The Lakeside Stadium' – that'd sound good, tripping off the tongue of John Motson or one of his ilk. The lake itself would want to be a key part of the development. I say 'of course', but there again, how many places are named after natural features that were obliterated to make way for them? Where, pray, lies the heath in Thornton Heath? No, any development in this park would have to enhance, not destroy, what was already here.

There was plenty, for sure, in *want* of enhancement, and not just in terms of the grass run wild. At the far end of the lake stood a folly, a miniature Doric temple; in its day, newly-built and brightly painted, it would've caressed the eye with the effect of its doubling in the water – now though, the paintwork was mossy, the reflection disrupted by a lakebed that had built up with autumns and autumns of fallen leaves.

'You know,' said Shelley, 'the house is haunted.'

'Oh?'

'Yes. One of them – one of the ghosts, I mean – well, not the *ghosts*, but one of the people who *became* the ghosts – he drowned in this lake. Only he *didn't*. He was a stable boy, and

he was beaten to death by his father. A terrible drunk, he was
– the *father*, I mean – and he beat the boy to death in a
drunken rage. Then, apparently, when he sobered up and
found what he'd done, he threw the body in the lake to make
it look as if the boy had drowned.'

'Did he get away with it?'

'Well, yes, in a manner of speaking. They didn't *hang* him,
at least – but the boy came back, as a ghost, to tell the tale.
He's *always* coming back; he shows off his scars and his
bruises.'

'Have you seen them?'

'Well, no. There's others, as well. There's a lady, and a
monk – the Black Friar.'

'Seen *them*?'

'No. No, I haven't. Look, I'm really sorry about this.'

'About *what*?'

'All this killing time. It can't be much fun for you.'

'No, no, it's fine. I'm enjoying it. In any case, I needed to
see the estate.'

'He's really so pleased – he's delighted you're on board
with the stadium.'

'It's a bit early to say I'm *on board*. I can certainly help with
the spa appeal, but...'

'Oh yes, the spa. You know, people around here – the
Council especially, they've always had it in for him. It's not as
if anyone can *see* the thing – not from the road, not from any
of the surrounding estates.'

'I'm not sure that's the point – not to the authorities, at
least.'

'Why don't they just leave him alone?'

She swung back up into her saddle; with considerably less poise, I followed suit.

'Trouble is,' she said, 'they've never forgiven him for that barbecue.'

Ah yes, the barbecue. *Bar-b-gate*, as it came to be known. Hardly surprising that should rankle still. Shelley, after all, was the one who'd had to deal with most of the fall-out from Reggie's great offence – the offence that had sealed the end of his original love affair with the British public: back in '97, on the day of Princess Di's funeral, while the rest of the nation were lining the streets or enjoying their grief via the TV, Reggie, God help him, had taken it upon himself to have *fun*.

Neighbours were first alerted by the sound of Frank Sinatra blaring disrespectfully out from the Cullen family patio. A photo was taken and sold to a number of papers. Snapped from a ludicrously long distance, Exhibit A depicted an anonymous blob looking down at another anonymous blob which might or might not have been a barbecue. Not that Reggie was denying anything: in a whole series of record-straightening interviews, he repeated over and over again that he had the greatest respect for Princess Di, and that the barbecue was simply his own way of dealing with his enormous grief (there was, he noted on more than one occasion, 'a new angel in Heaven'). He had, in fact, met the princess at a number of charity events, and, as he assured his inquisitors, she was 'a lovely girl, real lovely, not just a looker but real *nice* an' all'. Unfortunately, for some at least, he dwelt rather too much on the looks thing, going on to say that if Prince Charles didn't want her the stupid berk was looking a gift horse in the mouth. 'He's a lovely bloke, our Charlie, but he should've known when he was on to a good thing. Still, there was plenty of others to fill in for him – know what I mean?'

From this, to nobody's surprise (but his), flowed a whole new torrent of abuse. 'YOU SICK PERV!' roared *The Sun*.

And who had responsibility for sorting through the mailbags – for separating fan mail from death threats? Not Reggie. No; he was in America with his family, two thirds of the way through an ill-fated engagement with some east coast soccer team (he'd flown out almost immediately after being dumped from Glenn Hoddle's England squad). Thus it was in upstate New York that the offending barbecue occurred, yet it was at Cullen Place – on Shelley's watch – that most of the shit hit the fan.

'Are you hungry?'

'I'm sorry?'

'Shall we head back in? There's plenty of food left from last night.'

'Oh, fine.'

'And then, after lunch, maybe I'll have another go at raising Reggie.'

'Oh. No. Sorry, I should've said: I found him. He's in the garage.'

'The garage? Oh, not the *Range Rover*? I'm so sorry, I should've thought of that.'

'He'd been there all night.'

'Yes, yes, he would. He's done it before. I do wish he'd get rid of that thing. Of course, he did *try*. I mean, he *wanted* to use it for the funeral. He wanted to send her off on a great big pyre – put her at the wheel and send her up in a cloud of smoke – like the Indians, he said.'

'Er...?'

'Not the *American* Indians.'

'No.'

'The Indians in *India*.'

'Right.'

'Everyone thought it a bad idea, Jack and Monica especially – Denise's parents; it wasn't what *they* wanted at all. In the end, of course, it came down to the car people – they couldn't get it ready in time. And, of course, there were questions about permits – the authorities; we'd need a permit, they said, even if it was done on the estate.'

'Pesky pen-pushers.'

'Exactly. They really *do* have it in for him, I don't know why.'

– Eternity –

12:13pm

How many ghosts? How many did she say?

Three. Three of 'em.

Lady Someone, broken-hearted.

Lady Someone, yeah; she hanged herself – and in my room. Strung herself up in a cupboard in the Blue Room. Freaky, that, though I never – no – never saw her. Saw or heard. Never lost a night's sleep – not over that, at least.

And there was...

Devere – that's it! Lady Alice Devere. Cupboard-Lady was Alice Devere.

Okay, so, there was, Lady Alice; there was a monk... I say 'was'; *'is'*, I suppose, though me, I never...

Bullshit, of course.

Reggie, mate, it's bullshit. I'm sorry. Just bullshit.

Mind, there *were* a couple of times, with the dogs... They used to be locked in the lounge at night, and a couple of times they *did* get out. Later, this was – later on, after Festus and Lilian had left and Reggie wasn't getting out of bed, so it was only me or Shelley who... who... Two or three times it happened, though, and Shelley swore – *she* swore and *I* swore – absolutely certain, I was...

Doesn't count, though. That's not ghosts, that's...

71

So there was Lady Whatsit. *Devere*, yeah. There was the Friar – the Black Friar – though I did a bit of research one time, on the internet, and the house is miles from the site of any religious ruins or anything. I mean, yeah, there's a priest hole in the dining-room, and that was used, apparently, by someone who later went on to be caught and tried and butchered at Tyburn. But why – of all the grand houses – many much grander than Reggie's... He'd have been – this guy – he'd have been all over the country, giving succour to the great and good of the Catholic underground. Why would he want to spend eternity at Cullen Place?

He wouldn't, that's the answer.

So, there's the Black Friar (or *priest*, or whatever); there's Lady Devere; and there's... come on, there's... there's – come on, you had it just a while ago – the lake – yes, of course! – yes, the little stable lad, showing off his bruises.

So that's three. Three of them:

1. the friar;

2. the lady;

3. the little stable boy.

Just the three. Oh, unless, of course, you're inclined to believe in anything that comes off the mouth of Reggie Cullen.

Three of 'em.

– Surplus –

I was a full day late returning to the office, and nobody gave a shit. Or, if they did, they weren't letting on.

But then, they weren't letting on about much at all.

As I wandered the central work zone, dispensing tardy New Year blessings from desk to desk, I perceived a peculiar diffidence afflicting even the most boisterous of my junior colleagues. Looking back now, of course, I get it: they were simply embarrassed to be talking to me.

At the time, though, I didn't pick up on these vibes; my mind was otherwise engaged with the knowledge that, sooner or later, I was going to have to venture into Charlotte's office – and the knowledge that, when I eventually did so, every pair of eyes in the place would go with me.

Smoked glass. Such a good idea it seemed at one time: smoky brown glass to wall off the execs. Not exactly new or radical (old hat, in fact, said Ollie the Nose), but it did the job: a sense of hierarchy; a sense of democracy. Brilliant. And now, in lovingly smoky detail, every bugger in the place could read the body language of me and my ex-lover.

I managed for some while to put off the moment – she helped by being perpetually on the phone – but finally I was obliged to grasp the nettle. As casually as I could, I rapped on the door and wandered into her enviably tidy workspace. Our eyes met; then, just as our lips parted to make some awkward utterance, her phone went again. She took the call, and I *pretended* to read a copy of *Building Design* whilst listening to her talk about the Terriss Centre. She seemed to have things very much in hand.

'Happy New Year,' I said, at last.

'Yes, happy New, uh...'

'Sorry I'm late.'

'Oh, not at all...'

'Been following up on a lead.'

'Right.'

'In Bedfordshire.'

I *hadn't*, of course. Despite my efforts, nothing at all had been followed up. Reggie, for all his promises, had proved no more significantly cooperative the day after New Year – not, at least, in the morning, when I was hoping to see him. It was in the late afternoon in fact, as I packed for home, that he finally made an appearance, bouncing into my room with all the hyped-up glee of a child on its birthday.

'Come on, then, come and see the sights! I'll show you the estate.'

I glanced out the window. Pitch black. 'You're mad.'

'No, come on – we'll do it by torchlight – be an adventure.'

I thanked him, but explained that in fact I'd already done some location-scouting, and, no matter my thirst for further adventure, could delay my departure no longer. 'I'm a day overdue at the office already.'

As it turned out, I needn't have worried.

'It's alright,' said Charlotte. 'I've just been getting on with things.'

'I can see you're well on top of it.'

An awkward silence.

'McAlpine's say they can start Phase 2 on 1st April.'

'Oh. Great. Great news. April Fools' Day.'

'Right, April Fools.'

Silence again.

'Oh,' she said, 'what'm I talking about? Why'm I telling you that? We knew before Christmas.'

'Did we? Oh, yeah, so we did.'

'They told us after the hearing.'

The hearing, yes. That fatal hearing, where victory was mine, and mine to squander – which I did with consummate ease.

What did I expect, returning home that evening? One of the highest courts in the land had decided in my favour – at the very public, very humiliating expense of my wife – and yet I remember imagining, as I stepped over the threshold that evening, that I might just get a word or two of resentful congratulation from Mog.

What I got, of course, was a showdown over Charlotte.

Charlotte? I said – that's insane. Just cos I – what, cos I hugged her – *kissed* her, even? We'd just won a massive court battle. Relief beyond measure. I recognise, of course, I said, you're not gonna like the verdict; but surely, at least, you – *you*, of all people, a lawyer with such a wealth of experience – you can surely understand the nature of our relief? I kissed her. So what? It didn't mean a thing – not a thing, except to say that we were *glad.*

Glad. A proper charlie moment, that. Glad. Not that I was using, but still, there was a *vibe*. Back when Oliver was at the height of his habit, I used to marvel at the enormity of the lies he'd seek to sell. Doubtless I was the same in my victory moment: high already on the thrill of the adventure with Charlotte, and now pumped up to new heights of arrogance by the ecstasy of that High Court decision. Facing my wife that night, it seemed to me that I could fool *all* of the people *all* of the time. Okay, she'd seen the kiss, but so what? A chaste expression of comradely joy, that's all it was.

She'd have to buy that, right?

No.

No *what*?

No, she said, not the kiss; that's not it at all.

By the time the judge pronounced on the case, she said – by the time she saw me lay that teary-eyed snog on my colleague – she'd known already for hours. She'd *seen us*. She'd seen us, she explained, in the canteen during recess: we were talking to our brief – it was me, Charlotte and Mr Adler. Charlotte was eating chocolate. She offered some to us: Adler declined; I said yes; so, she broke off a piece... and placed it in my mouth.

Fucking *chocolate*.

'Exciting, don't you think?'

'I'm sorry?'

'Exciting – we're really going ahead with it.'

'Oh. Yes, that's right. Yes. I mean, unless... Mog...'

'*Mog*...?'

'On the legal side – she could always pull another fast one, bring it grinding to a halt again.'

'D'you think she will?'

'If she *can*, absolutely. Especially after...'

'After...?'

'Y'know...'

'Oh. God. Yes...'

'Which is why I was late back.'

'Right. Yes. I mean, no. Sorry, no, I don't follow...? You

were late back because... because she...?'

'Well, she's... y'know, she's really...'

'Angry.'

'Yeah, about... *us* – us – us – y'know...'

'Right. So, she...?'

'She'll do anything – anything, y'know, to... to...'

'To *derail*...?'

'Exactly.'

'Right.'

'So, y'know, we need... need more...'

'More...?'

'More balls.'

'Sorry?'

'In the air.'

'Right.'

'More balls in the air – and, so, that's why, y'see, that's why I was late back. I've been checking out this old school friend – I'll tell you who it is...'

The phone rang.

'Sorry, better...'

'Yes, of course.'

The call went on. There being only so much interest I could feign in *Building Design*, I mouthed an awkward 'see-you-later' and wandered out – straight into the path of Rocky. Dear, dear Rocky. Oliver's chief acolyte. Least, he *was*. Dead now, no doubt. Rowland. That was his real name – Rowland – but people called him Rocky because... well, come to think of it, because he *asked* them to.

'Alex! My man! How's it hanging?' He threw his bony arms around me, gave me a faceful of his Christmas after-shave, and then, as if not already way over the line, he dropped his voice and added, 'Or should I be addressing that question to Charlotte?'

'No,' I said, scarcely believing. Wavy-permed little shitbum, where in the name of Christ did he get off?

'Alex!'

And then there were two.

'We've been expecting you,' said Oliver, taking my hand in his icy grip.

Once there was a time when we did showbiz hugs. Long, long past.

'I've been in Bedfordshire,' I said. 'Possible – just *possible* we're gonna be building a football stadium.'

'*Really*? Tell me more.'

'Well...'

'Sorry...' He whipped out his Blackberry '... better take this.'

I'd swear on the Bible it hadn't even rung.

'*Stadium*?' said Rocky. He took a step toward me. 'Who...?'

'You'll hear all about it, don't worry.'

I moved away, quickly and purposefully heading for the office of the Velvet Fist. I knocked and entered uninvited, hoping to give the impression, to all who might be watching, of urgent business. I knew, of course, that I was safe to barge in: Maurice is never busy. He's the boss because his father was the boss, but he doesn't do any real managing. The wearer of the pants is Trevor Crisp, officially head of Accounting. Maurice is there purely to rubber-stamp the prevailing wind.

'Alex!' He jumped to his feet. 'Good to see you, *really*

good.'

He came round from behind the desk and shook my hand. The Judas Handshake, yeah. Mind, when Judas kissed JC that time, it was probably a pretty butch affair – a rugged, decisive kind of kiss. Shaking hands with Maurice, that was like fondling a wilted lettuce – and why, indeed, would you do such a thing?

Not that I'm Jesus or anything.

Uh... Uh... Where...? Where...?

Oh yeah – Maurice's office.

'I hope your Christmas was a pleasant one.'

'Yeah, thanks, it was, um... No. No, come to think of it, no, it wasn't that pleasant – but listen – never mind – listen: guess where I went for New Year? Reggie Cullen's house.' His face was a blank. 'Reggie Cullen, the footballer...?'

'Oh, yes, the fellow whose wife...'

'Exactly.'

'Just down the street.'

'Right. Yeah, we were at school together, me and Reggie.'

'Oh, how interesting.'

'We got back in touch over Christmas. I spent the New Year at his place in Bedfordshire – he's got this Jacobean mansion – well, Jacobean/baroque/mock Tudor, to be specific. Anyway, he's got a bit of a passion for building things, and, well...' I laughed self-consciously. '...he reckons he's going to put up a football stadium.'

'Oh?'

'Sounds crazy, I know – his own football stadium – but he might just be serious. So, that's why I was there. That's why I'm late back.'

'Oh, please, no need to explain.'

'Obviously I wouldn't want to waste too much time on it, not at this stage, especially with the need to proceed with the Terriss Centre...'

'Oh, well, I wouldn't worry too much about that.'

'No, I'm not *worried*, but...'

'Charlotte's got things very much in hand.'

'Course she has. She's well on the ball. In fact...'

'In fact, I wanted to talk to you about that. Y'see, we've been discussing the project, with a view to the next stage of proceedings – *vis-a-vis* taking it through to that stage and indeed carrying it *beyond* that stage to...'

Here I begin to switch off. I'm thinking, Oh dear, it's one of *those* sentences – one of those Maurice sentences, stringy as a clause in a contract. I drift away, as ever, supposing I can tune in again later without having missed anything of substance. Then, just as my mind's almost out the door, I reach back, grab a hold of two words – 'Charlotte' and 'piloting'.

'Sorry – what did you say?'

'She's certainly *more* than capable.'

'*Capable*? Sorry – capable of *what*?'

'Oh. Well, like I said, we thought it'd be good if she were to pilot Phase 2 from here on in. That way you'd be free to...'

'I beg your pardon?'

He hesitated. I was presumably reacting just the way he'd feared.

'You're so talented, Alex, it seems a waste to have you tied down on one project...'

'*One project*? What d'you mean? It's not *one project*. It's the

Terriss Centre. It's our flagship.'

'Oh, no question, no question at all – but, now it's got to this rather mundane stage of development –'

'Are you telling me I'm off the project?'

'No, no, not off the project, absolutely not; just –'

'It's my project.'

'Alex...'

'It's *my* project.'

'With the greatest respect, no individual in this practice...'

'*Respect!* You take a decision like this, without...'

'I assure you, full discussion...'

'Oh, you'll *get* a full discussion, don't you worry. Full discussion? Wait till the partners' meeting. If you think...'

'It was the *partners* who decided.'

'Believe me, first on the agenda – What? Sorry, what did you say? The partners...?'

'The partners decided. Yesterday.'

'What? I mean, no. I mean, how? The partners – the meeting; that's *today*.'

'Yes, well, I'm afraid it was decided to, er, to bring it forward. You see, there was a majority of the partners present in the office, and, well, as you were the only one who, er...'

Chancing, at that moment, to glance through the smoky office wall, I beheld a scene of uncommonly fanatical industry: twenty or so colleagues were buried deep, deep, deep in tasks which I knew, just a nanosecond earlier, would have been subject to complete neglect. In the foreground of the scene stood Oliver Grant. His mobile was pressed against his ear, but unlike the others, he made no bones about keeping his eyes firmly on me.

'Ah,' I said, quieter now, turning my attention back to Maurice. 'Yes, I see. I understand.'

'I'm not sure you do. We're not taking you off the project, you see, we're just...'

I wanted so badly to tell him where to stick the project. I'd have done it too, if only I could speak – *speak*, I mean, without the risk of tears. It was the second time in a week, this, and it troubled me. New Year, that was understandable, there was alcohol involved. This, though – in full sobriety?

'Honestly, nobody wants to take you off the project.' Maurice, it seemed, was still talking. 'We all respect your work so much – you've done such a... such a... well, such a *lovely* design...'

Lovely? Did I hear that right? He really said I'd 'done' a 'lovely' design?

'We just want to give you a bit more freedom.'

I laughed. That helped – it broke the spell. At last I managed to get out a few words, imparted slowly through a succession of deep breaths. 'I have sweated blood... I have given... everything. Everything. Even my... my *marriage*, quite possibly...'

'Yes, well, that's part of the problem. We feel you may have given too much.'

'*What?*'

'We...'

'*What?*'

'We...'

'You don't trust me?'

'It's not so much that *we* – absolutely not; not *we* – but, but you see...'

'What, then?'

82

'It's just, the *client*...'

'The client? What – the fucking Council? *They* don't trust me?'

'Oh, well, they didn't actually *say*, in so many words...'

'What, then? What's the problem? Cos *Mog* – I mean, *Mog*, she – she... Have I not, over and over, proved my loyalty? I *left* her, remember – I *chose* – because of this project...'

'Ah, well, now, Alex, you see...'

'*What? What?*'

'Well, it's just that, with the greatest respect, our understanding...'

'*Respect!*'

'...our general understanding was that, in actual fact, in as much as it's our business, *Imogen* was actually... was actually the one who...'

'Alright, yes, okay. Okay, it was *her* – she chucked me out – and yes, before you say it, yes, technically because of Charlotte, but – but, but, but – if not for this project, none of it would've happened in the first place.'

'Alex, believe me – please, believe me – nobody appreciates your sacrifices more than...'

'This,' I said, rising now to my feet, 'is bullshit. Bullshit. Just stop it. Tell me why you've done this.'

'Well, as I say, some people – not myself in particular, but some people, at certain levels, including but not exclusive to those speaking for the client, were fearful that, if it came to a choice between saving your marriage and saving the project...'

'So what d'you want me to do?'

'Beg your pardon?'

'What d'you want of me? Assuming you don't actually

want me to leave the practice...?'

'Oh, God forbid, no.'

'*What*, then?'

'What we... Well, what we'd like you, er – and thanks for asking, thanks for being so... I mean, what we'd like you to *do*, as such, for a *while* at least – say until construction has started on Phase 2 – we'd like you to, er, well, how can I put this...?'

'I'm sure someone's *told* you.'

'Oh. Well, er, yes. What we'd like, more than anything, would be for you to act as a, er... a sort of ambassador at large...'

'An ambassador?'

'Exactly, yes. At large. In other words, we're giving you the freedom – full, unfettered freedom – to go out and find us new projects, wherever they may be. And I must say, by the sound of it, you've already made a jolly good start!'

***

I was glad. Strangely glad. Angry, too, but with an anger fuelled more by pride than desolation. Naturally, I did the strutting-out-of-the-office thing – *naturally*. I wouldn't have known how to smile off an insult of such magnitude – and yet, sitting and fuming thereafter in the car, I had the unmistakable sense of a great weight lifting from my shoulders. A long, long time I'd been helming this project, and a great, great deal had it cost me... so, even as I sat there, my two hands jabbing at the steering-wheel to the rhythm of the word 'Cunts!', I was starting to see that this new situation might yet prove a blessing, however cunningly disguised.

I called Imogen.

'Can you talk?'

'Depends what you want.'

'*Want?* What I want is to make peace.'

She laughed. 'Just like that?'

'Is it beyond the realms of feasibility?'

'I really don't know. Last time I saw you, the hatred in those eyes...'

'*Hatred?* Hardly hatred.'

'No?'

'*Frustration*, for sure, but... But, look, let me get to the point: I've quit the project.'

'Oh?'

'I mean, I know it's not much of a gesture now, with Phase 2 going ahead, but at least *I* won't be involved any more. Matter of fact I'm going to... well, believe it or not, I'm gonna build a football stadium!'

'Football stadium? Where?'

'Well, not so much a *where* as a *who*. See, I bumped into *Reggie Cullen*, and...'

'Reggie Cullen – the footballer?'

'Of *course* Reggie Cullen the...'

'Reggie Cullen the *violent* footballer?'

'I think that's a bit...'

'Oh, but of course, it's a 'contact sport'. So, anyway, you bumped into Reggie Cullen...?'

'Right, yeah, on Boxing Day – just after...'

'*The* Reggie Cullen?'

'*What?*'

'*The* Reggie Cullen?'

'Yes – we've already established: *the* Reggie Cullen, who –'

'*The* Reggie Cullen who was your dearest childhood friend then dumped you in favour of cooler people – dumped your entire family and left you all for dead – *that* Reggie Cullen?'

'Yes,' I said. 'Yes. Yes, right: *that* Reggie Cullen.'

'Right. Well. So, you're off the project?'

'Yeah. Yeah, I'm done with it. Wish I could say I was done with the practice as well – the whole bloody thing – but I'm not quite that noble.'

'Nor that reckless.'

'Well, no. I mean, I'm not gonna cut off my nose to spite my face.'

'I should hope not. After all, it wouldn't be *your* face alone – not if we got back together.'

'*What?* Well, no. I... I, er... No – and that's the point. That's why I quit the project; it's done enough damage already. I can't let it do any more.'

'That right?'

'Yes,' I said. 'Yes, that's right.'

'Oh, okay, fine. Well, listen, I have to leave for court in a moment, but just before I go, what would you say if I told you I already *knew* you were off the Terriss project...?'

'I'm sorry?'

'...and that, the way I understand it, you didn't jump, you were *pushed*.'

'Where'd you hear that?'

She laughed. '*Where'd I hear that?* That's your answer?'

What could I say? I mean, where *had* she heard it?

'Well...?'

'Well *what?* You obviously know it's true. Why, if you knew already, why on earth would you allow me to...?'

'No, no, no, no, no, don't make this about me. What about *you*? Why didn't you just tell me the truth? Why didn't you say, 'I've been chucked off the project, but that's okay, I'm cool with it, cos it gives us a chance to make a new start?'

The question hung in the air for a number of seconds before I grabbed at it.

'Alright,' I said, 'how about this: I've been chucked off the project, but that's okay, I'm, uh, I'm 'cool' with it, cos, y'know, it... it gives us, er... er...'

A deep sigh drifted down the line.

'If only it were that simple,' she said. 'If only it were purely about the theatre.'

'What else is it...? Oh. What – you mean me and...?'

'You and Charlotte, yes.'

'Yeah, well, I *am* sorry about that, but...'

'That's a start.'

'I've said it *repeatedly*, over and over. I'm desperately, sincerely sorry – but, the fact remains, if you and I, if things between us had, y'know, had been...'

'Oh dear...'

'What?'

'Nothing's *ever* your fault.'

'Oh, change the fucking record.'

'*Record? Record*, you say? Why, Alexis, my love, I don't *do* records. Perhaps you remember: we replaced them with CDs – just as we replaced the tradition of husbands being able to demand sex on tap.'

'No, not on tap, just occasionally – if only to prove the equipment still works.'

'You hardly need a woman for that. Anyway, sorry, look,

I've got to go – Christ, look at the time! Due in court – really sorry, got to go get an injunction against a wife-beater! Talk soon!'

And that was it.

Textbook Mog. Absolutely textbook: *à propos* absolutely nothing at all she lobs that in the mix – *injunction against a wife-beater* – imply some kind of revolting kinship between me and that creep. And that's if the creep existed in the first place! For all I knew, there *was* no wife-beater; for all I knew, she'd conjured him out of the air, just so as to end the conversation from an artificially constructed region of moral high ground – which she didn't even need to do, cos let's face it, I'd just tried to lie myself back into her pants. She was already in command of a perfectly genuine piece of prime, unassailable moral high ground – with planning permission pre-granted.

– Divergence –

Mog doesn't even *like* theatre. That's what's absurd. Well, *ironic*, at least: all that argy-bargy – all the way to the High Court – and she's not even a fan, not really. I remember, when first we were going out – back in those glory days when she'd do almost anything to spend time with me – live drama was her line in the sand.

A two-hour lecture on brutalism at RIBA? No problem at all, she could handle that. Try and get her along to a *play?* Not a chance.

'For one thing,' she'd say, 'the seats are always uncomfortable.' (True enough, and it's a point we addressed in the Terriss refurb.) 'For another, I don't see why I should have to make so much effort. The moment the lights go down, I'm working even harder than the actors – working my arse off to suspend my disbelief, struggling like mad to get used to the fact that everyone's *shouting*. They don't do that in films. Why do they do it in the theatre? I don't pay good money to be shouted at.'

Compare and contrast with the messianic zeal of later years: the way she'd force me, in her capacity as President of the Friends of Godham Theatres – *force* me, she would, once a week at least – to do pilgrimage to the Terriss; be it some creaky thriller wall-to-wall with soap stars, or some such clueless soapie trashing *Lear* or *Macbeth*, she was ever-present, relentless in support of the cause.

What happened, one might ask, to bring on such a change?

Our marriage – that's what happened. Or rather, the *fruit* of that marriage. She had a couple of kids then lost interest in sex – and no, that's not just my misogynistic, paterna-phallocentric interpretation: she's said as much herself. As for her new theatrical zeal, that was less a case of changing taste than changing status: emerging as a pillar of the community, she found things thrust upon her, and one of them happened to be the Presidency of the Friends. Once appointed, though, she made like Thomas à Becket, pursuing the cause with a passion far beyond anyone's expectations.

In this context, I could have been forgiven for seeing the Civic Centre competition as a chance for vengeance. In fact I approached it as a means of mending bridges. Despite the fact that the Terriss Theatre was of no real architectural interest (even Matcham had his off days), I submitted a design which, alone amongst all the entries, aimed to preserve the existing building and make it the centrepiece of the new one.

It was naïve to imagine that this sensitivity would be appreciated by anyone beyond the membership of the judging panel. Like all fence-sitters, I was assailed from both sides: condemned by such as *Blueprint* for my architectural conservatism, and by the Friends (especially by their President) for my tendency toward architectural vandalism.

As for the other thing, there was actually a brief, thrilling period of reconflagration, when the ferocious passion of our arguments spilled over into the bedroom. That, however, was before I actually won the competition. Thereafter the debate moved on from harmless theory: as the years went by and the project got nearer to green-light status, so it ate away at our relationship: lack of sex turned to lack of touch turned to lack of any kind of communication whatsoever.

Who knows? It was maybe inevitable, this alienation. Who am I to say it wouldn't in time have crept into our lives without the help of some old playhouse? Well, this isn't *Star Trek*, sadly, so I've only the one reality to explore: the one that occurred, the one in which my marriage was seen to disintegrate even as my architectural career moved remorselessly on to its greatest triumph.

Charlottegate was an incident waiting to happen.

– Huh –

Looking back now on those early days of 2007, I all too clearly see how once again I squandered a chance to shun this dismal destiny of mine.

All I had to do was reassert control of the Civic Centre project. Instead I sulked – I did a Reggie: stayed in bed, declined to go to work... waited, basically, for those fuckers to ring up and grovel. It was a strategy of sorts, but here's the thing: when, in the wake of his New Year meltdown, Reggie proceeded to shrink back into himself, people were anxious to coax him out again – 'Please, Reggie, *say* something, *eat* something.' When *I* did it, no one even noticed. All morning I festered, entirely untroubled by either of my parents, and when my mobile eventually rang, it wasn't the office, it was Mog, asking could I ferry the girls to a birthday party that afternoon? She was wanted, it seemed, up in town: some big deal at the RCJ.

Nice to be popular.

'Dad, what's that under your jumper – is that your pyjamas?'

'Yes, Rachel, well observed.'

'Why?'

'Why what – the pyjamas? Cos I'm achingly trendy, and I'm going back to bed when I get home.'

'Are you sick?' asked Lulu.

'No, just sulking.'

'Why're you sulking?' said Rachel. 'Is it because you got the sack?'

'*What?* What're you on about? *Sacked?*'

'Mummy says you've been sacked,' said Lulu.

'Mummy has an axe to grind.'

'What d'you mean an axe to grind?'

'Never mind.'

'He means she's angry with him because of the theatre and because of that lady.'

'What – the lady he kissed?'

'Hey, never mind the lady. Just get this: I have *not* been sacked, I've been taken off the Civic Centre – that's all.'

'But you really *liked* the Civic Centre,' said Lulu. 'You said it was the best thing you'd ever done.'

'Well, yes, it *was* – it *is*. It's... I don't know – it's caused a lot of trouble. Maybe I'm better off without it.'

'Do you really *think* that?' Rachel, of late, has developed an alarming capacity – a capacity mainlined straight from her mother – for knowing when people are full of shit. 'Cos if *I* cared that much about something, I'd tell them they're wrong and get them to change their minds.'

I didn't bother going home again. I dropped the girls at their party then made for the office.

'I want another partners' meeting.'

'Yes, of course,' said Maurice, 'there's another one next Wednesday.'

'No, not Wednesday. *Now.*'

'Oh, well, I'm afraid that's not really possible.'

'Why? We've had emergency meetings before.'

'Absolutely. Only, right now, you see, it's not *physically* possible. We'd not be quorate – a number of our colleagues are on holiday.'

'Oh, is that right? Interesting. New Year getaways, yeah? That means they must've altered their plans – they must've actually come in specially for the other meeting – for the one the other day, the one you rescheduled to... to... I mean, such dedication – coming in specially, just to stitch me up before they fuck off on their hols.'

'Alex, how could you *think...?* Believe me, it wasn't like that at all.'

By now I wasn't listening; by now I was sailing proudly out of Maurice's office and setting course for mine, dismissing en route an enquiry from Kelly, the receptionist, as to when the water cooler people might be arriving.

I sat down to look at some emails. Nothing much got taken in. Too busy, I was, looking forward to the partners' meeting.

Flawless logic, breath-taking rhetoric – these, I vowed, would be my weapons.

A throat was cleared.

Kelly, slouched on the threshold of my fishbowl. 'It's just, people've been asking.'

'I'm sorry?'

'About the water cooler.'

'*What?* Why're you asking me? Just ring the water people.'

'Yeah, alright then. Nice PJs, by the way.'

'Thanks.'

No time to waste. I'd the gift of a week; I must use it to the full, use it to devise a cast-iron strategy for the meeting, whilst of course proceeding in a mature, constructive way with my interim tasks. Those tasks were crucial: if I were to take back the Terriss Centre I'd need something to swap for it – thus, the Reggie stuff had to move forward at speed.

Having already done a few rough (and, at this stage, purely generic) sketches for the stadium, I emailed them to Reggie then got on with the matter of the spa block appeal. This, if less glamorous than the other thing, should at least have been more straightforward, entailing for now a simple series of document requests to the professionals involved, i.e. the original architects, the local council, and of course Reggie's lawyers, the grand old firm of Ferris, Pettit and Fain.

I got not a peep from any of them.

Reggie was equally hard to pin down: he didn't respond to my emails, his mobile was going straight to voicemail, and when I rang the house all I could get was Shelley – who, despite her best efforts, had no success in locating him.

Still, if nothing else, I had the attention of my colleagues. Constant surveillance. Those glass walls – I felt like some kind of zoo beast. *Architectus pyjamarus*. God forbid they should get on with a bit of work.

But they were only half the problem. As well as being naturewatched through the front wall, I had the extra challenge of trying to keep my eyes away from the side wall, and the view it gave me through to Charlotte's office. Every time I looked up I found myself fuming afresh at the sight of my one-time protégée – the one I'd favoured; the one I'd fast-tracked over all protests (because, and *only* because she was exceptionally bright and able and keen) – getting on with the job – *the* job – of making a reality of *my* conference centre. I knew, of course (pretty sure, at least) that she'd done nothing underhand to upgrade her already high status on the project, notwithstanding, I'd have welcomed from her just a little bit more awkwardness about the whole thing.

Fret not, Alexis – that's what I told myself: a week from now – the partners' meeting – once more will the world be puddle-luscious. *Justice, after all, is on your side.*

Justice, yeah. Nice idea. It's hard to believe in justice, though – in the ultimate triumph of right – when all things point the other way: when you're watching your erstwhile lieutenant assert command over your pet project; when you and all the people about you can see she's doing it with effortless charm and efficiency; and, above all, when certain of those people appear to think you've nothing better to do than deputise for the office manager.

'Al, we need some toilet paper.'

'*And*...?'

'Well, Sheila's away...'

'Yes...?'

'Well, she's got the key to the petty cash...'

'Look, Kelly, I'm trying to... Oh, never mind: here...'

I plonked a tenner in her hand. It might just as well have been a turd, fresh and steaming.

'What – d'you want more?'

'No,' she said. 'It's fine.'

Only when she'd gone did the penny drop: Kelly actually thought *I* should volunteer to go out and get the bog paper.

I mean, Christ, does Richard Rogers do that? Maybe so, who knows? Maybe that's why everyone thinks he's so great, 'cos he can walk with kings yet keep the common touch as he pops down to Budgens and stands in the queue with his overpriced Andrex, trading gossip with Zaha Hadid, who just came out to stock up on tea, milk and Jaffa cakes.

Kelly, clearly, was not alone in the perception that I'd nothing much to do with myself. Mog kept me keenly in the loop with a series of text updates on her progress in London, so that it became gradually apparent that I, having delivered the girls to their party, would be picking them up as well.

In the interim, I pressed on – or *sought* to, at least – with the spa block work...

I tried Reggie again – in vain. Likewise the architects, the lawyers and the Bedfordshire bureaucrats. Silence all round. Barely 4pm on a Wednesday, and everyone, it seemed, had gone home. Except for Reggie. He, I assumed, was *away* from home.

My phone did a shimmy on the desk. Text!

'Pls pick up girls ASAP.'

Unbeknownst to Mog, of course, there was nothing at that moment I'd rather do than accede to her request. Anything – just *anything* to get me out and away from this putrid stew of failure. And yet, having so visibly started my working day at lunchtime, the idea of leaving early and thus confirming the popular belief that I'd nothing to do...

I picked up the phone and called her.

'I'm busy,' she whispered.

'So am I, believe me. This party: I thought it was going on till six?'

'It is,' she said, 'but Rachel just texted me: Lulu's not enjoying it.'

'So, in other words, *Rachel's* not enjoying it...?'

'Whatever. Look, I've got to go. You got me out of chambers–'

'*I* got *you* out of...?

'Alex, I'm in conference.'

'Fine, fine, go back to the conference. I'll pick 'em up.'

'You're sure?'

'Yes, I'm sure.'

'I'm sorry about this.'

'Don't worry. I'll get them – *ASAP*.'

Ooh, sarky. Yeah, I know, but really, I mean, okay, so they're my kids, why should I *not* be their chauffeur? I'm the one who failed to use adequate protection. Not that I – *We* – No, no, they're the best thing that ever happened to me, how can I think like that? I'm *not*, though – I'm not – I'm *not*, but –

'Alex...?'

A sour-faced angel hovering once more by my door. It seemed the water people had been and gone. Kelly was wondering, would I like to replace the empty tank?

But there again, nobody really *needed* confirmation. They already knew it. That's why Kelly, further to the long-awaited visitation of the water people, asked me could I do the honours in replacing the empty tank?

'Why didn't they put one in while they were here?'

'Dunno. Not their job, I suppose.'

'More theirs than mine, I'd have thought.'

'Oh, come on, Al, big strong man like you...'

I should, I suppose, have got on and replaced the thing without comment. My protestations served only to focus attention on the coming spectacle: before the minute was out the water cooler was broken, the refill was rolling across the floor, and there was Alex, pegging around in his loungewear, rending the air with the most colourful terms of sorrow.

Of course, I can laugh about it now (I *could*, at least, were laughter not so painful), but at that moment, with insubordinate mirth breaking out all around me, I was more than ready to deliver the Lear-like rant that all had been expecting. Just as I was about to whirl round, however, and launch into a full-on rage, I became aware that my phone was ringing; thus it was Reggie who bore the brunt of my toe-smarting ire.

'Where the fuck've you been?'

'What d'you mean? *Here*. I've been here.'

'Why haven't you returned my calls?'

'What am I doing *now?*'

'Yeah. No. I mean, what about all the others? I've been trying to get you all day.'

'All day? I didn't get any messages till after lunch.'

'So you *did* get the messages?'

'Never said I didn't.'

'Don't bandy words, you fucker. Just answer the phone when I call you!'

'Alright, mate, alright. What's wrong, you having your period?'

Well, how to react to that? It was *funny* – by any objective assessment it was funny. There's a perilously thin line, though, between mirth and tears, and suddenly I found myself unsure what might happen if I were to open my mouth.

I said nothing, therefore; just looked out the window and took some deep breaths.

The citizens were walking up and down.

Going about their business.

Blithely unaware of my sufferings on their behalf.

'*Mate...?* You still there?'

I turned back from the window, peripherally aware as I did so of 20-plus sets of eyes swivelling away from me.

'*Mate...?*'

'Yes,' I said. 'Yes, I'm here.'

'That's alright, then. So, any news?'

'What – about your...?'

'Yeah, yeah.'

'Well, I've put in document requests – to your previous architect, to your local authority...'

'Never mind that, what about the stadium?'

'Well, quite – what *about* the stadium? D'you see my sketches?'

'*Sketches?* Dunno. Shelley does the post – I'll ask her.'

'No, no, no, they were *emails* – PDFs.'

'Oh, fuck that. I don't know one end of a computer from another.'

'Oh. Well, in that case...' I looked through to Charlotte's office; our eyes locked for one awkward moment. 'In that case,' I said, looking away and out to the work zone, where, once again, absolutely *no one* was watching me intently, 'maybe you'd like me to come and show you which end is which?'

'*What?* Oh, yeah, alright.'

— Dress Code —

Albert Speer never went to work in his pyjamas.

Such were my thoughts as I watched Oliver Grant's poison lips smile forth my sugar-coated death sentence. I should, in that instant, have been girding my loins for the fightback; instead I was drawing comparisons between myself and Hitler's architect. No matter his conviction for war crimes, Speer would still have fared better with the board of Ingalls Broughton Grant, if only because he could say, by contrast with myself, that he'd *never* been to work in his nightwear. The *Führer* maybe, towards the end, when living and working in the same convenient bunker... But Speer? No way. Not with Werner March lurking in the wings.

It's fair, I suppose, to note that all were in attendance at the meeting. An effort was made. All my good friends and colleagues were back from their travels and ready to give me the fair hearing I'd requested.

And yes, I *was* heard. My address – five finely crafted minutes of clear, concise and emotionally disciplined argument – was repaid with rapt attention and followed by an extended silence; a silence seemingly eloquent with respect, humility and just a little guilt. Everything was going to be alright.

And then Oliver spoke.

Oliver. Oliver spoke. Not Trevor. The venerable Trevor Crisp, sole surviving original contemporary of Velvet Fist Senior – it should've been he who spoke; Trevor, co-founder of the company that had bailed out me and my coke-beaked albatross of a partner; Trevor, the man widely regarded as the wearer of the pants and the power behind the velvet throne – he should be the one that pronounced on this divisive and potentially damaging matter. Yet the spotlight fell not on Trevor but on the aforementioned albatross, and as soon as he started squawking, I knew I was in trouble – I knew that nobody was going to change their minds, for those minds had all too clearly been made up before we commenced.

I did wonder, while my fucked-up friend was busy hailing the brilliant 'groundwork' I'd done on the Terriss Centre, whether I ought to intervene with a point of order? Surely, if the Velvet Fist was in the chair, it was for he, Maurice, to recognise Oliver and give him clearance to speak; it was not for Oliver simply to launch straight into an oration. Just as I was pondering on this, however, I heard him say something about 'the toll' – the toll, he was saying, that the project had taken on 'our dear friend Alex – not just on his marriage but also, I fear, on his health'.

My *health*?

The allusion, of course, was to my *mental* health – and that's when I knew the game was up; when I realised that any attempt to thwart him would unleash and evoke the spectre of Alex in his nightwear.

I had now to concede that the pyjama protest had been a severe miscalculation.

And yet, *why*? I could make a perfectly sound case for coming to work in pyjamas *every single day*. Why waste time changing when you could apply that time instead to the pursuit of architectural excellence? And anyway, what bearing has the way you dress on your capacity to do your job?

Cue the Führer's architect. Ever smartly dressed, our Albert – in or out of uniform; but did that, in itself, make him a great exponent of our craft? A great human being? And what – while I'm here – what about the creep who designed Ronan Point? He'd a whole neckful, I'm sure, of really natty, really swingin' Carnaby Street ties; big comfort to the poor fuckers who died on his watch – died because he couldn't be arsed to make his buildings kettle-proof.

No point speaking these thoughts aloud, though. True as they were, their airing could only give credence to the argument that I needed to take things just a little bit easy.

Aside from which, I couldn't be bothered. It takes energy to fight someone like Oliver, and in such energy I was, I now came to realise, sadly deficient. Even before he'd completed his grand address, I knew that I would accede to whatever these people wanted.

A roving ambassador? Fine. Fine. I would *be* their roving ambassador. The only question was how much of a fuss I should make for the sake of appearance.

– Base Football –

I hope... Any rate, I *suppose* I hope... hope I'll... I'll 'make it'. I suppose... Living, I suppose – even in the face of endless interrogation and blame – living *would* be better than... than...

Better to live a poor bondsman – Achilles, I think – than be king of all the shadows. *Was* it Achilles? *Poor bondsman?* Doesn't sound like him.

Achilles.

Hector.

Cassandra.

King Priam.

Ajax.

Helen, of course.

Paris.

Odysseus. Or *Ulysses*. I prefer Ulysses.

Helen. No, done Helen. What's the wife? The *king*'s wife, I mean?

Anyway, if – here's the point – if I can't live – if such a half-arsed wish were too ambitious, then the next best will be to live long enough to know that Oliver is dead. Just to hear some traumatised voice seek solace in a sharing of the horror.

'Yeah, an RSJ – poor fucker: hit full-on by an RSJ – they found his face on a different floor.'

Bit negative, I suppose. Bit... petty... spiteful... unworthy, for sure. Maybe I ought to be rising above it. Oh, but what's a bit of spite – what harm can it do? My wife and kids are safe – my parents too; they left before the main event – so it isn't as if I can't afford to waste a wish or three on spite-led projects. Besides, I'd be more than justified in blaming this thing on Oliver – he and his Mandelsonian acts of manipulation.

As it happens, I don't. I no more blame Oliver than I blame Reggie or Mog or anyone other than my feeble, weak-willed self; and yet, having called up the memory of that fateful partners' meeting, it's hard for me to shift the mental image of Oliver's victory grin – even (now I think of it), even though the most recent image in my mind, coined this very morning, depicts my erstwhile tormentor crumpled against a pillar, barely conscious of the opening ceremony that blessed my new ascendancy; *there*, if I care to look, is Oliver Grant, every inch the boy on best behaviour, sagging against that pillar, saying nothing, simply longing for the cutting of that ribbon so he can muster the energy to get him upstairs and see him first to the refreshment table.

It's a pleasing (if admittedly rather poignant) image – but it does only so much to cancel out the vision, indelibly branded on my brain, of Oliver the smug-faced conqueror grinning me back into exile at that partners' meeting.

What a dildo. He surely must have known the score? Even with his long history of nasal abuse, he'd surely enough left of his brains to know I'd *handed* him his triumph? Had I wanted – had I cared to muster all my rhetorical skills – I could've torn him to shivering pieces in front of our colleagues; it was with my blessing (more or less) that he'd prevailed – but still he couldn't resist giving me that look of his.

Well, it was entirely counter-productive: that fleeting, ill-considered smirk stripped away all the apathy I'd accumulated over the foregoing days with Reggie, and it revived my determination to tear down my tormentor and place myself back on high.

Heading back to Bedfordshire the following week, I resolved to get straight down to business with the client. Soon as he bounded forth from the house, dog pack doubtless in tow, I'd confront him with my sketches and demand at once to know his thoughts.

Reality was less heroically satisfying.

For sure, the canine greeting was every bit as fulsome as expected. When I arose, however, from gathering up my fallen sketches, it was Shelley, not Reggie, attempting to bring the reception committee to heel.

'I'm afraid it's not the ideal day,' she said. 'His drama coach is here.'

I laughed. *'Drama coach?'*

'Oh, yes, he's very excited. It's his first lesson today. You see, he's going to be in a film – I mean, that's to say he's *been* in a film; they shot it a while back, it's about to be released, so, well, y'know...'

'Not sure I do.'

'The *offers* – y'know: he's got to be *prepared...'*

'Oh, right – for Hollywood?'

'Exactly.'

By now we're in the hallway. From beyond the ballroom doors, Reggie could be heard, grappling, in the dim echo, with what sounded strangely like poetry. Hard to tell, though, with the dogs sniffing and whining for admittance.

Their master's voice rang forth – 'Fuck off!' – before shifting clunkily back into lyrical mode. 'Yet in these thoughts myself almost despising, Happily I think on thee –'

'Haply!'

'...Happily I think on thee –'

'Haply, dammit!'

I looked to Shelley.

'*Shakespeare?*'

'Oh yes.'

'How's that gonna help him in Hollywood?'

'The *antitheses*, darling! What did I tell you?'

'That's Carla,' said Shelley. 'She's with the RSC.'

'The *antitheses*! Serve 'em up to me!'

'Is that what he wants to do, then – the RSC?'

'Oh, well, I mean, the Shakespeare, that's really about building confidence – but he *did* say he'd like to do a bit of theatre once he's –'

A door flew open.

'Fuck's sake, will you people...? *Aaaaa!* Al, mate, good to see ya! But all the same, look, no offence, but we *are* working in here...'

'Absolutely. When're we gonna talk?'

'*Talk?*'

'About the stadium.'

He shook his head. 'Not today, mate. Up to my eyes.'

'Right. So, why'd you ask me to come? You specifically asked me to come today.'

'That's true,' said Shelley, 'you *did*.'

Reggie sighed, as if in the presence of an over-zealous autograph hound. 'Look, I don't have time for this. We're right in the middle of...'

'*No hurry, darling!*' A tutorly voice from beyond.

'At the very least,' I said, 'I need to show you these sketches.'

'Come on, then.' He pulled wide the door. 'Come on – show us – quick!'

'Oh. I... I thought we could go in the lounge.'

'No, no, come on, you're among friends – come on in.'

I wandered through, more than a little self-conscious beneath the inquiring eye of the frizzily grey-haired form standing centre-parquet. A mass of scarves and ponchos bulked out what, to judge from her face, must have been a perilously meagre frame. Clutched at her side, between saffron fingers, a cigarette was busily supplementing the already formidable banks of smoke that hung in the air.

'Meet Carla,' said Reggie – then adding, as the lady swapped fag hands in order to shake, 'Look at her – *cancer*! Nearly died of cancer, but still she's puffing away!'

'That's very personal,' I sputtered.

'First thing she told me, mate – soon's she got in the door.'

'Not *quite* true,' said Carla, 'but in any case, it was only the ol' breasties – not me lungs.' Thus clarified, she let forth a chain of rasping coughs.

As I extracted my drawings, the master's eyes widened with excitement.

'C'mon, hurry up, let's have a look...'

I spread out the sketches on a table by the fireplace.

'What's *this*?'

'What d'you mean *what's this*?'

'Exactly what I say: what *is* it?'

Carla barged in between us. 'The Globe! It's the Bankside Globe! How wonderful!'

'No,' I stammered, 'it's – it's a football stadium.'

'A football stadium? A *Tudor* football stadium?'

'Well, come to think of it, they did *have* football in Shakespeare's time – *thou base football player!*'

'Aha!' she crowed. 'The man knows his *Lear*! Jolly good!'

I smiled, triumphant. Maybe those nights at the Terriss had been good for something after all.

'Even so,' she murmured, glancing again at the sketches, 'this *is* ridiculous, is it not?'

'I'm sorry?'

'Not what *I* had in mind, for sure,' said Reggie. 'I mean, they're really *nice* and everything, but to be honest, I *was* hoping for something a bit more like the Emirates.'

'The *Emirates*? Since when is the Emirates mock Tudor?'

'What d'you mean?'

'You said you wanted a mock Tudor football stadium.'

'Did I?'

'Yes, you did. You insisted on it. *I* said no, it's a bad idea, but –'

'There you go, then: you was right!'

'*What*? Yeah, but... I mean, yeah, but...'

'Look, mate, what you gonna do – you gonna whine, or you gonna move on? Just ask Carla, she'll tell you: these things can't be set in stone...'

'But they *will* be; something, eventually, *will* be set in stone.'

'Not *yet*, not *yet*, mate. Meantime, you've gotta be willing to adapt, try new ideas – ain't that right, Carla?'

'Absolutely, my darling.'

'Fine,' I said. 'Fine.' I collated the papers, scrunching them just as sulkily and noisily and passive-aggressively as I could. The gesture, of course, was in vain; for all its lack of subtlety, it was still too subtle for Reggie – way, way over it went, just like the Wembley arch.

He walked me to the door, friendly paw upon my shoulder.

'You're doing good, mate. You've just got to open your mind, let the creative juices flow. Now you're here, just relax – make the place your own, come up with a few new ideas.'

New ideas. My God, how profoundly I longed to strike out and 're-imagine' that big jolly face.

'Go on, now,' he said, propelling me gently through the door. 'Go do a bit of thinking, like what you're good at. We'll hook up later, talk it over. No more of that Tudor shit, though!'

The Tudor shit, bitterly scrunched, went back into my case, and, along with everything else, stayed there. I spent the afternoon enjoying the facilities of the estate, first going for a ride with Shelley, then undertaking a few leisurely lengths of the pool (post-receipt of my long-awaited induction from Curtis, the desperately keen young spa manager). In none of this was there the remotest pretence of even seeking inspiration; it was purely fun on the client's account.

That evening, in the lounge, while Festus and a bellyful of dogs attended nearby to *Holby City*, I reported back.

'So,' said Reggie, 'what you got for me?'

'Nothing.'

'*Nothing?*'

'I told you, we need to talk about this. Last thing I heard, you wanted something like the Emirates, so until...'

'The Emirates? No. No way.'

'What?'

'I *never* said something like the Emirates. All it was –'

'You said, not ten hours ago, you said –'

'No, no, no, listen: all it was, the other night – Saturday, it was – we had *Match of the Day* on the telly – yeah? – and they'd the Gooners on, and they did one of them aerial shots of the Emirates, and I thought, that looks nice – that sort of egg-shape thing – something like that'd be nice.'

'Right. So, let's be clear: you want something like the Emirates, or you *don't* want something like the Emirates?'

He pondered for a moment, then, just as I thought he was on the cusp of a decision, he pointed at the screen. 'There!'

'Where?'

'There, on *Holby*. That bloke, the line he just said. Clear as day he ain't thought about what he was saying.'

'Why's it clear as day?'

'He put the stress on the wrong word. It's what Carla said to me this morning: ninety per cent of the battle is understanding what you're saying – whether it's Shakespeare or some bollocks like this on the box. If *you* don't understand what you're saying, how's your *audience* gonna understand?'

'How, indeed?'

'It's fascinating, though, I've gotta say, with the Shakespeare. All them different words. Like 'bark', for instance, that come up this afternoon. 'Bark'. D'you know what that means? It don't mean what you get on a tree. Sure as fuck it don't mean 'woof-woof', not in that context. D'you know what it means? It means...'

'Boat.'

'Oh. Yeah, it means boat. Who told you?'

'No one told me.'

'Course they did. You couldn't just know.'

'No, you're right, I couldn't. I probably learned it at school; someone probably told me – one of those *teachers* –

while you were busy day-dreaming about football – or, no: maybe it was on one of those outings to the theatre, maybe I picked it up while you were busy throwing Smarties.'

'*Me* – Smarties?'

'Not only did you *throw* them...'

'Bollocks!'

'Not only did you throw them; not only did you encourage *others* to throw them; you got the whole class in detention, cos you were too chicken to admit responsibility.'

'That don't sound like me; that's more like you.'

'Look, never mind all this ancient history...'

'Ancient history! Hear that, Fes? Soon as he's rumbled, he changes the subject!'

'Look, seriously, I'm not kidding now. I need to know what you want.'

'I want you to admit it was *you* throwing Smarties.'

I jumped to my feet. 'As you wish,' I said, 'it was me throwing Smarties.'

'Where you going?'

'Bed.'

'What – already?'

'Sorry, I'm exhausted – between the riding and the swimming and the intellectual rigour of your discourse...'

'Fair enough, mate. We'll talk some more tomorrow.'

'Looking forward.'

I would learn the hard way to consult Shelley on matters of scheduling. Far from talking to Reggie the next day, I barely even got to see him. This time he was busy with his dialect coach – a 'world-renowned' dialect coach by the name of Matt Lloyd. I didn't even know he *had* a dialect coach (of whatever renown) – much less that he was planning to see one the following day.

Now, I'm used to the low-level noise pollution of an open-plan office, and I've endured the more intense aggravation of my parents' TV and hi-fi in competition, but nothing could prepare me for the sounds conjured forth by Maestro Lloyd.

There's me, in my room, beavering away on the laptop, with an oak door, a corridor, a staircase, a hallway and another oak door to dull the noise – and still I was privy to every sound that Reggie produced. How many times did I read and re- and re- and re-read that particular sentence on the Wembley website – the one about the arch? Twenty, I'd say – a conservative estimate – before I managed to absorb the fairly simple fact that said arch, which might to some read as no more than a pretty embellishment, actually carries 75% of the weight of the roof. Up until that moment, of course, I'd no particular reason *myself* to know such a fact, but now all of a sudden there was a ton of catching up to do, and it was pretty much impossible, so full was the air of Reggie's humming and buzzing and tongue-twisting. And that was just the *warm-up*; once he started repeating actual words and phrases in questionable accents, I had to admit defeat.

I'd have packed up and headed home, if not for Shelley, who, being of similar mind, invited me once again to go with her for a spin on the horses.

'I'm sorry,' she said as we set off. 'All this trouble you're having. I should've warned you. It's just – well, he's such a *perfectionist...*'

'I don't follow...?'

'It's that film – I told you about that film, *Easy Meat* – the one he shot last autumn? We heard last week – the day you left, in fact – they're bringing forward the release to this Easter. The director's thrilled with his performance – absolutely *thrilled* – but Reggie, as I say, he's a...'

'A perfectionist.'

'Well, yes – and of course he'll need a wider range of skills if he's going to take advantage of all the offers; because really, once the film comes out, he's going to be inundated.'

'Really – it's that good?'

'The film? Oh, I've not seen it – but Reggie says it's wonderful. I mean, I suppose he *would* say that – he's not always entirely objective about these things, but...'

'Offers...'

'I'm sorry?'

'Offers, you say – all those opportunities. He's not gonna have much time for football – not if he's making films all over the place.'

'Oh, no, he's *very* keen on the stadium – and the films will help to pay for it, you see.'

'He's gonna need a lot of films.'

'I'm sure he'll get them.'

'Are you?'

'Alex, forgive me, but sometimes it seems to me you're a little bit... ambivalent about Reggie.'

'That's one word.'

'I thought he was your best friend. Why d'you laugh? He's been so happy since he met up with you again. I know he's not had much time...'

'Listen,' I said, 'you ought to know – cos Reggie's not gonna tell you: he's been feeding you a load of bullshit about me and him.'

My God, the look on that face – anguish and rage fighting for control. I set at once to back-pedalling.

'No, look, forget I said that. I just... Honestly, it's great being here, I'm having a wonderful time – but I'm here to *work* – that's the point: to save the spa block and make plans for the stadium. As soon as I get some sense out of Reggie, I can do the rest from my office.'

I didn't trouble to reveal that, at this moment, the office was the last place in the world I wanted to be.

'But you *are* his friend, aren't you?'

I remember thinking, as we headed home in the gathering dusk, that Shelley, by way of looks and nature and a dozen other things besides, had all that almost any man could crave in a woman – save for the fact that she had the utmost trouble talking about anything other than Reggie. A bit like Reggie, in that regard.

Back at the ranch, and ready to relax with a cup of cocoa (it's a tiring thing, is sitting on a horse), I found myself instead being dragged into the sitting-room and pressed into the service of Reggie's voice lesson. The world-renowned Mr Lloyd wanted me to read with the pupil, and thus allow him to apply an outside ear. We did a couple of pages from an Arthur Miller play – which one I can't now recall, though, in any case, it's academic. This, let it be noted, came at the end of a day in which Reggie and his mentor had been working almost exclusively on American accents – and yet, for any progress made, you'd be forgiven for thinking they'd spent the whole time down the pub. Reggie's Jewish New Yorker came out sounding, at least to *my* inexperienced ears, like an Irishman chewing on a mouthful of bees.

It was with a certain reluctant sympathy that I watched the maestro struggle to find some kind of positive feedback. Reggie was waiting like a puppy. Lloyd, clearly playing for time, directed his gaze away from the client and onto me. I gazed back, pleading through my eyes for a gentle let-down.

'I do believe he's *got* it!'

What?

I glanced at Reggie, then back at Lloyd, then back to Reggie again. He wasn't going to buy that? I mean, there's 'gentle let-down' and there's 'insulting dishonesty'. Reggie, surely, could not be fooled by such flagrant brown-nosing? His face, however, was a picture of proud delight. I looked once again at Lloyd, curious to see how long he could keep a straight face in all of this. The maestro met my gaze, and, in the full glare of my clear disbelief, held firm with his look of tutorly pride. Then, dismissively withdrawing his attention from me, he advised Reggie to book him in for another couple of sessions right away.

'I'm free tomorrow,' said Reggie.

Yes, indeed: even as I sat there, Reggie made plans that would once again keep me from consulting with him.

Thus, several further days went by without the merest hint of architectural discussion – and I refused absolutely to let it bother me. After all, I'd plenty to be getting on with – not least the gathering of evidence for the spa block appeal, in pursuit of which I was blessedly independent of the need for my client's cooperation.

In these new laid-back circumstances it was all too easy to be seduced by the facilities of the house: swimming, riding, a bit of working out in the gym... and also, of course, there was the martial arts thing.

Reggie, destined for a career in Hollywood action flicks, had tasked his trusty assistant with organising a course of Kung Fu tuition. Attendance was to vary over the months, but the line-up at Captain Walcott's inaugural class comprised Reggie, Shelley, myself and Festus, the latter blackmailed into action by his old team-mate, through the simple expedient of confiscating the TV remote. It was a ploy never to be repeated, for Festus nearly died during that first lesson. Captain Walcott, as the title implied, was ex-military – and though superficially as mild as David Niven, he drove a very, very hard bargain. Festus was by no means the only one to suffer. For me too it was a punishingly harsh regime; muscles were used that day that I'd never even known I had, and when I awoke the next morning, every one of these new muscles was screaming to be put out of its misery.

No thoughts, in that moment, of trying to engage the client. I just took myself off out for a wander.

Shelley was in the stables, mucking out the equines.

'What're you doing?'

She gave a joyous laugh. 'What's it look like?'

'No,' I said. 'I can see what you're... What I mean is, what happened to, er... to...?'

'Harriet? She's not coming anymore.'

'Oh. She get another job?'

'Yes. Yes, I think so. Of course, I do it at the weekends anyway, but...'

'But it's Friday.'

'Exactly.'

'So she's gone – and Reggie's got you filling in for her?'

'No, no, he doesn't know yet. Anyway, it's not such a... I mean, it's fine; it's good to get the fresh air!'

'Fresh air – in here?'

'Oh, well, yes – no – well, you know what I mean. I'm pretty much finished, anyway. D'you fancy a hack?'

Jasper and Dobbin were saddled and led out into the yard.

'*There* you are!'

And there, indeed, was *he*: the lord of the manor, bounding forth from the house, moving as if on a low-lying cloud of dogs.

'C'mon, then, mate, let's have that talk.'

'Oh, yeah, Okay. Only, I'm just off for a ride with Shelley. Why don't we do it when I come back?'

'No, c'mon, I'm in the mood. Let's walk and talk. Wander round the grounds, yeah? Sniff out a few locations?'

'Yeah, sure – only, y'know, we've got the saddles on now.'

'Why don't you two take the horses?' said Shelley.

'Because,' said Reggie, spelling it out as to a child, 'I don't *want* to take the horses. I wanna take the dogs. They need a run.'

'I know, but so do Jasper and Dobbin. Look, you two go – the dogs can run along behind you.'

Reggie darkened.

'Ain't you got some letters to type?'

'Well, yes, but I've got to see to the horses as well.'

'No you don't. We've got Harriet.'

'Not anymore.'

'Oh. She gone?'

'I'm afraid so. She...'

'That's gonna save us a bob or two. Right, then, come on, Al.'

And, clearly expecting no further dissent, he set off across the deer park, hounds leaping and sniffing in his slipstream.

I looked to Shelley in my awkwardness.

'Go on,' she said. 'He's the client, after all.'

I'd made up about half the ground when suddenly – 'Shit!' – I landed in what surely must be the most enormous batch of excrement yet brought forth by earthly beast – and, judging by the richly rising aroma, the beast at fault was canine.

I stood there, fuming, only now fully aware of being in a

minefield – a full-on shitcake minefield; surrounded, I was, by jobtrot young and old.

My host retraced his steps. 'Sorry about that.'

'No you're not. Just look at this place! It's ridiculous.'

'Well, you wanna look where you're treading – dodge the fuckers. That, or make with the wellies, like me!'

'Yeah, thanks for the warning. Why don't you clear up after them?'

'Listen, when *you*'ve got a country estate, you can shovel shit till your heart's content. Till then...'

'I don't know why you've got so many dogs, anyway.'

'Don't blame me, blame the wife. Junked up on mutts, she was. Blimey!' He was looking now at the still substantial remains of what I was trying to wipe off my shoe. 'That'll be *him*, I reckon.' He pointed across the deer park to a hound of semi-ursine appearance. 'Yogi, yeah, too big for any other. Tell you what – we'll get a sample to the lab boys – yeah? – CSI, yeah? If he's the one, I'll take my Purdey to him.'

He barked out a laugh and bounded off in a lakeward direction. The dogs fell in and followed. Just as I was about to give chase, however, Reggie stopped and spun round.

'Fuck it,' he said, passing me en route back to the house. 'Come on, guys! Come on, you're going in!'

'What? No,' I said. 'No, that's okay. Don't worry, I was just being...'

'No, no, we'll do it in the car. More sense. Stay where you are.'

Moments later, he was sailing back toward me at the helm of the late Mrs Cullen's Range Rover.

I hopped in and held on tight as Reggie, to my great confusion, hung a U and propelled us away from the direction of the lake. Through the courtyard we screeched, round to the front of the house, then on down the winding driveway and out onto the road.

'Where we going?'

'It's a surprise!'

'Yes, it is. Where're you taking me?'

'Magical mystery tour.'

'Where to?'

'Hendon. Oh, fuck, I wasn't gonna say.'

'Why're we going to Hendon?'

'See the planes.'

'Oh, come on, Reggie, I don't want to go to London. We're meant to be discussing your stadium.'

'We *will* discuss it. I'll get inspiration.'

'What – from a bunch of old bombers?'

'No, no, they've got some really cool hangars there.'

'*Cool*, are they? *Cool?*'

'You know what I mean.'

'I know you're full of shit. Days I've been here, waiting for you to talk to me about this thing...'

'So? So? Who's the client? *Me*, that's who. We'll talk when *I* wanna talk –when *and* where.'

'Fine.'

I sulked as he yakked us onto the M1.

'Honestly, mate, it's better this way – I'm no good just sitting there trying to think, trying to come up with ideas. Besides, a bit of R'n'R, it's important; I tell you, since I lost Denz, I've really learned to step back and look at my life. You only live once, after all – and *you*'re starting to see that as well

– I can tell: with the swimming and the riding and –'

'There's only one reason I'm swimming and riding – cos I can't get any sense out of you. Now, if you don't mind, it's about time you gave me something to tell my colleagues.'

Reggie snorted.

'*What?*'

'Your colleagues? From what you told me, mate, I'd say they're not all that desperate to hear from you.'

Reggie, on occasion, can be as gratingly perceptive as my eldest daughter.

'Besides, mate, what's the hurry? I mean, Chrissake, you're in paradise: you can swim, you can ride, you can get your end away...'

'I beg your pardon?'

'Reckon Shelley's up for it.'

'*What?*'

'I know she ain't no supermodel or anything, but...'

'Chrissake, show a bit of respect!'

'I *am*. I'm respecting you both. I'm very protective of Shelley. I wouldn't try and palm her off on anyone. Festus – if *he* tried it, I'd kill him.'

'Not much chance, is there?'

'Nah, she'd get in the way of the TV.'

I tried not to let on to Reggie, but by the time we reached the RAF Museum, I was nigh-on wet with excitement. For all my desire to rise above his massive lack of maturity, he was punching every one of my buttons. How could I not thrill to the sight of these majestically gorgeous engines of death? The Heinkel, especially, with its great glass egg of a nose. A full-on design classic.

My elation, however, was tinged with melancholy. I couldn't help but think of Mog. I'd come here with her when we were first going out (funny kind of date, I suppose, but we'd have done something grown-up the week before – that's how it worked). Were she with us now, I figured, she'd be saying, much as she did the first time round, that we boys were too obsessed with war; while I, in return, would of course point out that a lot of war-mongering boys, many just out of school, had died in planes like these so as to save our nation from tyranny and oppression, and thus preserve the freedom under which she could express her Jewish-Bolshevist propaganda unmolested.

I used to enjoy those kinds of exchanges. There was an affection – a passion – dammit, a *love*, let's face it – which underscored the duelling; a sense of fun and friskiness which would come to be woefully lacking in our many arguments over the Terriss project.

'Achtung! Alex! Stuka! Over here!'

A Stuka? A Stuka! *Achtung* – and so, dear sadness, farewell.

Of course, by the time we left, he'd managed to piss me off again: piling up an armful of models at the gift shop, and once more getting me to pay for them; then, having promised we'd talk stadium that evening (little of worth had arisen at the museum), he reneged before we were even halfway home.

'Bit tired, mate; let's do it tomorrow.'

So much for taking it easy. What a waste of time – not just that afternoon; all those past few days with nothing to show. By the time we pulled up again in front of Cullen Place, I could barely contain my rage. Hitting the gravel, I stomped upstairs, grabbed my stuff, chucked it in the car, and, dispensing neither thanks nor goodbyes, set off for the coast.

And yet, by the time the M1 became the M25, I knew I'd be returning; by the time I got on the A24 I was pretty sure I'd be coming back that very night. Notwithstanding his unwillingness to validate my presence by talking architecture, I'd just had a more relaxed and relaxing week than I'd enjoyed for many a long month. Godham, by contrast, offered nothing but stress, conflict and almost inevitable humiliation on a daily basis.

Yes, it was my mission and my destiny to unmount my foes at the office and win back my position of advantage; for the moment, though, all the weapons in my armoury were situated north of London. The sole exception, I realised, was the latest edition of AutoCad. If I had that, I could be generating design ideas anywhere on the planet (though Bedfordshire would do just fine).

Thus I made straight for the office, loaded the new software onto my laptop, locked up my goldfish bowl, and headed back from whence I'd come.

– Going Native –

It would in time be alleged – by my wife, amongst others – that I'd 'moved in' at Cullen Place. It wasn't true.

I *never* moved in. I spent a lot of time there, no question, but only by default – and I *never* moved in. I was there to work, and that's what I did – far more effectively than ever I could've done back in Godham at the time. Sat on my bed in the Blue Room, laptop before me, mobile at my side, I could do everything I needed right there, without office and marital politics getting in the way.

For all that, I continued to make regular trips back to the coast; and if, after a while, my visits grew less frequent, it was only because they came to seem more and more redundant. When I showed my face at the office, even the nicer people seemed surprised to see it, and while there was always a welcome at my parents' hearthside, they were also happy to think I was 'having a good time with your friend'. As for the marital home, I'd have hardly been spending much time there either way.

Thus Cullen Place came to seem progressively more inviting, and not just as a work venue. For all my single-minded devotion to the cause, boundaries were blurred. It was one thing, for instance, to fork out for Airfix models at Hendon (chips too, come to think of it); but light bulbs? toilet paper? dog food? I'd never have had the balls to claim for such things, and yet these were the kinds of expenses I all too frequently incurred. It really was remarkable, now I come to look on it, how many times Reggie found himself without 'readies' or Shelley claimed to have mislaid the petty cash key.

By this point, though, I was beyond fretting about a bit of pocket money. That first full month on-site flew by in a glorious whizz of ruthless efficiency. Granted, I didn't advance too far on the spa job (thanks to the various slothful jobsworths in possession of the various documents needed); on the stadium, though, I made major strides. The secret, I now saw, was in referring as little as possible to Reggie – who, as long as he was in thrall to the idea of Hollywood stardom, would be of minimal help. I was at liberty, it seemed to me, just to forge ahead on my own.

Taking inspiration from the world of Palladian follies, the proposal I eventually came up with was, essentially (and this I can admit now I'm dying and well past giving a shit), a drastically scaled-down version of the Olympiastadion. Well, he'd given me so little to go on: Berlin's was a stadium he liked – that was a matter of record – and if he'd expressed objections to its fascist origins, I was happy to gamble he'd have forgotten all about it by now.

I was a couple of days away from presenting the client with my design when, one unseasonably sunny Monday, quite out of the blue, we had a couple of visitors turn up at the gate.

'Friends of yours,' said Shelley.

Friends? No, nothing of the sort. Oliver and Rocky; passing through, they said, on the way to a meeting in Luton.

'*Meeting?* What meeting? Say I'm away.'

'But, Alex...'

'They're here to check up on me. Please, please – get rid of them, just get rid of them.'

She tried, too, but Reggie had different ideas.

'Any friend of Alex...' he said, whilst warmly gladding the royal hands and yanking the visitors over the threshold.

This, I could see, was going to be bad. Reggie was on his best behaviour – I'd never seen him like that before. No, tell a lie, there *was* a TV news clip I saw one time: Reggie and the Queen Mother – everybody's favourite sporting thug meekly lining up to meet the Queen Mum at some charity do. And that's how he was with Oliver – fawning, simpering, laughing indulgently at every one of his lettuce-lame witticisms. It did give me a bit of pleasure, though, to see the way he patronised Rocky – 'Where're you at school – sorry, *college* – no: *uni*, yeah? *Uni*. What's your team? You're a Chelsea boy, yeah? Bet you're a Chelsea boy?' I almost expected to see him produce a half-crown and do 'Which hand?'. He clearly thought the little shit was Oliver's son – and Oliver, to my amusement, said nothing to put him right.

'So,' said Ollie, 'how're you finding him?'

'What – Alex? No complaints, not so far. He's come up with a fuckin' magic plan for the stadium.'

I almost choked on my sherry.

'I *have*?'

'We'd love to see,' said Oliver.

'Hasn't he shown you?'

'Alex? No, indeed. Quite the dark horse, our Alex – keeps the old cards very close to his chest.'

'Does, doesn't he. Go on, mate, get your stuff. Gi's a demo.'

As I climbed the stairs to fetch my laptop, I could feel my face burning red with embarrassment. Thirty years had fallen away; it was Parents' Night all over again. Who, though, in this scenario, was the headmaster – Reggie or Oliver? It wasn't an exact fit, but, yes, probably Reggie – making Ollie my father, and Rocky, by extension, my kid brother.

Oh, I do hope he's dead.

When I came back down, they'd migrated to the lounge. Festus, though visibly peeved at having to watch *Jeremy Kyle* with the sound down, brightened somewhat when I set up my laptop on the table, and happily transferred his allegiance from the TV to my flythrough of the stadium.

'Look at that,' said Reggie, 'fuckin' magic – pardon my French.'

'Indeed,' said Oliver, 'it really is most impressive. So tell me: where are you planning to *put* this stadium?'

I looked to Reggie. This was just one of many things I'd given up trying to discuss with him.

'By the lake,' he said, without hesitation. 'We'll pump in water from the lake to irrigate the pitch. It's gonna be really green – the stadium, I mean, not the water! Why don't we go and have a look? Tell you what, I'll give you a ride round the estate.'

'That'd be delightful, Mr Cullen.'

'Call me Reggie, mate.'

Yes, call him Reggie. *Do* call him Reggie. Don't mind me – I'll go and fucking pack.

The grand tour saw my self-esteem yet further downgraded, I, being forced to sit in the back of the Range Rover – squashed in the back, with Rocky and a couple of stowaway dogs, listening in fury as the big boys up front proceeded in their dialogue of mutual admiration. Still, I couldn't help being impressed by Reggie's continued bluffing about the stadium – you'd scarcely believe he'd only just set eyes on my new design. Who'd have thought he even *knew* a word like 'irrigate'? It was good stuff, I had to admit, very impressive – excellent improv work, as Carla the raspy drama coach might well have observed. Only thing was, I couldn't imagine why he was doing it. Why didn't he just say, 'Ask Alex'? Why should it matter to Reggie if those creeps knew he hadn't a clue about the stadium? Could it be that somehow he perceived in Oliver something worthy of his respect, something that made him eager to appear engaged and on top of the game?

Yeah, right, I thought; had he shown this level of interest with me, the thing'd be up by now.

What a surprise, then, when Reggie, having tried and failed to get my colleagues to stay for lunch, waved them off then stepped back into the house, looked at me and said, 'What a pair of wankers.'

'I'm sorry?'

'Don't you think?'

'*Me*? Yes, of course, *I* think so, but...'

'Like a pair of football agents. Fucking creeps. No wonder you don't want to go home, if they're all like that.'

'Who said I don't want to go home?'

'I tell you, I'd half a mind to dunk 'em in the lake, the smarmy fuckers.'

'What d'you mean? You were absolutely charming with them.'

'Only for *your* sake, mate.'

'*My* sake?'

'Course. They came to check up on you. What d'you think – I'm gonna set the dogs on 'em? No, I was looking out for you, mate.'

'Oh. Well. Thanks.'

'Welcome. That design, though – you'll have to do better than that.'

'Oh. Well, obviously I wasn't *ready*; I didn't intend, at this stage...'

'Doesn't matter how ready it is. I ain't having no Nazi stadium on my estate.'

'What? No, no, it's not a *Nazi* stadium. It's...'

'Forget it, mate. And listen – don't try pulling the wool over my eyes again, alright? I'm not as daft as you think.'

Embarrassing, that. Still, my heart lifted to reflect on his razor-sharp assessment of my colleagues. I'd feared a repeat of my schooldays experience; this time, though, he'd not only seen through the 'cool people', he'd actually expressed a distinct preference in my direction.

Then, just as I was basking in the glow of Reggie's Christ-like love, Kelvin Sperring bumbled onto the scene and spoiled it all. Mr Sperring, according to the voicemail I retrieved on the way back to my room, was Reggie's solicitor. Good news, I thought: at last I was going to see some of the documents I'd for so long been requesting in vain. However, though the message did indeed relate to the spa block, it wasn't quite in the way I'd anticipated.

'Re: the forthcoming assault case,' intoned the plummy voice, 'Mr Cullen tells me you've expressed a readiness to speak on his behalf at the trial. I hope you might be good enough to call me back, in order that we might discuss the matter.'

Reggie, in spite of my barging in on yet another voice lesson, was only too happy to provide an explanation. The case, he told me (in the most astoundingly casual manner), resulted from an incident that occurred some months previously: it seemed that the local council, weary of seeing their letters go unanswered (praise from Caesar there!), had sent a planning officer to talk to Reggie about the extension; and, as Reggie described it, 'One thing led to another'.

'What d'you mean? You *shagged* him?'

'He should be so lucky. Nah, it was just a couple of taps. He went home with his teeth in a bag, that's all.'

'*What?*'

'I'm kidding, for Chrissake – he had a black eye.'

'Oh, well, that's alright, then! Just a black eye! Fuck's sake, why didn't you tell me?'

'What – so now I've got to tell you everything?'

'Yes, actually! Yes. You want me to help you keep your gym? Then yes, it really would be as well to let me know which officials you've roughed up.'

He shrugged. 'Sorry, mate, I assumed you knew about it. It was in the papers.'

'In the papers, was it?'

'Tabloids, yeah.'

'The tabloids. Oh, well, in that case, the apologies are all mine. I must take it up with my cuttings agency.'

'Alright, don't get sarky.'

'No, seriously, I retain a cuttings agency, devoted exclusively to matters Cullenesque. They've always been highly reliable in the past, but...'

'Oh, fuck off.'

'When did I ever say I'd testify for you?'

'What?'

'When did I say...?'

'It goes *without* saying. If you wanna help me keep the spa block...'

'The planning committee. I said I'd speak for you at the planning committee; I never said anything about any *court*.'

'What's the difference? You're gonna get paid.'

'What – to perjure myself?'

'Don't be daft. Just tell the truth.'

'The truth?' I laughed. 'The truth,' I said, 'is that you're famous for hitting people. What could I possibly say to counter that?'

He sighed theatrically. 'Alex, mate, you're enough to try the patience of a fucking saint. Just stand up and say exactly what you're gonna say to the planning committee: that my spa block's great, it's a fucking beautiful building, and if anyone was crazy enough to try and knock it down, you'd understand why a bloke might feel like hitting them.'

Now, it happens that I've actually met a lot of planning officers, and some of them are in fact *well* worth hitting. Indeed, if one or two lie crushed in the rubble around me, this whole thing won't have been in vain. Nevertheless, I didn't think it wise to impart such sentiments to my client. On the contrary, I told him I'd no intention whatever of lending him my testimony; if he'd any sense at all, I said, he'd simply go to court, grovel for mercy and promise forthwith to mend his ways.

He gave a gormless chuckle. 'That's what I *always* say.'

And that was the end of the matter. At least for the moment. He was still laughing as he went back to rejoin Maestro Lloyd in the lounge. I, however, was just a little bit shocked. Had I understood him correctly? What did he mean 'That's what I always say'?

Did he mean he always said it but, while meaning it most sincerely, he hadn't the willpower to keep his word?

Or did he mean he always said it, with absolutely no intention of trying to make good on his promise?

Either way, it hardly seemed to bode well for the future.

– Fathers' Days –

Reggie, it seemed to me, was more than content to carry on billeting his kids with the in-laws, back there in Godham. He'd not seen them since Christmas, and though I offered, every time I set off on a trip back down to the coast, I was never once burdened with gifts or sweets or anything else he might've wanted them to have.

Well, I figured, it wasn't my business; he obviously had issues still to work out.

I, however, was rather less content to... to... *My* offspring... Of course, to *them*, it may well have seemed... If I'd *known* I was... I was... Away so long, I...

Think. *Think.*

Vanity? Yes, of course, there was vanity – a fear that... that the girls, they might get used to my absence, get to be 'cool' with it.

One time, just before Easter – yes, yes, I remember this – I went down home to take them – '*specially* – a special, *dedicated* trip, for the purposes of... of... Esmeralda's – Esmeralda's Zoo – I took them to Esmeralda's; they'd been asking for ages, and – I mean, God knows how many times they've been, since they were little – maybe that was the thing, maybe it just wasn't, once they got there and remembered, maybe – maybe, I don't know, maybe it didn't live up to... Cos I mean, Jesus, it's barely much more than a playground and a rabbit hutch – and yet the *prices*...

Anyway, afterwards – here's the point at last – afterwards,

132

when I dropped them off home, I had a cuppa with Mog – a polite but awkward cuppa with their mum – while they went off to watch TV. When I made to leave, neither of them could be arsed to look up from the screen.

'Forty millionth rerun of *Friends*,' I said, as I made for the door.

'What d'you expect?', said Mog. 'You can't just dip into their lives on a whim and expect to be treated like a film star. They've seen you, they've done the zoo, now they're getting back to normal without you.'

Soon enough, of course, our conversation degenerated into talk of theatres and marital infidelity, but still I took on board her earlier point; it was well made, and I resolved thereafter to keep more actively in touch with the girls.

I decided to start by getting them up to Bedfordshire for a weekend.

They didn't need much persuading – certainly not once horses were mentioned – but Reggie, to my surprise, proved a bit of a challenge.

'I don't know, mate, we've a lot of work to do – all that architecture, and me with my drama studies...'

The real objection, of course (though he'd die before admitting it), was simply one of jealousy. The big man wanted me to himself. Foul vanity, I know, that's what it sounds like; it's true, though. From a weirdly early stage, he showed himself reluctant to share me. Whether off on a non-Reggie mission for the firm (they came up occasionally), or away on family business, my absences were resented.

'Oh, look who it is,' he'd quip, on my return. 'Who're you – Alex, is it? Nice of you to show your face.'

This, though, with the girls; this was a new low.

'What the fuck is wrong with you?' I said. 'I hardly ever see them. Just cos *you*'re content to keep your kids in exile...'

'Alright, mate, alright, chill out.'

'Why? Why? Why should I *chill out*? Why should I put up with this shit?'

'Look, if it's that important, bring 'em, fuck's sake bring 'em up.'

'It's not as if there isn't room.'

'Right, so bring 'em.'

'I never ask you for anything.'

'*Bring 'em*, I said!'

'Alright, I will.'

And I did. They came the weekend before Easter.

Mog agreed to drive them up. She insisted, in fact. I don't know what she expected to discover, but her disapproval was fully on record; Reggie was a bad enough influence on *me*, she said, never mind the girls.

She didn't linger long. They were together for just a few minutes, she and my friend, but the hostility was almost tangible, and, in spite of friendly encouragement from Shelley, she declined to stay for lunch.

Given his initial reluctance, it was surprising to find that no one was more delighted than Reggie to have the girls there that weekend. In fact, I had trouble getting a look-in. He gave them a riding lesson (with Shelley for support); he took them for a spin round the deer park in the DeLorean; he insisted on their joining us for a specially convened Kung Fu class with Captain Walcott; he masterminded a rather damp barbecue on the Saturday evening (Lilian had to finish off the chicken breasts in the oven); and on the Sunday he took us all on a magical mystery tour.

Well, not quite *all*: Lilian declined, and Festus, having expressed a degree of willingness in principle, was on the day unable to roll off the sofa to meet the departure deadline. So in the end it was Shelley, the girls and me who piled into the Range Rover with Reggie and set off for Woburn.

Yeah, *Woburn;* it was Woburn, the secret destination – we weren't even out on the public highway before that one leaked.

My own very genuine excitement was dented by the eventual realisation that the trip, though Reggie's treat in theory, was mine in practice. Forty quid it cost me – and *that* was just to get us in, never mind the inevitable chicken nuggets. Our host, it seemed, had failed to bring sufficient cash – *any* cash, in fact – and, as he once again fatuously explained, he doesn't 'believe' in credit cards.

I wasn't surprised, of course – rich people are always pulling these stunts; it's how they stay rich.

Despite the financial embarrassment, Reggie was very much still in charge of the venture, and it was his decreed opinion that we should start with the zoo and leave the safari – the 'best bit' – till last. Thus agreed, he parked up, decanted his complement, locked the car, then declaimed, 'Last one to the sealions is a bag of shit!' And off he went, balletically weaving his way across the car park, effortlessly dodging the other patrons and leaving us in his dust. Well, *me* at least. Rachel and Lulu were giving good chase, tearing after 'Uncle Reggie', giggling their way out of sight.

'Why doesn't he get some kids of his own?' I muttered.

'He's *got* some kids of his own,' said Shelley.

'Yeah, I know.'

We followed at a more leisurely pace, eventually separating completely from the advance party, with agreement to reconvene later for lunch. Mog would've been horrified at my leaving the girls to the immature care of Reggie Cullen. Maybe that made me more inclined to do it – that and the realisation that he and the girls were similarly slight of attention-span. While they raced through every enclosure and on to the next,

Shelley and I were able to devote some proper quality time to the more quality creatures – the lemurs, for example.

In any case, 'Uncle Reggie' was going down a storm with the girls – I really couldn't compete, and I wasn't at that point inclined to try. Maybe I *should*'ve done. Maybe what later occurred was inevitable; Reggie never could resist the encouragement of an adoring crowd.

I remember one time, years ago, reading an interview with him in one of the Sunday papers. It was never a good thing to do: invariably, the slights of teenhood would rear up again in my mind, and I'd find myself angered anew, not only by his almost universal popularity, but also by the instinctive knowledge that, despite my residual bitterness, I'd forgive him all in a second were he, by some unlikely circumstance, to stroll back now into my life. Best, then, to avoid reading about him – and yet, I rarely did. *Avoid* it, I mean. I guess I enjoyed the fury.

They asked him, in this interview, why he thought he had such a tendency to get into trouble on the football field – as he'd done once again just lately, incurring a ban and a fine for flicking the Vs at a reprimanding ref. He said he'd no idea, though he noted that it was rare for him to get into rows during training; it was more usually on match days that his demons found their way out of the bottle.

The interviewer wondered if perhaps the crucial ingredient was the presence of an indulgent audience?

'What d'you mean?' said Reggie. 'You mean I start showing off? Yeah, that's probably it.'

Showing off, indeed. Never had he a more indulgent audience than he did that day at Woburn. It was bad enough out in the open, but once back in the car, as we plied the Safari Trail, things reached a whole new level of ghastly. Like a latter-day Percy Edwards he was; for every beast there was a mimicking, and every mimicking, no matter how inept, brought forth screams of laughter from the back seat. This, in turn, egged Reggie on to be more and more outrageously hilarious, thus generating more viciously circular giggling from Rachel and Lulu. I thought I was going to have to say something, but in the end it was Shelley, wedged between them in the back, who stepped up instinctively to play the bad guy.

'Shut up! Will you shut up, *please*! I can't hear myself think!'

'*Think*?' said Reggie. 'What d'you want to think for – pretty girl like you? You wanna...'

'Please, Reggie, please, just shut up for a minute! I can't stand it. Please, just... just... just shut up.'

And so he did. They all did. A silence descended on the entire party, a deep, sulky silence which wasn't to be broken until we were fully inside the heart of beastly darkness.

There on the Safari Trail, an expansive ring of steel creates the illusion of 'free range' existence for a wide variety of deadly creatures. Within that ring of steel, however, the most vicious and unpredictable of all the beasts are confined within a further ring of steel, a special enclosure unto themselves; it's called the Tiger Woods (ho-ho), and in order to gain access you have to make your way through two sets of electric gates.

It was once through the second set of gates that Reggie stopped the car.

I thought nothing of it at first; there's no rule against stopping, as long as you leave room for other cars to get past you (though, in fact, he hadn't bothered).

'It's a bit *small*,' said Rachel.

'What is?' I said.

'The space they've got. In the jungle –'

'Oh, not again! We had this at Esmeralda's – the rabbits; their hutches...'

'The hutches *were* too small. And here – just look; in the

137

jungle they'd have a *lot* more room.'

'Right – and you'd never see them.'

'They're not here on Earth just to be *seen* by the likes of us.'

'True. Very true. So why don't you get out? Go on – go set 'em free!'

'Oh, ha ha.'

'You're right, not a good idea – next thing, you'd be asking to keep one in the house.'

'Look!' said Lulu, 'there's one!'

'Oh, so there is. D'you see it, Rae?'

'Yes, of course I do. I'm not blind.'

'You don't *have* to be. He's got stripes; they're for a purpose.'

'Alex...'

I looked sideways at Reggie, surprised to hear him speak for the first time since Shelley's outburst.

'What're you doing?' I said – though I could see *exactly* what he was doing: slowly and deliberately, well-nigh stripteasingly, he was removing his seatbelt, smiling all the while a wicked smile the like of which I'd never seen before. Just for a brief, stupid moment I imagined he was going to kiss me.

'Alex,' he purred, 'd'you dare me to run round the car?'

'Eh?' I was still thinking about the kiss.

'D'you dare me to run round the car?'

I laughed. 'No, I don't. Don't be stupid.'

He turned and looked to his fan club in the back.

'What about you, girls? Shall I? Shall I do it?'

'Yes!' said a two-thirds majority.

'Come to think of it,' I said, 'I don't even like being stopped here. Come on, let's go.'

'*Go*? You're mad!'

'No, really, what if you couldn't get it started again? Come on, let's just – What're you – ? Jesus Christ!'

He was out and slamming the door.

'Reggie! Fucking stop it! Get back in! Reggie!'

In the ten or so seconds it took him to circle the car, I was afflicted with a series of visions: first I was forced to break the news to Reggie's children; then I'd to explain to my colleagues how I'd carelessly thrown away their next meal ticket; and finally must I tell all to the slavering press beast, seeing my honest words twisted to condemn me out of my own mouth for having lost our nation 'the best prime minister we never had'. Worse than all this, though, was the thought that Mog, for ever more unto Doomsday, could hold me responsible for any and every problem with the girls, caused as it surely would be by the everlasting trauma of seeing a man eaten alive.

'Fucking 'ell, that was great!'

'Reggie! Fuck! Fuck! Don't ever –'

'What a buzz! Fuckin' 'ell. You've gotta get some!'

'*What*?'

'Go on – *you* now!'

'Fuck off!'

'Go on.'

'Go on, Dad!'

'Yes, go on!'

'You two shut up. And you – get us out of here; come on, let's go.'

139

'Not till *you* do it, chickenshit.'

'Call me what you like. I'd rather be live chickenshit than dead tiger food.'

Even as I said this, I was aware that the nearest tiger had batted barely an eyelid throughout Reggie's little stunt. That, though, was not the point. Who could say what other stripey meatseekers might've been lurking amidst the trees?

'Just drive, will you!'

After all, that's what they're made for, to blend in.

'No,' he said. 'No way. I ain't going nowhere, not till you do it too.'

Shelley now joined the debate. 'Really, I think Alex is right.'

'Shut up, bitch.'

'Do NOT talk to Shelley like that.'

'Sorry, love, you know I don't mean it.' He turned round, took Shelley's hand and kissed it. 'You know that, don't you?'

'Yes,' she said.

'I love her,' he said to the girls. 'I'd be nothing without my Shel.'

Then he turned round to face me again.

'Right, then – you gonna have a go?'

'Jesus Christ, you're not still on that, are you? Start the car!'

And he did – he *did* start the car – but only when the next one back came and honked him on his way.

'Right, then, Chicken-boy, reckon we've earned ourselves a cup of char, don't you?'

'No, I don't. I just want to go home, if you don't mind.'

'Oh. Did I overstep the mark?'

'Yes.'

'Blimey, anybody'd think *you* was the one in danger.'

'Can we just go, please.'

I know I come out of this story as a bit of a sourpuss, but the way I was seeing things, I was the founder of the feast: yet again I'd paid for a trip suggested by Reggie, and – more to the point – I'd been made to look a dick in front of my kids – who – and here's – here's – here's another point: that fucker put my kids in danger. Okay, so it all ended happily – the girls had a laugh, Reggie got to show off, no harm done; but what if one of those monsters had got him? Much as he deserved his mauling, there's no way I wouldn't have jumped out and tried to help – Christ knows what I'd have *done* – maybe I'm deluding myself, but delusions, in *my* situation – my mind's all over the place, but still, I'd have tried – I'd have *tried* to do something – I'd have leapt out of that car, and in my panic... All I'm saying is, in all the confusion, with other tigers creeping around the undergrowth, it's not too much to suppose another of those sneaky fuckers might've got into the car and had a right royal picnic.

I didn't say much on the way back to Cullen Place, nor, indeed, much more when we got there, aside from, 'Girls, get your stuff.'

'Oh, *Dad...*'

'Get upstairs and get your stuff.'

They sulkingly obeyed, stomping up the staircase as Reggie bounded into the hallway.

'Leaving already?' he said. 'They've only just got here.'

'Yeah, well, that's not true, is it – and besides, just mind your own business. I'm taking my kids home.'

'Oh, come on, don't be a spoilsport; just cos they find me more entertaining than you!'

That's when I lost it.

'Yes!' I yelled. 'Yes, that's right – more entertaining. My kids – *my* kids, they come up to see me, and you – you – you – I mean, fuck's sake, what about *your* kids?'

'What about them?'

'What *about* them? You never see the fuckers!'

'Well, I'm busy.'

'*Busy*? Busy taunting tigers! Busy trying to get yourself eaten. Fuck's sake, you've got three kids down there, you haven't seen them in months.'

'Yeah, well, it's very, y'know...'

'Very what?'

'Poignant. Y'know, it's... it's *poignant*.'

He meant, I suppose, that seeing them reminded him of his wife, reminded him of the good times they used to have when they weren't getting drunk or hitting each other or going out dogging in car parks.

'Look,' I said, 'you have nothing to do that won't wait till next week. Go upstairs, chuck some clothes in a bag, and come with me. See your kids.'

'They might have something on.'

'Let's take a chance.'

And chance it we did.

When I dropped off the girls, I cautioned them against telling their mother about the tiger thing.

'D'you mean about Reggie running round the car...?' said Rachel.

'That's right.'

'...or,' added Lulu, 'do you mean about saying *fuck* a lot?'

142

'Yeah, actually, both of those – oh, and don't go copying me, alright? I know it's hypocritical, but you shouldn't.'

'Right,' said Lulu.

'And should we tell her about you and Shelley?'

'*What*? What *about* me and Shelley?'

'You were walking around the zoo with her, all morning.'

'*So*? What does that prove?'

'Brilliant!' said Reggie.

'Shut up.'

'No question, mate, you're gonna have to pay 'em off.'

'Thanks, I've spent enough already. Go on, you two. Thank your Uncle Reggie and bugger off.'

I moved on then to offload my final passenger – and it was during this short journey, to the in-laws', that Reggie informed me, ever so casually, that he might not after all be wanting a football stadium.

'*What*?'

He'd been wondering, given his recent forays into show business, whether perhaps he shouldn't think about pouring his money and his energy into something more relevant to this new life – the construction, say, of... an arts centre...?

'Let's face it, mate, it's more in *your* line an' all. You're more experienced with theatres than sporty places.'

He'd timed it to perfection, this announcement. The bomb was dropped just as we pulled up outside the in-laws'; thus, with beings of various sizes running out to greet the prodigal father, I was cheated of the chance to blow my top (again).

The following day, being as I was in the neighbourhood, I took the opportunity to show my face at the office. It was a face more welcome now: frost a-plenty still, for sure, but less of the impending drama that my presence would once have seemed to guarantee. My lengthy absence had meant I was neither an awkwardness for Charlotte nor a threat to Oliver as he extended his inevitable influence over the Terriss project.

Furthermore, if my occasional appearances now tended to raise fewer hackles at management level, they aroused outright curiosity among the star-struck junior staff. Alex, after all, was hanging out with someone 'cool' (well, *famous*, at least). I didn't feel the need to tell them, on this particular occasion, that Mr Cool had cooled off on the stadium. I just got out the laptop and showed them where I'd got to: by now the thing was looking like a mock Tudor version of the original Wembley (I'd added a couple of towers half-way up one side of the existing 'Nazi' design), and as I exhibited the flythrough I found myself repeating, with perhaps an excess of studied contempt, that this abomination was 'what the client wants'. Or *doesn't*, as the case may be.

Later on I went round to retrieve Reggie from his in-laws.

Not unlike my own dear mum and dad, Denise's parents Jack and Monica seemed to abound in warmth and good will – and though Reggie would soon come to cast dark aspersions upon them, they've never really done anything since to alter that first impression I had of them.

I joined them on the patio, where they were watching Reggie play football with his kids. It was him versus the other three – and he gave pretty much no quarter. To Reggie, clearly, an opponent – be it Tony Adams or 6-year-old Chico Cullen – is an opponent.

'He's so good with them,' said Monica.

'Yes, he is.'

'Y'know,' said Jack, 'we love having them here...'

'That's right, we do.'

'...they'll always be welcome, of course, but I don't

understand why he doesn't want them back.'

I shrugged, and offered a simpering smile, realising only after a moment that some kind of insight was desired.

'Oh, I don't think it's that he doesn't want them back; it's just he doesn't... doesn't feel the time is right yet.' *Time.* Not 'right'. He just didn't want the hassle. 'It's still very painful for him,' I continued. 'I think they remind him of her.'

Monica laughed. 'And that's a *bad* thing?'

'Well, no, of course...' I flushed in my trapped stupidity.

'I mean, how're *we* meant to feel? We lost a *daughter*. If he thinks...'

'Monica, love...' Jack placed a gentle hand upon her shoulder.

'No,' she said, equally gently shrugging him off. 'No, I'm just saying...'

'I *know*, love.'

The game went on well past dusk. Not even a potential penalty incident – little Chico went face-down in the mud – could halt the action for long, though it was to have both short- and long-term repercussions. The short-term derived from Chico's perception that his father had done him wrong; as a result, he blanked out his two siblings and focused solely on tackling Reggie. Unfortunately, the more angrily persistent he got, the more gracefully evasive his father became.

Finally, Chico got so browned off with his dad's effortless skill that, in exasperation, he attached himself fully to Reggie's famous left leg and refused to let go. You had to pity the big man, at least to a degree: whilst hobbling around with a small boy limpeted to his leg, he was also trying to fight off the attentions of the much larger and more formidable Conrad. When Daisy also saw an opportunity to move in on the ball, Reggie finally lost patience, reached down and scooped Chico away, face-first. It was only after sinking one home between the plant-pots that he realised the child was in hysterics on the ground.

He swept him up and held him to his chest.

'Where's it hurt? I'll kiss it better.'

The wailing persisted.

Reggie was forced to resort to flattery.

'Listen... Listen to me... Chico, listen to me. Listen, I'm sorry, mate, but you've got to see it from *my* angle. You're just so *good* – so *talented*, so... *formidable*. D'you know what that means – formidable?'

A barely audible 'No' came forth from the heaving bundle.

'Unbeatable, that's what it means: unbeatable, unstoppable – and that's *you*. You're so *formidable* – yeah? – so blinkin' formidable, the only way I could beat you was to cheat. That's how good you are.'

Chico was now grinning through the sniffles.

'Course, holding on to my leg, that wasn't fair neither – yellow card, no question – but what *I* did, that was red, clear and simple; that's why I'm gonna let you have a penalty.'

When it came to it, Reggie couldn't quite bring himself to fall on his sword – 'Oooooh yes! Nice try, not quite nice enough!' – but it didn't matter; the crisis was over.

Only when the world was fully black did the game conclude.

'That was great,' said Reggie, thawing out in the kitchen. 'I could've played all night.'

'No you couldn't,' said Daisy. 'It's too dark.'

'No, but if there was proper *lighting*...' He turned to his in-laws. 'D'you want me to install some floodlights in the garden?'

Jack laughed nervously. 'I think the neighbours'd have something to say.'

'He's right,' said Monica, with nicely feigned regret. 'We'd need planning permission.'

'Oh, well, never mind. We can play all night once we get the stadium. Did I tell you about that? Alex is building me a stadium on the estate – 'ere, Al, have we talked about floodlighting?'

'Last thing I remember,' I said, 'we were talking more in terms of *stage* lighting.'

'Eh?'

It startled me to see that he'd no idea – genuinely no idea – what I was talking about. No recollection whatsoever of a conversation barely 24 hours old.

'Listen...' He was already off on another tack. 'Listen,' he said to the in-laws, 'is there anything you need?'

'*Need?*'

'Anything I can get you?' He turned to me. 'I got them a sunbed a while ago.'

'Yes,' said Monica, 'he did. It's wonderful.' Her pale complexion attested to the use it was getting.

'I want you to have something. You've been so good to my kids.'

'It's a pleasure, really.'

'And don't worry, you'll not be stuck with 'em forever!'

'We're not worried,' said Jack.

'Really, the state of things right now, you're giving 'em a much more stable home than I could. You're a pair of fucking diamonds, I mean that – pardon my French.'

***

147

Shut up. Shut the fuck up.

'*What shall we do with a drunken sailor? What shall we do with a drunk* – Come on, people!'

Unless my ears deceive me, that's Mister Mayor – a voice in the dark, seeking through song to revive the Dunkirk spirit.

'Whoever's out there, come on, let's keep each other going!'

Fuck off.

'Come on, we'll get through this together! Join in with me! *What shall we do with a drunken sailor...* Come on, we've got to stay awake!'

Stay awake? The nerve of the man. Not two hours back, that voice – that booming, bloated voice now exhorting us to stay awake – was boring us all to tears and hunger and doziness as we waited for him – *pleeeeease* – to stop talking, just pass the big scissors to Reggie, let him cut the ribbon, so we can all get upstairs for wine and cake.

Not that I *got* any. Cake, I mean. I bought it myself, that cake – a *special* cake, from Choccywoccydoodah. Stupid name, fantastic cakes. I knew there'd be poncey canapés, but no, I wanted something *real* with which to celebrate. Fifty quid – fifty bloody quid's worth of Belgian chocolate – in three tiers.

Yeah, that's right, it all ends in tiers – and *I* didn't get a mouthful.

'*My old man said follow the van...*'

Music hall now. And, God help us, people are joining in.

'Shut up!' I shout. 'Shut up!' I *try*, at any rate. I try to cry out my dissent – even as I die I refuse to fall into line – but all that comes is a cracked whisper.

'*My old man...*'

148

Don't listen.

'...*follow the van...*'

Easily said – 'don't listen' – but... but the thing is, I can only get one hand over one ear. The other one's... well, it's just awkward.

'...*don't dilly-dally on the way-ay-ay!*'

Think. Just. Any. Just *anything* to...

Gobstopper. Jack Russell. Used to sit on Festus. I think. Think that was Gobstopper. *Was? Is. Is,* yeah, he was here just an hour ago, they *all* were. *Is,* yeah, but no... no longer... no longer Festus with the stomach.

So. Gobstopper, yeah. Who else? Gobstopper, yeah, but...

Yogi! That's it – Yogi, the big mongrel – more of a bear than a dog.

Oh, and Terry, of course. Terry the greyhound. He's the one who kicked it off, says Reggie. Went to the races – Walthamstow – with Keith Allen and 'Damien from Blur'. You mean *Damon?* Yeah, whatever. So there's a dog up for auction; Reggie, drunk, egged on by his celebrity mates, he splashes out on this dog – takes it home, certain his wife's gonna kill him, only of course she falls in love at once; over her dead body, she says, over my dead body are they gonna race this dog; fuck your 'investment', she says. She just – Denz – apparently – she wraps her arms around this soppy mutt: 'He's my baby now,' she says.

Come on, what else? There's seven of the buggers – six or seven.

'My baby!' says Reggie, 'My baby! She'd three of 'em already – three of 'em, real babies: Conrad and Chico and Daisy – why do we need a dog?'

Why indeed? After that, apparently, he couldn't hold her back: especially once she became patron of the local dog

149

shelter.

Oh, yeah – Doggy. Doggy, yeah. Doggy, the Dalmatian –
named by one of his genius kids.

Don't be horrible. Just cos Reggie's a twat who got you
buried alive in a tomb of bricks and powdered concrete; just
cos he's the nobber of the age, don't take it out on...

Yeah, dogs. Dogs.

Pixie. Yorkshire terrier. Little one. I know they're *all* little –
most of them, at least – but she... yappy little – tiny little...
Used to sit on top of Festus, along with...

So, yeah, that's Pixie and Yogi and Gobstopper and Terry
and... and Doggy and... and...

'Mummy!'

Mummy?

'Mumm...myyyy!'

Is that the Mayor again? What became of the singing?

***

I woke to find the house in uproar.

'Bastards! Fucking nosy bastards!'

The place was all but shaking to the sound of Reggie's
voice. I hurried downstairs and found him there pacing the
hall. He was deaf to all calming entreaties.

'Those fucking nosy bastards!'

This was just a few weeks on from our trip to Godham –
when, it might be recalled, he'd taken leave of his in-laws
offering gifts and lauding them as 'diamonds'. Surprising,
then, to find him directing his present ire at what turned out
(once unscrunched) to be a letter from Monica.

The substance of this letter related to Daisy, the middle
child. She had, it seemed, been reprimanded at school for the

use of 'a rude word' – one which transpired to have been learned at her father's knee. When exactly she *learned* it, no one could say, but it was to be noted that, in recent weeks, since Reggie's rebirth as a father, his kids had seen a lot more of him. They'd twice been up to the ranch, and, as yet, the novelty had by no means worn off (for *him*, I mean); Reggie was, without doubt, having a wonderful time – though, even before Monica's letter, I'd begun to wonder what effect he might be having in turn on the children.

'I don't know if you've noticed,' he said to me one time, 'but they're always a bit subdued when they come here; by the time they leave, they're a lot more upbeat and outgoing.'

Well, now, it appeared, this upness of beat had got one of them into trouble – hence the letter, wherein Monica very tactfully requested Reggie to take greater care what he said in the presence of his offspring.

'Fucking bitch! MY kids – my fucking kids – want to tell ME how to raise MY kids?'

'Yeah, but...'

'MY kids!'

'Yeah, but you're *not.*'

'What?'

'*You*'re not raising them – *she* is.'

He stared at me, weighing (I assumed) the question of whether to hit me or not. Then he said, 'Exactly'.

'I'm sorry?'

'Exactly, mate, that's the problem. We've got to get 'em back – back here, and fast, or those snobs are gonna ruin them for ever.'

'I think you're being a bit harsh. She's only saying...'

'Who gives a fuck what you *think*?'

Oh. Well, foolishly, I'd lulled myself into the belief that *he* gave a fuck. Finding myself wrong and at a loss for words, I shrugged and walked away.

I was halfway across the hall when he skipped round into my line of vision.

'Sorry mate!'

I tried to move around him.

'Sorry, I'm just a bit...'

'I'm going to the kitchen.'

'Look, that was rude of me. Sorry, okay? I'm just a bit upset – *you* can understand, *you*'ve got kids...'

'Yes, I do – and I don't teach them to swear.'

'You *do*. I've heard you.'

'Not on purpose.'

'What's wrong with swearing, anyway?'

'Nothing,' I said. 'Nothing at all. Swearing's great. I do it all the time; but you have to know how to use it – when *not* to use it, too. Now, if you don't mind, I'd like some breakfast.'

'Don't you mean 'some fucking breakfast'?'

'Exactly.'

He stood aside, then followed, yakking on as we descended to the kitchen.

'Okay, maybe I was a bit hasty. Maybe she's got a point. I'll tell her sorry, all that. But *I*'ve got a point too. They're *my* kids and they should be with *me*. They *will* be, an' all, just as soon as I'm in a position to take responsibility for them.'

'And when d'you think that's going to be?'

'Soon, mate, very soon. All I have to do is crack Hollywood. Once I do that, everything's gonna be alright.'

– Illusionment –

Now, of course, I know he's a psycho. *Now*. *Now* it's all too obvious. Back then, though...

I don't know... even back then, I probably should've seen the signs.

Okay, not a *psycho*, not literally; no one's getting chopped up. *Probably* not. Even so, knowing now what I didn't know then, I seriously doubt... I mean, *children*...? Look after children? He can't even look after *himself*, let alone...

Back then, though... Well, maybe I was having too much fun to think about it. Or maybe I *thought* about it, only then to put those thoughts aside. After all, there weren't huge crowds of other people vying with Reggie for my friendship.

Even so, I should've seen something was up.

That time at Chesham Hall, for instance.

Just after Easter, it was: the client, reluctant as ever to sit down and talk, whisked us off on another of his magical mystery tours. A country house this time – 'somewhere architectural – help me think'. Our destination, he explained, was a little bit older than his place and therefore ideal inspiration for the Tudoresque stadium to whose construction he was now yet again fully committed.

As it turned out, the house was a mish-mash of styles, all of them mish-mashed together in the late Victorian period. The frontage, half-timbered, was flanked by a pair of pointed towers the like of which are more usually found on a Scottish castle. The interior was scarcely less eccentric: the baronial hall, complete with minstrels' gallery, was the only part entirely free of fan vaulting (even the subterranean service corridors were subject to it).

So, there's us – me and Reggie – floating about the fan-vaulted drawing room, intensively examining the items on display, not so much through keen interest as through a desire to avoid the eye of the resident volunteer and thus escape a long, over-detailed lecture, when Reggie, flipping through a folder of ancient photos, suddenly beckons me over.

'Look at this.'

I found him paused on a group portrait: a large assemblage of householders, guests and servants at a hunting weekend sometime in the 1890s.

'Edward VII,' I murmured, recognising the Falstaffian hulk in the middle. 'Course, at that point he'd have been Prince of –'

'Never mind him. Look, in the row behind – next to Ali Baba!'

The so-called 'Ali Baba' figure was clearly some kind of Indian prince, judging by his patrician demeanour and the relative prominence of his positioning, just behind the Empire's heir apparent. Next to him, in any case, was a pretty young woman in a white dress.

'Spooky, innit?'

'What d'you mean?'

'Denz. Just like Denz. Don't you think?'

'Well, I don't know. I never met her.'

'You seen her in the papers.'

I had indeed, and allowing even for the fact that the girl in the picture had moved a fraction, and blurred herself in the process, I could be sure she looked absolutely nothing like the late Mrs Cullen.

Still, I did what I could.

'I suppose there's a very mild resemblance.'

'*Mild*? I tell you, mate, she's the fucking spit.'

From the corner of the room came a most emphatic throat-clearing. I smiled at the volunteer and tugged at Reggie's sleeve.

'Let's move on.'

'Tell you, mate, you got funny eyes.'

He didn't talk to me the rest of the way round the building.

When we were browsing in the gift shop, however, he drifted up beside me, a postcard in his hand. It was a reproduction of the hunting party scene.

'Weird,' he said. 'You were right. She don't look *nothing* like her. I could've sworn...'

It was, I now see, a sign of things to come – a sign I should and maybe *would* have read at the time, had we not been pushed for it. *Time*, I mean. We were due back for a lesson with Captain Walcott, and anxious not to be late, for lateness incurred a penance: you were obliged to walk up to the front of the class, put your hands humbly together, bow in apology to the teacher and then do likewise for your fellow students. Actually, it didn't bother *me* so much, but Reggie, as the lord of the manor, clearly found it degrading. For him it was another example of the namby-pamby elements which tainted an otherwise excellent method of learning to 'kick arse'.

'It's like them eighteen tenants, when he...'

'*Tenets.*'

'When he makes us say the eighteen tenants of...'

'*Tenets!*'

'What?'

'The eighteen *tenets*.'

'Alright, tenets, tenets, whatever – still the same old bollocks. Spiritual bollocks, that's all.'

'Oh, come on,' I said. 'The tenets, okay, that's maybe a bit airy-fairy, but the *bowing* – that's just good manners.'

'Yeah, s'pose – only, what's so wrong with *sorry I'm late*?'

'What's so wrong with not *being* late?'

'Fuck you.'

There might have been more of this witty banter, but for the call that came through from Gordon, Reggie's agent, just as we pulled through the gates at Cullen Place.

As far as I could gather – 'You what? You fucking WHAT?' – it was bad news about *Easy Meat*. This, of course, was the film which, according to Shelley, was destined to make Reggie a movie star and bring on the succession of roles that would pay for the building of the stadium. Unfortunately, it was looking ever more unlikely that anyone would actually get to *see* this film. Several times the release date had changed, and just lately there'd been a threat from the distribution company to shelve it altogether.

This latest from Gordon, however, turned out to be good news – at least, by any rational estimation: the distributors, under threat of legal strife from the producers, had with ill grace agreed to reschedule the release for late June.

Why, then, I wondered, the foul-tongued tirade? 'Your film is being *released*,' I said. 'That's good, isn't it?'

'I'll believe it when I see it. They've fucked us over so many times – so many, I've lost count.'

And, as if to prove the point, he attempted to list all the various delays and double-crosses, growing yet more frustrated when it turned out that there had indeed been too many twists and turns to remember.

By the time the second call came, he was wound up like a watch.

Expecting, presumably, yet more from the long-suffering Gordon, he answered with an unpleasant 'What?' It wasn't his agent, though. Who it was, I couldn't tell, but by the time we came to a halt in front of Cullen Place, the expression on his face had journeyed far, from belligerence to concern to moist-eyed fear.

Climbing out of the Range Rover, he ended the call with a meek thank you.

'They've set a court date,' he said, trying to smile as he did so.

'Oh. Right.'

'Three weeks from now.'

He had another go at smiling.

'I'll be glad,' he said. 'Glad to get it over with. It's been hanging over me for ages.'

Then he started crying. I'd known he was going to, but still it was somehow a surprise.

You always think you'll know what to do next time – next time some blokey hard-man friend starts bawling in close proximity – but, when it comes down to it, all you can actually do is to look intently at a brick wall and note how much of it needs repointing.

'Sorry,' he sniffled. 'It's not the poofters – you know that, yeah?'

'I'm... I'm sorry?'

'It's not the poofters I'm worried about. I mean, I'm not worried *at all*, not as such, and as for the poofters, I can take care of that, no problem. No, it's just the thought of being locked up twenty-three hours a day with six other blokes and a bucket of shit.'

'I don't think they do slopping-out anymore.'

'Six blokes and a *bog*, then. There'll still be a fucking *bog* in the room.' He laughed. 'Maybe I should start sleeping in the bathroom – get used to it.'

The tears started flowing again.

I thought I'd have a go at saying something.

'It's gonna be okay.'

He laughed a snotty laugh. 'Course,' he said. 'Course it is – for *you*: you ain't going to jail.'

'*No one*'s going to jail.'

'They'll fucking kill me. Everyone's gonna want to have a go, just cos I'm a celeb. *Who's gonna take out Reggie Cullen?* They'll be taking bets.'

'Reggie, mate, you are *not* going to jail. Believe me, I will do anything and everything in my power to help you. I will say whatever it takes.' *Please, just stop crying.* 'Me and your lawyer: we'll build a cast-iron case for you – I promise By the time I'm through, they'll be ready to lynch that planning inspector.'

Reggie looked me in the eye – *did I really mean it?* I nodded reassuringly. His lower lip quivered dangerously, then he broke into another laugh, a real one this time, full of hope and blessment.

He reached for my hand, clasped it in both of his, and kissed it.

'Thank you,' he said – just as Shelley and the dogs poured forth from the front door.

'Oh,' said Shelley, as Reggie snatched his hand away. 'Oh,' she said again. 'Oh, I was just wondering, are you coming to Kung Fu?'

'Yeah,' said Reggie, in a voice more gruff than his usual. 'Absolutely,' he boomed. 'Let's kick a bit of arse!'

– Smarties Ascendant–

There's a story I read once in a history textbook...

It seems that, back in the darkest days of the Second World War, when the Germans were sweeping through the lands of their former Soviet allies, Joseph Stalin learned that his son Yakov was among those who'd fallen before the Nazi killing machine. Himself, of course, a cold-hearted killer on an already record-breaking scale, Stalin nevertheless retained enough of a soul to be devastated by this personal blow, and in his moment of despair, the General Secretary of the Communist Party of the Soviet Union offered to resign as his nation's leader.

The Politburo turned him down.

That's right: he offered to quit, and they turned him down. Or at least, that's how the story goes. For all I know it may be apocryphal, but, if otherwise... well, you've got to wonder, how many millions might have lived that perished instead because Stalin was gifted another decade in power?

Idiots. Apocryphal idiots.

And yet I can sort of relate to those poor Politburo lickspittles in their moment of epic dilemma. For I too had such a moment. When I told Reggie I'd do 'anything' – by making that promise to do and say 'anything' to keep him from jail – what was I doing but passing up the chance to change the future.

If there might at that stage have been any doubt at all about how our destinies were entwined, within a few days the deal was sealed. At the Court of Appeal in London, at a hearing I thought it best not to attend, Mog lost her final bid to derail the second phase of the Terriss project.

Phase 1, completed the previous summer, had involved putting three storeys of underground parking below my home town high street, to serve the theatre and the two council buildings to which it would eventually be linked. Though hardly the most glamorous part of the project, it was quite the engineering feat, involving as it did the extension and deepening of the pre-existing car park under the main council building – and all this executed with the minimum of disruption to the everyday workings of the road above.

On, then, to Phase 2: we had the go-ahead, and soon a great hedge of scaffolding and blue netting would rise around the William Terriss Memorial Theatre. My dream was about to become reality – and all of a sudden I couldn't be far enough away. To be there but not in charge – to be, at best, a mere consultant; that would be unbearable. More to the point, as things moved forward, relations between me and Mog could only worsen. Even if I was no longer directly involved in the project, I'd still be blamed for having once again caused her humiliation: as lawyer, as civic pillar, as wife, as mother, as sentient being.

Aside from which, I couldn't realistically have decamped, even had it suited me, not before Reggie had his day in court. I'd made him a promise, and for all my other faults I am, in most things at least, a man of my word.

The next few weeks I worked pretty much round the clock, collating all the data I had about the spa block and selecting precedents for 'inappropriate' juxtaposition (Pei's pyramids, for instance, at the Louvre), thus arming myself with everything I'd need to go into a planning appeal and win. Eventually I'd have to do just that, so it was worth the effort, though its direct relevance to Reggie's criminal case was actually pretty tenuous: however one chose to rationalise the decisions that drove the building of the spa block, Reggie was surely not justified in hitting that planning officer (not *legally*, at any rate). He may well have been provoked beyond endurance, but as I pointed out to his solicitor, I'd not been present and therefore couldn't comment.

'True,' said Mr Sperring, 'but you can at least appear as a character witness.'

'And say what?'

'That he's not naturally violent.'

I nearly spat out my coffee.

'Sorry – I thought we were talking about *Reggie*?'

'Yes...?'

'Reggie, yeah? The same Reggie who sat out half a season cos he bit a referee?'

'Did you see him do that?'

'No.'

'Stick to what you know, then. Millions have read about him. Few know him like you do.'

'I've only known him a few months. Prior to that we were at school together. In between...'

'Yes, yes, school,' he said. 'Was he violent at school?'

'Let me put it this way: does the term 'Piss-Ears' mean anything to you?'

Unsurprisingly, it didn't.

The first thing I (and many others) noticed about Reggie the schoolboy was that he smelled of urine. It was subtle but unmistakable. Not his fault, of course; it was the fault of his parents – or, more specifically, that of his brutalitarian father, who'd been in sole command ever since his wife found the sense to walk out. Unfortunately, though, kids don't tend to look for underlying causes; they look at hard facts, then use them as sticks with which to beat people. In Reggie's case they had two such sticks to work with: his rich aroma, and the generous cut of his ears. For a while, then, his persecutors were spoilt for choice: ears or piss – take your pick – but *do* choose, because, as it turned out, you wouldn't get away with both. When someone was unwise enough to combine the two traits and go public with that term *Piss-Ears*, he wound up losing his incisors.

Sperring, unimpressed: 'And you were witness to this incident?'

'Well, no, I didn't actually *see* it – but plenty did: he kicked the guy in the stomach – repeatedly – and then moved on to his head. Apparently, there were teeth everywhere.'

'*Apparently*? So, if I have it right, you saw *none* of this?'

'I don't think he'd deny it happened.'

'But you didn't *see* it?'

'I saw the blood in the playground.'

'Could've been *anyone*'s blood.'

'But it *wasn't*.'

'Unless you know that for a fact, it's hearsay.'

'Look, you're asking me to say whether he's known for being violent...'

'I'm asking whether you, personally, Mr Alexis Broughton, have ever personally seen Mr Cullen engage in physical violence.'

'Then the answer's no.'

'Good. We got there in the end. You'll be perfect.'

'But what if I'm asked about his *reputation*? The other guy – the prosecution – what if I'm *asked* about hearsay?'

'Simple. In that case you say that, putting aside a few

unfortunate incidents brought on by extreme stress or on-pitch adrenaline overload, you understand his violent image to be just that – an *image*, carefully cultivated for PR purposes, and with no basis in reality.'

I stared at him, awestruck. The clever fucker. I almost said it. Come to think of it, I probably did.

***

Thus, sucked free of all my finer scruples, I turned up to court ready and willing to be the very Chancellor of truthful economy – only to learn I'd not be needed.

At the magistrates' the previous autumn, Reggie had insisted on pleading Not Guilty; he was provoked, he insisted, and he wasn't going to say otherwise. As far as I knew, that remained the official line; *un*officially, though, the official line had changed – and all because of a stupid film. *Easy Meat* being once again slated for release, Gordon the agent was expecting a flood of offers from 'across the pond'. The last thing Reggie needed, therefore, was a prison record to pique the interest of the US Immigration Service.

Hence, the plea was changed, Sperring bullshat the court about his client's dead wife, and the judge came up trumps with a community service order.

Brilliant.

No, really, I was glad for him; glad, too, not to have to speak in court (I'd have fucked it up, I know) – but *when*, I wondered, had the official line been changed? Precisely when had Reggie and his upstanding, incorruptible advocate decided they were going to throw in the towel? And why did I have to learn about it through the proceedings of the court?

There was further frustration to come. I'd assumed that now, with the spectre of prison happily banished, I'd get some quality time together with Reggie on the stadium project. Who could've known that community service was going to take up so much of his energy, or indeed how joyously he'd embrace the experience?

Given the wide variety of activities his penance encompassed – he was never in the same location two days running – it was strange the number of times the paparazzi turned up in just the right place to find him cleaning toilets or weeding flower beds or whitewashing graffiti.

'What can you do?' he shrugged. 'Some fucker must be tipping 'em off.' In time, of course, I realised the 'fucker' in question was Shelley. Reggie, it transpired, worked on the celebrated principle that all publicity is good publicity. The same seemed to be true of the thoroughly compliant authorities; on one occasion, sent to do some odd-jobbing at a retirement home, Reggie was even able to blag entry for a local BBC camera crew.

The results were on the regional news that very same evening – and, as Reggie himself admitted, they couldn't have done him better PR if they'd been on the Cullen payroll.

At one point in this courageous piece (destined to be played, rewound and played again so many times over the ensuing days), the camera finds our hero in the process of touching up paintwork in the TV lounge, while oldies in oversized armchairs look on.

'This work,' he says – he's talking to a presence just offscreen – 'this stuff, it sort of brings out my artistic side. Brings out a sort of pride in my work – like the old days, when I was chipping in goals on the field. Artistic, yeah.' Then, just when you wonder if he could possibly get any further up his own arse, he tips a self-satirising wink into the camera.

Elsewhere, a bit less flippant if no less media-savvy, he speaks of the assault on the planning officer. 'I don't know what gets into me,' he sighs, eyes yearning moistly into the middle distance. 'I mean, the guy was just doing his job...'

This, it seems, is the moment – the golden moment –

when Reggie Cullen's all set to grant his audience the tears to which they're so richly entitled. Instead he whips himself out of frame. When the camera catches up, he's revealed to be opening a door for one of the ancient residents. Close-up of Reggie, watching her recede very slowly from view. 'Puts it in perspective,' he mutters.

'So,' says the offscreen brown-nose, 'what does the future hold?'

'Well,' he replies, 'I've done a bit of *acting...*'

At this point, Reggie – the *real* Reggie, the one next to me on the sofa – gives me a nudge. 'Look,' he says, 'they're gonna show a bit of *Easy Meat!*'

They don't, though. Instead, they cut to a scene in the garden, where assorted hard nuts in matching hi-vis tabards are taking tea and enjoying exposure to Reggie's new-found accent skills; while Voice-over Reggie talks of conquering Hollywood, On-screen Reggie reproduces a scene (the tiresomely obvious one) from *Taxi Driver*.

Sofa Reggie's having a ball. 'Good, eh?'

From the neighbouring sofa, there's input from Festus. 'That Robert de Niro?' he mutters.

'You talking to me, mate? You talking to me?'

Great. Two of them now – on-screen and on-sofa. Then, as if that weren't enough, Festus joins in. Not that he managed to work up a great deal of lung-power, poor sod, stretched there on his sofa with dogs atop, but he made a bit of an effort, so in the end it was a full aural triptych of shit de Niro.

Ungracious? Okay, maybe. It's just, y'know, that Travis Bickle thing, it's so over-done; even the original's hard to take these days – and what eventually emerged, to top off my irritation, was the revelation that Reggie's never even seen the film. 'I just picked it up from other people!'

Even more irksome were the comments that followed our watching (and three-time *re*-watching on tape) of the report. Referring back to his on-screen words of contemplation, I asked him had he actually learnt anything from his experience thus far?

'Well, one thing I realise is, I *could've* handled prison, no problem. I get on fine with those lads: they like me, they respect me, I cheer them up. It's like the school bully, at school; long as you make 'em laugh, they won't, y'know...'

'...rape you?'

'Well, that's another matter; I mean, obviously, if I got sent down I'd have to use my fists to keep the queers at bay, but apart from that... What? What's so funny?'

'*You.*'

'*Me*? What d'you mean?'

'You've not the slightest idea what it's like in prison.'

'I do. More than you, at least. You – *you'd* be dead within the hour. You couldn't take it; you'd hang yourself with your own knickers. Me, though – I'd just give 'em the Cullen charm, like I do with the lads on the chain-gang.'

Chain-gang. He was really getting into this thing. He actually thought it was *cool.*

Next day, he brought 'the lads' back to the house after work. Needless to say, de Niro was back on the bill (special treat for Alex, says Reggie), and extra laughs were achieved through the inspiration of directing the speech at Pixie, the miniature Yorkie. I was charmed, I admit: little ball of fluff moving her head from one side to the other, trying to make sense of what her master was saying – but that was the *dog*, not Reggie; the dog was the making of the act. Nonetheless, Reggie's little turn went down a storm, and we even got an encore in the form of an Oscars speech.

'Thank you, thank you,' said Reggie, in what I think was

meant to be a sort of breathy Marilyn (it came out closer to Frank Spencer). 'I'd just like to say: this award doesn't belong to me. It belongs to everyone who worked on the film.'

Gales of mirth from the wrong 'un hordes.

'It belongs to my director, Alfred Hitchcock, and my co-stars, Brad and Angelina, but also to all the people who believed in me down the years...' By this time his accent's heading south, inexplicably south '– mah ma an' mah pa, mah wife and mah wunnerful children – mah best friend Festus, all the boys on the chain-gang...'

Another huge wave of laughter.

'Everyone except my supposed friend Alexis Broughton, who thought my Robert de Niro was a big pile of shee-yit! He didn't *say*, but I could tell. Well, Alex, here's me at the Academy Awards, and where are you? You're nowhere. You're nothing. You're NOBODY!'

By now his eyes are burning into mine; the smile long gone.

Only of course he couldn't hold that pissy face, not for long – he was just too thrilled by the final whoop of delight coming forth from the criminal assembly. He'd made his point, though, I realised, as I attempted to simper along with the surrounding hilarity, that I was now sweating like a little piggy. Yes, Reggie Cullen had once more made me feel like shit for the joy of other people – for *lesser* people, at that; for the dregs of society. And then, just as these unworthy, uncharitable, un*Guardian*-y thoughts were passing through my mind, one of those useless lumps of shit actually took it upon himself to tousle my hair. This guy – let's be clear – this guy did not know me from a hole in the ground – nor I him, in strict fairness, so whether he was a car thief or a crack-merchant or a wife-basher, I really couldn't say; all I knew was that his new-found friendship with Reggie apparently gave him clear rights of access to my person.

'Get off me, you cretin!'

The cretin in question was actually rather a sizely lad, but he didn't seem to mind too much; he just joined in gamely with the chorus of high-pitched undulating 'woooooo!'s that greeted my outburst.

Even so, I thought it wise at this point to withdraw, before I say something truly punchworthy. And so, to a predictable reprise of the great 'wooooo!' that had gone before, I vacated the room and went upstairs to make love with Shelley.

Oh no. No I didn't. That was a bit later.

– Sleep No More –

For the first ten years or so of my existence, I took it that William Terriss – he who lent his name to one of my home town's principal landmarks – was some kind of bushy-whiskered, chain-wearing civic handshaker of days past.

I'd ice cream to thank for my enlightenment.

There was a lolly, back in the '70s; a Lyons Maid ice lolly called Haunted House. Vanilla, ghost-sheet white, with a spooky picture inked on in lines of bloodiest red. It came in a range of wrappers, each one bearing what the manufacturers seemed to suggest was a true-life ghost story – and among these wrapper-bound tales was that of William Terriss, a Victorian actor whose ghost was said to keep vigil at the theatre where he died.

I inevitably got to wondering if Terriss the spook might be in any way connected with the Terriss Theatre? Surely not. The lolly wrapper talked of his haunting the Adelphi in London – the *West End*; why would he have anything to do with a dump like Godham? Next time I was at the Terriss, however, lining up with Mum and Dad to see Peter Butterworth as Widow Twankey, I noticed a plaque on the foyer wall. Though it was semi-obscured by the confectionery kiosk, I was able to make out a tribute to 'the much-esteemed actor and manager' William Terriss, a 'popular visitor to this town' and a man 'taken tragically before his time'.

Poor old Peter Butterworth. I mean, he *was* good, of course he was, but he could hardly expect my full attention; pretty much the whole first half of *Aladdin* was spent inside my head, obsessing over an actor from an age long past. How exactly had this Terriss guy been 'taken'? Cancer, perhaps – a courageous battle with cancer? Or maybe just a cold – they weren't very hardy in those days (I'd heard all about the Brontës). Or even an on-stage accident: a falling sandbag, or a ghastly mishap with a prop gun that wasn't in fact a prop?

In the interval, I sought out the manager. Big disappointment. Terriss, he revealed, had actually been *murdered*, but he'd no idea how – nor, from the sound of it, was he all that curious. All he knew was that the people of Godham Malpass had clubbed together to build a theatre in the great man's memory.

I asked if his ghost had ever been seen hereabouts?

'Don't be silly.'

'Why?' I said. 'Why silly? He haunts the Adelphi in London.'

I was told to run along, and did so. It didn't occur to me then – cos it never *does*, not when you're a kid – to stand my ground and ask him *why*? *Why* don't you know how he was murdered? Where's your professional curiosity? *Mine* – when I grow up to be an architect – mine will cause me to find out all I can; I'll be right on the case.

Cos I *was*: as soon as I started in on the conference centre project, I wanted to know *everything* about that theatre, and especially about the guy for whom it was named. What I discovered, first and foremost, was that Terriss was *huge*. Today he's the stuff of plaques half obscured by pricey ice cream kiosks, but back then, in late Victorian England, he was second only in popularity to Sir Henry Irving. That's pretty much like being second in popularity to the Beatles. Sadly for Breezy Bill (as he was affectionately known), he managed to *lose* popularity with one of his fellow actors, a sort of Oliver Grant character by the name of Richard Archer Prince. Actually, it was *he* who got on the wrong side of Terriss. Bit lippy, old Prince, especially for a minor member of the

172

company (which he was). Apparently Terriss, at first, turned a blind eye, but eventually he had to let the guy go. Even so, he felt bad about it, and for a while afterwards sought to keep Prince apprised of any opportunities that came to ear. It wasn't appreciated, of course; in fact, far from acknowledging his ex-employer's efforts, Prince conceived the idea that Terriss was actively conspiring to *deprive* him of work.

And so, one night in mid-December 1897, as Terriss arrived at the Adelphi to prepare for that evening's performance, he was accosted by Prince and stabbed to death.

Cue national outflush of grief – and just make sure you're not enjoying a barbecue on the day of the funeral!

As for that smarmy '70s theatre manager, so full of shit and ignorance, the ghost thing was only the half of what he didn't know. According to my later researches, Terriss was indeed a popular visitor to the genteel and cultured holiday resort of Godham Malpass. He stopped along the way with most of his touring shows, and his loss was undoubtedly met with shock and genuine grief by his many local fans. Other than possibly defraying the cost of the nice plaque, however, the people of Godham 'clubbed together' for sod all: the sum of their tribute was to shove his name on a theatre which was already half-built when he died.

But, hey, print the legend, why not? That's Mog's policy. I can see her now, in one of those courtroom spoiling missions, standing up and insisting, in a voice heavy with emotion, that the William Terriss Memorial Theatre was built by public subscription. This she said in spite of my presence mere yards away – in spite – *unbelievable!* – in spite of the fact that she knew I knew *she* knew it was a load of steaming horseshit: the Terriss Theatre was the work of a consortium of businessmen reacting to what were then very favourable market conditions.

I did actually scribble a note to that effect and pass it along to our counsel, but he, quite rightly, ignored it. As he was shortly to point out to the judge, the theatre's origins and heritage were immaterial. We weren't, after all, planning its removal – far from it: the plan was to preserve it for the people, enrobed in a coating that would keep it secure for centuries to come.

In fact, he might justly have added, if ever they should bulldoze the Adelphi, the shade of William Terriss could float on down to the coast and take up residence in his namesake playhouse, there for ever more to shake his gory locks at the seaside sun-seekers.

– Idyllia –

Kung Fu people are strange. Nice, by and large, but rather sharply focused. At least, that's what I found in downtown Luton. The people there, at the Whittaker Centre, had only one topic of conversation: be it in the dojo or the pub post-class, all they could ever talk about was martial arts. Even the Captain; he must have had a lifetime of interesting stories to tell, yet he chose not to tell a single one of them. Even if you managed to break out and lead the conversation into the realm of, say, cinema, you'd sooner or later end up focusing specifically on the exploits of Jet Li or Jackie Chan.

That's why Shelley and I got together.

Well, not *just* because of that. Clearly there was some attraction involved – and, let's face it, but for Reggie and his high-vis fan club, we wouldn't've been spending so much time together in the first place; it was only because of him – because he'd started encouraging his new 'friends' to attend the Kung Fu classes at the house – that the two of us started hanging out together in town.

And no, it was nothing to do with snobbery, nor indeed my reluctance (as Reggie so piously put it) to 'rejoice in the saving of sinners'. For me, it was simply about a certain person having found a new forum to make catty quips at my expense. I'd endured that stuff at school; now I didn't *have* to, if only because of the Captain and his twice-weekly drop-in classes at the Whittaker Centre.

As I say, though, the post-class conversation could be a bit limited, hence the growing tendency for me and Shelley to divide off from the rest, become a kind of two-strong fringe meeting. Between the pair of us, of course, the focus was almost as narrow as on the Kung Fu table; long after the others had departed, we'd be sat there still, swapping tales about the atrocities of Reggie Cullen. I was appalled if not surprised to learn that my schoolboy humiliations were nothing to the trials endured by Shelley in the line of duty.

'You know, one time,' she told me, 'when they were doing their thing with the... the, y'know, the 'dogging'; one night they were drunk, both of them – too drunk to drive – so they made me run them up to the golf club.'

'The *golf club*?'

'That's where it used to happen.'

'Oh, right.'

'In the car park. All these couples with torches, scurrying around between cars.'

'Right. And... and... you...?'

'God, no. No, certainly not... but I had to sit there and wait while *they*...'

'Right.'

'Every so often, of course, someone would come and tap on the window, and I'd have to explain that I wasn't there for the actual...'

'No.'

'They got quite annoyed, some of them.'

I'd nothing quite so stark to impart back to Shelley, though I tended to be equally candid in other areas, especially regarding what I sought to paint as my shamelessly mercenary attitude toward the great man. Now the court case was done, I said, and now Reggie had once again found new friends, I had no reason to hang around... at least (I found myself confessing), no reason apart from the knowledge that if I went home, I'd be nothing but a gooseberry, impotently watching as other people gave life to my dream.

My only solution, therefore, was to find a whole new dream to dream – and Reggie's stadium, however fanciful, was the only dream in town.

Only, of course, this was bullshit – for as soon as I got The Word, I jumped.

A call came through one day from the Velvet Fist. They were planning a photoshoot, he said, to mark the start of construction proper – was there any chance I could be there?

My intention, that night, was to go to Kung Fu with Shelley, as planned, then set out immediately afterwards on the road for Godham.

'Sorry,' I said, 'can't do the pub.' We were leaving the Centre, heading for the car. 'I'll drop you home, though, of course.'

'Oh. Fine. Thanks. If you don't mind.'

'Not at all.'

'Couldn't you go in the morning, though? It's a long drive tonight.'

'No. No, they want me there first thing.'

'Oh. Right. So... does this mean they want you back on the project?'

'I don't know. I hope so. I shouldn't flatter myself. They probably just got cold feet. Charlotte's very good – she can handle it, no question, but who knows? Maybe they're feeling a bit funny about not having me on the ground.'

'So, what will you do?'

'*Do?*'

'If they ask you to...?'

'Oh. Well, obviously, I'll, um... I'll, er...' I was fumbling with the lock, trying to open the door for her. 'Obviously I'll...'

'Will you be going back to, er, to...?'

'To Mog?' I laughed. 'I doubt very much if...'

'You – you seem to be having a bit of trouble there, with the, er...'

'No, no, it's just a bit... No. No, to be honest, if I get back – if I get back on the Terriss Project, it's pretty sure to be the last nail in the coffin – y'know, the, um, the coffin of our, er...'

'Yes. Yes.'

The door came open.

'Right,' said Shelley, edging only slowly toward the beckoning passenger seat; 'Right, so, if you stayed here for a bit, you've probably more chance of...'

'Well, yes...'

'More chance of...'

'Ironically, yes.'

'Of saving your...'

'Exactly.'

'Of saving your mramwruuh...'

***

Small mercies. Thank Heaven. Shelley. Shelley, wherever you are, thank God. Thank God you're there and not here. Just think, if you and I... if things between us had... I shudder to think. You might've been here now beside me: coughing and broken, waiting in the gloom for International Rescue to get their arse in gear... A blessing. That's what it is – if only you could hear me tell you that. A blessing. A sign. And no, I don't believe in that bullshit, but still I say it's a sign. You've

178

been delivered, so stay away. From him, I mean. Don't let him tempt you back. You're worth so much more than...

Cos me, of course, I was never gonna... Not as long as he... I mean, the way you were with him, and me with Mog, it was never gonna... never...

Not that I saw it that way at the time. Not that first morning, at least – that morning after the Kung Fu class. Setting off for Godham, well... who needs a car? I was riding a cloud. Down the driveway it carried me. All was suddenly spring at Cullen Place: the grass was lush, and glowing ranks of crocus had the dogshit surrounded in purple and orange. It was a glorious sight to see me off back to my real life – and it tempered my dismay when I beheld the line-up at the newly buzzing construction site.

I'd expected, of course, to be posing with the Velvet Fist – with Charlotte too – and if I was surprised to see Oliver there, I assumed (as nobody had told me otherwise) that he was present simply as a senior partner with a legitimate interest in a major company project. Only whilst being conducted on a tour by the foreman did I come to understand the full reality. Thinking of the project still as being my baby (notwithstanding custody issues), I naturally asked a lot of questions, however, though these questions were heard with respect and answered in full, the answers invariably reached me second-hand. Every time, without fail, the foreman's gaze would start with me, but shift instinctively unto Oliver – not to Charlotte (which would've made a rude kind of sense), but to Oliver.

And so I came to understand: I'd been invited purely for the piccies – for the sake of appearance, and nothing more.

Informal shots were taken throughout the tour, but the official one – the *grinner* – that was done up at top level; the photographer thought we'd look good against the panorama of the town and the sea beyond. I was surprised, and pleasantly so, to be placed emphatically at the centre of the line-up – 'Say cheese!' – big laughs; and yet, job done, those fuckers – my God – they could not get away fast enough. It was well-nigh supernatural: I dawdled for just a few moments, gazing out on the drama of the storm clouds and the sea, and when I looked round again, I was alone.

Well, they'd got what they wanted – a nice, cheery picture, exuding confidence and continuity. What were they wanting now? Who knows, maybe I was meant to do the decent thing and throw myself over the side.

It didn't matter, anyway. It *really* didn't matter. I realised as much in those four or five seconds of care-free cloud-watching. It suddenly struck me – and with no sour grapes involved – that I really, genuinely didn't mind being off the project. Despite what I might have said to numerous people down the years about my love for the construction part of the process, I finally accepted, in that epiphanic rooftop moment, that I actually *hate* the construction part of the process.

I hate the cold and dampness that so often prevails.

I hate the smell and taste of plaster dust that *eternally* prevails.

I hate the sense of impotence when things are going slower than expected – no matter that experience tells you to *expect* things to go slower than expected.

I hate – I *really* hate – the stupid big clothes they make you wear. I know they're to protect you, but by the time you've got yourself into the big clompy boots, the one-size-fits-most gloves, the hard hat and goggles, the blinding high-vis vest that so utterly negates the effect of the Paul Smith suit you bought to keep up with the Grants... by the time they've finished with you, you don't feel like an architect, you feel like a ten-year-old on *Jim'll Fix It*.

Above all, though, what I hate is feeling inadequate among builders. I know I shouldn't. I know they're no more 'real men' than I am, and yet, despite my membership of the officer class – my god-like status as the man on whom everybody else's job depends – despite the fact, above all, that I don't need Page 3 on my office wall to confirm me in my sexual security...

I think I've always felt these things, but I never before allowed myself to knit them all together in my mind and accept the truth. I didn't *need* to, I suppose: my on-site lack of enjoyment and self-esteem was counterbalanced by the respect and loyalty I enjoyed back at Base Camp.

Not now.

Now, oh no, not at all.

Farewell and adieu, compensating loyalty and respect.

As I withdrew once more to Cullen Place, I continued to congratulate myself on dodging a poisoned chalice. I'd done the best bit, I told myself, and now it was for more workaday talents to oversee the execution while I went on to new challenges.

And yet, I wondered... If not for the unexpected privilege of carnal relations the night before, would I now be saying such things to myself? In other circumstances, would I not, at the very least, have taken the Velvet Fist aside and sought once more to convince him of his error? The answer must surely be yes; after all, I skipped town without even trying to see my kids – an extremely rare occurrence – so it's fair to assume there was pretty much the one thing on my mind that day.

Not that I was wrong in my conclusions. Not at all. Even were I said to have been swayed by sex and spring flowers, the sex and spring flowers turned out to be right on the money – for shortly thereafter, something surprising occurred: Reggie started cooperating.

This was due in part to the conclusion of his stint on community service. Though the miscreants had pledged themselves to amity eternal – martial arts would bond this band of brothers – in practice, attendance at the Kung Fu sessions quickly dropped off. As it turned out, only a few had actually made it past their first class, and in time the remainder too fell away – though whether through sloth, competing commitments or mere resentment at the tenner a head Reggie had started charging them, it was impossible to know.

In any case, the release of *Easy Meat* was imminent. Reggie's acting career was about to go stratospheric – he assured me of this – and his income was set to go with it. Thus, with a newly enhanced belief in his ability to pay for it, he became more seriously focused than ever on the stadium. Though many of the coming days were due to be spent doing media interviews, he and I would meet religiously for an hour every morning and another in the evening; I would show him my work, listen to his thoughts, then go away and labour some more in response.

While I filled my days in architectural grindstoning, Shelley was busy masterminding Reggie's press schedule. On top of her ever-expanding estate workload, she'd been roped in as an unpaid adjunct to the *Easy Meat* PR machine.

There were still the nights, though, and most of those we would spend together, using a mixture of texts, emails and notes under doors to decide whose room played host. Secrecy was fun and, by common consent, a simpler way of doing things: it allowed Shelley to carry on holding a torch for Reggie while I continued to harbour delusions of reunion with my wife.

One way or another, then, Cullen Place unexpectedly went through a bit of a golden age, a bit of a kind of Bloomsbury thing. *Rural* Bloomsbury, I mean. I'm thinking of the Charleston Farmhouse – all those proto-hippies getting back to nature and making her their muse. Okay, so we weren't writing books and daubing cupboards, but we *were* building a stadium and promoting a film (if only a film about putting people in pies).

Similarly, Charlestonian was the sense of unreality that pervaded, the sense (within *my* mind, at least) that somehow this golden age could last for ever. Even as I continued to crave a new beginning with their mother, I found myself observing how well the girls got on with Shelley – more like a big sister than a potential step mum – and in those moments I would dream of something radically different.

In the very perfection of the idyll, however, was its undoing.

It struck me as a shame that, though the girls had started coming up quite often to visit, they were never there at the same time as Reggie's kids.

'We should get them all together.'

'Why?' said Reggie. 'It's not like we're getting married.'

'No, though of course we *could* – civil partnership, at least.'

'You what?'

'Never mind. What d'you think?'

'Yeah, alright. Yeah, it's a good idea. Tell you what – let's do something special for midsummer. Like we did last year!'

'Oh. Yeah. Yeah, I heard about that.'

'No, no, it's okay, I won't cry this time. It'll be great – we'll have fireworks, and a barbecue, and... I dunno, loads of stuff. We could have a football match!'

'Yeah, okay.'

'Cullens versus Broughtons!'

'Ah, well, I don't know about that. I've seen you in action against your kids, I wouldn't want to let you loose on mine.'

'Y'know your problem, mate? You worry too much. Now, you've had a great idea, just be pleased with that.'

And I was – very pleased indeed – for at that point I'd not

an inkling (why should I?) that in arranging for all the kids to be brought together, and in appointing Reggie Cullen as master of ceremonies, I was creating the perfect storm.

– Celebrity –

Uncle Flesh works for Bradshaw's, an old family firm in Yorkshire with a small chain of butcher's shops. Their speciality is black pudding. They also have their fingers, metaphorically speaking, in certain other pies – considerably meatier, more lucrative pies. Anybody who threatens the family's livelihood ends up in the black pudding; whether rival gangsters or men from the Ministry, they all become part of the rich, tasty mixture.

That's the basic premise of *Easy Meat*, which finally found its way onto selected cinema screens in the early summer, and in so doing ended my golden age.

Reaction to the film as a whole was tepid, but Reggie caused a sensation with his small but crucial turn as the aforementioned Uncle Flesh, chainsaw-wielding fixer by appointment to the Bradshaw family. The papers showered him with good will. Not only had he done his penance for the planning officer punch-up, but, more importantly, Bar-b-gate could now be regarded as forgiven and all but forgotten. As if to underline his redemption, the *Daily Mail* ran a full centre spread commenting in good humour on the gulf between his real-life criminal past and the wages of his cinematic sin; images of his community service activities were juxtaposed with snaps of his red-carpet appearance at the star-studded premiere in Leicester Square.

I was meant to be at that premiere. Not a month before, Reggie had apologised for neglecting me with his chain-gang chums, and promised to atone by taking me along to the big bash. I wasn't that fussed, in truth, but I appreciated the

185

gesture, or at any rate, I *would've* done, except that in the end there *was* no gesture. He took Shelley instead.

I didn't begrudge her, of course; the way she sweated for Reggie, it was good to see her getting some appreciation. I just resented being lied to, that's all – having Reggie tell me, 'Sorry, mate, I tried to get you an extra ticket', then later hearing the truth from Shelley: sweetly oblivious to the party line, she told me, 'I don't really want to go – all that fuss and noise – but Reggie said he can't take you in case people think you're gay lovers.'

So, to prove he's not gay... to prove – I mean, as if people even *care* these days – he blows me out, and in my place he takes my – my – yeah – she – she – all that, just to prove he's not gay – takes her down to London, twirls her on his arm for the media scrum – all that – all that, just to...

Okay, okay, so I was jealous, I admit, I freely admit it. At any rate, it's no coincidence, I'm sure, that Shelley and I had our first falling-out the night before the premiere.

Summoned by email, I entered her boudoir, and found her there, lying on the bed, reading a book. Curled up like a croissant, she was, her body nestled cosily in folds of blue and white. I'd not seen her in pyjamas before. They were several sizes too big. You could've got two of her in there.

'Hello,' she said.

She closed her book, dropped it over the side of the bed, and opened her arms.

'Nice,' I said.

'Thank you,' she beamed.

'The PJs, I mean.'

'Yes, I know.'

Without further ado, I launched myself into an ostentatious vault for the bed; I was somewhere in mid-air when I heard her say, 'They're Reggie's.'

I crash-landed beside her.

'I'm sorry?'

'They're Reggie's. At least, they *used* to be.'

'Reggie's pyjamas? You're wearing...?'

'No, no, they're *mine*. They *used* to be his, but...'

'He gave them to you?'

'I didn't *steal* them.'

'No, no, course not.'

'He was going to throw them out. It was after Denise... He was having a clear-out. One of those sort-of 'new broom' kind of things.'

'Right.'

'He wanted me to take them to Oxfam, but they'd hardly been worn – I mean, they're really good ones – *Jermyn Street*; it says on the label.'

'Right.'

'If you don't like them, though, you could always, y'know... take them off me.'

'Right. Yes, of course. Yeah, I'll do that.'

'You don't seem very enthusiastic.'

'What? No. I mean, yes, of course – of course I'm...'

I kissed her, and considered reaching for the first button. It didn't happen.

'What's wrong?'

'Sorry,' I said. 'It's just...'

'Just what...?'

'The pyjamas. You're wearing *his* pyjamas.'

187

'No, Alex, they're *my* pyjamas.'

'Yeah, but he... he... Look, I'm not trying to make us out to be more than we are. Y'know, we have fun and that's great, but all the same... I mean, I know they're only pyjamas...'

'Yes, exactly. Pyjamas, that's all they are.'

I bounced up off the bed.

'Look, I'm sorry, I'm gonna go.'

'I'll take them off. It's not a problem.'

'No, that's okay. No. I mean, I'm sorry, I know it's... I'm sorry.'

I *was*, too. If not then, at any rate very shortly afterwards. Before I was halfway back to my room, I was cursing my pettiness and my insecurity, as well as the deeply unattractive harshness of tone they seemed to have unleashed.

Even as my bedroom door closed behind me, I resolved to open it up again, rush back and beg her pardon for my pathetic insecurity.

But no, I thought – I'll send her a text.

A *text?* A snivelling, cowardly text? That, surely, would be even more pathetic than the offence for which I was seeking absolution. I must face her straight-off, and take it from there.

My fist was hovering, poised to knock on her door, when I was stilled to breathless by the sound of a whispering voice; a voice which I took, at the time, to be Shelley's. Now I can't be so sure. All I knew then was this: the voice I took to be Shelley's had come not from Shelley's room, but from *Reggie's*.

The following day was pretty much a write-off. I did my best to work, but I couldn't concentrate.

I sat in a meeting with Reggie, striving to listen to his pronouncements when in fact all I could effectively do was hate him. 'Gay lovers?' I thought. 'You should be so lucky, mate. If I were gay, I wouldn't touch you with yours – and – and – and – and tell you what else; if I were you – if I were a sad, pathetic, sexually insecure macho man like you, I certainly wouldn't be shagging my assistant, who I don't even fancy, just to reassure myself of something I couldn't – I couldn't – I couldn't...'

I couldn't concentrate – just couldn't take in a word. I kept having to ask him to repeat stuff – then, when he repeated it, I'd get just a few words in before I started telling myself, 'Right, make sure you *listen* this time and don't get side-tracked into thinking about the fucker walking down the red carpet with Shelley in pyjamas on his arm while I'm sitting here like Cinderella, waiting for them to...'

It was no better once they'd departed. I tried again to work, mucking around on AutoCad, factoring in whichever of the fucker's comments I'd actually managed to catch. Too often, though, I found myself jumping up off my bed and pacing like a zoo-bound animal, raging out loud at the injustice of it all.

Eventually, I took myself downstairs in search of company, no matter whose.

In the lounge, Festus was stretched out on his sofa, half-consciously flicking from channel to channel. On any normal day his viewing habits would move me to silent rage – the way he'd linger on a programme just long enough to inspire your curiosity, then snatch it away again. This, however, was no normal day. So total was my preoccupation, I barely registered how much the room stank of his sweat and his farts and his feet. I plopped down on the secondary sofa, displacing a couple of dogs but not troubling to discourage them (as I normally would) from jumping back up and sitting with me.

What, I wondered, was my problem? 42 years old and almost crying with rage because a client – not a *friend*, a *client* – had taken someone else to a stupid film premiere.

Yeah, but also – *maybe* – I couldn't be sure – but who else?

189

– who else? – who else could it be? – *she* was in his room last night.

And *so*? So what? Why not? She's his PA. She lives on the premises – up the corridor, no less. He probably wanted to dictate a letter.

At THAT time of night?!

Yeah, *that* time of night.

But she was WHISPERING!

Oh fuck off. Fuck off and grow up.

No sooner had I resolved to do this – yes, okay, I'd grow up, I would – than I was met with the sight of Reggie on the *News at Ten*.

'Eeeey!' said Festus, sitting almost upright. 'Ey, there's our boy!'

There indeed was Reggie, basking in the light of his completed rehabilitation. And this was no 'And finally...'; this was a full-blown news story (at least in the wonky perception of ITN). Footage of our hero in his Premier League prime was juxtaposed with images borrowed from the BBC 'chain-gang' piece, this in turn contrasted with shots taken just a few hours earlier, of Reggie gliding **down** the red carpet, trading quips with reporters and wolfing down autograph books while Shelley stood demurely by.

She didn't *look* all that demure, mind. She was in this metallic green dress – one of those strapless things. Stunning. She looked stunning. No other word. Well, *radiant*, maybe.

Festus was also impressed.

'Someone must've put a couple of turnips down her dress! Look – she's got tits!'

I'd never before heard him string so many words together, nor longed so passionately to crush his disrespecting windpipe.

'Look at her! She's fuckin' gorgeous!'

I drifted downstairs to bother Lilian. She was in her parlour, watching a little black and white TV – the *News at Ten* again, though Reggie was gone now, succeeded by an apparently less important story about sectarian violence in Baghdad.

She wasn't exactly over-friendly, but she wasn't hostile either – she just told me to exclude the mutts that had followed me down to her lair. That done, I was assigned a chair.

Noting the elementary nature of her entertainment system, I pondered if she wouldn't prefer a colour TV?

'No,' she said. 'The licence is cheaper.'

'But, surely, Reggie gets one for the whole house?'

'Maybe. Maybe not – but I ain't going to rely on him. I don't want to get no fine.'

'Fair enough.'

We weren't, I could see, going to have the game-changingly life-affirming conversation I may have been craving when I came down. Still, there were worse things I could do than share the kitchen cosiness; in the fullness of time, she even made us some cocoa. It was a bit watery, but otherwise quite palatable, or at any rate *potable*.

And then she struck. She'd reeled me in with her cocoa, and now, with my defences down, she went for the jugular.

'So, how much longer you staying here?'

'I'm sorry?'

'When you going home to your wife and children?'

'Oh. Er, well, I mean, well, that's – yeah – that's a very good question. Certainly not before I've done the basic design for the stadium.'

191

She laughed. 'I tell you before, you ain't gonna build no stadium.'

I laughed back, with all the good spirit I could fake. 'You may well be right,' I said. 'The history of architecture's littered with grand designs that never came to fruition. Edwin Lutyens, for instance...'

'Why don't you just go home to your family?'

'I wish I could. I really wish it were that simple.'

'It's real simple. You don't make it less simple hanging around here, that's for sure.'

I really was beginning to dislike that old woman – that rude, nosey, self-righteously perceptive old woman who can't even make a cup of cocoa to save her life.

I downed my warm brown water and made my excuses.

The next day, I was working in my room when I heard Reggie's car crunch to a halt outside the house. I rushed out with a view to joining the doggy throng, albeit not to greet but to confront. I'd had a whole night to gnaw at my wounds, and I was ready to tell him I knew bloody well what was going on.

'You could've got any number of tickets for that premiere. I've got you sussed. You're edging me out of your life to make room for a whole new batch of celebrity friends – trendy celebrity coke-head friends!'

Probably just as well I didn't get to Reggie without first meeting Shelley, who'd bounded into the house, raced up the stairs and was now backing me into the discretion of the corridor and kissing me heartily.

'It was wonderful,' she said. 'I had such fun. I just wish you'd been there.'

'Yeah, well...'

'You really *should've* been there.'

'Yeah, well, there... there wasn't a ticket.'

'Oh, come on, don't sulk. Be happy for me.'

'I *am*,' I lied. Then, more sincerely, 'you looked really nice on the TV.'

'Oh, you saw me?'

'Yeah. Stole the show. Lovely dress. Was it one of Reggie's?'

'I'm sorry...? Oh, shut up!'

'No, really, you looked wonderful. Sensational.'

'Oh, well, thank you.'

'So, who'd you meet?'

'*Meet?*'

'Celebs...?'

'Oh, no one. He ignored me most of the evening. It was such fun, though.'

Ignored her?

I flew down the stairs.

Ignored her?

Reggie was beating off the last of the dogs.

'Leave me alone, you fuckers!'

I moved on in, ready to unleash hell.

'Alex, my friend, we are going to Hollywood!'

'*What?*'

'Hollywood! Pack your bags!'

'Hollywood? When?'

'What d'you mean *when*? I don't know. What's it matter? All I know is, we're going, so pack your bags!'

'I will, don't worry; that's just what I'm gonna do. Pack my bags

193

and fuck off home.'

Again, that's what I *should've* said, but in truth I'd already allowed him to steal my thunder (and my lightning too).

'Y'know what, mate? I was fucking magic in that film – everyone said so; said I stole the show. This is it, believe me: we're moving to California. *I* am, leastways and you're coming too.'

'*Really*, Reggie?' Here's my chance. 'Me as well? But, Reggie, what if – *oh, my God, the shame of it!* – what if people think we're *gay?*'

'*What?* Oh, that. Don't worry about that. We're *all* going – *my* family, *your* family, the whole kit and caboodle.'

Kit and caboodle. Ridiculous. Totally unrealistic – for *me* at least. If Reggie wished to plan his entire future on the presumption of offers that might never materialise, so be it. For me, though... well, a new start in a new world had its attractions, for sure, but Mog would never come, nor, in a million years, would she let me take the girls.

'Last night, mate, I tell you, the people I met: Jude Law, Madonna, Stephen Fry, Jonathan Ross – he fucking loved that film – *me* above all. They *all* did; everybody loved Uncle Flesh. Here's the thing, though: get this – I told 'em about our fireworks party, and they're coming, all of 'em!'

'I'm sorry?'

'They're coming up, next weekend. I don't have precise numbers yet, but...'

'Hang on, what *fireworks party?*'

'Y'know, like we talked about...'

'No, what we talked about was having the kids up for midsummer, having a barbecue and a few fireworks – just a *few*. A small display. That's what we talked about – a family affair.'

'Yeah, well, now it's an *extended* family affair.'

'Oh, for fuck's sake!'

'What? What is it with you? You should be pleased. There'll be so many faces here – real thrill for the kids.'

'It's not what we discussed.'

'So? So? It's my house, mate.'

'Right, and you can do what you like with it – only don't expect me to bring my kids here to hang out with a bunch of coke-heads.'

'*What*? Is that what's bothering you? I tell you, mate, you want to get a fucking life. Listen to Radio 5. *Charlie*? Never mind the Charlie. Your kids, believe me, every day at school they're doing spicier stuff than that.'

Stuff.

'Stuff,' he says.

What kind of *stuff* – I wondered – what 'stuff' are you on right now, Reggie Cullen?

But the answer, I feared, would be: *nothing*. Nothing chemical. Just a little bit of praise... mainlining praise, that's all – and he was eight miles high on it.

– Opposing Forces –

1:38pm

Friends.

The Friends.

Friends of the Terriss Memorial Theatre.

FRITS.

That's what they called themselves. Better than
FOTWTMT, they said – it should, strictly speaking, be
FOTWTMT – Friends of the William Terriss Memorial
Theatre – but this was more streamlined: first three letters of
'FRIends' appended to the T of 'Terriss', with an added S for
plurality.

So where, says I, is the M for Memorial? Mind your own
business, they said, though it seemed to me it *was* my business,
as it was in opposition to *my* project that the whole thing was
formed. Okay, so strictly speaking that's a lie. FRITS was
actually founded, a good two decades back, in response to the
Council's first disclosure of the Civic Centre idea. When
things went quiet on that for a while, the organisation adapted
to encompass a range of worthy activities – awkward first
night events, for instance, with cheese and wine and small talk
for weary actors. In the end, though, with the revival and full-
on prosecution of the Civic Centre plan, FRITS came more
than anything to be an anti-Alex campaign group.

For Christ's sake, they met at *our house* – within my very
own castle keep, they were invited to plot my downfall.

I don't recall the precise chronology of things. Was it pre- or post- my winning of the competition that they asked Mog to be their leader? Pre-, probably. Yes, of course, it was *years* before, back then, when she was first starting to emerge as a young citizen of prominence. In *her* view, therefore, the provocation was all mine – a great big two-fingered salute to her, and all because I was no longer getting sex on tap. Bullshit, of course, but... but...

I mean, what am I meant to do? It's *my* town too. She's not the family's only citizen of prominence; I'm a major player in Godham's foremost architectural practice. The local authority announces a project – a huge and hugely significant project destined to change the face of the town centre; potentially the project of a lifetime – and I should *abstain*?

Apparently, yes.

Anyway, they met at our house. Frequently. More and more frequently as things went on. At any time I could come home, weary at the day's end, and find them draped around the sitting-room, none of them remotely concerned – because *Mog* was so clearly unconcerned – that I might overhear their schemings.

So there was...

Who was...?

Well, Mog, obviously: Mog Whose Husband Is The Devil.

There was Harry. Yeah, Harry Who Used To Be A Dresser At Chichester.

Carole. Poor old Carole. Carole Whose Husband Left Her. She always used to smile at me when I came in; I don't think she can help being civil to people. She'd smile, and then of course she'd look away, embarrassed to be giving succour to the enemy. Oh, Carole. She could get another one, I'm sure – another husband. She thinks it's a weight thing. I'm fairly sure it's a won't-stop-talking-about-her-ex thing.

So, there was Mog, there was Harry, there was Carole – oh, and Leslie, don't forget Leslie. Leslie Who Got A Knighthood For Being In The Civil Service. Doesn't use the title, of course – oh, apart from when he's telling people he doesn't use the title.

He it was – Leslie – who insisted on the name: FRITS. 'Does what it says on the box,' he argued.

– A Midsummer Triptych –

For all my protestations, it might've been good after all to have a few celebs in attendance at the midsummer do. Who knows, Reggie might just have behaved a little better. No one could make it, though; not one of his new showbiz mates was able to attend. In fact, when Shelley made some follow-up phone calls, most of them didn't even remember having been asked.

Notwithstanding, the master threw himself valiantly into preparations for 'a weekend them kids'll never forget'.

If only he could've applied the same intensive energy to the stadium as he did to planning the firework display. Having splashed out two hundred quid on rockets (we'd 'settle up later', I was told), we spent the best part of a day arranging them in the walled kitchen garden, spaced sufficiently to allow us to run around and set them off safely without bumping into each other or scorching out our eyes. Each piece of ordnance was assigned its own jam jar or beer bottle, and finished off with a taped-over bin-liner to guard against rain in the interim.

The full itinerary was to comprise a Kung Fu class on the Saturday morning, a film that afternoon, a barbecue in the evening followed by fireworks once the sun was fully down, then finally a football match on the Sunday before our guests headed south once again.

Reggie went down on the Friday to fetch the kids. As soon as he returned – as soon as the Range Rover disgorged its load – I knew this was going to be a long, long weekend. Reggie, his kids and mine, after two hours in a metal box, bouncing like molecules off each other's excitement; it was hard to say which was the rowdiest child – but the one in the driver's seat was a contender, no question.

Friday night was disarmingly mellow. My two went for a sunset clop on Jasper and Dobbin, while the others played in the car museum. Then, after a banquet of chicken nuggets (singed but eatable), everyone slobbed out in front of the TV – or to one side of it, at least, Festus naturally making no concession to circumstance.

It was on the Saturday morning that things started heating up. Since his last Kung Fu session with Captain Walcott, Reggie had become a major movie star (or so he perceived), and this, together with his compulsion to show off in front of the kids, made him even more reluctant than usual to subdue the 'I'.

We were faced up already with the Captain – Shelley, me and the five kids, going through some gentle stretches – when Reggie jogged into the ballroom, tipped me a chummy wink, fell in behind Shelley and set about copying what the rest of us were doing.

'Hang on,' said the Captain. 'Reggie, if you're late, you don't just form up, you know that. You come up beside me here...'

'Yeah, sorry, mate, I've just been...'

'*Why* you were late doesn't matter. You asked me to take a class at twelve. We started at twelve and you came after. If you're late, you come up the front, bow to the teacher, then bow to...'

'Alright, alright.'

He strode across the room, positioned himself in the corner, tossed a bow to the Captain, another to us, then fell in again behind me; as he did so, he muttered, 'Bollocks', just loud enough to win a titter from the kids.

The warm-up continued, but it wasn't long before Reggie found another cause for mutiny. The Captain had adjusted the intensity of the warm-up (his youngest student was five, after all), but for Reggie the adjustment was insufficient.

We'd been running round the room, dropping down and doing squat-jumps to order; now, after maybe four or five circuits, Reggie came to a halt.

'Okay, mate, that's fine.'

'What's that, Reggie?'

'No more... no more warming up. The kids – they've had enough.'

The Captain laughed. '*They've* had enough or *you've* had enough?'

There ensued an ominous Reggie Cullen pause, in tandem with a fuming Reggie Cullen smile.

'Look, mate, we're warm enough, okay?'

'No, Reggie, not okay. If you want me to teach you martial arts, you'll learn *my* way.'

'I already know *My Way*. I done it on *Parky*!' Another cackle from some of the kids. 'No, seriously, that's what I *want* to do. I *want* to learn your way – *I* wanna know what *you* know. I wanna be able to kick arse like you do – pardon my French, kids!'

'Reggie, it's not about *kicking*... It's not about that.'

'No, no, of course, I know you've got to *say* that, but...'

'Let me tell you something – and it's important the young people should hear this. I've been practising Nam Pai Chuan for 26 years, I've been a black belt for 22 of those years, and I've never been in a proper fight.'

'What – *never?* What about the Gulf?'

'Oh, well, yes, of course...'

'So you've shot people and that?'

The Captain smiled bashfully. 'In the context of my job,' he sighed, 'I did what I needed to do. In a civil context, however – which is what we're talking about here...'

'What – you've never...?'

'Never.'

'*Never?*'

'Never. Now, shall we get on?'

And so we went back to the warm-up – though, perhaps by way of compromise, the Captain moved on swiftly to doing some actual moves. There were front kicks, there were turning kicks, there were back kicks – but none of it was good enough for Reggie, who, every time we spent more than a few minutes on any particular move, would make it clear he was getting bored. Finally he felt compelled to explain to our instructor that he was pretty soon going to be asked to appear in some Hollywood action movies, and that he'd need more than just these disjointed actions; he wanted to work on some proper routines.

A less saintly man might at this moment have used his special powers to snap his tormentor's neck. The Captain, however, simply paused to gather his thoughts, then announced that, okay, we would spend the rest of the session working on a takedown.

'At last,' said Reggie, facing up to help him demonstrate. 'Now then, give me something real – something I can use in my next movie.' Seconds later he was on the mat, the bony point of the Captain's elbow hovering barely an inch from his nose.

'Great!' said Reggie, jumping to his feet.

His enthusiasm was soon to fade.

So fast had it unfolded, this last move, that it was

impossible to say on one viewing what we'd actually seen. No problem, said the Captain, proceeding then to fell his partner once again, this time in slow motion. The routine involved his grabbing hold of Reggie's arm, gently twisting it in such a way that it felt liable to snap at any moment, then sweeping the great man's feet from under him before concluding with that elbow to the face.

The Captain, I came to realise, was more greatly irked than he cared to admit by Reggie's attitude problem; it must have been so, for he proceeded to demonstrate that take-down over and over again, never once asking Shelley or me or any of the kids to substitute as guinea-pig. Reggie could hardly complain – we were now being taught to kick arse, just as he'd requested; sadly, *his* was the arse being kicked, or at any rate brought into repeated contact with the mat. I could see that however much he tried to keep smiling, he was *not* having a good time.

Reggie's simmering anger was compounded when, at the end of the class, we were invited to assume the lotus position and close our eyes.

'We'll underline our studies,' said the Captain, 'with a statement of the principles of Nam Pai Chuan Shaolin Kung Fu.'

Ignoring the deep sigh that emanated from Reggie's part of the darkness, the Captain launched into the routine.

'Revere your ancestor.'

'Revere your ancestor.'

'Respect your guide.'

'Respect your guide.'

'Train with your mind.'

'Train with your mind.'

And so on, through all the tenets.

'Act with earnestness.'

'Act with earnestness.'

'Covet nothing.'

'Covet nothing.'

'Subdue the I.'

'Subdue the I.'

With each repetition I became more aware of the sighing, sarcastic tone with which Reggie, just behind me, was obliging our teacher.

'Life is death.'

'Life is DEATH!'

'Death is life.'

'Death IS Life!'

By the time we got to the climax, Reggie's was the loudest, most belligerently zenless voice in the room.

'Learn always.'

'LEARN ALWAYS!'

'Assume nothing.'

'ASSUME FUCK ALL!'

'Sorry, Reggie?'

'No, nothing, mate. Thanks a lot. Great class.'

He saw the Captain to the door, just so as to have the satisfaction of shaking his hand, patting him on the back, then saying 'Fucking wanker' as the door slammed shut.

'Christ, d'you hear him? Never been in a fight!'

'He didn't actually *say* that.'

'He *did*. He said he's never been in a fight.'

'A *proper* fight.'

'What's that mean – a *proper* fight?'

'Probably that, on the rare occasions he's had to use his skills, he's had the guy down and out on the floor before it even *becomes* a fight.'

'Bollocks. Big ponce.'

'I'd like to see you call him that to his face.'

'I *would* – I *would*, mate – only he'd come over all Jesus and tell me I've a perfect right to my opinion. I mean, clearly, that's how he works: try and stay out of trouble at all costs.'

'And that's a bad idea, is it?'

'Sometimes, mate, as Kenny Rogers so aptly put it, sometimes you've got to fight to prove you're a man.'

'Oh, right, right. Prove you're a man; valiant struggles with planning officers, that kind of thing?'

***

2:07pm

The North Wind is on his bike.

Did I imagine that?

No.

No.

I mean *yes*. Yes, you did.

Stay with me, Alex.

Bite yourself.

Harder.

Harder.

Ow!

Good.

***

Luton. That was next. The next – the next part of the... the...
Luton, yeah. We went into Luton. Lunch at... at... at Nando's
– Nando's, yeah, that was it. Reggie and Conrad – how could
I forget? Father and son, vying to see who could talk the most
bollocks the loudest.

While Papa Reggie held forth in turn about over-zealous
bureaucrats, peacenik army officers and spineless football
managers, his eldest and brightest invariably offered solutions
involving thermo-nuclear weaponry. Their loud macho
posturing, while causing my girls initially to retreat into their
shells, had the opposite effect with Daisy and Chico, who
shrieked to be heard, and, when failing in this, took to chasing
each other round the restaurant. Reggie made no attempt to
control them, nor did he offer support to Shelley when she
had a go. If this had the knock-on effect of bringing my two
out of their shells, it was only a good thing till gentle
exuberance grew into squealing boisterousness.

In truth, few covered themselves in glory that afternoon,
but the later shames at the cinema were, without question,
entirely down to Reggie.

He'd been in a mood ever since Kung Fu; I suppose I
made it worse by insisting that we *weren't* going to see *Easy
Meat*. It was never a serious option, though; the film was an
'18'. Nevertheless, once at the cinema, the self-appointed 'star'
of the film started lobbying for his kids 'to be able to watch
their old man on the big screen'.

'Do what you like,' I said. 'Mine aren't seeing it.'

A swift and whiny protest came forth from Rachel and
Lulu; Reggie's kids were seeing it, why couldn't *they*?

'Because,' I said, 'it's incredibly violent – and you get quite
enough of that kind of thing at home. *Joke! Joke! Joke!* Don't
tell your mother I said that. Look at you; you're storing it all

up.'

'We won't tell her,' said Rachel. '*If* you let us see the film.'

'Forget it, okay? Choose something else. What about *Shrek 3*?'

'It's called *Shrek the Third.*'

'Alright, then, how about *Shrek the Third*?'

'No, it's rubbish.'

'Oh, you've seen it?'

'No, I just know it's rubbish.'

Shelley intervened. Having already seen *Easy Meat*, she'd be glad to come with us to something else – *if* they wanted. That shut them up as if by magic: the girls seemed to think Shelley the best thing since camera phones.

So, that was all sorted, at least till Reggie stepped up to the booth and demanded 'One adult and three kids' for *Easy Meat*.

'It's an *18*,' said the weary-voiced woman behind the glass.

'Alright, then – four *adults*, if you like.'

The ticket lady looked at Chico – or, rather, at what little showed of him above the counter. 'Is *that* one of the adults?' she witheringly enquired.

'Oh, lighten up, for Christ's sake. I'm *in the film*. I'm *Reggie Cullen!!!*'

'I'm sorry, they're too young.'

Reggie heaved a sigh and appealed to Chico and Daisy. 'Listen,' he said, 'you two go with Uncle Alex, okay?' He turned back to the counter. 'Right, then, let's make it *two* for *Easy Meat*.'

Ticket lady cocked an eye at Conrad. 'And how old's *he*?'

The boy had the presence of mind to lie, if not the brainpower.

'Sixteen,' he said.

'*Stupid*!' hissed Reggie.

'I'm sorry, you have to be 18 to...'

'Alright, just give us a load of tickets for... I dunno, whatever fucking crap *they're* seeing.'

'*Shrek The Third,*' I said, sweating forward to take control.

By the time I had the tickets, he'd moved on, and was busy raging at some luckless teen about the price of the Pick and Mix.

'If you wanna mug people, mate, you should go out and do it in the street. You won't have the overheads there.'

I pulled him aside.

'Look,' I said, 'I know you're annoyed about the film...'

'Fucking jobsworths.'

'What's the problem? You can get a DVD from the producers.'

'I've *got* one. It's not the same, and you know it.'

'Alright then,' I said. 'We'll build you a cinema of your own. How's that?'

Reggie smiled.

'Crafty sod. I know what you're up to.'

'I'm sorry?'

'Don't worry, I'll be good. Come on, kids, let's be 'avin' yah!'

He *wasn't* good, of course – and I don't even know where he got the popcorn from. *I* didn't pay for it, I know that much.

He started out just throwing it at Conrad, but inevitably, once the boy began returning fire, other patrons became involved. Result? A group eviction, the innocent along with the guilty.

Artistically speaking, it was actually no bad thing. *Shrek the Third? Shrek the TURD.* Annoying, though, to have forked out all that money, especially as Reggie, true to form, made no attempt to settle up for his share; too focused, I suppose, on improving his popcorn marksmanship. Cos, yeah, that's right, they carried on, all the way across the foyer and into the car park.

As I opened up the car for Shelley and the girls, I watched the others head off in the Range Rover: Conrad, I could see, was still coming on with the Sweet 'n' Salty, joyously pelting his old man from the close range of the front passenger seat. Reggie, as far as I could tell at that point, was taking it still in good heart.

Surprising, then, to arrive back at Cullen Place, just a few minutes later, and see Conrad stumble down from the Reggiemobile with a face smeared in blood.

'Have you got a hanky?' said Reggie, getting out the other side. So matter-of-fact was the question, I assumed the boy had suffered a nose-bleed. 'You should always have two hankies with you, that's what they used to tell us in Cubs – in't that right, Al? – one for your schnozzer; one for an emergency like this. Let's see...' He rummaged in his pocket. 'Here we are. See – *Be prepared!*'

He clasped a grubby-looking tissue over the boy's face and directed him toward the house.

'Go on, go wash yourself. You'll be alright.'

It was only now that Reggie released the small ones from the back of the Range Rover. Chico climbed down and bounded up to me.

'Daddy hit Conrad!' he chuckled.

'What? Why?'

Reggie laughed. 'Little fucker was throwing popcorn.'

'*Everyone* was throwing popcorn!'

'Not in the car. I'm not having it in the car. Anyway, it was only a little slap with the back of me hand.'

'He's got blood all over his face!'

'Don't worry, it was just my wedding ring – forgot I had it on. C'mon, let's get some tea and crumpets.'

However Reggie might affect to laugh off the incident, I think it freaked him more than a little. Might well explain his readiness to pander to the whims of the children later that evening.

We'd everything carefully planned: there'd be a barbecue on the patio, then when it got dark, Reggie and I would slip off to the kitchen garden and unleash two hundred quid's worth of hell. That, indeed, remained the plan, right up until the moment we set off from the patio with our torches – at which point, Conrad said he wanted to help.

'No, that's okay,' I said, 'me and your dad have it all figured out.'

'Well,' said Reggie, 'I suppose he can let off a *few*.'

'*What?*'

'It won't do any harm. He's a big lad.'

'No he's not – not legally.'

'Ah, come on, don't be such an old woman.'

Cue gigglings from the patio.

'Fine,' I hissed. 'Let him blind himself.'

I was just preparing to huff off down the garden when Rachel said, 'Dad, *I* want to let off some fireworks.'

'So do I,' said Lulu.

'Uh-uh. Absolutely not.'

'Why?' said Rachel. '*He*'s allowed to.'

'Yeah, cos his dad's even more stupid than he is.'

'Just cos we're *girls*...'

'No, not cos you're girls; cos I want to keep you *alive* and in one piece.'

'Oh, pleeeeeeease. We'll be really careful.'

Now the little ones joined in.

'*I* want to let off a firework,' said Chico.

'So do I,' said Daisy.

'Listen to me, people. No one is letting off fireworks. No one except for us three.'

'All the *men*,' muttered Rachel.

'That's right, all the men.'

To my surprise, there was no comeback, only silence. Then, just as I seemed to have quelled the mutiny, leading feminist Reggie Cullen put in his two penn'orth.

'I don't see why Rachel shouldn't do a couple. What d'you say, Al?'

I heaved a weary sigh, intended as a prelude to telling Reggie, in the gentlest, most child-friendly way, to fuck right off. Lulu, however, must have read it as a sigh of resignation, for before I could say a word, she was away and into the house, snarling, 'That's not fair'.

I turned to Reggie.

'Listen,' I said, 'neither of them are doing it. So, if we can just *please –*'

More welly now scraping on flagstone, as Rachel follows her sister indoors.

'Chrissake,' said Reggie, 'let's just go back to plan A – you and me alone.'

'What?' said Conrad. 'Just you two? So *I* don't get to do it?'

'No, son. Sorry. Just watch, Okay?'

'*Watch*? Why? Why? Just cos of those little cunts?'

Reggie reacted with frightening speed. Before the offending word was fully out of the boy's mouth, his father had him round the neck and was doing that thing – that thing his yobby friend did to me that time, with the 'affectionate' ruffling of the hair.

'Listen,' he said, 'those ain't no *cunts*, alright? They're young ladies – *young ladies* – and they're entitled to respect. Alright? Respect! What'd I say?'

'Wrspct.'

'That's right. Now you say sorry to Uncle Alex.'

'Fsurry.'

'That's better.'

Reggie cut the boy loose, only to see him retreat immediately into the house.

Daisy started crying – 'We're not going to see the fireworks!' – and was soon enough joined in the sobfest by Chico.

'Oh, fuck,' said the Master of the Revels.

The ensuing peace offensive was of a complexity and fragility not seen since the negotiations for the Good Friday Agreement. Shelley, Reggie and I undertook a series of proximity talks which eventually bore fruit with the household re-assembled on the patio – the *entire* household, in fact, now with Festus and Lilian as part of the line-up.

Reggie and I were firmly in control this time – no help from the minors – and, though you don't get that much for two hundred quid you'll never see again, we gave them a night I'll remember till the now fast-approaching end of my days.

If only we'd packed everyone off home immediately afterwards.

***

'Don't be such an old woman!'

'I am *not* being an old woman – and will you *please* stop calling me that, especially in front of the kids.'

'There aren't any kids around.'

'Even so...'

'What's wrong with old women, anyway? Your mum's an old woman. Come on, help me with these goalposts.'

'No, not till you help me check for dogshit.'

'I'm telling you, a bit of dogshit never did anyone any harm.'

'Yes, actually, it *did*. It can make you go blind.'

'Never! Blind? You're kidding?' He riffed extensively on the matter as we scoured the park for doggage. 'D'you think that's why they see in black and white? Cos I heard they see in black and white...'

'Yeah, that's true.'

'... and, now you come to say that about the shit, it kinda makes sense. So, d'you think their eyesight's affected by their shit?'

I'd created a monster.

After a Sunday roast from Iceland, the household was assembled on the field. Only Lilian refused to take part, though she *did* set up a refreshment table with tea and squash and traditional half-time oranges. Ah, had we only *reached* half-time...

Reggie proudly issued us with team shirts – he'd had them specially made for the occasion: red ones for the Cullen team

213

(or Cullen's Kings, as the print on the front would have it), and green for the Broughton team (Broughton's Budgies, for Chrissake!). Reggie's squad consisted of himself and his three kids, plus Shelley. I, having proved less fecund than my opponent, had only two family team members, with the thankless addition of Festus. This left us one down on the opposition.

'It's not *unfair*,' insisted Reggie. 'It's your clan versus my clan, with one each extra from the household.'

'But you've got *more* than us – including an England international.'

'*Ex*-international – and don't forget, Festus played for Spurs.'

'In what capacity?'

'He was an apprentice, like me. Anyway, think yourself lucky. *We've* got Shelley.'

'Don't give me that. She knows more about football than you do.'

'Yes,' said Shelley, 'but I can't really *play* it, not very well. I just know how to talk about it!'

'Sorry,' I said, 'I hate to be an 'old woman', but we're not doing this till you balance things up.'

So he gave us Conrad – much as I'd hoped he would, if only because I thought it'd reduce the potential for trouble. I'd been aware all morning of an acrid vibe between Reggie's eldest and my own. Clearly, he blamed Rachel for coming between him and the fireworks. I reasoned, however, that if they were playing on the same side, they'd surely have to shelve their differences and work together. *Surely,* they would.

The fact that Reggie was a world-class player among infants, girls and no-hopers drew not the slightest concession from the man: he put ball after ball after ball into our goal, so that it quickly became very, very boring. For Conrad it must've been particularly frustrating – not just to see how good his father remained, even after years in retirement, but also to know that, at 15, he had nothing like the talent his dad had enjoyed at a similar age. It made him ever more ill-disposed to tolerate the incompetence of what he quickly came to regard as *his* team. He seemed unable to appreciate that we were *trying* – yes, even poor wheezing Festus – but that it was hard to put up any kind of meaningful show against Reggie.

Finally I took the opposing captain to one side. Could he not just go a little bit easier? No way could we beat him now – Cullen's Kings were heading into the mid-teens; surely he could lighten up just a teeny-tiny bit?

'Take a dive? Fuck off.'

'No, not a *dive*. Just let the rest of us have a chance.'

His hard-won agreement was to prove counter-productive. Yes, he held back a bit, but he continued to ensure that no more than a few balls actually made it through the Cullen goal-mouth; thus Conrad, enjoying more possession but still being thwarted, could only grow yet more hot-headed. Every time another of our team got the ball, he would demand they pass it on to him. Personally I couldn't care enough to resist, but his relentless barkings incensed Rachel, and with ever greater determination she defied his claims for sole possession. Whenever she got a chance, she would go all the way, dodging round Chico and Shelley then punting the ball toward goalkeeper Daisy, only to have Reggie streak in at the last moment and head it off.

'Why don't you fucking pass?'

'Cos I don't *fucking* want to.'

'Hey, hey,' says Reggie, 'come on, now, break it up.'

'She won't pass. She keeps going it alone.'

'So do *you*,' said Rachel.

'Yeah, but *I* can play.'

'So can *I.*'

'No you can't. You're crap.'

Just a couple of minutes before the scheduled end of the first half, I somehow inherited the ball – and, along therewith, the obligatory tirade from Conrad.

'*Pass*! Pass, will you!'

Conscious that his father was bearing down on me, I was only too eager to oblige; in my panic, however, I misdirected the ball, passing it not to Conrad but to Rachel. No sooner had she started toward the enemy goal than she was subjected to the most brutal scything tackle – not from Reggie but from her own team-mate, Conrad. She hit the ground wrist-first.

While Conrad hovered around, seeking desperately to apologise, I cradled his victim in my arms, waiting in ear-bleeding hope for her piercing screeches to abate just a little. It was a forlorn hope, given the unmistakable snapping noise that had echoed so vividly about the park a few seconds before.

Still, at least I was taking the situation a bit more seriously than Reggie.

'Come on! Come on – she's time-wasting! Yellow card!'

Naturally inviting him to fuck off, I was, equally naturally, exhorted in return not to be *an old woman*. 'Fuck's sake,' he said, 'it's a contact sport!'

Though I persisted in telling him to go away, it *did* seem like a good idea to at least get Rachel up off the soggy ground. In so doing – gently taking hold of the afflicted hand – I induced a new and newly piercing tower of screams.

Reggie, suddenly relieved of any lingering doubts, lashed out at Conrad, shoving him with both hands.

'What you done, you stupid little sod? Eh? Eh? What's

wrong with you?'

A vision now came before my eyes: it was of a long white convoy of ambulances, snaking down the drive to convey our children to hospital one by one. Or *was* it? *Was* that the vision? In truth, I don't know what I saw or thought or felt in that moment; I only know that, having seen Reggie administer a second violent shove to his son, I found myself deserting Rachel, walking toward the new centre of conflict, and, without any planning aforethought, launching myself into the air. Such a move – a jumping kick to the back – would've seen me disqualified from any sparring match, but, here in the (comparatively) real world, it did the trick. Reggie wound up face down in the mud.

By the time he'd unstuck himself, I was standing over him, feeling the raw red rage in my face as I yelled: 'Don't pick on him! *He*'s not the problem; *you* are. Now stop wasting time. Go in the house, get your keys, drive us to A&E.'

I suppose he was too shocked to do other than as told. I was pretty shocked myself. *Everybody* was – even Rachel, whose screaming seemed to have been shocked down to a level of hyper-ventilational sobs.

At the hospital, Reggie attempted to throw his weight around: where were people on *BUPA* meant to go? He was amazed to learn he couldn't jump the queue.

'Blimey,' he said, slumping down beside me, 'what's this country coming to?'

As it turned out, the doctor who set Rachel's arm was an old friend. At least, that's the way Reggie told it. I got the impression it was more of a nodding acquaintance; still, it *did* seem to help a bit when Reggie got to lying about the cause of the accident.

'What happened to *you*, then, young lady?'

'She fell off one of my horses.'

Another medic – one perhaps less blinded than he by celebrity – might have invited Rachel to answer for herself. This one, though, accepted what he was told, and as I didn't immediately break ranks to set the record straight, the patient took up the lie and ran with it.

'It was Dobbin,' she said. 'I was riding him and he – he sort of stumbled, and I fell off. I think he was frightened by a bird!'

'Yeah,' said Reggie, 'that's right. He's always been easily spooked. I told you, didn't I? I said you should take Jasper.'

'No, but *Lulu* was on Jasper.'

'Oh. Oh, yeah, that's right.'

Citing the need for coffee, I dragged Reggie out into the corridor.

'What is this?'

'What d'you mean?'

'What do I *mean*? Getting my daughter to lie – *that*'s what I mean.'

'She seems pretty cool about it.'

'Yeah, well *I'm* not. Give me one reason why I shouldn't go back in and tell them what really happened.'

'I'll give you more than that. For one thing, you've already gone along with it this far; you'll look pretty bad if you tell the truth now.'

'But what's the big deal? It was an accident – pretty much – and it's not as if *you* did it to her.'

'Exactly. I'm protecting my son.'

'*Protecting*? That's a good one.'

'What d'you mean?'

'He can do without *your* kind of protection. Twice in as

218

many days I've seen you hit that kid.'

'Oh yeah? How's that when you wasn't even in the same car as us?'

'Alright, it's circumstantial, but...'

'What d'you care about him, anyway? You should be kicking his teeth in after what he done to your little girl.'

'Right, I'm going back in.'

He zipped round in front of me.

'Look,' he said, 'I know I've got a bit of a temper problem, but –'

'A *bit?*'

'But – but – no, listen – look, I've got a lot to deal with at the moment; you know how much I've got to deal with, I'm very highly stressed. But I promise you – and he'll bear me out on this – I never hit that kid before yesterday. Never did, and never will again. Okay? Look, things're happening for me. *Hollywood,* yeah? It's gonna happen, mate – for *all* of us. But listen, if this shit gets in the press...'

Even as I stood there in neutral, struggling to filter this emotionally charged hogwash and formulate some kind of response, Reggie was busy shifting the nature of the debate. Given how stupid he sounds so much of the time, it never fails to amaze me when he occasionally comes up with something completely irrefutable.

'Look,' he said, placing a gentle hand upon my shoulder, 'what's done is done. Them lot in there seem happy enough, and I know what I'm telling the grandparents. The kids'll back me up – just like your Rachel. Question is, what do we tell your old lady? Eh? Seems to me, y'see, that your *Mog,* she approves of riding – am I right? Leastways, she don't *dis*approve. So tell me, what goes best with the wife – what's gonna cause the least grief for you? Rachel falling off a horse? Or Rachel breaking her arm playing football with an oiky ex-pro and his moronic son – in a game where her loving father could've stopped things at any time, as soon as it started getting nasty... Only, he *didn't?'*

– A New World –

I don't know how I ever imagined the horse-fall story was
going to stick. It wasn't only *my* kids who had to hold the line;
Reggie's too would be flapping their mouths all over Godham.
If, in the short term, Mog did *seem* to buy the story being sold,
it was probably because she was a more than willing
consumer: she'd expected something to go wrong, and when
it did, it confirmed everything she wanted about me and the
company I was keeping. She wasn't bothered with the details
of my incompetence, nor would it have lowered me further in
her estimation to have known of the intensive story-
straightening that took place in the car on the journey home.

All, then, was well, in a sort of way. I dropped off the girls,
delivered Reggie's lot to his in-laws, stayed a night at Mum
and Dad's, then headed off back to Bedfordshire.

And there, at Cullen Place on that cloudy midsummer
morning, I was greeted by Reggie with the news that the
stadium project was off (again).

'Sorry, mate – I really *am* – but I did a lot of thinking last
night. I hardly slept at all. I feel very, very bad about yesterday.
Now, I'm not saying football's a violent sport – you only have
to look at the Brazilians to see how graceful it can be – but it's
a sport that attracts a lot of violent people. People like *me*, let's
face it – and *this*, mate, is where it stops. There's no shortage
in this world of monuments to violence, and far as I'm
concerned, this football stadium's just one more.'

'Oh, look...'

'No, listen, I've thought it all out. Now, there ain't no

shortage of monuments to violence...'

'As you said.'

'Right, then, so shut up a minute. Now, there's plenty of monuments to violence, right...?'

'*Right...*'

'...but, the way I see it, there's precious few monuments to *peace*. That's why we're gonna build one – you and me. Only, not just a monument: a living, breathing peace factory.'

'*Peace factory?*'

'The Denise Cullen Centre for Peace Studies.'

'Oh, fucking hell!'

'Yeah, I think she'd approve: a place, made in her name, where people can come, from all over the world and just, y'know... *talk*. Settle their problems in a peaceful way.'

'Right. So... no more UN?'

'Oh, there'll always be a place for the UN. No question. But, y'know, why go to New York when we've got an airport on our doorstep – when delegates can fly straight into Luton? Eh? Job done!'

I was caught about equally between my dual desires to laugh and to punch his peace centre down his throat. Knowing, however, of his capacity for discarding his fads as quickly as they're conceived, I simply heaved a theatrical sigh of resignation and offered to schedule a meeting.

'*Meeting?* Schedule a meeting? Next you'll be getting 'your people' to talk to 'my people'. Come on, we're here now. Let's talk.'

And we did, for several hours. He gave me, as demanded, his full and exclusive attention, and I made full and exclusive use of it. I was determined, given the severity of the policy swerve, to cover every angle of the new project before committing myself. How, for instance, was the centre to be staffed?'

'Easy. Put Shelley in charge – to start with, at least.'

'Have you discussed it with her?'

'Not yet.'

'Don't you think you should? Bit more of an add-on than mucking out the horses.'

Shelley, of course, was immensely flattered. If also perturbed by the extra potential workload, she kept it well hidden from Reggie. In any case, she came up with some good ideas, suggesting, for instance, that he link the centre to Bedfordshire University, endow a chair in peace studies. Such was her zeal, she well-nigh succeeded in convincing me it wouldn't be a total waste of time and resources. Not, of course, that it should matter to me; what was I, after all, but a hired hand? As a wise man once told me – Geoffrey Bede, in fact, father to The Velvet Fist – if you're worried how your client spends his money, you're getting too close.

By the end of the afternoon I'd a brief to design a three-storey mixed-use building comprising office space, accommodation, catering facilities, meeting rooms, and, of course, a conference hall. It would occupy a clearing in the wooded area to the north of the kitchen garden, accessed via a road which would extend round from the driveway, circumventing the main house and skirting the western edge of the estate.

Over the ensuing days there were regular progress meetings. Reggie was as focused as ever I've seen him. Deadly serious. The third day came, and then the fourth and the fifth, without him changing his mind and demanding another stadium – or, indeed, a theatre or a cinema or a hospice for puppies with cancer.

Even when he got the call from his agent, he didn't just drop everything.

'I don't want any slouching while I'm away,' he said. 'When I come back, I want to see real progress, yeah? Cos I'm coming back a movie star – a rich, fuck-off loaded movie star!'

The reason for this surge of confidence? *Easy Meat* had come to the attention of no less a personage than Jerry Bruckheimer. He'd seen it and he'd hated it. Tediously predictable, he said; embarrassingly provincial, and desperate in its sensationalism. Or was that *me*? No, I'd not yet seen it at that point. Anyway, Bruckheimer: hated the film, liked Reggie – *loved* him, in fact, or so it was said – and thus our man was whisked off to LA for an audition.

It was really starting to happen, just like he'd said it would.

***

Surprised he didn't take Shelley. Glad, but surprised. Confused, really. Well, *intrigued*. Frustrated. I wanted to know what was going on. *Was* there something going on? Had I even the right to ask? No, and nor would I, as long as Reggie was out of the picture and the house was ours in which to frolic.

Frolic.

Frolic.

Frolic and fun.

Same thing?

All over the place...

1. Down by the lake. Idyllic.

2. The spa. That was good, as well. Bit of a faff, though: before doing anything, we had to take the cover off the pool. Curtis – eager young Curtis – he'd stopped coming a few weeks prior, and the pool was in mothballs.

So, yeah... fun, that, albeit a bit of a palaver.

3. The stable. Oh yes, the stable. Not a success. We

thought we'd be emulating a certain scene from *Goldfinger*, but reality proved damper and whiffier than expected.

Better offer. *Curtis*. He'd had a better offer, or so I was told. *Very* much better: he'd gone to work for the Beckhams, said Reggie. They could offer him a full-time residential position at 'Beckingham Palace'.

But sex, yeah, sex. Where else...?

Well, let's see, there was:

1. By the lake.

2. The spa.

3. The stable.

4. Yes, of course, I remember – the *attic*. Warm, dry, a bit of dusty sunlight from a convenient dormer window, and best of all, there was plenty in the way of post-coital entertainments.

All kinds of stuff you get when you're famous. I remember Reggie telling me *people just give you stuff*. And what a collection he'd amassed: phones and razors, family duvet sets – it was like *The Generation Game*, and so much of it still boxed up as new.

'You could make a fortune on eBay,' I said.

'We may yet have to.'

'Is that how he's going to finance the peace centre?'

'Oh. No, no, I'm only joking.'

The biggest and least shiftable commodity was the consignment of books – boxes and boxes – all of the one title: *Pitch Black*, the alleged autobiography of Reggie Cullen.

'Oh yes, he *did* write it himself,' said Shelley. 'With a bit of help.'

'From you?'

'Mostly from Denise. She read through, told him what needed work, which bits were, y'know, 'the crappiest', as she put it. I did a bit of that as well, though mostly my job was just getting him to sit down and do the work. It wasn't easy.'

'No, it's not.'

'As you can see, it's a bit on the short side.'

Indeed, the pages of lavish illustration were only barely outnumbered by the pages of text.

'Where're you, then?' I pondered aloud, flicking through one of the many picture sections.

'Oh, I'm not in there. Any with me were taken out – Denise insisted.'

'Why? What – because...?'

'She was *convinced*. And yet, there was never an ugly word between us, me and Denise. That's what's odd, she was never anything but kindness to me, and yet, the *rows* they had... I think they argued more over me than over anything else. So many times I said I'd go, but no, he said, *absolutely not* – just wouldn't have it. He's so terribly loyal.'

I laughed. 'More the old Cullen stubbornness, I'd imagine. He doesn't like being told what to do.'

'Yes, well, you don't really *know* him, do you?'

'Mi-aow!'

'Well, honestly, these things you say...'

'Okay. Okay, maybe I don't; I don't know him as well as you, but believe me, I know *enough*. One of the first lessons I ever learned about loyalty was from Reggie Cullen. See this...' I thumbed ostentatiously through the book. 'The index – I just had a look. See if there's anything about me or my parents in here. The only happiness he knew as a kid he owes to my mum and dad. But no: nothing. Just as I thought – like Stalin, simply writes them out. That's how *terribly loyal* he is.'

I could've gone on, but I didn't. The look on her face: dangerous. Either ready to cry or throw me a punch. Instead there was a snog.

'Of course,' she said, eventually, 'it was all fantasy.'

'What was?'

'Denise. You remember, we were talking about Denise – or *I* was, at least, before being so rudely contradicted. She was convinced, you see, absolutely convinced there was something going on. But of course there wasn't. He never laid a finger on me, before or since.'

'What – *never*?'

'Me and Reggie? You're joking?'

And she laughed. I wondered what it meant, this laugh? An expression of frustrated bitterness? A laugh at me, perhaps – *prove me a liar, why don't you!* Difficult. A difficult laugh to read. And why did I want to 'read' it in the first place? Why should it be any more required reading than Reggie's not-too-crappy book, with its extensive range of full-colour pictures which Shelley was now so hungrily browsing?

'Oh, look, that's him at Fulham. And that's him at Celtic. They, in turn, after a few months, they sold him to... there we are – to *Sunderland.*'

The author, rather bizarrely, had included a picture section exclusively comprising mementoes of his various ill-starred signings-on. Page after page of cheesy grins and brand-new shirts; new beginnings and pledges of eternal loyalty.

'That's him at Forest, with Brian Clough. "I'll never leave," he said. "I've found my true home." He was gone in six weeks!'

It was interesting to observe, as the pages turned, that she was reading none of this: the captions were minimal to the point of non-existence. Her commentary came straight from the hard disc of her adoring memory.

****

There were several days of blissful radio silence before Reggie rang, great with glad tidings.

'Say hello to Bulldog Pinto!'

'I'm sorry?'

'Bulldog Pinto! That's who I'm playing – in the film. Mental, he is, completely mental – he's this scuba-diving treasure-seeker – right? – and he's so fucking reckless, he's so in love with danger that, when he goes on a dive down to a sunken wreck or whatever, he's so nutty, he only fills his tank three quarters with the amount of air he's gonna need!'

'Why?'

'*Why? Why?* Cos he's mental, that's why. *And* to see if he can do the job quicker.'

'Oh, okay. So, er, have you ever *done* any scuba diving?'

'What? What's that got to do with it?'

'I just...'

'Don't be so fuckin' negative.'

'Sorry, I just...'

'Why've you got to piss on my chips all the time? I mean, *no*, alright? No, I've not done any scuba diving. What's it matter?'

'Well, it doesn't, not really.'

'Mind, there *was* that time – one time, in Callor Millor – when I was with Cloughie, in Callor Millor, before I got sent home – I *did*, on that occasion, do a bit of snorkelling, though of course it's not the same – but what's it matter, anyway? I'll *learn*. They're gonna *teach* me – teach me all I need to know. A lot of it's gonna be shot in a tank at Culver City. There's a coupla weeks in the Bahamas, but most of the time we'll be here. Six months, mate, starting February fifth.'

February fifth. Fresh in the job, and already he's speaking American.

'Start packing, mate – the whole team's coming out: you, Shel, Festus, Lilian...'

'Carla?

'Carla? Too right – gotta have me drama coach. And Matt, of course.'

'*Matt?*'

'The voice bloke.'

'Oh. Yeah.'

'The whole team's going Stateside – UKPLC can eat our dust!'

'For six months, at least.'

'*Six months?* Shit on six months! I'm making it permanent. Buy a nice little house in the hills – plenty of spare land, we can build the stadium here.'

'*Stadium?*'

'Just cos I'm moving, don't mean...'

'*Stadium?* I thought you wanted a peace centre?'

'Yeah, yeah, course, we'll have that as well, but the stadium, that goes without saying. 'Ere, guess who I played with the other day? Fucking Robbie Williams. He's not bad, either. Got his own pitch an' all, but I'll tell you what he *ain't* got: a stadium!'

Shelley, I suppose unsurprisingly, was almost as thrilled as Reggie.

'It's going to be great,' she said. 'I know everyone's really down on America, but let's face it, that's where all the 'movers and shakers' are. It'll be far more convenient – a peace centre in LA, instead of Bedfordshire.'

I laughed.

'What? What's so funny?'

'Oh, you're actually *serious?* I thought you were... You actually believe there's going to be a peace centre?'

'Why not?'

'There'll no more be a peace centre than a stadium.'

'No, no – he wants both.'

'*Both.* Exactly: this time last week it was the peace centre – that and nothing else. *Football?* Football – remember this, all of a week ago? – football was *violent*, he wanted nothing more to do with it. *Now*, all of a sudden...'

'Alex, he's an emotional man. You can't blame him for that. Footballers are emotional people. Ian Rush, after Hillsborough, he said he'd never play again. The following week...'

'I don't care. Okay? I mean, sorry, but, *football* – I'm just not interested. No offence. I know I should be – *Grrrr! Football!* I'm a big, beefy, macho man – but sorry, I really don't care. I'm here to work, that's all.'

'Oh. Oh. That's *all?*'

'No. Look. I mean... I... I didn't mean...'

The phone rang. Thank Christ, the phone rang. She grabbed it. It was Reggie, and Reggie, I could tell, was in a strop; that much was clear from her inability to gush more than a few words at him. By the time she managed to get off the line, she was looking quite shaken.

'You alright?'

'Oh, yes, fine, he wasn't having a go, not at me. It's just, apparently, just now, he's been talking to the grandparents...'

My mobile went (or should that be 'cellphone'?). Reggie again – my turn to hear exactly what he'd just said to Shelley;

ranting through it the once had not been sufficient.

'Did she tell you? Did she? She – she – she tell you what they said?'

'She didn't really have time.'

'You'd think they'd be happy, right? I mean, *you* were, *you* were happy. Worried, maybe, yeah – about the peace centre and the stadium...'

'Well...'

'But *happy*? Course you were. And who wouldn't? Who wouldn't be? Not *them*, as it goes. I mean, sure, they *pretended* – 'Well done', all that, but soon as I say I want to take the kids, suddenly it's 'Ooh, is that a good idea?' 'What d'you mean,' I said. They say, is it wise – 'Is it *wise*, taking them out of school for six months?' '*Six months*?' I said. 'Never mind six months, we're going for good – and don't worry, they'll be in school. They do *have* schools there.' I said to 'em, I said, 'I know you *Guardian*-readers think America's a pile of shit, but – 'Oh no,' they say, 'no, we don't think that at all. It's just, well, they've been with us so long now'. 'So what?' I said. 'So fucking what?' They say, 'Well, you didn't want them living with you in Bedfordshire, what's so special about California?' DIDN'T WANT THEM LIVING WITH ME?!!!'

I yanked the phone far from my ear. Even at arm's length, he was all too distinct.

'I said to them, 'My wife died, I've got *issues*'. 'Yes, yes,' they say, 'and we want to *help* with those issues. That's why we were thinking' – they actually *said* this, they said, 'That's why we were thinking – by coincidence, like – we was thinking of asking if maybe you wanted to make our arrangement official, like – y'know: permanent'. '*Permanent?*' I says. 'Permanent?' 'Ooh, well, no, not *permanent*, as such.' Now, y'see, they're *backsliding*. 'No,' they say, 'no, we don't mean permanent, but *official*, certainly; if you made us their legal guardians...' *Legal guardians* – believe it? – try and take my fucking kids?! I said to them, 'I'm coming back, tomorrow – you have my kids ready – ready and waiting by the door, cos soon as I touch down, I'm coming to get 'em, and if you try and stand in my way...' I said to them, 'You try and stop me, I'll fucking kill you.'

***

Shelley took the LA ball and ran with it. Whole days came to be filled with trans-Atlantic calls to 'realty' folk. She'd a natural instinct for the task: how to push the right buttons, declining at first to divulge the identity of 'her client' whilst explaining that, whoever it was, he'd need a base for at least six months, with a view to a possible purchase longer-term. She was also wont to throw in the need for a bit of spare land, as the building of a peace centre was on the cards. I sought to convince her that, if anything at all got built over there, more likely it'd be the stadium. I guess she knew, though, that a peace centre would play better with folk used to dealing with hippy-dippy actors.

In any case, it was none of my business. *I* was not going to LA – that much was clear. I'd never be allowed to take the kids, and there was no way I'd consider going half-way round the world without them. Nor should I, for by any rational assessment I was in far too deep already with Reggie Cullen. Instead of trying for real to retrieve my once-happy and secure home life (not to mention my sparkling career), I'd willingly embraced a second-childhood existence at Cullen Place – and were that not quite stupid enough, I'd also managed of late to hook myself into a growing attachment to a woman whose sole devotion was to another man.

In short, the imminent departure of the whole Cullen circus could not be better timed. The only problem was this: what to tell the gang at the office? A partners' meeting was at hand. In a few days I was due to drive down to Godham Malpass and report on my progress – to explain to a meeting of my senior colleagues exactly what we'd gained from my six months of 'field work'.

I called Imogen. That's how depressed I was: nothing, I felt, could bring me any lower.

I told her I'd been wasting my time at Cullen Place. That nothing – be it a stadium, a cinema, a theatre or a peace centre – would ever get built, especially now the client was moving to LA – a move which, I confidently predicted, would result in his dropping me for a whole new army of cooler, richer, more *famous* friends – oh, and of course there'd be an achingly trendy new architectural adviser; that was a given.

Despite the undoubted tediousness of this self-indulgent whingefest, I found Mog to be in more than expectedly conciliatory mood. I was met, in fact, to my great surprise, with an acknowledgement of defeat. The Civic Centre, she said, was now surging ahead – and thus, with heavy heart, she must concede the battle was lost.

'Some of the other Friends are hoping it'll fall down,' she said. 'Not me. I can't – I can't hope for that. It's not as if the extra bits are going to fall off and leave the theatre in one piece.'

'No,' I said, 'that's not going to happen.'

'Well, you'd know.'

'Listen,' I said, 'I'm down for a partners' meeting tomorrow. Would you have time for a coffee?'

'Don't be silly,' she said. 'Come and have dinner.'

'At the house?'

'Course at the house. Unless you've other plans?'

I didn't.

– Homeward Bound –

I was on the M25 when I had the first call of the morning from Reggie.

'Guess where I am?'

'Heathrow.'

'Yeah, Heathrow. Just off the plane. Guess what I'm wearing.'

'What *are* you wearing?'

'I told you to guess. Fucking hell, how much longer we gotta walk? *Terminal* building? More like *in*terminal building.'

'So, what're you wearing?'

'Eh?'

'What're you *wearing*?'

'Oh, yeah, right. T-shirt. I'm wearing a T-shirt – Union Jack T-shirt. Only guess what: I had it over-printed – got a slogan. *Apathy in the UK*, it says. D'you get it?'

'Er, yeah...'

'Gonna be fantastic. If Shel's been about her business, they'll be waiting for me – loads of 'em.'

'Who?'

'See, what it is, this shirt, it's an ironic comment on all the moaners – all them people in this country who never get off their arses and do anything. Oh, hang on, better go. Coming up to Immigration. Last time I gotta bother with *that* bullshit.

234

See ya.'

I moved on south.

It was maybe 20 minutes later when he called again. The voice was very different.

'Al, where are you?'

'On the way to Godham.'

'Great. Come pick me up.'

'I can't. I've a meeting.'

'Never mind that. They wanna take my kids!'

'*Who* do?'

'Who d'you *think*? The in-laws, of course – and guess how I heard? These press fuckers: I stroll on out of Customs, ready to talk about the film; all they wanna know is how I 'feel' about my wife's parents. What *about* 'em? I said. 'Ain't you heard? They're gonna file some application in court.' Fucking *court!* And how'd they know, these fuckers? Cos the cunts *told* 'em. They *told* the fuckers. No, no, no, don't bother telling *me* – I'm just the father – I've got to get it from Lunchtime O'Fuckin' Booze.'

He stopped to clear his throat – or was he choking back a sob? In the brief hiatus I became aware of other sounds, of cameras clicking and clicking, of people yelping for Reggie's attention.

He was still, I realised, in the midst of the 'fuckers'.

'Reggie...?'

'So you'll pick me up, yeah?'

'No, I can't. Listen, Reggie, fuck's sake, get away from those reporters.'

'Oh, they're cool, don't worry.'

'They're not *cool*. You just called them 'fuckers' –

'Lunchtime O'Booze', for Chrissake!'

'Never mind that. Just get up here, quick as you can.'

'Reggie, I can't. I've got this meeting...'

'Where? Godham?'

'Yeah, but...'

'Perfect.'

'No, it's not. I'm miles past you already. I'm nearly in Sussex.'

'Oh, right, well, thanks a lot, mate, thanks a bundle.'

'In any case, I really don't think you should do anything hasty. Give it a day or two. Go home and cool off, then –'

'Fuck you.'

Oh.

Oh, okay.

Having hit town and the office, I donned my big-kid building gear and, in company with Charlotte, descended upon the site. Progress was being made. Impressive progress. They were nicely on schedule – the *dream* was on schedule, and everyone was happy! Everyone but me. Me and maybe Charlotte as well. She, I could see, was doing a first-rate job, keeping the office efficiently in touch with both the site and the construction brass in London, but though she made no complaint at the time, I could see that she was also devoting a growing abundance of energy to the handling of Oliver.

I lost sight, on that visit, of the number of times I heard the phrase, 'Yeah, well, see, *Mr Grant* said...' And always, it seemed, even as Charlotte was politely but firmly putting people right, I'd be aware of Oliver somewhere in the background; there he was, on his own independent site tour, talking to some or other member of the building team, without authority, quite clearly charming the pants off them even as he muddied the waters yet further.

The way he was putting himself about, you'd be forgiven for thinking he was the architect of record – except that the *real* architect of record would never have behaved in such an irrational and unprofessional manner.

Irrational and unprofessional. That's what they'll say, all the same. Not Oliver; *me*. Me: poor old me; poor old Alex. Hot pants too hot – got into trouble, had to stand in the corner – got to like it too much; took his eye off the ball, started mixing his metaphors – deadly, that.

Anyway, I wanted back on the project.

Wanted? Never mind wanted – they *needed* me, they needed me desperately back on that project, and I told them as much at the partners' meeting. Well, more or less. I couldn't come right out and accuse Oliver of misbehaviour, let alone misconduct. No, I had to put my case in a more positive light. Now the project was well under way, I said, and in no possible danger from the state of my marriage, there could surely be no reason not to bring me back on board.

'But what about your work in Bedfordshire?' said Maurice.

'Well, of course – and thanks, Maurice, for raising that very important point. Things are now at a stage, I'm pleased to say, where I can confidently open up the Cullen project to one or more of my colleagues. I've laid the groundwork, and...'

'Sorry, Alex...' The Velvet Fist again. 'Sorry to interrupt, but I think we'd be grateful if you could give us a brief account of the state of play there. We're a little unclear, you see – I'm sure it's *us*, not you, but if you wouldn't mind...'

'No, not at all. There are currently three strands to the...'

'Three?'

'Yes, three. There's the stadium – that's coming to be increasingly solid in its conception; there's the spa block appeal – I'm very optimistic about that; and there's the

237

prospect of a second development on the estate, a conference facility dedicated to the client's late wife.'

I congratulated myself on having avoided the use of the phrase 'peace centre'.

Oliver cleared his throat. 'That all sounds very good,' he said. 'Really very good indeed. I just wonder, could Alex tell us: these developments – the stadium and the conference centre – are they liable to end up being built in Bedfordshire or, say... Los Angeles?'

Bastard.

'I'm sorry?'

'Well, I rather thought I heard your Mr Cullen was about to depart for "Tinseltown".'

'Er, well, yes, it's true, he's landed a part in a film – but he's only going for six months.'

'Of course. Of course he is. *At first*. But, should things go the way he wants – which, I presume, would mean more "movies" – he'll surely be wanting to base himself permanently in California?'

'I suppose, theoretically, that *could* be the case, but I've no reason to believe he's going to do so.'

Oliver chortled. *'No reason to believe.* Alex, you're a true politician.'

'Praise from Caesar.'

Trevor Crisp weighed in.

'If you'll forgive me, Oliver...'

'Oh, go ahead, TC...'

'If you'll forgive me, this is something of a conversational backwater. If Mr Cullen does indeed move to the Big Orange, or whatever they call it, he will without doubt sling us overboard and seek out the services of... well, Mr *Gehry*, let's say...'

'Indeed, TC. Or at any rate, some or other much bigger fish than little old us!'

'Well, quite. For the moment, though, we must assume we're still on the project – and I think I speak for all when I say there's currently no question of Alex being relieved of his command.'

It's not (they allege) what you say, it's the way you *say* it – and the way he said it, I was lulled for just a moment into thinking I'd been handed a compliment. But then, that's Trevor's way – feint with the left, flatten with the right.

'The thing is, Alex, before you can hand over to anyone else, there has to be something definitive *to* hand over.'

'Well, of course.'

'And frankly, all those months up there in Bedfordshire... Well, I'm sorry, but we need a lot more evidence that you've actually been *doing* something.'

I couldn't speak. For a few moments I simply could not begin to try and articulate – to even form the thoughts I required to encompass the enormity of this belittlement.

Doing something?

Evidence?

'I thought I was being given free rein.' That's all I could splutter.

'Free rein, yes. That still means proper records of time you've spent, not to mention...'

'No, no,' I said, 'look, the thing is, he's incredibly difficult to pin down.' My front was gone. All I had left was the truth. 'He changes his mind on almost a daily basis. I warned you what he was like; you told me it was worth the risk – you *all* did. Who knows, maybe you were just eager to have me out of the way, whatever the...'

'No, no, no, not at all,' said Maurice.

'I didn't want to do it, I wanted to be here working on the Terriss Centre; *you* lot – you decided I was better off with Cullen. Why? Cos of our history, me and him: we're friends – at least we *were* – and that's exactly why it's been almost impossible logging time. A lot of our discussions take place in a social context.'

'Yes,' said Trevor. 'Yes, indeed. You put in an expense claim for...'

'For Woburn, yes.'

'Right, yes, and for some model kits. Airfix model kits.'

A mirthful bark from Oliver.

'It's a very unconventional job,' I said. 'I've had to *estimate* the time spent – and those estimates, I freely admit, have been crude; very, very crude, but...'

'We don't mind the crudity,' said Trevor. 'We've accepted your estimates, and used them as the basis for the bills we've sent. The problem is, he's got you, effectively, as his personal architect; and yet, in the last three months he's paid not a penny for your services.'

'*What*? You...? That... that can't be right.'

'I'm afraid it is.'

'Why didn't someone tell me? There's a mistake; there must be.'

'No mistake.'

'Well, if you'd *told* me –'

'Believe me, I would,' said Trevor. 'I'd have told you long ago but I only learned of it yesterday.'

He uttered these words like a trump card – then, clearly realising how badly out of touch they made him look, he took refuge in his figures.

'Yes,' he said, after some ostentatiously intense scrutiny of the papers before him, 'yes, definitely: the last payment we had was in April. We need you to sort it out, Alex. Until you do so – until you get your project on a much firmer footing, I really don't think it would be fair to expect anyone else to shoulder the burden.'

***

That evening, after the partners' pow-wow, we played Sorry. Me and Mog, I mean – us and the girls; we played Sorry, and it was great.

It *wasn't*, of course. It seemed so, but the joy of the occasion was nothing but a false prophesy.

I really should've known. There's *something* about that game, and I'm not just thinking of the Boxing Day trauma, with the board on the floor, the screaming walk-outs, the doorstep tug-of-war. No, no; since way, way back it's been a source of controversy.

Maybe I'd had a premonition, that first Christmas morning, back in the early '70s. Sat with Mum and Dad amidst a landscape of toys and ravaged wrapping paper, I suddenly became aware that there was one present as yet unclaimed beneath the tree.

Mum picked it up. 'Oh, it's from Auntie Astrid. It's for the whole family.'

'*Boring*,' I said.

'Don't be so ungrateful. She doesn't have a lot of money, poor old Astrid.'

So there it was, generating guilt and disharmony even before it was opened. And indeed, knowing that Auntie Astrid *didn't* have a lot of money, it feels bad even now to remember how much more vehemently I repeated the word 'Boring!' once I'd stripped back the paper. What a sorry-looking game was this Sorry: a slightly trendier version of Ludo, that's how it appeared, with three-dimensional counters and circular cards in place of dice. Turned out, though, that there were several rather mischievous variations. For instance the cards, as well as directing a player to advance so many spaces, could also order you back on yourself. Then of course there were the titular 'Sorry!' cards which allowed you – no, *compelled* you – to set one of your four counters on the road to victory by liquidating someone else's.

That's what caused the trouble later, of course, with my own kids. You need a bit of viciousness with Sorry, same as you do with Monopoly; Lulu and Rachel, though, they play like a pair of Switzerlands.

'Sorry, Lu, I really *am* sorry.'

'Oh, that's okay, *I* sent you home before.'

'No, really, I wish I didn't have to.'

'Well, I don't suppose you *have* to...'

'Yes,' I'd say, 'she *does*; she *does* have to. You're the only one with counters on the board.'

And then, on that apocalyptic Boxing Day:

'The rules!'

'What?'

'Let's look at the rules. Where're the rules?'

That was it – what finally shattered the fragile peace.

'Sod the rules' I said. 'You've *got* to send her home.'

'We want the rules.'

'There *aren't* any.'

'Don't be silly. You can't have games without rules. Besides, *you* said –'

'Yeah, you said she's *got* to, so there *must* be rules –'

'Of course there are, but they're gone – the actual, written-down rules with this set...'

'Let's look online.'

'*What?*'

'We'll Google it!'

'Oh, just play the fucking game, will you.'

And that's it. In no time at all, I'm picking up the pieces, screaming at Mog about the screaming kids, how I'll talk to them how I fucking want – and she – *she, she*, the lawyer – she's threatening injunctions – stop me even seeing them if I can't control my tongue. *Fine*, I say; I'm off now up the corridor, saying, fine, so do your worst, I'll see you in court. And *then* she says – as if threats and injunctions aren't bad enough – she says, hey, what you doing – where d'you think you're going with my Sorry set?

Hers, yeah. On that she always insisted: *her* Sorry set – not mine. For so long it was just a gag – a fondly shared running joke. 'It's mine,' she'd say: 'It's the one I got at the Spastics Society in Cambridge.' Apparently, she and her housemates, back in those carefree student days, they used to stay up half the night playing Sorry. So hooked were they, in the end – such a threat did it pose to their studies – that one of the team eventually took it to the bank and lodged it in a strong-box, not to be redeemed till after their final exams.

Nice, I said; nice story – but here's the thing: *my* set – *my* set, the one I brought from my parents' when we set up home together – was unmistakable in its very specific tattiness, its cards not merely old and frayed but organically microchipped by the unique nibblings of certain silverfish.

Hence the bitter doorstep wrangling of that Boxing Day.

This next time we played, things were different. Very different. So different, in fact, that I allowed myself to be lulled by a sense of glaringly false security into thinking my luck had changed.

After the bleakness of that partners' forum, my welcome at the old marital homestead was an unfamiliar joy. The time we spent together that afternoon – just me and Mog and a bottle of wine – was quite the most civilised in months. *Years*, really.

Though she laughed to hear of my colleagues' knife-twisting ways, she was at the same time strangely incensed.

'Did you not point out,' she said, 'that the Terriss Centre – the project that's going to cement their rotten, festering reputation – is almost entirely your work?'

'D'you know, I didn't even think to say that. It's so long since I've had anything directly to do with it...'

'No, no, no! You can't absolve yourself that easily.'

'What? I'm not *trying* – Jesus, I'm just saying...'

'Lighten up, fuck's sake. I'm only kidding.'

She *was*, too.

At this point we're in the kitchen – the memsahib chopping mushrooms for coq au vin, me slouched at the table, enjoying a glass of the 'vin' not yet assigned to the 'coq'. It was... well, it was... *normal*.

And then, of course, my mind starts racing: I see myself back for good with Mog and wondering what to do about Shelley? Most likely it wouldn't be a problem – she'd follow Reggie out to LA. But what if she *didn't*? What if it didn't *happen*, any of that stuff? The last thing I wanted was to hurt Shelley. But then, if I were really so concerned about that, maybe I should never, in the first place, have...

'Alex!'

'Sorry?'

'I asked if you wanted more wine.'

'Sorry, I was daydreaming.'

'About what?'

'Oh, er... Is that the girls?'

It was.

'Dad!'

'Daddy!'

'Are you staying the night?'

'Er, no, no, I, er...'

'You're welcome,' said Mog.

'I... Uh... I...'

'Well, see how you feel after dinner.'

What I felt after dinner was the need for sleep – a cup of strong coffee, a long drive back to Bedfordshire, a good eight hours, then a fresh morning's start on planning my exit strategy. The girls, however, were intent on a round of the fateful board game. The last time, we'd ended in nuclear meltdown. This time, despite the usual sisterly agonies, and despite my sarcastic asides (cheerfully ignored by all), the game went off without incident.

'Nighty-night,' I said, as the girls headed bedward. 'Thanks for the game – it was a triumph for fair play.'

I watched them go, then turned back to encounter the frostiest of glares from my wife.

'Only kidding,' I ventured.

Her glare became a smile – though laced, as yet, with ice.

'Another game before you go?'

'You have *got* to be kidding.'

'Never more serious. Now we're alone, the gloves can come off.'

'Oh, I see. Reckon you're hard enough?'

'Twenty quid says I am.'

Never has the word 'Sorry' been uttered in so many different shades and depths of dripping sarcasm; rarely has it been met with such glowingly, joyously abusive expressions of mock indignation.

'Sor-*ry*!'

'You vicious *cow!*'

'Up yours, cock-face!'

And so we proceeded, growing steadily more drunkenly obnoxious, and, as time went by, more obnoxiously flirtatious.

'Look, just while you're losing so badly, let me say, cos, I mean, you're obviously too pissed to drive back home – *home*, I say; *home*, as I assume you'd call your Bedfordshire grief-hole...'

'It's not *my*... It's not *my* Bedfordshire... But, anyway, it's fine, I can sleep at Mum and Dad's.'

'Oh, come now, you don't want to go all the way up the road...'

'What're you... what're you saying?'

'What'm I saying? I'm saying, let's raise the stakes a bit. If I win, you sleep on the sofa. If *you* win...'

'Yes...?'

'If you win, you can sleep... wherever you fucking like.'

'Dear, dear, Imogen, such... such *tartness*. You'd not, I'm sure, be using that kind of language in front of a judge?'

'Ah, well, that would rather depend.'

'On what?'

'On *where* I was in front of him...'

– Paradise Revoked–

Mog was up and dressing; I was still in bed.

'Where to, m'lady?'

'Taking the girls to school, then I'm off to work.'

'You coming back after?'

'Well, yeah. I *usually* come back after work.'

I pawed at her hand. 'No, when you've taken the girls, I mean...?'

She sat on the edge of the bed and stroked my face.

'Quickie over breakfast, that the idea?'

It was indeed the idea, but, in seeking to confirm it I merely gave vent to a cavernous yawn.

'Y'know what,' she said, 'I think I had the best of you last night.'

'Mmm, think you did. Still, if you fancy... fancy...'

She laughed. 'You can't even finish the sentence. Will I see you later?'

'Yeah, after you take the girls.'

'No. *Later* later. Tell you what: give me a call when you rise, like a lion from your slumber. I'll have a kiss, for now.'

I responded, tight-mouthed.

'Come on, gimme a proper one.'

'Not brushed my teeth.'

'Don't care, you silly sod.'

The next thing to breach my consciousness was the sound of the front door banging shut. I assumed at first that she was still on the way out – that mere seconds had passed since I drifted off again. Grouchily peeking up at the alarm clock, I found that in fact a full half-hour had elapsed.

On the stairs now, hurried footsteps.

Changed her mind!

I wriggled back beneath the duvet and pretended, in my simply hi-*larious* way, to be asleep.

The bedroom door wheezed open, then all was silence. I listened for the sound of shoes, abandoned, hitting the floor. Nothing. All I got was my own undisciplined sniggering.

'Amazing the shit they put on the front of the *Guardian* these days.' As she spoke, something landed on top of me. 'Time was, you'd only find that kind of crap in *The Sun.*'

I awaited the next line, hoping to hear it delivered in a tone just a *little* less icy.

Silence.

Finally I emerged from beneath the duvet.

There was the face, every bit as sour as the voice.

I sat up a little more, and, hoping to find some clue to her simmering rage, focused on the front page before me.

Indeed, what *was* the *Guardian* coming to? There, up front in frozen colour, was Reggie, mid-mouth-off at the airport, his chest ablaze in the red, white and blue of that Union Jack T-shirt. Regrettably, his witty punning comment on 'Apathy in the UK' turned out a waste of time and money; the way they'd cropped the picture, the slogan was all but lost. Thus the T-shirt, together with the raging red face of its owner, made him appear like nothing more than a fascist bully-boy. Even to *me*, knowing he *isn't* a fascist bully-boy, he looked *uncannily* like a fascist bully-boy.

The picture, though, that was just *embarrassing*; the neighbouring prose...

Whatever Reggie might have hoped, the coverage was never going to be about his latest movie role; the kids and the in-laws, *they* were the story. Moreover, that story had moved on apace since his impromptu press conference – and I couldn't help feeling in some way responsible for its doing so. For it seemed that while Reggie, acting on my advice, had gone home from the airport to cool off, his in-laws had talked tirelessly to anyone and everyone willing to listen to their case. Crucially, they'd gone very, very public on the events of the midsummer weekend, talking not only of Reggie's violence toward his son, but also of his *influence* on said son – an influence which, they said, was no better exemplified than that son's vicious assault on a certain young girl during a football match.

My first, irrational, unfair reaction was directed at Reggie's kids: the little fuckers – they'd spilt *every one* of the beans! Next, of course, I got to shifting the blame a little closer to home, i.e. Reggie. Only *then* did my thoughts get round to the question of how I could possibly salvage things with the glaring, seething, terrifyingly brilliant and unfoolable woman standing at the foot of the bed.

I decided to have a go.

'You're right,' I said. 'The *Guardian*, of all papers!'

'*What*? That's *it*?'

'I'm sorry?'

'That's your line? *It's not true? The press are liars?*'

'Well, they *are*, you *know* they are. It's in their blood.'

'So what're you saying – it's all bullshit?'

'What I'm...'

'No, fuck that, just tell me about Rachel.'

'What *about*...?'

'Her *arm*. What happened to her arm?'

'You *know* what happened.'

'I know what she *told* me. I thought at the time – I remember thinking – how *funny* she didn't break anything else – not so much as a bruise anywhere else on her body. I mean, it's a long way to fall, isn't it, from a horse?'

'She was lucky.'

'*That*'s what I decided. I decided I should put my suspicions aside. Whatever else, I told myself, it wasn't fair to think you wouldn't look after your own kids.'

'Well, of *course* I look after my –'

'Fuck's sake, Alex, she could've *died*. She could've *died*. You put her up against the biggest thug in the whole moronic world of football.'

'Oh, come on. It's not as if it was *him* who... who... who, uh...'

'Who *what*, Alex?'

She couldn't help smiling just a little bit at this, the moment of teased-out truth.

'It wasn't Reggie,' I muttered. 'It was Conrad, his son.'

'Right. Right. So, just to be clear, you put your daughters in a game with a pair of hulking yobs, then got them to lie about it.'

'Well... yeah. Yeah. But only cos Reggie –'

'Please, Miss, it was Reggie, not me!'

'Well, it *was*. He lied to the doctor, we went along with it. I'm not saying it was *right* –'

'Big of you.'

'And besides, look, it's not like it was on purpose. It was an accident.'

'Accident? Right. And how's that meant to make me feel better?'

'It's *not*; it just... I'm just saying, if he'd done it on purpose, you'd have *known*; I'd have *told* you. As it was... I mean, these things can get blown out of proportion, y'know – especially when someone like Reggie – a *celeb*... Let's face it: case in point...'

So saying, I picked up the *Guardian,* gestured to the shamelessly frivolous lead story, then, with a case-resting tut, allowed the paper to drop back onto the duvet.

Mog gave a sigh. 'Well,' she said, 'I suppose when you put it like that...'

'You see what I mean?'

'I do, I absolutely do.'

'I know it was wrong to lie to you, of course it was, but...'

'Hey, look, if it was just about protecting the boy...'

'Well, I don't want to claim it was *just* about that...'

'Of course not, no. No. You were protecting *Reggie* too.'

'What?'

'Well, *weren't* you? Let's face it: if it was just about the boy – about protecting Conrad – you'd have told someone about his nose.'

'His *nose?*'

'The police...? Social services...?'

'What d'you mean his *nose?*'

'There, in the *Guardian*, it says – I mean, maybe it's bullshit: more press bullshit, but –'

'Oh, right – his *nose!*'

'Yeah. Yeah – Reggie broke his nose, it says.'

'*What?* Christ! *Broke* it? No, he never *broke* it. He... He just... he...'

'He *what...?*'

'He... Yes. I mean, he *hit* him, yes – there *was* blood, but...'

'Oh, that's okay, then.'

'No, not at all.'

'No breakage? That's fine.'

'No. No, I'm not *saying* –'

'What *are* you saying?'

'I'm saying, since you *asked...*'

'Actually, no – I've heard enough. No further questions.'

'Look –'

'I mean it. Just get dressed. Go on.'

So I did. Of course I did. At least, I *tried.* But things had been messy the night before; garments were liberally sprinkled around, her office gear mixed up with mine and hard to tell apart in the curtained gloom. Thus, while I sweated and searched for the unforgiving sock, she took the opportunity to subject me to further harassment and harangue.

'*Kids?*' she says.

'What?'

'Never mind his influence on the *kids;* his influence on *you* is testament enough.'

'To *what?* Testament to what?'

'I can't do anything about it, of course – not about you hanging around with that oaf – but I'll be buggered if I'm going to let my kids have anything more to do with him.

Matter of fact,' she said, producing her mobile, 'if I have my way, *nobody*'s kids...'

The voice trailed off as she dialled.

'What're you doing?' I said. 'What d'you mean *nobody's*...?'

'Oh, you're still here. Why's that?'

'Listen...'

'Do me a favour; be gone by the time I finish this call.'

I didn't seek to establish the possible consequences of failure to oblige. They would, I assumed, be the terrors of the earth.

As I headed for the stairs, I heard her establish contact.

'Oh, hi, Terri. ... Fine, thanks. Listen, you know that footballer, Reggie Cullen...? ... Exactly, that's the one – the *children*. ... Yeah, listen, do me a favour: can you find out who's acting for his in-laws? ... *Any way I can help* – just tell them that.'

***

Returning that afternoon to Cullen Place, I was obliged, in order to get through the gates, to honk my way past a seething mob of news-hounds. As I squeezed through, they plastered themselves like suckerfish on the windows, one or two shouting for quotes – though most lost interest as soon as it became clear I wasn't a member of the family.

Reggie proved to be in a surprisingly positive mood. 'Upbeat', I think that's what they say. Maybe a little *too* upbeat; when I got to the house, Shelley was trying to talk him down from the idea of giving another of his matey press conferences.

'It'll give me a chance to put my side of the story.'

'No,' said Shelley, 'don't, please don't. You'll play into their hands, that's all. They'll get you out there, get you mouthing off, then print exactly what *they* want to say.'

'Mouthing off? That what I do – *mouth off?*'

'You know what I mean.'

'*Do* I, though? *Do* I? And what about *your* mouth? Eh? Eh? Tell you what, love, you wanna spend a bit less time with lippy architects.'

'Yes, well, look, I didn't mean...'

'So, what d'you suggest? Eh? Eh? You don't want me *mouthing off* to the press...'

'I suggest – if you'll give me a moment – I suggest – and don't get angry, please, but I suggest...'

'Yes?'

'... that you forget about the press for now. I think you'd do far better just to pick up the phone and... and... and *talk*... talk... to Jack and Monica.'

'*What?* Those fuckers? After what they said about me?'

Shelley, stepping back just a little as she spoke, pointed out that, strictly speaking, nothing they'd said was in essence untrue; un*fair*, perhaps – grossly, horribly unfair, but not, in any fundamental way, untrue.

He took some convincing, of course, but in the end he made the call.

'Hi, Jack, how's it going? Listen, I thought we should try and, y'know, bring down the temperature a bit – just talk things over like civilised human beings...'

That was the last truly civilised thing he said. Within minutes he was yelling down the line, irked beyond measure (or so I surmised) by the other man's natural civility and cool-headedness. Jack, of course, could to some extent *afford* to be cool, being the one with the upper hand. As Reggie so sagely noted, 'You've got my fucking kids!'. This was followed by a period of silence, during which the point was evidently made that the kids had been in Godham for a great many months, without any indication from their father, at least until now, that he wanted them back.

'*Course* I want them back. I've *always* wanted 'em back – just a question of *when*. I lost my wife, that's what you forget... I know. I *know* she was your daughter, but she was *my* wife. ... Yeah, well, that's ironic, innit, that's really ironic, cos you're standing there telling me I don't know what it's like to lose a daughter, when you're showing me *exactly* what it's like to lose a daughter – and two sons as well!'

Good point, that, but it was to be the last with any merit. Before long there were tears, there were death threats, and, before much longer, there was a gentle but persistent humming on the line.

Replacing the receiver, Reggie heaved a sigh of re-stabilisation, then as calmly as he could reported, 'They're gonna go to court.' He was trying his best to smile away the absurdity of the notion. 'They're gonna try and get a... a... What'd that fucker say...?'

'A residence order?'

'Exactly! A residence order! Listen, Al, mate, I'm gonna need some real good legal help. Your old lady, she's a barrister, right? She's based down there, an' all; she'll know the local judges, she'll be perfect. I know she don't like me, but that's okay, she don't *have* to, long as she does her job. D'you think she'll take the case?'

I took a deep breath and explained to him exactly why it would be impossible for her to do so. I then attempted, through force of reason, to dampen the inevitable rage. She's a *lawyer*, I said: they're like architects and footballers, they'll work for anyone, it's nothing personal – Cherie Blair, for instance, she's acted again and again in cases against her husband's government.

Reggie, however, was beyond placating. Hitler in his bunker could scarcely have appeared more paranoid.

'Is that why you came back? Eh? To get the goods on me? Dig up dirt for yer old woman?'

'No, of course not.'

'She paying you – expenses, at least? Petrol, that kind of thing? Or maybe you're working for free, wiggle your way back into her good books – yeah? – back into her knick-knacks?'

'Stop it, you're being ridiculous.'

'*Ridiculous? Ridiculous?* Y'know what's ridiculous? You, the other day, telling me to take it easy – nothing *hasty*, you say – give your mates a bit of time to go to the papers with all that stuff about...'

'Oh yeah, that's been great, that stuff in the papers; that's helped me no end. Thanks to your in-laws, my wife knows all about Rachel, about her broken arm...'

'Exactly! All the more reason for you to suck up, to do whatever it takes...'

'Bullshit! Bullshit! Suck up – to Mog? You've no idea! The things I've thrown away for you... I was on the verge of getting *everything* – everything I'd lost I could've had back, and guess what? I *walked*. As soon as she started talking about those people – bloody Jack and bloody Monica... She thought I'd let her screw you over, just so... just so I could... D'you get what I'm telling you, Reggie? I well-nigh sealed the deal – but no, I walked away – and why? Cos you're my *friend*. My *friend*. So don't you dare... don't you... don't you...'

Good job he chose that moment to clasp me to his manly bosom. Just a few seconds more and I'd be gone, either in tears or fits of helpless laughter. There's a perilously thin line. In fact, I think it was Reggie who told me – yeah, he got it from Carla, the drama coach – an actorly tip: the common key to laughter and tears is control of the breath. And my breathing, at that moment, could've taken me either way. I could've cracked up laughing, but just as easily I could have broken down in tears. For I really had thrown away all I held dear – and even if I hadn't, as claimed, 'walked' away on principle, there could be no doubt that my loss of Eden was down to my friendship with Reggie.

There again, pretty much everything's Reggie's fault, let's face it.

I can blame myself. I can blame Oliver. I can blame Mog. I can blame Richard Archer fucking Prince. But more than anyone, it's Reggie who's put me under this building and left me to wonder how my family are going to survive. Not, of course, that anyone's gonna starve – Mog's a good earner – but belts will have to be tightened. Seems to me the least Reggie could do would be to marry my widow and befather my children. But that's just the delirium talking. Reggie shouldn't be raising his *own* kids, let alone exerting his rancid influence over mine.

So anyway, there's Reggie, grasping manly hold of me as if to say thanks for standing tall with him. Then, releasing his grip and smiling down through watery eyes, he proclaims his intention to go out and set the record straight. It's nearly six, he observes: time for the news!

Turning from the window, having watched as he jogged off down the driveway and out of sight, I found myself face-to-face with a most unhappy-looking Shelley. It struck me only then that my blustering talk of familial reunions had been perhaps a mite insensitive.

'You okay?'

'Yes, of course. Why shouldn't I be?'

'Oh, y'know, I just...'

'I wonder if I should go out there with him? He's so unpredictable. I got a real earful yesterday, when he got back.

He said I should've briefed the press about the film – but I *did;* I *did* brief the press. I emailed everyone; that's how they knew where he'd be, and when. I did exactly what he asked. Only then, of course, he turns on a sixpence, says I shouldn't have told them he was going to be at the airport.'

'What – so *you* get the blame, cos *he* failed to get his message across? That's crazy.'

'I know.'

'Well, you want to tell him so.'

'Do I?'

'*Don't* you? He's got you doing stuff that's not your job –'

'My job is whatever he says it is.'

'Right. Right. Fine. So, if he said your job was –'

'It's none of your business, Alex.'

The air, at this moment, was rent by a whoop of excitement from the lounge. Not a *big* whoop – it came from Festus, after all, and he was never wont to expend too much energy on anything other than gathering food. Still, it was a welcome distraction, and we hurried into the lounge to see 'the former England football international Reggie Cullen' on the lunchtime news.

There he was, chatting to the assembled media, batting back answers to their questions in what, considering his all-too-recent state of rage, was an astoundingly easy and relaxed manner. The only thing undermining that sense of ease was the fact of having chosen to stay on the inside of the gates.

Shelley groaned. 'He looks like he's in prison.'

True, but for all that, he was handling himself okay. The day before he'd let the journos run the game. This time *he* was in charge. Asked about the dispute, he said he'd had 'a very constructive chat' just now with his in-laws, and he was confident all would be sorted in time for the start of principal photography; thus, having deftly shifted the agenda, he talked in detail about *Treasure Raiders*, and his excitement at the prospect of working with Brad and Angelina.

After a while, the Beeb, perhaps growing bored of the film plug, cut back to the studio for the next item – though it was suggested that they might return later in the programme for an update.

'That went rather well,' I said.

'Yes, maybe he did the right thing after all.'

'Of course, Brad Pitt's not in the film, but...'

'No, nor Angelina. Doesn't really matter, though. It's not as if it was libellous.'

'Depends.'

'On what?'

'On how bad the script is.'

'Yes, well. Anyway, he managed to do what he wanted to do yesterday: talk about the film. In fact, he talked a lot more about the film than he did about the kids. Hopefully, in a day or two, they'll find somewhere else to camp out.'

No sooner had these words left her mouth than the TV people made good on their promise to return to 'that story'. This time, however, they had an exclusive. The BBC crew had been invited through the gates, and Reggie was now talking directly to Sophie Raworth in the studio. If it no longer seemed as if they were coming live from San Quentin, that's where the good news ended. Raworth briskly scotched his renewed attempts to plug the film, and homed in on the allegations of what she called 'child abuse'. The magic buzz-phrase had the desired effect on Reggie: though trying his best to convey reassurance, he quickly began to panic.

'Look,' he told the nation, 'I know people worry about this stuff, 'specially if there's kiddy-fiddlers involved, which people always assume – I mean, you say 'child abuse', he's scarcely a *child* anyway, you wanna see the size of him – but that's not the point, I *know* that's not the point – yeah, yeah, just let me finish: I just wanna say – yeah? – that if there was any abuse – and I'm not saying there *was* – but if there *was* abuse, I can assure you, it was *not* sexual, it was *physical*, pure and simple.'

***

News travels fast in today's global media village. Within just a few hours of 'putting his side' to the BBC, word of Reggie's *faux pas* had made it across the Atlantic and back again.

I was in the lounge, drinking in a bit of *EastEnders* with Festus and the mutts, when Reggie wandered in, looking like someone had died. Shelley came in his wake, wittering nervously.

'Don't worry,' she said. 'It's going be fine. Your agent – Gordon, he'll – he'll – please, don't worry – he'll find you something else, I'm sure.'

'What's up?' I said.

'*Treasure Raiders.*'

'What about it?'

'They sacked me – they've torn up the contract.'

'Oh, *Reggie...*'

'They said I was perfect. Exactly what they were looking for.'

'Yes,' said Shelley, 'that's what they said.'

'It's my brand.'

'Your *what?*'

'My *brand*,' he said, his voice now quavering. 'According to *them* – 'Ere, Fes, turn it down a bit. They say it's *damaged* – my brand, it's damaged.'

260

'What does that mean? *Brand?* I mean, I know what it *means,* but...'

'They said I was perfect. They said – the guy who wrote the script, he said... Festus, mate, please...'

The Mockneys on the telly were being more than usually shrill. Not that such would normally be cause for comment; indeed, even now it probably wasn't troubling Reggie half as much as the failure of Festus even to acknowledge, let alone commiserate over, the devastating news his patron was struggling to digest.

'Hey, Fes, guess what – I got sacked again!'

'Yeah, shame.' The eyes remained fixed on the telly.

'*Shame*, you say? Is that it?'

Festus twitched his uppermost shoulder.

Reggie turned to Shelley. 'There – y'see? Everything's fine. You run along now, I'll be okay.'

Reluctantly, she withdrew.

Reggie sat down on the spare sofa.

'Really, mate, it's a bit loud. Where's the clicker?'

'Dunno.'

'What d'you mean you don't know? It's the tools of your trade.'

The line was delivered entirely deadpan.

Festus, with a weary sigh, tilted his head and made a cursory sweep of the floor directly in front of the sofa. The gesture made, he refocused attention on the TV.

Sometimes, when occasionally berating myself for 'sponging' off Reggie (never having fully bought my own spin about being there to work), I've eased my conscience by thinking of Festus – of his barely concealed contempt for the friend who provided his meals and his viewing and his sofa space. Compared to Festus I was a model guest and a model friend. He so filled me with rage, this man, I sometimes found it difficult to share the same space without acting on the desire to hit him, repeatedly and thoroughly. I *didn't*, of course – I *didn't* act on it, but I spent an unhealthy amount of time thinking about it.

'So, you don't know what's happened to the clicker?'

'No.'

'No? Then, you'd better fucking LOOK FOR IT!'

Upon which, he ducked round behind the sofa, gripped the underneath, and tipped it over.

That, at least, is what he *tried* to do; even for a big boy like him, though, fat shit plus sofa plus three dogs equates to immovable object. The mutts, at least, had the sense to hop down, but the main ballast remained in place, compounding his patron's steam-faced ire by chuckling, 'What you doing?' (even as his eyes remained fixed on the telly).

Resuming his full height, Reggie strode round in front of Festus. He clearly didn't know at this point what he was going to do, but inspiration was quickly forthcoming.

'Mind out,' said Festus, 'I can't see.'

'Can't see? Can you not?'

'No.'

'So fucking *move!*'

And, without further ado, Reggie Cullen raised up his famous left foot and stamped his best friend in the stomach.

'Go on, *move!*'

He did it again.

'Fucking *move!*'

And again he did it – again and again and again.

'Move, you cunt!'

'I'm *trying*!' He was, too, by now, but of course his every effort was impeded.

'Move, you lazy fat cunt!'

Oh, to be able to say how bravely I waded in on behalf of that corpulent fool. To be able to say I *wanted* to help, that'd be something, but even *that*'d be only half-true; for in addition to the part of me that thought this spectacle long overdue, there was another, even less distinguished part of me that was simply fascinated by the vision now unfolding. Maybe it was the same instinct that had motivated so many people down the years to defend Reggie's on-pitch excesses because he was, 'at the end of the day, a great entertainer'.

Festus at last managed to turn himself over onto his front and crawl off the sofa. I expected the assault to continue all across the floor and out into the hallway; in the event, it ceased almost immediately.

'There it is!' said Reggie, with apparently unaffected delight. 'It was there the whole time, you silly fat fuck. It was *under* you!'

Festus did not respond. He was hugging his guts on the floor, too shocked and pained to brush off the dogs as they rallied round to lick him better.

– Fit –

Let's see: there was a rowing machine. There...

Is. Not *was;* there *is.* Still there. There *is* a rowing machine. Or did he sell it?

Well, anyway...

A rowing machine.

A couple of treadmills – one for him, one for Denz, that was the original idea.

A rowing – No, had that.

There was the pool, of course, and the sauna – the whirlpool too, but in terms of... of *machines*, of specific gym stuff...

And Curtis, he never went to the *Beckhams*. He *left*, that's all. Just left.

So there was...

Rowing. Treadmills.

1. rowing machine.

2. treadmill one.

3. treadmill two.

4. ...what else?

He had to keep *fit*, he said – Reggie, said he'd to keep fit, 'in case my country calls again'.

Jesus. If ever I pondered his mental stability, *that* surely... I mean, he's *40* for goodness sake. No, he's not, he's nearly *42,* but back then, when I first...

Teddy Sheringham, he said – I *think* it was Teddy Sheringham – still playing at 40 – still up there, playing professional competitive football at 40.

For *England?*

He wouldn't answer that; he'd just go back to the point. 'El Tel', he said – this with deadly straight face – he had to keep fit, he said, cos El Tel had assured him, 'The door remains open'.

Yes, I'd say – on thin ice here cos I know bugger all, though I know at least this much: El Tel's not in charge any more. Not for *years.* How many managers, I'd say – how many – cos we had this conversation all the time – how many England managers since 'El Tel'?

Yeah, we had that conversation a lot. Sometimes he'd get mad, say I was 'pissing on his chips'. Other times he'd just shrug, mutter something about being 'kept on file'.

– Falling Scales –

That business with Festus – the thing on the sofa, with the kicking. One thing it brought into sharp relief: there was no way – no way in the world – I could possibly get anyone else to replace me on this job. Not, I mean, that it was *unfeasible* – I could win myself a transfer simply by obtaining settlement of those unpaid invoices – no, what I mean is, having seen what happened to Festus, I couldn't possibly contemplate unleashing Reggie on any of my colleagues – not even Oliver.

Well, *maybe* Oliver. Might've saved a few lives, come to think of it now.

Festus, of course, was very much less bothered than I about the whole thing; Reggie bought him some sweets and a cake, and all was apparently forgiven. Indeed, aside from the fact that I started going more regularly to the Kung Fu classes in Luton (the Captain hadn't been back to Cullen Place since midsummer), things went on pretty much as abnormal.

Reggie was determined, he said, not to be beaten by those who would stop him expressing himself. Along with America, he said, the stadium and the peace centre were dead – but the *acting career* was not. If they wouldn't let him into films, he'd work on 'the boards' instead – and if they wouldn't let him on the boards either, he'd get his *own* boards. A theatre. A *playhouse*.

I was more than a little taken with this one. Not the least of its attractions were scale and scope: more realistic than the stadium, and indeed far more in keeping with the country house tradition (Glyndebourne, I noted, had started out as a family's private theatre). Aside from that, there was an all-too-rare logic to this latest brainwave: Reggie's desire was to build a scaled-down version of Shakespeare's Globe, positioned on the far flank of the house from the spa block, thus answering one piece of mock Tudor with another.

At his behest, I got in touch with Carla, not only to pick her brains but also to moot the possibility of her coming on board as artistic director. This, it might be said, was a little beyond my pay grade – doing HR for a building I'd barely started sketching – but I was happy enough to give her a call, and delighted when I found her so thrilled by the offer.

'Wonderful!' she said. 'Just wonderful! A wonderful idea – and such a wonder to be flattered like this. But really, you know, you ought to get someone more famous.'

'No, really, Reggie wants *you*.'

'Well, in that case, of course, I accept. An honour. Just hope I live long enough to see you get it up!'

'I'm sorry?'

'Joke, my darling. Dirty joke. But with a grain of truth, I fear. Cancer, y'see: got a touch of the old cancer – yet again! Lungs this time – *quelle surprise!*'

'Oh, God, I'm so sorry.'

'Don't be, darling. I've had a wonderful life – and it's not over yet. This playhouse of yours, it'll give me something to fight for. Assuming, of course, he's not just full of shit.'

'I'm sorry?'

'Oh, come on, my love. Reggie's an angel, but he's like a mixer-tap – hot and cold, hot and cold. You know the way he is. He'll have me up there three times in a week – 'Teach me all you know!' he says – and then for months I don't hear a peep. But of course *you* know all this; now I come to think of it, weren't you building him a stadium? A mock Tudor football stadium?'

'Well, yes,' I said, pained to recall it. 'Yes, that *was*, at one time, a thing that we, er... But really, this playhouse, he's really keen – and I know, for sure, he'll be all the keener when I tell him *you*'re on board.'

All the keener. Alex, how could you?

I don't know. I suppose I was 'in the moment' – that's the thing, right, being *in the moment*? And in that moment there, no question, I *believed* what I was saying. He'd *made* me believe – though most of all, I guess I was channelling my own hopes and enthusiasms. There were those, after all – quite a few of them, not least within my family – who viewed Alex Broughton as nothing more than a vandal, a destroyer of venerable theatres; here was a chance for me to build one from scratch of my own. Who could blame me for believing, if only for 48 hours?

Cos that's how long it lasted before the mixer-tap swung back from hot to cold.

I can't actually recall what directly succeeded the playhouse idea. Too much to remember. Too many big ideas. All I know is that, post-America, not a week went by without my client conceiving some new, more exciting thing to build: an aeronautical museum, a recording complex, a motion-capture film studio... None of these projects lasted more than a few days at most; nevertheless, I had to go through the motions of discussing every one, knowing that the stadium would sooner or later return to the top of the pile.

Though each new project of course brought new annoyance, it also brought a measure of relief; for when he wasn't enthusing about something new to build, he was increasingly likely to be afflicted by bouts of despondency, more often than not brought on by the antics of the media.

We'd expected a bit of a firestorm in response to his wise words on child abuse (*only physical*, for Chrissake!), but the scale of the backlash took all by surprise. As news-hounds continued to picket the gates, their colleagues back at unit base went into overdrive. Hacks and columnists who only a few days earlier had been talking of a 'national treasure' were now piling up the faggots for the *auto da fe*.

No story, no matter how old or inaccurate, was deemed beyond resurrection – though, oddly, it was one of the most innocuous that pierced his armour.

One morning, long ago and far away, Reggie, then at an early point in his playing career, had awoken from a drunken slumber to find himself in a strange bed, in an unfamiliar part of London, with an important match little more than an hour hence. So he'd got a cab to the ground – on the other side of the city – and, being in possession of just enough cash to pay the driver, he'd told the guy to keep the change; this, it seems, had amounted to only 10p.

That was it. *That* was the story. A tiny piece of nothing – and yet it ate him alive.

'I gave him all I had,' he'd say. 'Okay it was only 10p – 10p change – but even so, it was all I had.'

It doesn't matter, you'd tell him; you paid the fare, you didn't have to tip him *at all*.

'But I *would*. I *would*, if I'd had it. Ten *quid* over, I'd still have told him keep the change.'

It doesn't *matter*, you'd say again – cos it *didn't;* this was by far the least harmful of all the shit being thrown at him. Most of the other stories were tales of violence and extra-marital sex, some of them true, most of them *un* – though it made little difference, for every negative story, true or not, threatened to make it that little bit harder for him to get his kids back.

Given all this, I could surely be forgiven for letting things drift on the payment front. In fact, as the weeks timesheeted by, and as three months' festering bills became four and then five, I grew ever less inclined to press the matter. Fact was, the more time we spent discussing these mayfly building projects, the more came to feel that Ingalls Broughton Grant was simply taking advantage. As it turned out, my guilt was without foundation, for nobody was taking more shameless advantage than Reggie. This I realised one day when, in the wake of yet another rantful email from Trevor Crisp, I went up to see Shelley in her office.

'Oh, yes, I'm so sorry, I promise we'll get something to them really soon. No. No, in fact I'll get something out *today* – only it won't be the whole lot, I'm afraid, it'll have to be something on account.'

'Thanks,' I said. 'I'm sorry to...'

'No, not at all.'

'It's not me, it's the guys at the office...'

'No, but they're entitled. It's just, cashflow's not as we expected – y'know, with that film role falling through.'

'Right. Still, I'm sure there'll be others.'

'Yes, yes, I'm sure there will.'

All a bit awkward, really. We'd not talked so much since Reggie's return from LA. Yes, there'd been the occasional night together, but there tended not to be a lot of conversation; once upon a time we'd enjoyed chatting ourselves to sleep in the dark, but of late there'd seemed too much we couldn't say to one another. We both had unanswered, unaskable questions about the other's future plans: mine in the wake of my comically brief ceasefire with Imogen; Shelley's in the light of her apparent assignations with her boss – for, though she continued to act as though nothing had changed, I had on several further occasions heard voices from Reggie's room – and they really *didn't* sound like they were engaged in business talk.

I mean, why would they *whisper*, for Chrissake?

'Oh!'

'Sorry?'

She jumped to her feet.

'Sorry, I just remembered, I've got to go up to the attic.'

'Is that an invitation?'

'What? Oh. Oh, no. No, sorry. Ha-ha, no – but I *could* do with a hand; I need to bring down all those gifts and things.'

Reggie, it seemed, had got to seeing that there was gold in them thar celebrity freebees – and to Shelley, naturally, had fallen the task of listing them on eBay.

It was now, as I helped her ferry down the phones and Teasmades and duvets and electric blankets from the attic, that I was initiated, more or less by accident, into the true state of the Cullen exchequer.

She was struggling, at the time, with a not-too-portable portable TV.

I said to her, 'He's happy for you to do this, then – on top of all your other duties?'

'Got to be done,' she puffed. 'We've got to get money from somewhere. He can't get any credit now; he's maxed out *so* many cards.'

'Has he, now? And there was me, thinking he doesn't 'believe' in credit cards.'

'Well, he doesn't – not anymore.'

'So, how bad's it getting?'

'Bad?' She laughed. 'Don't tell him I said this, but, between the household bills, the outstanding debts, the money I'm sending to the in-laws for the kids... Frankly, if I were taking a salary, I'd have to recommend sacking me!'

'*What?* What did you say?'

'Oh, he'd never actually *do* it – he'd be left having do all the credit control himself.'

'Well, quite,' I said, 'you're indispensable. That's why I'm sure I can't've heard you right. I thought for a moment you said you don't get a salary...?'

'Oh, of course I do – of *course* I get a salary.'

'Right.'

'It's just, I haven't drawn it for a while.'

'Does *he* know that?'

'Oh yes,' she said, with frankly infuriating jollity. 'But it's not as if I need it at the moment. I get room and board and the chance to... to, er...'

Be near to him, she was probably minded to say. Or maybe she *did* say it – who knows? By this point I was halfway out of earshot already, stalking down the corridor with a mission to find and kill her lord and master.

I found him in the ballroom. He was practising a sonnet.

'You don't have a pot to piss in, do you?'

'What?' he said. 'Why d'you say that?'

'*Teasmades? Electric razors?* You're down to selling trinkets on eBay – and meanwhile, you can't even pay your PA.'

'Who says I can't –?'

'She's not drawn her salary in weeks. You've nothing coming in, bills piling up – not least from *my* lot – and you're acting like everything's normal. You need to wake up. Do something!'

'What d'you suggest?'

'Well, for one thing, you've got a whole barnful of cars out there –'

'The cars? I'm not selling the cars.'

'You never even *look* at them.'

272

'Not the point. They're an investment.'

'An *indulgence* – same as having a personal architect and a cook who never cooks.'

'*Lilian?* She cooks.'

'*When?* When d'you last get her to cook you anything?'

'She cooks all the time – for *Festus*. He loves her stuff. It's daft, I know, but it was Denz took her on – I *know*, I *know*, but what can I say, I'm a sentimental guy, I make no apology for that.'

'So, just for the sake of nostalgia, you're gonna keep on a full-time chef to service the most unproductive member of the household; meanwhile, Shelley –?'

'*Unproductive?* Festus, you mean?'

'Who else?'

'Well, I really don't know. Cos it seems to me, mate, the pot may just be calling the kettle black. I mean, *unproductive?* What about you? Let's face it: you come here to build a stadium –'

'Absolutely.'

'And what've we got to show? *Nothing!* Absolutely nothing. You sit about, month after month, twiddling on yer laptop –'

'You know as well as I do –'

'Months and months, and what's the result? Nothing. Nothing at all but great big fucking invoices!'

I sighed, deeply and with feeling.

'There are reasons,' I said, 'why nothing so far has come of our discussions. I do not propose to go into those reasons now, tempting as it might be to clear my name and slander yours. The point, though, is this: no matter what we may or may not have achieved, my presence here is an indulgence – and you, my friend, do not have room for indulgences, not

273

anymore.'

Now there was silence. I fancied, just for a moment, that, against all odds, my words of wisdom had found their mark, and that a radical plan of action was even now taking shape within his fevered brain. More than likely, though, he was pondering whether to hit me.

'D'you know what, mate? D'you know what's good about Festus? I mean, cos I know *you* think he's shit, but –'

'I never said –'

'*The most unproductive member of the household* – you said that, right? You said that. But, see, what's great about Festus – okay, so he costs me a bit, with the beans and the telly juice and that; and okay, so he lies around hogging the sofa, wearing the same old kit for days on end – I mean, let's face it, he stinks; *but*, apart from that, d'you know what's good? He never, ever tries to make out he's *better* than me.'

'Look, I'm just trying to point out –'

'No question, he's got his faults, but at least, mate, at least he *knows* what a leech he is.'

'A leech? Right. And *I* don't?'

He said nothing.

I started for the door.

'Where you off to?'

'Home.'

'Just like that?'

'Well, hey, who needs another leech?'

'Okay, maybe I was a bit...'

'No, no, you're right, I'm a leech – and that's why I'm slithering away: you've no money left, and no prospect of making any, certainly not now you've been outed as a child-abuser – only *physical*, of course, as you say, but still...'

I suppose, the mood I was in, I *wanted* him to attack me – he'd just called me a leech, after all, and my choice of response was guaranteed to have an effect. No sooner had the phrase left my lips – 'child-abuser' – than he was grabbing at my shirt. Two good handfuls of cloth he got. Perfect – it couldn't be simpler. I raised my arms above me, drew my elbows in toward one another and dropped to my knees, dragging his bundled fists along with me. Then, as he looked down in surprise, I shoved up with my open palms.

He stumbled back against the mantelpiece, grimacing as the elegant rococo marblework dug into his ribs. I paused just long enough to make sure I'd done no major damage, then turned away again.

His farmyard grunts of discomfort were easy enough to disregard, but, just as I was reaching for the door handle, I became aware that the grunting had evolved into something different.

At first I thought it was laughter; relief and new annoyance flooded through me – but something in the quality of that laughter compelled me to turn for confirmation.

He was crumpled on the floor beside the mantelpiece. *Not* laughing.

I'd seen him cry before – that time when he learned about the court date – but this was different. This was a succession of large, dry, soul-searingly dreadful sobs, primal in their intensity and openness. I knew he'd have given anything not to be doing this. I also knew instinctively that, at this moment, there was nothing he *could* give.

I wandered awkwardly back and crouched down beside him.

What to say? Maybe I should give him a hug or something...?

Thanks be, *he* knew what to do. He took the initiative – reached up, pawed my head. All I had to do was crouch down, lay my arm around, let him bury his face in my shoulder.

A few sobs more, and he began to get a bit of control – at least, enough to be able to speak.

'I'm sorry, mate, I'm sorry. I don't know what gets into me.'

'Don't worry,' I said. 'I'm... *I'm* sorry, too. I was being a dick.'

'Don't go.'

'I think I *ought* to, really, cos...'

'Please, mate, don't... I can't take it. I'll die without you. You're my only friend.'

'Oh, come on, that's not true. There's...'

'Please. You're the only one I can talk to.'

'Look, I know Festus isn't a great communicator, but Shelley...'

'Please – don't leave me alone with her.'

'*What*? What's wrong with Shelley? Y'know, it's about time you made up your mind –'

'Not Shelley. *Denise*. I'm talking about Denise.'

For a moment, I just didn't *get* it. I couldn't think who he meant.

'Denise...?'

'*Denz*. My wife.'

'What about her?'

'She's here.'

'I'm sorry?'

'She's *here*. In the house.'

276

'What... you mean she's... *alive?*'

'No, you thick doss. She's fucking dead. She's a *ghost*. She comes to me at night. She *talks* to me. Just *talks, talks*. I can't stand it. I bury my head in the pillows – don't make no difference.'

'Right. I see. And... and you're *quite sure...*'

'No, it's not a *dream!*'

'Okay, fine.'

'It's not just in the bedroom, y'see. She's all over the place. Comes to me in pictures. *Pictures*, mate – plays tricks. That time at Whatsit Hall – remember? With the hunting picture?'

'Oh, right... And that time in the pub – Boxing Day – at The Geese...?'

'Exactly.'

'The cricket team?'

'Cricket, right; hunting, whatever – all the time – just, *all the time* she pulls that shit. You see a picture: there she is – it's *her* – she's there, she's bang in the middle – you stare and you stare – it *can't* be her – but it *is*, it's her. And *then*, you look away a sec, and when you look again, she's got a moustache! I mean, she's *hasn't*, of course – it isn't *her*, it's the – the – the Sultan of Simbu, whatever. *Her?* I mean, *her*, she's gone, of course. But there she *was* – she *was*... she was there.'

Breathless, he paused, located a hankie, blew his nose and wiped his eyes.

'You *do* believe me, don't you? I mean, you don't think I'm... I'm...?'

I answered as carefully and truthfully as I could.

'Put it like this. I've never seen a ghost myself – surprising, given all the time I've spent in *this* place – but I certainly don't think it's any more outlandish than, well, believing in God, for

277

instance – maybe *less* so. And, to answer your question more directly, I certainly believe *you* believe in what you've seen.'

'*Heard*. I don't *see* her. She don't *appear*.'

'Right. Right. *Heard*. Right.'

'So, you'll stay?'

'What?'

'You'll stay? You won't go?'

'Well, at some point, inevitably, I'm gonna have to...'

'Course. Of course. But now – just for now, please, mate, say you'll stay. Please. Please – I won't be afraid, not as long as I've got a friend here in the place.'

***

My promise not to leave – at least not *yet* – was subject to the condition that he come clean with the rest of the household about his financial situation.

He convened a meeting the following day. It didn't go quite as he planned. No sooner had he finished his speech about empty coffers and tightening belts than Lilian piped up and suggested he give her the push.

'I'll take a month's wages,' she said.

Reggie turned his gaze on me; there was murder in his eyes. I tried, by means of a helpless shrug, to indicate that though great minds may well think alike, this was nothing to do with me.

He turned back to Lilian, charm incarnate.

'Bless you,' he said. 'Really, bless you, Lil, that's such a generous gesture, but no, I wouldn't think of it.'

'Why not?'

'Well, er...'

'Maybe you can't *raise* a month's wages...?'

'What? No. Yes. No. I mean, yes, of course I can.'

'So, why? It sure ain't cos you love my cooking.'

'That's not true. Not true at all.'

'All them take-aways you eat...'

'Exactly. Good point. That's gonna have to stop. Cut right down on the take-aways!'

'Why don't you sell some of them cars?'

'Eh? What cars?'

'You know what cars – in that old rusty shed.'

He directed another murderous look in my direction before saying to Lilian, 'Sell the cars? You're out of your mind. They're my pride and joy.'

'What pride you got? A silly children's movie car! A Nazi motorcycle!'

'*German*, if you please – a *German* motorcycle.'

'With swastikas everywhere!' She looked at me. 'My grandpa, you know – my Grandpa Dennis – he flew in the Royal Air Force!'

'Really?' I said. 'I didn't know that.'

'He fought against the Nazis. Came all the way from the Caribbean to join the RAF and kill Germans.'

'Gosh, how interesting,' said Shelley.

'Yes,' said Reggie; 'yes, it is, it's very interesting, but no matter whose grandpa did what, I'm not selling that bike, or anything else. Okay, we've got to make economies, but it's not gonna mean letting go of anything I love – least of all *you*, you daft old bag!'

And thus, by means of wrapping her in an affectionately asphyxiating hug, he brought the debate to an end.

It was unfortunate, really, that the economic strategy he

eventually produced contained no element at all of motor marketry, because, as Lilian had suggested, there was little of value beyond the walls of that rusty barn. Nevertheless, we did what we could. The horses were first to go, being offloaded to a local riding school for kids. Shelley was devastated at having to say farewell to Dobbin and Jasper – and all for the sake of a few hundred quid; that's what we got for the pair of them. Still, they did better than the donkey; for Henry there were no takers at all, not even on eBay. At least the stuff from the attic brought forth a few bob; I helped Shelley get it all online, and in return I was moved to the top of the creditors' list, thus being able to toss a bone to Crisp and his acolytes.

I don't know if Reggie actually managed to scrape together a month's wages, but, in spite of his sentimental protestations, he *did* end up accepting Lilian's generous offer – and with almost instant effect. One day she was cooking beans for Festus, the next, thanks to one of Reggie's celeb chef chums, she was starting work at one of London's most pretentiously trendy restaurants. Not, in fact, in the kitchen, but front-of-house, where her withering gaze and her merciless tongue made her an instant hit with all the rich fools she refused to suffer.

The day after Lilian decamped, I heard more from Festus than I'd heard him say in total over the past eight months. 'I'm hungry!' That was the gist. 'I'm hungry!', over and over again. A kind of keening, I suppose. 'I'm hungry!' Finally Reggie dragged him off the sofa and told him to go and make himself something to eat. No supplementary violence this time – no need, for the *coup de grâce* was a verbal one: as Festus was slobbing his way to the door, Reggie called after him, 'And you'd better get used to doing stuff, an' all.'

Festus, with surprising poise and agility, swivelled on his axis.

'What d'you mean, *stuff*? Cooking, y'mean?'

'Not just cooking, mate. People round here've taken the piss for too long. If you wanna stay *chez* Cullen, from now on you're gonna make a contribution. At the very least you can expect to do some chores – muck out the donkey, that kind of thing.'

If Festus was alarmed by the prospect of his new duties, he didn't make it obvious. A shrug of resignation and he turned to go.

But the Squire wasn't finished.

'Course,' he said, 'it might not be enough, we'll have to see. I might need some help with the bills. Could be you'll have to go out and get a *job*.'

Two days later, Festus was gone.

It was a characteristically thoughtless exit – tough not only on the poor, perchless dogs, but also on those of us who, in the absence of any kind of clue to his actions, had to search the estate for his possibly lifeless form. When our efforts failed to produce results, the police were informed. Their reluctantly initiated enquiries were abandoned again when, after a few days more, a lazily-scrawled postcard arrived from Hartlepool, with postage to pay. Festus, it seemed, had gone home to 'visit' his elderly parents.

'He was my only friend,' said Reggie.

'I thought *I* was your only friend?'

'Yeah, you and him. Don't leave me, mate – promise you won't leave me.'

'I already *said* I'm not leaving.'

'Not *yet*, you said. Not *yet*. I want more than that.'

'How much more can I give you? It's not like we're married.'

'Alright, then, when're you leaving? Today?'

'Course not.'

'Tomorrow? Next week? Next month? The month after that?'

'You're being stupid.'

'No I'm not. I'm trying to organise my life. Now, tell me: are you gonna be here this time next month?'

'Fuck's sake, I don't know. You're asking me to promise...'

'I *am*, right: a promise between friends. Just promise me you'll stay, for the next month, at least. Come on, you can do that, can't you?'

It seemed so important to him, just to hear me say it. And, given the way the year so far had played out, wasn't it a fair bet that, whatever I said, I'd still be there on the Cullen estate a month hence?

I had nothing to lose.

'Yes,' I said. 'I promise.'

– Beckonings–

Early in September, just after I'd forgone the latest in a growing line of partners' meetings, I got a call from Charlotte.

'I *know* I wasn't there,' I said. 'Why *should* I be? If *they* don't want me, why should *I*...?'

'No, no, that's fine,' she said. Her voice went quiet. 'Are you okay to talk?'

'Talk? Yeah, course I am – just as long as you don't mind a bit of barking.'

I was, at this moment, wading across the kitchen through a sea of snouts, mobile deftly cupped between ear and shoulder as I worked to open two king-size cans of budget dog food.

'Go on,' I said. 'What's up?'

'Oliver is.'

'*Oliver?*'

'He's... he's getting out of control. I *think*... I'm pretty *sure*...' The voice became extra-intimate. 'Look, we went to this party, the other week, me and Ollie...'

'Oh, *yeah*...?'

'*What?* Oh, shut up, it's not like that.'

'Sorry.'

'A Council do, that's all it was – the Mayor in his parlour, something to do with 'stakeholders'. Ollie thought we ought to attend – for the booze if nothing else, he said. But the thing is, he didn't actually drink all that much...'

'Right...?'

'Barely a sip, in fact – but he went to the toilet an *awful* lot.'

'I see.'

'Bouncing off the walls he was, by the end; and, ever since that night, I've been noticing, more and more, the same kind of... Well, I don't need to tell *you* the kind of...'

'No. Right. So, is it affecting his work?'

'Oh, come on, Alex, what do *you* think? Of course it is. We're a week ahead of schedule!'

I laughed; I couldn't help it. '*A week ahead?* That's *good*, isn't it?'

'Don't be so disingenuous.'

'I'm *not*. Why's it not a good thing to be a week ahead? Just cos he's using again...'

'Shhh!'

'Don't shushh me!'

'Sorry. I'm sorry.'

'They may be all ears where you are, but here it's just me and the mutts – and believe me, these guys're giving *all* their attention to shapes in gravy.'

'Okay, okay, I'm sorry, it's just... Look, he's getting people's backs up – not just *mine*, it's *everyone*. All the time, he's down the site... far more than he needs to be. He struts around, harassing the builders – completely ignores the site manager – just wades on in. F'rinstance, he's got this thing – well, more than a *thing*, an *obsession* – about the time people spend in the toilet...'

'Ironic.'

'What?'

'A coke-head getting riled about...'

'I'm serious, Alex.'

'So am I.'

'And you know, of course, who always has to clear up the mess, calm people down. For the most part, I manage; but a couple of times they've taken their complaints to the top. Last week, at the partners' meeting, they showed him a letter from McAlpine.'

'Shit.'

'Oh, nothing happened; all he had to do was say we're *a week ahead*, and that was it, they just rolled over. But then, he comes out of the meeting, bawls me out – in front of everyone – *you're* in charge of the project, he says, *you* should be keeping the workforce in line. But I'm *not* in charge, that's the thing – not in practice; *he* is.'

'Well,' I said, 'it's a tough one.' I grabbed a couple of carrots from the fridge. 'A tough one, no question – and you *do* have my sympathy, but...'

'*Sympathy?*'

'Well, what else d'you want?'

'He's *taken over*. I thought... I thought you'd be, y'know...'

'Outraged?'

'Well, yeah.'

'And I *would*, I'm sure, if not for having a donkey to feed. Henry, old boy, how are you?'

'You're feeding *donkeys*? I'm trying to talk to you about...'

'Of *course* I'm feeding donkeys. We've done the dogs... you join me now in the stable. We'll give him these carrots, then see if he wants to go out in the field. He's an old boy, is Henry; we keep him inside a fair bit but on day like *today*...'

'Alex...'

'*What*, Charly? *What*? What d'you want me to do?'

'What d'you *think*? Talk to the other partners, of course.'

'To what end? They're not stupid – many things else, but not stupid. They can see as well as you what's happened, and they're very clearly cool with it.'

'But *they* don't see the effect he's having. *They* don't have to pick up the pieces, mend fences...'

'Believe me, there's nothing you can tell me about Oliver...'

'He's damaging the long-term reputation of the firm.'

'Of course he is – and I'm the *one* person who can't say so.'

'Why?'

'Are you familiar with the term *sour grapes*?'

'Look, Alex...'

'I've tried once already to get back on the project. If I go to them now...'

'I'm sorry, I know I let you down, but...'

'*What*?'

'I should've supported you, I know, but...'

'Don't be daft. That's nothing to do with it. That's not... Believe me, it's not that at all.'

So what *was* it? What was it caused me to dismiss this chance to get Oliver? For dismiss it I did: *keep me apprised*, I said, but really there's nothing more I can do.

Why? Why did I tell her that?

Well, partly because it was true. If my colleagues even listened to me – and that was a *very* big 'if' – they'd hardly take action against Oliver. They might, at a stretch, bring me back to lord it over him, but as for getting *rid* – well, I knew those guys too well; if anyone were going over the side, it'd most likely be the one who'd rocked the boat, i.e. Charlotte.

Of course, if my colleagues were to decide, independently, without the need for scheming on my part, that they wanted me back, well, that'd be another matter; *then*, perhaps, I could do something. But, as I explained (whilst leading Henry out to the West Field), in the absence of any such offer, I couldn't just uproot and return to Godham.

Uproot. What a strange phrase to find working its way through my mind. I didn't use it to Charlotte, of course. I simply told her my stadium design was coming on in leaps and bounds (though it wasn't), and noted that there was still the spa block case to conclude.

'But surely...'

'Yes...?'

'Surely, if Mr Cullen's having trouble paying our invoices...?'

'Yes...?'

'Well, then, how's he going to pay for a *football stadium*?'

'My dear Charlotte, have you not heard of the *National Lottery*?'

She *had*, of course. What's more, she knew very, very well that *I* knew very, very well that even if the Lottery were amenable, you'd still have to find at least half your millions from elsewhere: they never front you the lot.

But whether or not the money could be found, things by now had moved on beyond the simple matter of having to design a football stadium. I'd made a promise to Reggie, and while, okay, I didn't expect to have to stay for ever, there seemed little prospect of being able to depart any time soon.

The *headlines* – that was the thing – they just kept on coming. Though the press pack at the gates had long since melted away, there was no let-up in the flow of stories – nor, for Reggie, any consolation in the fact that most of them were as old as the Chiltern hills. Quite a few of these stories were actually breaches of copyright, lifted verbatim from his own stupid book. All the more surprising, then, that he took them so much to heart. Just a few short months before, this man had been actively courting publicity – even *bad* publicity; now it worked only to make him retreat further and further into himself. When Shelley asked why he'd stopped coming down to breakfast, he said he didn't want to see himself in the papers. So she *cancelled* the papers – but still he stayed away, and still the bad news flowed in.

It was via breakfast TV, for instance, that he learned of Festus selling his 'story' to the *Daily Sport*. When the fucker left Cullen Place it was too much of an effort even to scrawl a goodbye note; for the *Sport*, though, he managed a whole four-page exclusive. I know, he probably didn't write a single word of it, but the effect was no less devastating to his old friend. Thereafter, Reggie took to emerging later and later every day, till soon enough he was skipping not just breakfast but every other meal as well.

And yet, he was still capable, every so often, of bouncing into your room at seven in the morning and announcing a day trip to Woburn or Hendon or Bletchley; and for all that I knew *I'd* be the one shelling out for any expenses, I was powerless to resist – his increasingly rare up days were just too precious to squander.

It didn't take a medical degree to see that we were dealing here with depression. I urged him to seek professional help, but he didn't want to know. Depending on his mood, he'd either laugh off my suggestions, or he'd clasp my face in his hands, lean his forehead against mine, and tremblingly assure me he'd be fine, just fine, as long as his *friends* stuck with him.

These, then, were not the ideal circumstances under which to tell him I was going home. And yet, as the Indian summer days grew shorter, I came under increasing pressure to do so.

For one thing, we saved the spa block – by *default*, it's true, but all the same, we won. It didn't even go to court. What happened was that the Council discovered itself to be in the midst of a severe cash crisis. The result was a raft of emergency measures, i.e. cuts and redundancies, affecting every department. Our friends in Planning found salvation in the simple expedient of dropping a load of cases, Reggie's included.

Good news, of course, but it eliminated my only real pretext for hanging around.

Soon thereafter, in downtown Godham Malpass, the hoardings were removed from around the Terriss Centre. Though it was months yet from completion, the superstructure was in place, and the client hoped it might reduce some of the residual opposition if the citizens could see the scheme nearing the end of the process.

It did the job for me, certainly. In fact, it well-nigh took my breath away when first I gazed on what we'd done. Granted, the glass was mired in masking tape and dust, but for all that, the magnificence of the thing was undeniable (except, of course, to our friends in FRITS).

Almost immediately, new expressions of interest began to roll in to the practice and, whether or not through Charlotte's influence, new expressions were heard from on high with regard to the idea of my helping shoulder the growing workload.

There were also signals, rather less vague and ambiguous, from the domestic front; they came, a few days into October, in the form of a chunky brown envelope from the firm of Haines Crompton Associates. It contained a set of divorce papers from my wife.

I'd not expected this. I don't know what I *had* expected; not this, though – not more than two months after my last chucking-out. As I told the complainant, over lunch in her favourite sterile-and-echoey restaurant back home, I'd kind of assumed that no news was, well, if not exactly *good* news...

'Oh, come on, Alex, what am I meant to do? You move four counties away, cease contact with your kids...'

'*Cease contact*? What're you...?'

'You sure haven't *seen* them much of late.'

'No – and not surprising, as you won't let them come to Cullen Place.'

'Well, I'm old-fashioned. I was brought up to believe that *one* broken arm's enough. And anyway, why should they come to *you*? *You're* the grown-up – *technically*; *you're* the one who should be making the effort.'

'I've been *working*.'

'At Woburn? And Duxford? And Whipsnade? Yeah, I've been looking at the Visa bills – that's what got me thinking. For someone who's been away on business, you've done an awful lot of entertaining – with *our* money, no less. Now, what was the other...? *Cineworld*, yes, that's it; Cineworld Luton.'

'There's nothing wrong with Cineworld! The *kids* – I took them to a film. *Shrek the Turd* – we went to see...'

'The kids and who else? It was nearly fifty quid. What did you do – pay for *everyone?*'

'Look, what *is* this? I come down here to – I mean, *yes*, alright, *yes*, I paid for everyone – so what? Reggie was meant to settle up with me.'

'Never *does*, though, does he?'

'Look...'

'You want to be Reggie's pet poodle, my love? That's fine, but *I'm* not going to pay for it.'

'Who's *asking* you...?'

'Wanna live there for ever, that's okay too, but...'

'Look,' I said, rather louder than intended. The echoey room fell silent. She watched me, smirking, as I took a last morsel of ciabatta roll and intently mopped up my *jus* (it's a *jus* kind of joint). 'Look,' I said, once the enveloping rhubarb had resumed, 'I don't *want* to live there. I've no choice. You chucked me out.'

'I chucked you out because...'

'I *know*, because of Charlotte, but...'

'Charlotte's not the reason I'm divorcing you.'

'Her name's on the papers.'

'Yes, it is, cos *something*'s got to be there. But let's be clear: I don't view Charlotte – or anyone else in the interim who I don't want to know about – as a long-term factor in the break-down of our marriage. Whereas, your decision to move half-way up the country...'

'I *had* to.'

'You *didn't*; you didn't *have* to move there, not at all. It's not like you were homeless. Had you only stayed put with your mum and dad...'

'How *could* I?'

'We could've avoided *all* of this.'

'The nature of my work with Reggie – the way he operates – not to mention... Sorry, what did you...? *Avoid...?*'

'We could've avoided this. That's all I'm saying.'

'What – if...?'

'You didn't *have* to go all that way.'

'So... what – so, if I'd hung around the neighbourhood – just on the off-chance – instead of getting on with my life, my *work*... you're saying...?'

'Who knows? Even as it was, we came pretty close that

time. But for the malign influence of Mr Cullen...'

'He's not *malign,* he's just –'

'Stick to the point! My God, you're a cool customer.'

'Yeah, that's been said before. Let's face it, though, there *were* some outstanding issues. I mean, yeah, we kinda dealt with them that last time, but...'

'What – you think just because we had sex on one occasion...?'

'No, no...'

'That doesn't give you the right to demand it every...'

'I've *never* demanded...'

'*Demanded*, no, but believe me, the power of your *sulk*...'

'Hang on! hang on!'

'What?'

'We're getting away from the point.'

'Which was...?'

'Do you, or do you not want a divorce?'

She pondered, took a deep breath, let it out again, thought for another long moment, opened her mouth to speak, and...

Her phone rang.

'Yes, I know... Yes, okay, I'll be there in five.'

Up on her feet, she was folding her Star Trek phone and grabbing her coat.

'What're you...?'

'Sorry, gotta dash.'

She flung a couple of 20s on the table.

'Don't be silly...'

'No. No, go on. It was my choice to eat poncey. Look, we'll talk, okay?'

I sat there, slightly dazed. Was it my imagination, or had we just danced, however lightly, around the idea of my coming home?

I asked for the bill.

Oh, Alex. Alex Broughton. What a nobber you are. Sitting there, fretting away, wondering how much of her change to leave as a tip – *is service included?* – when what you should've done (as just about anyone else would've recognised) was leave the stupid money and run from that restaurant. Run! Run! Run! – catch her up and *kiss her*. She'd all but *asked* you to.

And yet, at the time, it seemed so complicated. Even without the tip politics, there was the matter of...

Of *what?* I mean, really, *what?* What was so terribly *complicated?*

Not, I suppose, that it matters now. It wouldn't have made any long-term difference, certainly not to the current situation. Whether in the design or the construction, or something in the earth we managed to miss, chances are the damage was done already by then.

Still, if nothing else, I might at least have enjoyed a few weeks' extra happiness with her.

– Heroes –

3:06pm

How many Tracy boys were there? Just while I'm on the subject.

Was I? Was I on the subject? No. But how many brothers, anyway? Jeff was the dad, I think, but his kids...?

Five, I suppose. Must've been five. Five Thunderbirds, *ipso facto...*

1. Thunderbird One was... was who? Can't remember. Can't even remember which one it was, let alone... A rocket, yes, I know, but which one – the orange or the silver?

2. Thunderbird Two. That's easy enough: big green froggy thing with a pod in the middle. Down it came and out popped Thunderbird Four. Well, sometimes. And who was inside – inside the inside?

Was it Alan? Scott? Gordon? John? I never could tell them apart.

Must be odd having brothers.

– Division of Labour –

Sat one morning at the kitchen table with Shelley, I got into a tug-of-love over donkey manure.

We were in the midst of our daily estate management meeting, about half-way down a list of chores to be divided.

'*Muck out Henry.* Shall I do that?'

'No,' I said, '*I'll* do it.'

'Fine. Oh, but didn't you do it yesterday?'

'Yeah, but...'

'*I'll* do it, then.'

'No, really...'

'No, you don't want to do that.'

'I'm really not bothered.'

'It's not nice, though, it's yukky.'

'Just put me down, I really don't mind.'

'No, but *I* don't, either.'

'Well, fine, I said, 'if you honestly don't.'

'I *don't,*' she said. And then she went a lie too far. 'In fact, I quite *like* doing it.'

'Oh, bullshit.'

She laughed.

'What?'

'*Donkey* shit, at least!'

I laughed too, weakly, and pondered for a moment, then I pushed back my chair and made for the stairs.

'Where're you going?'

'Get us some help.'

Ignoring her flustered imprecations – 'Don't wake Reggie!' – I ascended to the master suite, entered without knocking, dragged the bedclothes onto the floor, and ordered the lord of the manor to go and muck out the donkey – *his* donkey.

He made no protestation; simply rolled off the bed and, without getting dressed – without shoes, slippers or even a pair of socks – he wandered downstairs to do as bidden.

Shelley, appalled, followed him out with a pair of wellies. For me though, it was gladdening to see how a 'tough love' approach could work (even if he *did*, as he returned to his room, mutter something about 'both barrels of my Purdey').

It was the first time in a week that he'd stirred from his room. A full week. Seven days – I counted them. It was getting to be just a little self-indulgent. It wasn't as if he could even claim to be hiding from the press. Not anymore; not since the focus of the media had shifted, so completely and so relentlessly, onto the slow-motion car crash of Paul McCartney's divorce. I understood, of course, that Reggie was troubled by his own increasingly rancorous family soap, but he could hardly expect to win back his kids by modelling himself on Howard Hughes.

He, however, was immune to such reason, and so, to my frustration, was Shelley. While he reclined upstairs with his celebrity melancholia, she and I were running the place between us – and for nothing. In *my* case, at least, someone *somewhere* was paying me a wage (in spite of my lack of sweat on the firm's behalf); she, however, was continuing to exist on the meagre expenses she would guiltily disburse to herself from petty cash. And yet there was never a word of complaint; she seemed, in fact, to grow more dedicated with every new task she took on, apparently oblivious to the irrational guilt which caused *me* to toil ever harder in response. Three times a day, for instance, I had to go and retrieve trays from Reggie's room – not an epic task, just another of so many little ones made necessary by Shelley's extra strivings, for now she was not only cooking his meals but actually providing them as room service.

'He's taking the piss,' I observed more than once.

'No, that's not fair, he's just got a lot on his plate.'

'In no *sense* is that the case,' I might reply, pointing to the tongue-swabbed utensils just collected.

For all my dry wit, I was getting progressively more angry – and, as so often is the case with bleeding-heart liberals irked by the conduct of even more gushingly bleeding-hearted liberals, the bulk of my anger was directed not at Reggie but at his faithful PA.

So far, this anger had stayed largely in check. We continued to 'see' each other, in spite of everything: in spite of my despair at our ever-expanding workload; in spite of my continuing concern about the household finances; even despite the knowledge that I wasn't the only one enjoying her favours – because I knew, I absolutely *knew* – deny it as she might, I *knew;* I'd heard the giggling behind his door (*ghosts?* oh, fuck off!) – and now, of course, in the wake of that tantalising, hope-inducing lunch with Mog...

Mog, indeed. *'Had you only stayed where you were...'* Everything had changed in that instant, and, unfair as it may be, it was hardly surprising if I should find myself increasingly impatient, for even as home appeared ever more attainable (at least in my fevered imagination), it became progressively more clear in reality that the final bar to leaving Cullen Place was not my loyalty to Reggie, but my reluctance to abandon Shelley.

The storm broke the morning after the bedclothes

incident. In spite of Reggie's muttered threats, I again made pilgrimage to the master bedroom.

'Come on, you lazy fucker, get yourself up.'

He didn't stir. I yanked open the curtains and let the day in.

Nothing.

I opened a window, then another.

Still nothing.

With the most ostentatiously weary of sighs, I approached the bed.

As I pulled away the sheets, he opened one eye; it looked at me for a moment in lazy defiance, then led my gaze down the bed. Only now did I perceive what the sheets had revealed: there it was, the promised shotgun, a finger resting ready on one of the triggers.

I gently replaced the sheets and withdrew.

'You've *got* to leave,' I told her.

'I *can't*,' she said flatly. 'There's too many others against him already.'

'Did you not hear what I just told you? The shotgun – the shotgun was *in his bed*. He must've had it there all night.'

'He might've shot his foot off.'

'Fuck his foot! What about my *head*? And *your* head?'

'I wasn't there.'

'Don't be obtuse. Christ, I'll bet it's not even licensed.'

'It *is*. I made sure of it.'

'Oh, yeah, I'll bet you did.'

'What does *that* mean?'

From there it escalated: the more I begged her to leave, the more she insisted she wouldn't; the more she insisted, the more I poured contempt on her blind devotion to Reggie; and the more I made free with my contempt, the more emphatically she assured me it was none of my business anyway.

'Of *course* it's my business,' I said. 'Don't you see, you're the only thing keeping me here.'

'*I* am?'

'Of course.'

'You're not serious?'

'Deadly.'

'Gosh. I'd... I'd no idea. None at all. Well, of course, you must go.'

'*What?*'

'Go, at once. I mean it.'

'*Go?*'

'Well, if, as you say —'

'That's not why I said it.'

'No, I'm sure, but really, you *should*. If that's what you want —'

'Is that what *you* want?'

'Well, I... I don't want to *stop* you, not if —'

'No. No, I don't suppose you do.'

'I'm not saying —'

'And why *would* you? What did you ever *get* from me, anyway?'

'*Get?*'

'I mean, what d'you get from being with me? *Him,* up there, the love of your life — him you can have any time you

299

want, so...'

'I *can't*. What on earth –?'

'Oh, *please!*'

'Please *what?* Look, Alex –'

'I've *heard* you. I've heard you in his room! The giggling!'

'*Giggling?*'

'I've heard you.'

'What *giggling?*'

'I've heard you together.'

'You're mad.'

'You deny it?'

'Of course I do. Of course.'

'You're saying –?'

'Oh, Alex, please, just leave me alone! I mean, really – just go, or stay, as you wish – but *me*, I'm staying, and that's my choice – and it's *nothing* to do with – with – with – And *you*, please, *I* never told – I never *forced* you –'

'Look –'

'No! Please! enough! Just, please – just – just – just... *fuck off!*'

Rows like that can clear the air. Rows like that can sour it too, beyond measure. This one had the latter effect. Shelley, so often so keen to kiss and make up, was in this instance entirely unforgiving, and as she brooded on what I'd said, I brooded back, both on her brooding and on my own inability to offer even a partial apology.

If we continued to meet every morning, it was only so as to divide up the chores and then retreat for the day into rebuking one another through ruthless efficiency.

In time she made even that redundant: I came down one morning to find the list ready-filled on the kitchen table – each chore assigned to one of us or the other, with 'Hope this okay' in a scrawl at the bottom. She was already out seeing to Henry.

For two full weeks that carried on – two full weeks of hideous, ghastly silence. Nor was the silence confined to the estate, for Godham Malpass had also gone eerily quiet: nothing more from Mog, and as for the practice, all I got there was a string of increasingly shirty messages about the invoices. And all the while, according to my back channel, i.e. Charlotte, Oliver was growing increasingly unstable, without even the initial efficiency gains to compensate. It seemed his obsessive interference was causing more and more delays.

Why did they not just cut him loose? A sub was ready, willing and waiting. If they'd only *say something*, I'd come – sod Reggie, and, yes, in all frankness, sod Shelley too.

And then, one evening, just when I was starting to think I really couldn't go on, Shelley came to a similar conclusion.

The night was all too apt to the moment, with lashing rain and a fierce wind doing its utmost to wrench the creaking eaves from their moorings.

I was in my room, exhausted after another pointless day of phone-jousting, dog-feeding and donkey-sanitising (actually, no, *not* the donkey; Shelley had taken full control of that particular privilege). So there's me, stretched out on my bed, half-reading a book and expecting it to fall from my hands as welcome slumber takes me – takes me in its arms and draws me down. I hear voices and think I'm drifting off to Dreamland – but as one of them grows louder, raised in anger, I suddenly realise: the voices are not voices from within my weary head.

As I reached the door of my room, I heard another door slam beyond. I poked my head out into the corridor. Nothing to see now. I made for the door of the master suite and stood there, hovering on the cusp of a knock (I knew better now than to go barging in). There was a noise from downstairs. I glanced over the balustrade, and there below saw Shelley, crumpled on the bottom step, apparently convulsed in tears.

Padding down the staircase, I took up position, loitering in front of her. She looked up, clocked my existence, then buried her face once again.

I sat down next to her. As with Reggie on those earlier occasions, I was clueless as to my next move. A fraternal hug, perhaps? I extended a cautious arm, just as she heaved another, seismically epic sob. My arm recoiled at the double. A hankie was offered instead, and accepted.

'What happened?'

'He... he was horrible. He said I've brought financial... financial ruin on him.'

'*What?* How'd he make that out?'

'He said I'm incompetent... He said I'm dishonest. He said I've been embezzling. I *must've* been. No one'd work for nothing, he said, not unless they were running a fiddle.'

'Jesus...'

'He said... he said, he said what's the point of having me around – an ugly, boring bitch like me – if I can't even be *honest,* if I haven't got *that* going for me at least.'

'He said *that?*'

'More than that. He's – he's – he's – he's fucked uglier than me – that's what he said – but only in car parks! Yes. Yes – and with *them* at least he didn't have to *talk* to them.' She laughed, launching a spray of snot and tears across the parquet. 'I knew he didn't *fancy* me, but...'

'Oh, come on, he's nuts, he's a complete whack-job. Doesn't *fancy* you? Chrissake, that's a *compliment,* if anything. I mean... Well, you know what I mean.'

She looked me in the eyes and tried a smile. It didn't really work.

'At least... at least I've woken up, at last. All the years I've been... I've been hanging around, doing his bidding, in the tiniest... slenderest hope that he might come to... Oh, God, it makes me sick to even... in the hope he might come to...'

There was another trauma-stricken intake of breath, followed by a big, self-deriding laugh. '*Love* me? He never even paid me the compliment of *fucking* me. Not once.'

'Oh,' I said. 'Oh, but I thought...'

'*What? What?* How many times do I have to TELL you?'

'No, I'm sorry, I...'

'Don't you think I'd *say?* I'd shout it to the world.' She wiped her nose and laughed again. 'D'you know what's really funny? Denise thought...'

'Yeah, I know.'

'*I* was the only woman he *didn't*... Even when they were doing it with *strangers*...'

'Right.'

'Even then, I never got a look-in.'

'Well, maybe he just, y'know... *respected* you too much.'

She laughed another shower of snot. 'Maybe *once* I could've... Back then, maybe, I could've believed that. But *now...?* She's been dead nearly three years.' She started crying again. 'That's not respect, that's contempt. I was too stupid to see it, that's all. He had to spell it out for me.'

I reached out and pulled her close, too dazed by now to fear she'd misinterpret. I say *dazed,* though — *dazed?* It was less about what he'd said to her — foul as it was — than about what *she'd* just said to *me*. If she really *was* telling the truth — if she wasn't simply as barking as Reggie — if she really *hadn't*... all

303

those times I thought I heard her...?

Gently disengaging from Shelley, I got to my feet. 'I'll go and talk to him. He'll have calmed down by now.'

'Don't bother,' she said. 'I'm going to pack.'

Pack?

Pack, she said?

Did she mean it?

Strange how things turn out. For weeks I'd been longing to escape, and now it was upon me. This time tomorrow, I could be back in the loving bosom of my family. No more dog food, no more donkey dung, no more shotguns...

And then it struck me, as horribly as if a lightning flash had pierced the roof and seared my brain: what if Shelley were *not,* after all, the reason I'd hung around? What if, in truth, despite what I'd told myself, it was *Reggie* for whom I'd stayed? What if I should awake the next morning and find myself more stuck than ever?

I had to stop her. We could leave together – a few days hence, a planned escape – an escape committee – but if she went right *now*...

I'll get her reinstated.

Two steps – even three – at a time, I upped and advanced on the master bedroom... my fist was raised to knock, my other hand poised to turn the handle, no matter the response.

My knuckles were an inch from the oak when I heard his voice from beyond.

'I just hope you're satisfied,' he said. 'That's all. I hope you're satisfied. All my friends are gone. All of them.'

I was about to try again when the second voice came.

'Not everyone.'

It was soft, low, barely audible; distinct from the other voice, but that's all I could establish. On it went, softer and lower than before, too low, in fact, for me to get more than a few words – something about 'your friend Alan'.

'Alex,' said Reggie, all too loud and clear. 'Fuck's sake: *Alex* – that's his name.' The other voice said something indistinct, then Reggie said, 'Yeah, but for how long?'

I strained to hear what the other voice – *was* it another voice? – came back with. All I got, though, was something about 'the way you alienate people'.

'Ooh, big word – *alienate*. Alienate, yeah, that's right, that's me. Yeah – and then you'll be satisfied, yeah?'

The response to this was as clear as I could have wished. No more mumbling now.

'Yeah,' said the voice, 'I will. I *will* be satisfied. I don't want to share you with anyone else. Ever again.'

– Arrival –

Nothing was said on the way to the station.

No, I lie.

I asked her, did she want dropping in Luton, or should I drive her into London – which, I said, was sort of on my way? Luton, she said, would be fine.

Beyond that, there was silence. I didn't ask where she was heading, and she didn't tell me.

At the station there was an awkward hug and a honk from a taxi. I made a weary gesture, left the engine humming, and lugged Shelley's cases into the ticket hall.

So that was that.

All the way down to Godham, I wrestled with what I'd heard at Reggie's door. Surely, I thought, he wasn't *really* talking with Denise? Not *really?*

And yet, why not? When Shelley told me, all those months ago, that the house was haunted, did I take her for a nutter? No, of course not. There again, she never claimed to have actually *seen* anything. That notwithstanding, the alleged history of these three spooks was well documented; why should there not – accepting the existence of the others – why, logically, should there not be a new one to keep the old'uns company?

Oh, fuck off, it was *him* – both of them – *both* voices – it was *him,* it had to be.

But *why?* I was never much impressed by the stuff he did

with that con-man voice coach; should I now believe he'd improved enough to sound so convincingly like a member of the opposite sex?

There again, how could *I* tell? There was so much mumbling involved, and besides, how would *I* know what Denise sounded like? I never met her.

No, I thought, that's true, but I *had* heard her voice, on tape. That time – just the *one* time, thank God – I was put through hours of Reggie's family videos. Birthday parties, anniversaries, all that tedious shit – and here's the point: Denise – the late Mrs Cullen – sounded nowhere near as sophisticated as that voice I'd lately heard from the master bedroom.

Yes, but surely – surely! – round and round! – one hand, the other hand, but surely, YES! – but *surely*, even a ghost can put on airs and graces.

Airs and graces? Fucking hell!

I sought to change the subject in my head – *just think of something else!* – but it was all in vain: as I sped through the night, putting ever greater distance between myself and Cullen Place, I found my guilt increasing with every mile covered. It was just as I'd feared; even with Shelley out of the picture, it was going to be no easy task to exorcise my needless sense of duty towards him.

But *why*? Why should I *not* walk out on him? I owe him nothing.

True. True. But still, the guy needs help, does he not?

That's none of my business. Social Services – them, or – them, or – them or the NHS, it's them – whoever – whoever it falls to – *Christ!* – I mean, *jurisdiction! Patches!*

Yeah. Yeah but still, at least, you can *call* them.

I will. I *will*. In the morning.

Tonight.

Tonight? There'll be no one in.

In *where?*

Wherever – wherever it's their jurisdiction – NHS, the Social lot, whatever – whatever – they'll not be there, just a message on the – the – the – but the point – the point – the point is this: it's why – *why* – why, just cos *he's* pissing his life down the drain – why should mine go with it? It *shouldn't.* It shouldn't – it *mustn't* – it *can't:* I've other obligations, far beyond Reggie – Reggie, who, never forget, was more than happy to run out on me when...

Thirty years! Don't be stupid! That was thirty years ago!

Easy to say, when it wasn't *you...*

It *was,* though, it was...

Exactly, it WAS – it WAS – *you're* the one who got the piss ripped in front of those girls, so don't stick up for the fucker. I mean – I mean – *coach trips,* too: another, y'know – coach trips, trying to get a place at the back with the cool kids and the tape-recorder playing Led Zeppelin – who – who – who was it, eh? – who was it always did the dirty work – 'Fuck off, Broughton, go sit somewhere else'? Why, Reggie, of course – of course it was – and all because I simply wasn't cool enough to sit with those people. Well, cool *enough?* Not cool *at all* – and not, back then, equipped with the personality to persuade myself I was actually much, much, much, much TOO cool to sit with those ludicrous fashion sheep.

And okay, I know, it's a long, long time gone past to find that even now, so pathetically I'm harbouring this stuff, but still, but still, but still I'll be fucked if I'm cool enough *now.* Let some of those other fuckers, those fuckers at the back of the bus, let *them* come forward now, identify themselves to the driver and take up the slack. Yeah, that's right: uncool Alex is going back to his humble home town, where he has *obligations* – to a wife, to a pair of lovely daughters, to a bunch of business partners, and yes, to the good, long-suffering Council Taxpayers of Godham Malpass.

But...

What? But *what?*

Well, the dogs? And the donkey?

Oh, sod the donkey. *And* the bloody dogs.

I *couldn't,* though. I couldn't 'sod' them, not that easily – no more than I might dismiss that Reggie fucker from my guilt-sodden mind. All the way down to the coast, the same stubborn arguments went festering round and round, sometimes swilling inside my head, more often declaimed out loud to the car, the empty road and the world beyond.

By the time I drove up onto the pavement outside Mog's – outside *mine,* that's to say – outside *the old Broughton place* – one in the morning, it was – by the time I finally got there I was wound up tighter than a watch spring. I'd just enough energy to raise a finger to the doorbell, and she – Mog – she'd just enough space to murmur, 'What time d'you call this?' before I lurched forward into her arms and commenced to howl.

– Journeys to Glory –

I awoke with a decision to make.

Two days I'd spent in bed, being there-there'd and pampered back to full strength, but I knew there'd be a reckoning of some kind. Sure enough, on the third day, when Mog yet again brought me breakfast in bed, there was more than just breakfast on the tray. Alongside the plate of bacon and eggs lay a set of legal documents. Her copy of the divorce papers.

She'd tear them up, she said – as long as I agreed to sever all relations with Reggie.

Sorry to say, I didn't need too much persuading. Well, a *little* bit sorry, at least.

'I'll have to see him *one* more time, though.'

'Yeah? Why's that?'

'Gotta get my stuff.' It was true: I'd brought not a thing. Even my laptop was still, to my knowledge, humming away on the desk in the Blue Room.

'I'll get some people to fetch it,' she said.

'Oh, I wouldn't like to...'

'I'll send someone.'

And so she did. A couple of bailiffs went up. Reggie, reportedly, came to the door in his pyjamas. He was carrying a shotgun, they said, though he made no attempt to use it: he just led them upstairs and told them to take what they needed.

Within a few days there was further news. In response to my lingering concerns, the RSPCA sent an inspection team to Cullen Place. Word came back to the effect that all beasts were in good health and adequately fed, suggesting that Reggie had finally forsaken his bedly cocoon and got back to life.

So that was it: me and Reggie done.

Finished.

Liberated.

I could settle down once more, both to family life and to re-engagement with my career.

If I expected, in my re-engagement, to meet opposition from Oliver – and I certainly *did* – it was perhaps because I'd underestimated the extent of his coke-bingeing. At any rate, I was unprepared for the bleary-eyed wreck who faced me across the table at my first partners' meeting. Far from throwing obstacles in my path, he welcomed my return to The Project. It would *lighten his load*, he said. He'd been 'overdoing it' lately.

Yes, I said, that's what I understood, and that's why I wanted now to suggest he be relieved entirely of any hands-on involvement with the Terriss Centre. After all, he'd never actually been formally assigned to it in the first place, so in truth he was putting in efforts far beyond the call of duty.

At this he exploded. What did I think? He'd been skimming off the top? Shoving it up his nose? No, I said, of course not. Nothing of the sort had even been suggested; in fact, I said, just to make it clear, we'd get Shana, Trevor's secretary, to read back the last few lines of her minutes, 'just to make it quite clear that nothing at all's been said about embezzlement from petty cash, or indeed about class A drugs'. Shana read, and as she did so, Oliver slipped further and further down in his chair; when she'd finished reading, I got her to minute the fact that the minutes had been successfully read back, just to make it explicitly clear for all time that nobody – absolutely *nobody* – thought there'd been *any* embezzlement from petty cash, or indeed any other kind of wrongdoing by our esteemed colleague.

'Oh, and please minute what I just said.'

'*About...?*'

'About embezzlement and drugs, yeah.'

'But you already...'

'Yes, I know, but it merits repetition, I'm sure we all agree.'

Oliver took no further part in proceedings, other than to drag his hand into the air and vote for the resolution I'd tabled.

And that, of course, was that.

It would emerge pretty swiftly that Oliver had helped himself to many, many thousands of pounds from company funds, and much as I expected, nothing at all came of the revelation. He wasn't prosecuted; he wasn't disciplined; he wasn't even obliged to repay the money he'd ingested – there was barely so much as a gentle request for him to go into rehab. According to the press release, he'd done 'a fantastic job' on the Terriss project, but sadly, 'health issues' had forced him to curtail his involvement. Thus, with immediate effect, he was to replace me as the company's roving ambassador. Yes, that's right: for having stolen a ton of money and upset just about everyone involved with our flagship project, he was to be allowed to spend more time at home.

Except that he *didn't*.

Whereas I, when surplus to requirements, had the dignity to take myself elsewhere, Oliver insisted on carrying out most of his ambassadorial duties from our offices – frequently, in fact, from *my* office. A common scenario would find me hard at work making up the time and ground he'd squandered, while the man himself lounged across the room, leafing through *Blueprint* while reflecting nostalgically and distractingly on our early, exciting days in practice together – those long-lost youthful glory days when we thought we were invincible and he didn't yet hate me.

There was no question, unfortunately, of his taking up residence at Cullen Place. For one thing, there was no longer a case to be made for our involvement there. For another, Reggie was the last person in the world I'd want to expose to Oliver's influence. So, to give him something to do (and, above all, to get him out of my bloody office) I put him in charge of liaising with the Council over the grand opening.

It was, I suspected, a fool's errand, but I could live with that: it was Oliver's own foolery, after all, that had caused so many delays to the project. I *know*, I *know* – there *had* been times when things were *ahead* of schedule, but those, as far as I could now discover, were the results of corner-cutting over-reactions to delays he himself had caused. In any case, here's the point: 15th December 2007 – that, as long as anyone could remember, was the agreed date on which the Borough of Godham Malpass was to celebrate the opening of its glorious new Civic Centre, and now, thanks overwhelmingly to Oliver, it was clear that we could not and *would* not meet the deadline. Thus, to our collective shame, the grand opening had to be put back from panto season to that most unfestive month of February.

Sufficient progress had at least been made to allow *Cinderella* to open in the theatre (new fancy sound-proofing meant site work could proceed, even during shows); nonetheless, the delay was embarrassing, and the blame for that embarrassment came down squarely upon the heads of me and Charlotte. *We* were the ones who took turns to go and grovel at Council Planning meetings; *we* the poor fools compelled to cower beneath the gaze of Councillor Kee, the big-specced, bad-breathed Deputy Mayor and Committee Chair, as we sought to explain the latest delay. Ah, had I only a shiny round pound for every time I sweated to the tune of his favourite catchphrase: 'It's not really *good enough,* is it Mister

Broughton?'

Reggie, meanwhile, was going from strength to unexpected strength. Just before Christmas, the BBC went public with the line-up for *Born to be Wild*, a shameless *I'm A Celebrity* rip-off, in which a bunch of C-listers (among them my former patron) would be flown to the States, plonked down in the middle of the Louisiana Bayou, and subjected to all kinds of indignities aimed at stirring them up to hate each other for the masses' delight.

I didn't see all that much of the show – I could only really watch it when Mog was out of the house – but I caught enough to ascertain that Reggie was doing okay. In fact he ended up the winner – they crowned him King Creole, largely by dint of the fact that he was slightly less of a wanker than most of his co-stars.

Not, of course, that the voting public assessed it in such terms.

Oh, voting public, have you no bounds? Your *shamelessness*, your... your...

King Creole! This *King Creole* – was this not the same individual – the same 'celebrity yob' – who, six months before, was being denounced in every quarter as a *child-abuser?* You could be forgiven for doubting it, or within a fortnight of his debut on *Born To Be Wild*, Reggie was apparently one of the best-loved people in Britain. The wheel of fire had come full-circle: the erstwhile public enemy was now a 'national treasure' – at least according to the tabloids that once had led the lynch mob.

That said, I *could* understand why it happened. The qualities I saw in Reggie on his good days were what came to the fore in the swampland environment. The boyish charm, the infectious enthusiasm – he lit people up in the most miserable situations (even though his competitive nature sometimes put his fellow campers at risk). Added to which, he got himself a whole load of sympathy points by talking with irresistible candour about his late wife and his absent, 'kidnapped' children.

The truth, of course, was that nobody had been kidnapped: Chico, Daisy and Conrad remained in Godham, under the loving care of their grandparents. They'd got their Residence Order and it was all fully legal. But who needs truth like that? Reggie, coming home with fame refreshed, was pleased to allow his new tabloid champions to trumpet his divine right of fatherhood. One even helped with his legal costs, encouraging readers to call a premium-rate phone line and 'REG-ister' their support.

None of this did me any favours with Mog. Okay, so yes, we were back together – sleeping as one, even making love from time to time – but you couldn't exactly talk of a second honeymoon. For all her 'resignation' to its fate, the theatre remained a sore point between us, and before long we'd yet another to deal with, this one courtesy of King Creole.

I knew, of course, that Mog was helping the in-laws (if only on an informal basis), but still, I was astounded when the 'ghost talk' thing made its way into the papers; even *The Sun*, Reggie's partner in justice, found it just too good a story to spike.

'How *could* you?' I said. 'How could you do that – just leak it to the press?'

She didn't trouble to deny it.

'I'm acting for the opposition.'

'I know,' I said, 'but Christ – I mean, Christ, what about lawyer-husband privilege?'

She laughed at that.

'I'm *serious,'* I said.

'So am I, my love. I'm trying to keep three kids away from a raving maniac – and you, despite knowing that to be the case, you *told* me...'

'Yeah, but...'

'You *told* me a story that...'

'Yeah, but...'

'At no point did you say it was off the record.'

'I didn't think I *had* to.'

'Oh, come on: he was talking to his dead wife. How could you think I was gonna keep quiet about that?'

In truth, I was less concerned about Reggie than I was about the prospect of having him shriek obscenities down the phone at me. In that, at least, I needn't have worried; being now able to afford it, he chose to speak to me through his legal representative.

'I'll be quite brutally frank with you,' said Mr Sperring, 'I advised my client to drop this case.'

'Oh, right.'

'Just press for *access*, I told him.'

'You *do* know my wife's an adviser to the in-laws?'

'*Access*', he said, blithely ignoring my caution. 'Just press for access,' I told him. D'you know what he said?'

'I can guess.'

'*Bollocks*'.

'I wasn't far off.'

'You see, Mr Broughton, he has — or at least, he *says* he has — a *secret weapon*.

'Oh yes — and what's that?'

'Not so much a *what* as a *who. You.*'

'*Me?*'

'You, Mr Broughton.'

'Me? But...'

'Your wife's involved with the opposition– indeed, as you just felt compelled to remind me. Yes, that's exactly why my client feels it'd make such a statement to have you in the witness box.'

There was, I must admit, a certain method in the madness, but madness it unquestionably was. The way I saw it, my presence in court could have only two possible outcomes:

1. I go in the box and express the belief that Reggie really *had* been talking to the ghost of Denise; or

2. I go in the box and, in spite of his counsel's best efforts, articulate the much more likely explanation that it was an acting *tour de force,* worthy of Alec Guinness or Peter Sellers, in which both starring roles were essayed by the man himself.

That was the choice: one way I'd paint him as a loony and lose him the case, the other way I'd paint us as a *pair* of loonies and *still* he'd lose the case.

My objections were heard with respect; indeed, said Mr Sperring, they were much as he'd anticipated, and much as he'd already told his client to expect. Noting my reluctance to be involved, he undertook not to trouble me again.

That, I assumed, was that.

Then Oliver told me who was going to open the Civic Centre.

'Your friend Reggie Cullen!'

I hit the roof. I very nearly did the same to Oliver.

'I thought you'd be *pleased,*' he said. 'So did Reggie.'

'Oh, I'll bet he did. I'll bet. I mean – *Reggie! Reggie!* Your mate Reggie. Believe me, he *knows* – he knows all about *you.* Knows just what I think of you, and you of me. He'll have known, be assured – known *exactly* why you asked him. So tell me – tell me, Ollie: what's the idea? What d'you hope to achieve with this?'

'Nothing. Nothing, apart from what you asked me to do. And please, Alex, whatever you think of this guy, he's a *name*, there's no denying it – a big, big name. It's a *coup.*'

'A *coup*? Right, right – a coup against *me*. How much did you offer? Eh? How much? How much? How much for this *coup*?'

'Well, that's just it, y'see. I didn't offer *anything*. *He* called *us.*'

'Oh, don't be... *What?*'

'He called *us.*'

'In *person?*'

'Absolutely. I'd have put you on, but you were at the Council.'

'Oh. Oh, right. So... So, how much are we giving him?'

'Nothing, like I say.'

'*Nothing?*'

'That's what he wanted: nothing. *Expenses,* of course...'

'Of course. Of course.'

'A bit of petrol, that's all. It's the *honour,* he said.'

'The honour?'

'The way he tells it, yes: he'll do it for the honour – the honour and the love of his home town!'

– Those Two Impostors –

3:14pm

We played Sorry last night. It was good. None of the usual from the girls. None of the sisterly schmaltz, none of the 'Sorry, Lu, I really am'. None of that – just clean, ruthless efficiency: each and every 'Sorry!' unleashed with the requisite spoonful of irony.

I did sort of wonder, was there maybe a similar irony at play this morning, with the Good Luck card on the breakfast table? It came from the girls, but Mog had signed it too.

'Don't be daft,' she said. 'Course I wish you luck. What am I gonna do – stab you in the eye?'

'You're not coming, though?'

'Don't push it. Just be grateful I'm not joining the protest.'

That's right, there was a protest. Proudly led by Carole, Whose Husband Left Her, a militant rump of Friends turned up, in full and feisty denial of the facts, to picket the opening ceremony. According to the security guys, they'd been at the site since before first light – since long, long before anything at all was scheduled to happen.

Still, they bagged a good spot, establishing themselves at the front of what turned out to be a heaving throng. As well as the gawpers who massed to get an eyeful of King Creole, there were also some 600 delegates from the Royal Benevolent Order of Beavers, whose annual jamboree was about to inaugurate the new conference chamber on the top floor.

As for the star attraction, he turned up late – of *course* he did – and managed to make himself yet later. According to the plan, Reggie was to drive into the new underground car park, there to be met by Security and brought up through the building. Instead, like the well-drilled professional celeb he's become, he maximised his exposure, parking in the street, buying a ticket from a machine (just like a *real* person!), and, then, to a constellation of camera flash, wading cheerily through the crowd, dogs at his heel.

Yeah, the mutts came too, the entire pack. He wasn't meant to do that – Guide Dogs Only – but what could I say? What could *anyone* say? Not even the protesters could resist his cheeky charm.

'Whassis, then? 'Give us back our theatre'? Bit late! Bit late, yeah? C'mon, stop whining – come on in, have a bit of cake!' Carole blushed and giggled at this unauthorised invitation, before attempting to issue a polite but firm refusal to his already retreating back.

Reggie squeezed through the high-vis cordon.

'Morning, mate! So this is it – the big day!'

'Yes. Yes, this is...'

He pulled me close and crushed me to his chest.

'And what a *building!*' He cut me loose. 'Fantastic – fucking lovely job. I never thought you had it in you! I'm kidding, mate, really. I'm proud of you!'

Oh, no. Was I about to cry? I couldn't string two words together.

'Mr B! *Mrs* B!' Thank God, he'd spotted Mum and Dad. 'Long time no see! Bet you're proud of your little boy!'

'We *are*,' said Dad, uncrimping himself, post-hug.

'We're proud of you *both,*' said Mum. 'Who'd have thought, all those years ago, when you were kids, making models on our kitchen table...'

'*So* pleased to meet you!'

An explosion in our midst: The Mayor – His Worship – efficiently obsequious as ever – 'Such a *treat!*' – cuts off my mum mid-sentence, grabs the guest of honour and drags him to the dais.

This urgent task accomplished, the Mayor then embarked on what he promised would be 'just a few words' of introduction; I in turn embarked on what I knew would be several long minutes of carefree daydreaming. What brought me back was the sound of laughter. *Laughter* – real, unforced laughter, from the crowd. Had the Mayor been *amusing* in my absence? No: the mirth, I now saw, derived exclusively from the work of Reggie Cullen. Standing just slightly back from His Worship's line of vision, he was giving a full-on clown show: feigning sleep, mimicking the Mayor's myopic speech-reading style, even wrapping an imaginary rope around his neck and launching himself into eternity (to use the sensational phrase of the Terriss/Prince era).

The Mayor, concluding at last, presented Reggie with a pair of big scissors.

'Blimey, look at these,' he said. He held them up aloft. 'Where's Delilah?'

The crowd went wild. Whether or not he was alluding to the Bible or to an ancient Tom Jones murder ballad, it clearly didn't matter, he'd warmed them up well. And there was more. 'What's this?' he larked, making ready to do his duty, 'A silver ribbon? I wanted a *scarlet* ribbon, for me hair!'

While the faithful were rocking with joy at this piece of comic treasure, I became aware of an eerie, braying laugh cutting through from somewhere in their midst. I wondered, for one irrational moment... Or *did* I? Maybe I'm projecting it now, looking back with the benefit of... of...

No, but I *did;* I *did* – just for a moment – I *did* wonder if

321

that creepy laugh was maybe a visitation from... well, *Denz*, for instance, bent on tormenting her husband – or maybe even Terriss himself, come to show spooky solidarity with the Friends of his memorial theatre.

The truth, of course, was nothing so exciting: a *live* ghost, that's all – a dishevelled figure propped, wild-eyed and tieless, against one of the gleaming new marble columns. It was Oliver.

Surprising to see him, really, given how badly he reacted earlier this week, when I removed him from his stewardship of the opening ceremony. 'You bastard,' he hissed. 'You vicious, vicious bastard! This is pure spite.' It wasn't, of course; not spite *alone*. The simple fact is that, for weeks now, he's not been turning up to the office. At all. That he honoured us this morning I can only put down to the free booze on offer. And how he *moved*, when the moment came! One floor up, on the stage of the Terriss Theatre, a refreshment table awaited; as soon as the silver ribbon was cut, Oliver surged ahead, leaving behind him a mob of honoured freeloaders no less eager yet forced, by dint of their sloth, to vie for stair space with the 600 Beavers bound for their conference on the top floor.

Nobody missed out, though – I can testify to that. Nobody went short. Nobody but the *architect*. The architect, that's right – the blood-sweating work-his-*arse*-off-architect – who foolishly allowed himself to be detained downstairs, saying ta-ta to his folks (not big on schmoozing, Mum and Dad) and seeking out space for a bunch of bloody dogs. For, yes: somehow that chore fell to me, and by the time I had it sorted – by the time I'd arranged to stash them in the box office (the staff are all *big* Reggie fans) – the goodies upstairs were significantly depleted. Okay, so the cake – *my* cake: three splendid tiers of Belgian chocolate – stood intact, but as for the sarnies and vol-au-vents, they by now were but a memory for a keenly greedy few.

Nothing, however – not even the rapaciousness of

freeloaders – could diminish my moment. While the gorging went on behind me, I wandered up to the front of the stage and gazed out at Matcham's auditorium, now fully returned to its original glory (but safer and more comfy). I thought of all the hard labour, of all the sacrifices, of all the compromises, not least the ones that had paid for Oliver to live the high life. Despite him, despite Mog, despite Carole Whose Husband Left Her, despite the Council and their ever-changing moods – despite everyone and everything, we'd *made it*.

It struck me now that Matcham himself, were he stood here beside me, would struggle to identify anything materially different from what he built; and yet, thanks to what we'd done, this playhouse was guaranteed a life far, far, far beyond what he could ever have imagined. No matter how the Friends might seek to defy and distort the facts, the pillars and the beams and the cantileverings would ensure – mostly in ways the eye could not discern – that not so much as a kilo of conference hall was actually being directly supported by the theatre itself. Thus, thanks to me and my colleagues *(most* of them, at least), Breezy Bill Terriss could go on being honoured in this building for centuries to come.

'What you thinking?'

Reggie now beside me.

'What am I *thinking...?* Well, I... I guess...'

'Listen, mate, can I have a word – somewhere private?'

'I thought you wanted to know what I was thinking?'

'Oh, alright, go on, then – what're you thinking?'

'I...'

'Hurry, though, cos I *do* want a word.'

'Fine. Fine. Okay, I'll be brief. What I'm thinking is this: I'm thinking how great it is not to be a spotty, greasy-haired teenager sitting down there in the stalls – in the very front row, sat there looking up, with a crick in his neck, too close to get any perspective on the play he's watching, though really he's not so much bothered about that – nor even about why he's the dick who got lumbered with the one, odd single ticket – *he's* the one marooned among strangers while everyone else is sitting together like one big happy scholastic family. One day, of course, things're gonna work out for him, but at this moment he has no such inkling; all he can do is sit there and wonder how he got to be so unpopular that people are willing to squander good confectionery as a means of taunting him.'

'*That*'s what you're thinking?'

'*That*'s what I'm thinking.'

He gave a big, gormless chuckle. 'Y'know, mate, you're a one-off, you really are.'

'Well, thanks.'

'Tell you what: d'you remember, all those years ago, us, down there – sat down there, in front of the stage – d'you remember, that time, throwing Smarties...?'

'*What?*'

'Us, when we came to that play...'

'You are *unbelievable!*'

'Eh?'

'*That*'s what I was *talking about.* That boy – the spotty, greasy kid – that's *me!* Not *throwing* Smarties – Smarties *thrown. At me.* Me with the Smarties bouncing off my head, my neck, my – my – my – Me: *I* was the target – you and your new-found trendy friends. *Hey, let's get Broughton!* Smarties! Smarties! And *I* ended up in detention!'

'We *all* got detention.'

'Right, right – but not *all* were guilty, least of all me!'

He smiled and shrugged. 'Gotta say, mate, that's not how I remember it, but...'

'Oh, believe me, that's how it happened – *and,* by the way, while we're on this general topic, we never – you and I – we never, *ever* played pool at The Geese.'

'Alright, mate, alright. What's wrong with you?'

'I just want to get things clear, before you start in with the moral blackmail.'

'What d'you mean?'

'You want *a word,* don't you?'

'Well, yeah.'

'Come on, then.'

With a bounciness borne of having let off a prodigious amount of steam, I led the way downstairs, to the relative privacy and comfort of the outer foyer. There, where Matcham's portico stood now shielded from the elements, we relaxed on one of the lush new Natuzzi sofas and Reggie presented his opening gambit.

It chilled my blood.

'Shelley's coming back.'

'*What?*'

'Yeah, she's coming back to Cullen Place. All is forgiven.'

'By *whom?*'

'Eh?'

'You don't mean to suggest that *she*'s done anything to forgive?'

'What? No, course not.'

'Good. So, what, you gonna *pay* her this time?'

'Well, yeah. Mind, if it goes the way I want, it's gonna be a *partnership.* No more master and servant – a real partnership. I've asked her to marry me.'

'You *what?*'

'Well, the kids need a mum, and besides, it's what she wants – what she *always* wanted.'

I laughed. 'Is that how you pitched it?'

'More or less.'

'And what did she say?'

'She's thinking about it. At the least, she's coming back to work, so, one way or another, there'll be someone to mind the kids, and that'll look good for the court case, so...'

'Right. Right.'

'So, you'll be there, yeah?'

'I'm sorry?'

'At the hearing?'

'Oh. No. Sorry, I can't. I mean, I did *tell* Mr Sperring...'

'I *know* you did. I know what you said, but look, I'm your *mate,* yeah? End of the day, we're mates – am I right?'

'Yes, right, of course, but...'

'Besides, you owe me. Oi – Oi – Oi – Don't give me that face: you *do,* you owe me – all that stuff you done with your wife.'

'What *stuff?*'

'That shit you spilled, about me and Denz.'

'Oh. That. Okay. I mean, I'm sorry, I *am,* really – but it's not like it was untrue.'

'Maybe not, but the fact is, you only heard that stuff cos you was spying on me.'

'I wasn't *spying.* I was coming in to talk to you about Shelley.'

'Whatever, mate; whatever the story, I'm in the shit cos of

you, so...'

'No...'

'*Yes.*'

'No, I'm sorry; the reason you're in the shit is cos you dumped your kids on your in-laws and let them think you didn't want them back.'

'Well, I *do* want 'em back, and unless you come and testify...'

'What should I tell them – you were talking to a ghost?'

'Why not? You know there are ghosts in the house: the boy in the lake; the bird who hung herself...'

'It's not gonna happen. I'm sorry.'

'But *why?* Why? I don't understand.'

'Because,' I said with patronising over-enunciation, 'I'd look like a *loony.*'

'You wouldn't. You *wouldn't.* You said yourself, it's no more nutty than...'

'*Believing in God*, I know. But see, it's not just about the ghosts. As it is, there's other stuff to think about – *Mog*, above all.'

He emitted a weary sigh.

'I'm sorry,' I said, 'she's my wife. I love her.'

'*Love* her? Sorry, mate, you got me there. Your *wife*, you say? For a moment there I thought you was talking about that bird who chucked you out of your house...'

'Yeah...'

'*...your* house, designed by *you* – the one you built with your own bare hands...'

'Not *quite* with my own...'

'Out on your arse, sent you cap in hand to your best and oldest friend...'

'And I'm grateful, I *am*, but...'

He jumped to his feet, started pacing the lobby.

'Where *is* she, anyway? Where's your wife? Not here! Not there! They seek her everywhere, but nowhere – nowhere to be seen. The biggest day of your life – where's she? Cos *me*, I'm here. Where's *she*?'

'At work, where I'd expect her to be. And that reminds me...' I stood up now myself, and, delving in my jacket pocket, located a fat brown envelope. 'Here you go: expenses. Five –'

'Fuck that! I'm not here for money!'

'No? Cos your agent was quite insistent. 'Five hundred,' he told me: 'no less – in cash.' So, if you *want* it...'

'I don't!'

And he slapped it from my hand. It flew through the air and landed on the carpet of the inner foyer; as it plopped to a halt, there came forth the sound of barking from the box office.

With a pointedly gentle sigh, I retrieved the envelope, and, returning to face up to Reggie, said, as calmly and unshakily as I could, 'Look, even if you were right, even if I owed you all my loyalty and none to Mog, it wouldn't matter, and I'll tell you why: I cannot, in good conscience, come and speak in your support, because – and I'm sorry – I really don't know if you're fit to have those kids in your care.'

'*What?*'

'I said...'

'WHAT?'

'I said...'

'What – you think I'm gonna fuck 'em?'

Faces now were vying to gawp through the tiny box office windows, while the mutts, in the background, were working up a pack-wide howl.

'No,' I said, 'I do *not* think you're going to... going to...'

'What, then? What d'you mean?'

'If you want a specific example...'

'Not *Conrad?* Not the nose thing?'

'Well, that's *one* example, but...'

'Fucking hell, that was months ago!'

'Yeah, but it's more than just... You've a *way* with those kids – a way that... I mean, I know you're probably no worse than a million other parents – *better*, in some ways, but...'

'A *tap,* that's all it was. Chrissake, a *tap.* I forgot I was wearing a ring.'

'Right; oh, right. So, a 'tap' *without* a ring, that would've been...'

'Whatever you say, they're *my* kids and I love 'em.'

'Do you? *Really?* Be honest, for once – with *yourself,* above all: the only reason you want those kids is cos *somebody else* wants them.'

It's not all that often I've seen Reggie speechless.

In the end he managed only, 'They're my kids.' Then 'They're MY kids.' And then, beating back tears through a scrunched-up face of rage, 'They're MY kids and they're gonna live with me, and no middle-class ponces are gonna take them away from me just cos they've got some cunt lawyer on their side.'

I turned for the stairs.

'Hey! Hey! I'm not finished!'

'Well, I *am*, especially if you're going to talk that way about my wife.'

'Your wife? Your wife? What about *my* wife? Eh? Eh? My Denz, more than anything, she would've wanted me to –'

'*Denz?* You're not serious? The last thing she did – Christ's sake! – the last thing, before she drove into the sea, she dumped those kids on her parents! How clear could she be?'

'Oh come on, that don't count. She didn't know what she was doing. The balance of her mind, it was – y'know – *disturbed,* all that...'

'The balance of her mind – that's what they said?'

'Too right.'

'So, tell me, then: how could you possibly know what *Denz would've wanted?*

To be honest, I too might well have been tempted to hit me at that point, so smug I must've seemed, delivering my logical *coup de grâce* then turning yet again for the stairs. In the end, of course, I *wouldn't*; I *wouldn't* have hit me. Recalling our previous form – recalling in particular that faceful of midsummer mud – I would, I think, have kept my powder dry. But, that's *me,* not Reggie.

In our earlier bouts, the shock of the downing had taken the wind from his sails. This time he was as a child mid-tantrum – punching and slapping and scratching up at me, without concern for dignity or fear of further harm.

'Stop it!' I said. Then louder. 'Stop it, calm down.' Then louder still, in a voice at least an octave higher than comfy: 'Just stop it! Stop it! Christ, will you stop it! Please, just stop it, *please!*'

How embarrassing.

After a while, though, he *did* start to quieten down, and as he did so, curious spectators began to emerge from the box office: the staff hovered nervously beside their fallen idol, while the dogs, more instinctive, went straight in for the lick.

'Get off! Get off me, you cunts!'

He was similarly gracious when one of the box office team tried to help him up.

'Fuck off! Just fuck off! You're all the same!'

Finally back on his feet, he essayed a dramatic exit, calling down the vengeance of the gods while seeking in vain to find the right door down to the car park. At last, having with much ill grace allowed someone to show him the way, he disappeared into the depths, only then to re-emerge a few moments later having remembered not just his pack of whining, stranded hounds, but also the fact that his wheels were in any case stashed not down below but on the street.

I watched from the first-floor bar as the Range Rover pulled away. He can't have known I was observing him, so perhaps it was for the benefit of Godham *en masse* that he held his arm out the window and flicked a V sign in his wake.

Either way, I reflected, the joke was on him: he'd departed without his expenses.

I turned, with a laugh, and wandered back into the theatre, entering via the authentically Victoriaesque new fire doors at the rear of the circle (installed, be it noted, with the guidance of the Theatres Trust). Apart from these, and a few other safety enhancements, the protesters would be hard put to say that anything substantial had changed – oh, apart from all the *improvements* they'd been demanding for years: re-upholstered seating, illuminated gangways, and, of course, a murderously expensive restoration of Felix de Jong's original internal decorations.

All of it done, I wryly observed to myself, as part of a process the 'Friends' had relentlessly opposed.

I trotted down the steps to the front of the circle, feeling for all the world like a Roman emperor coming to take his just acclaim from the Senate. I stood there, fancying perhaps that, at any moment, those lesser beings now milling around the stage would turn to applaud me. And then my triumph turned to horror.

The cake – *my* cake; my ridiculously costly cake which *I* myself had ordered and paid for from Choccywoccy-bloody-fucking-doodah in Brighton – was, I could all too clearly see, in a terminal state of shrinkage. It was meant, that cake, to go with my speech – they *knew* that, every one – and yet, while Reggie and I were spatting and sparring in the foyer, these people had taken it upon themselves to move in like a swarm of complacent, talentless, freeloading, uncreative locusts.

I dashed through a side door, took the winding stairs a couple at a time, and launched myself down the sloping passage to the stalls, all the time muttering darkly about wolves and jackals – *wolves and jackals,* yes, that's it, not *locusts,* no, not – *Jesus!* the years I'd given to this project – *years!* – all the years – could they really not wait just a few pissy minutes?

Unstoppable now in my rage and wounded pride, I soared down the centre aisle and launched myself toward the stage.

A totally stupid thing to do. I mean, yes, okay, I'm fitter now than in many a year – and I thank Captain Walcott for that – but still it was stupid, I was lucky to get away with it – so lucky, in fact, that in the moment I naturally ascribed my dodgy landing to dodgy leaping. Whereas now I know pretty much for sure that as I came to rest on 'the boards', they shifted under my feet.

'What's that?' said a nearby cake thief.

I said, *'Me* – that's what: the Architect of Record!'

They said, 'No. No: what was *that* just now?'

'Don't care,' I said. 'Want cake.'

And so I did. Not even the distant sounds of alarm – they seemed, I supposed, to be coming from the stairs outside –

could sway me from my mission.

The crowd of liggers parted before me as I homed in on the table. Last line of defence was a cake-eating coven made up of Oliver, Rocky and the Deputy Mayor. They gave me no trouble.

'Oh, fuck!' I said, as they moved aside. 'You bastards!'

That's the last thing I ever said to another human being – 'Oh, fuck! You bastards!' – and no one even noticed. While I stood there, bemoaning my devastation of crumbs, the rest of the assembled were turning their collective attention to the auditorium – to the circle, in fact, from which, just a few moments before, I'd been looking in imperial wonder upon my achievements. I followed their gaze, up to the back of the circle and on through those fine new fire doors, past which a foaming mass of humanity was now streaming... a full-on river of suits, flowing down as one from the conference hall toward the next set of stairs.

The Beavers were moving en masse; a coffee break, I might've guessed, if not for their collective vibe. *Panic,* it was – a clear vibe of panic in no sense eased by the voice of common sense so shrilly urging calm. I wonder if it was the same altruistic person, this voice of common sense, who peeled off from the stampede, dashed down to the front of the circle and urged us to 'Get out – now!'?

Nice thing to do. Really nice. Probably cost him his life.

Anyway, that's the point at which the borough's gleaming new conference centre fell through the roof and then the auditorium and finally the basement of the William Terriss Memorial Theatre.

How long was I out?

Don't know. Not long, perhaps. I only know that once there had been reds and golds and bright lights and cake crumbs, and now, only dust and darkness. Dust and darkness all around. And silence. No, not *silence,* as such: a constant deep background, in fact, of people screaming and crying and yelling – but only *up there,* among the gawpers and the helpers. Down here, for sure, the odd moan, the occasional cry for 'Mummy!', and later, of course, those bursts of unwelcome song. Mostly, though, just the sound of my own laboured thinking.

I was lucky, I suppose. Came to rest between a couple of cars. Good, that. Broke the fall of the lighting rig. Less lucky, though, with all the hard, unyielding objects encountered on my descent: judging by the pain in drawing breath, I reckon I smashed at least a half-rack of ribs. My arms still work, but as for my legs... well, one way or another, they're not taking me anywhere in a hurry – certainly not with a combination of masonry, stage equipment and corpses pinning them down. At least I've got my head, though. Not *my* head, I mean – the *other* head, the severed one, the one under mine. But for that, I'd be in a right state.

God.

The protesters, they'll be loving this. They're only human. 'We *told* them... we *said* this was going to happen.' And true, they *did;* they saw it all. But they were *wrong.* I *know* they were. This thing, done right – I *know* – it could and would and *should* have stood for centuries.

So who fucked up? Me? The builders? Oliver? No, not him. *Fuck up?* No. No, he'd have done it on *purpose* – he'd – he'd – he'd –

Oh, don't talk bollocks.

There'll be an inquiry. *Have* to be – so many corpses; have to find a scapegoat amongst them. *Me,* I suppose – the ideal candidate: Architect of Record. Who will there be to denounce me, though – to stamp on my grave and damn me for ever? Just about everyone with anything to say is under here somewhere.

The only ones who *aren't,* thank Christ...

1. Mum and Dad. Well clear, yeah. Yeah, brilliant – saved by their lack of social skills: but for that – but for their awkwardness, scurrying off home as soon as...

2. Mog, of course, thank God. If she... if she... But more to the point, the *kids*... The kids. 3 and 4. Rachel and Lulu. *Desperate,* they were: desperate to come and support their dad. *No,* she said: no you're going to *school.* 'And no, don't give me that: it's nothing at all to do with whether I approve or disapprove. It's much more simple: under the Education Act of... of... of...'

Oh, I don't remember the year, but *she* did, of course. Of course she did.

My God, I was so pissed off with you. Mog. My love. I didn't let on, but I *was.* Even to the last, I longed for you to swallow your pride and come along to this thing. This stupid ribbon-cutting bullshit. Mum and Dad were gonna be there, and, well, I don't know, I just...

Pride. Thank Christ for that pride of yours. Maybe if I'd had just a little bit more myself...

What do I mean, though? What do I *mean* by that?

Don't know. Just thoughts. Just...

'Imogen! *Here!'* A voice. A woman. 'Over here, *Imogen!'*

Sounds like – yes – it's Carole, it *is,* Whose Husband Left Her – though why I ever thought it big and clever to take the piss out of her *loneliness*... It's her, though, it *is,* it's Carole – and, more importantly...

'Imogen! Imogen!'

Why so formal? It's Mog. *Mog.* She's here. At last.

'Alex...? Alex...?'

And there she is. Above me now: her voice up there,

335

among the points of fading winter light. She's up there, mere metres hence – and she might as well be on the moon.

I want to say her name, but I can't. Can't do it. Just can't make a sound. I want to tell her careful – *be careful, don't get too close, not safe* – but I open my mouth and... No. Nothing. Barely a breath, let alone...

The dust: my mouth, my tongue...

It's like a dream. Can't speak.

A *dream?* If only.

'There! Over there! Why aren't you trying over there?'

Oh, no. What's this? She's started being *forthright:* into management mode already – the diggers, the medics, she's telling them what to do – *pro bono* advice. Please, Mog, just leave them alone! Okay, I know, you're *scared*. Believe me, *I* am too, but...

Ah. Ah, right... okay, now they're trying to... to... No, not *them,* not the ambulance people, but someone – *someone,* at least, is trying to calm her down, to move her clear and –

'You?! *You*, of all people – don't you *dare* tell me to – to – to – Just get out of here. Go on – fuck off!'

'Look, I know you're upset...' *What?* 'Of *course* you're upset...' *What?* 'You're not gonna help him like this, though.'

It's *him*. He's back. It's King Creole. No wonder she's mad: the King is back and giving advice.

Advice on anger management from a man who sleeps with a shotgun.

'Just calm down. Okay? Cos, listen, you and me, I know we've got form – all that stuff with the kids – but for *his* sake, at least, just for now – for *Al*'s sake, wherever he is...'

'*Wherever he is?* He's down *there* – and *you* put him there!'

'Don't know about that, love. But what I *do* know is this:

336

there's a guy down there somewhere, and there's two people up here who love him and want to help. Now, where do we start?'

You could start by being honest. *Love? Help?* You came back for your money. Your *expenses*. Am I right? Got halfway home, remembered, did a Starsky. Well, good luck, my friend. You'll have to be digging very, very deep. Cos here's the thing: just after you left – just as you were storming out with all your threats and dogs – I ran into the Chief Exec. I gave him back your envelope. *Safe keeping*, I said. He was heading for the car park at the time. Why stay? He'd had his cake. *My* cake. He stuffed his face then scarpered – and, okay, he *might*, for all I know, have made it out, but I doubt it. There were three floors of underground parking. I should know, I put them there.

Safe keeping.

***

3:37pm

Oh.

Oh, I must've been out. How long? Don't know. Reggie and 'Becks' were crawling across the desert. No. No, it wasn't David Beckham – well, it *was,* but it was him and Reggie at the same time, only then it changed – changed to just the one of them, but *still* it was both, and yet... His *face,* that's the thing: I could see his face, even at the same time as my eyes... *his* eyes... *his* point of view was... was... But whoever it was, he was made of fibreglass. Of course. Of course he was. Though his eyes were real.

But anyway, how long...? How long was I...?

A while, for sure. Those little specks of light before. Specks through the wreckage. There's nothing now.

'Come on, people, don't give up! My mate's down there – keep digging!'

Right, so now *he's* giving orders as well. As if they haven't counsel enough from Mog.

I mean, it's *nice,* of course. It's nice to know he cares – but fuck's sake, Reggie, all you're doing is putting lives at risk, encouraging other people to put *their* lives in… in… And not just *any* other people…

'Mog!'

Yes! I did it. Yes, that's good: a crack of angry breath to croak my fears.

'Alex? Alex! Oh God! He's down there! I heard him.'

'You *heard* him? You sure?'

'Of course. He called my name.'

'That's great! Fantastic! Brilliant! Told you, didn't I? Didn't I tell you? Didn't I say he'd be alright?'

'Yes,' she says. 'You did.'

I'm *sorry?* Just how long have I been asleep? How long was I with puppet Reggie-Becks? Last time I heard those voices together, she was hurling *fucks* and *dare-yous* at him.

'Mog, *please!* Not safe…'

'What's that? What's that, my love??'

'Not… Not…'

But I can't say more. I *want* to: *Go! Get clear!* But still, no breath, or not *enough.* Too dry. Need water. Must… get water.

'Go!' Okay, that's something. 'Go! Please!'

'Go?' That's Reggie. 'D'you hear him? *Go?'*

Mog laughs. I *think* that's what it is, a laugh.

'She ain't goin' nowhere, mate! She's your *wife.* And fuck me gently, what a wife she is! Seriously, mate, talk about arm-candy! Talk about punching above your weight!' Well, thanks. 'You've gotta get out of the ground, okay? You've gotta fight

338

– *fight!* Just to be able to look at this gorgeous face again...'

If I know that gorgeous face, old chum, it's about to scrunch up and gob in your patronising, oafish...

'Ere, what you doing?'

'What d'you think?'

'Blimey! Al, mate, you should see her – your old lady, digging away nineteen to the dozen. It's Wonder Woman! Look at that girl! You're Wonder Woman – yes you are! – or – no – no: *Bionic!* The Bionic Woman! Look at you! *Jaime Sommers!*'

'Well, I *do* work out!'

'Oh, I can see you're well fit.'

Fit. Did he say *fit?* Was there a pun intended there? Is it just my fevered imagination, or... or...? And, what's she *doing* about it? Nothing, by the sound of it. This, surely – surely, would it not? – would this not be the ideal moment for Reggie Cullen to learn how it feels to be slapped across the face with a wedding ring?

I mean, Christ, Mog, remember what you *said!* Whose fault is this? It's *his*. It's *his*. Your new mate Reggie. Him and his stupid stadium! His stupid, his stupid...

Stay calm!

Okay. Of course, be calm. But awake. Calm but awake. Awake and alert. Like the *Thunderbirds* man – whatever it takes to keep him alert. For him it was water. For me... For me...

I mean, who the fuck died and appointed him cheerleader? Mog, please, please, don't let him... I know: a truce, just for one day, just to... just for my sake. And I *do* understand: you're crouching up there in the dusk, scrabbling around, trying to feel useful when in truth there's nothing much you can do – nothing except, perhaps, to open your mind and accept that this friend of your husband... that maybe, just maybe there might be a good side after all to... to...

But no! No! Not in my name! It cannot be. Don't let your guard down now! Remember, he's the reason... No, of course, I know, he's not the *only* reason, but... Cos I... I have been a complete and utter... He never could've tempted me if I, in the first place... Oh, God, I've been such a... such a... I see it now – I see the little chinks of light poke through again, they show me how... Cos you know – I *hope* you know, that I... that I love *nothing* in this world so well as you. And if...

What's this...? What's...? Water? Water... must get water. Running down my dusty cheeks. A little bit of lubricant if I can just... That's it – catch them on my tongue, and...

'Mo-o-o-g!'

'Alex...?'

'There he is again! He's hanging in there! See? Y'see?'

Oh, fuck off, Reggie. Well and truly off. We're trying to talk. Not talk – not face to face, of course, though soon enough... Those lights... They brought those lamps, did they? The point is, Mog – my love – the point is this: I want to start again. I know we patched it up – you took me back, but still I've never said... I've never actually said the words – and if I ever had to say to this to your face I'd die of blushing, but no matter, let me say it in my fashion, let me thank you for... for... You have been my – corny as it sounds, but what the fuck – my *lightship*. Always. Always that – but since... since I... You led me back to shore, thank Christ. He tempted me, that fucker there beside you, but I'm back – I'm back and awake and alive, and I'm going to live.

I'm going to live. I *will*. The lights are brightening. That fire across the sand.

'Alex...? Alex, are you there...?'

Yes, I'm here and alive and feeling the sun on my face. They slag it off, some people – yes, of course it burns, and yet you've got to accept, no life is possible without that roaring ball of... of... And I'm crawling now towards it. I am. I'm leaving him behind – just you and me, my love, that's how it'll be. I'm crawling. It's all I have to do. Keep crawling – crawling across the sand, cos I know that even if they don't turn up – they – *them,* I mean, the Tracy boys – International... International...

But what am I...? Stupid! Fantasy. Just fantasy. Kids' stuff. *Thunderbirds?* Stupid. They're not coming. But *you*, my love – you're for real, and I know, if I keep, keep, keep on pushing forward, you'll be there.

You'll be there, my love. And I promise. I promise – please believe me – I'll never, ever fail you again.

***

Printed in Great Britain
by Amazon

18900782R00200